The Magic of Us

OTHER TITLES BY BETH MERLIN AND DANIELLE MODAFFERI

The Last Phone Booth in Manhattan

Heart Restoration Project

Breakup Boot Camp

Life Derailed

The Campfire Series

One S'more Summer

S'more to Lose

Love You S'more

Tell Me S'more

The Magic of Us

BETH MERLIN

DANIELLE MODAFFERI

Published by Montlake, Seattle

www.apub.com

EU product safety contact:
Amazon Media EU S. à r.l.
38, avenue John F. Kennedy, L-1855 Luxembourg
amazonpublishing-gpsr@amazon.com

ISBN-13: 9781662535239 (paperback)
ISBN-13: 9781662535246 (digital)

Cover design and illustration by Leah Jacobs-Gordon

Printed in the United States of America

To the ones who run beside us

Elliot West's Ten Commandments of Love and Dating

1. *Thou shalt not audition for the role of someone's peace.*
   You're not their therapist. Or their mother.

2. *Put thyself first. If you don't, no one else will.*
   It's not selfish, it's survival. Oxygen masks, people.

3. *Thou shalt not put all thy eggs in one emotionally unavailable basket.*
   Translation: Don't date red flags and confuse them for roses.

4. *Thou shalt not mistake potential for partnership.*
   You're dating a person (an adult, no less), not an HGTV fixer-upper.

5. *Thou shalt not chase what does not choose you.*
   If you're begging to be picked, it's already a no.

6. *Thou shalt not water dead plants.*
   Stop pouring love into someone who won't grow with you.

7. *Thou shalt not resurrect an ex.*
   They're an ex for a reason. Don't go grave digging. It will unearth nothing but disaster.

8. *Thou shalt not stay for potential, memories, or promises.*
   You live in the now, not in the maybe.

9. *Thou shalt not confuse being wanted with being valued.*
   Desire is easy. Respect is rare.

10. *Thou shalt know thy worth—and add tax.*
    You are the prize. Don't become less, become even more.

Chapter One

Hurrying into the studio, already late, I tossed my bag and coat onto the nearest chair. I kicked off my shoes without a second thought, and they hit the wall with a soft thud.

"Easy there, tiger!" Ravi's voice carried through the intercom from the sound booth. "We've already had to replace three mics this month thanks to your flying UGGs."

I called over my shoulder at him while pantomiming, "No, see? My aim's getting better. They completely sailed over the desk this time and hit the wall. All good."

He rolled his eyes and turned back to his coffee mug, the words PROBABLY VODKA emblazoned on the front, before taking a long, intentional sip. I tried desperately to calm my sweat-kinked blowout and slid the familiar headphones over my ears, the soothing static hum drowning out the rest of the world.

"Okay, El, system's all checked. You're live in five. Remember, watch your time with the callers during the first segment. We've got a hard break at ten past for a sponsor mention and commercial."

"Yeah, yeah, yeah, I got it," I said, adjusting the microphone, and racked the deck of index cards on the desk with a satisfying tap. I shuffled through quickly to review my show notes and some of the random ideas I'd jotted down in the margins. As I traced my fingers over the switchboard while I skimmed, the red light illuminated, catching my eye, and I reordered my thoughts just before it flashed three times, signaling my cue. Ravi pointed over to me.

"Hello, my loyal listeners! Whew, it has *been* a morning. First, my coffee machine met its untimely demise, taking my will to function right along with it. And though Keurigs aren't the most environmentally friendly, as you know, I'm a single pringle who just wants one damn cup, not a whole pot. But today it decided no coffee for me. Miserable and jarring start to the morning, I can assure you that. So I do this lumbering-style zombie walk all the way to the 4 train, only to find out it's a crawling local instead of an express *and* packed tighter than my prepandemic skinny jeans. And because the universe is apparently a two-bit comedian, those very jeans decided to split right up the ass as I stepped onto the platform."

I stood up, folded in half, and flashed the damage to Ravi. He cracked a wide smile (wider than my own crack), rolled his eyes at me for the second time that morning, and shook his head like I was some kind of walking disaster, which today was fair.

"So naturally, with my best Hanky Panky panties out on full blast, I got catcalled and ogled across six blocks and two avenues. Just another day in the glamorous life of yours truly, Elliot West, host of *Love Is a Four-Letter Word*."

Ravi hit play on the show's clubby techno intro music, then shot me a quick nod when it was time to take over again. Glancing at the bullet points on my first note card, I was already preparing for the pulsing energy of the show ahead, hot opinions flying, tempers flaring, and callers ready to turn the high holy day of "love" into an all-out battleground.

"Good morning, everyone. So glad you're tuning in. Tomorrow, as you all know, is Valentine's Day—the Hallmark holiday of all Hallmark holidays. So to celebrate or not to celebrate? That is the question. And I've got your answer, ladies. I say: No. Hard pass. You can keep your overpriced roses, overcooked filet mignon, and overstuffed animals the size of my first studio apartment. I mean, is it really a gesture of love if a pop-up ad from 1-800-Flowers.com has to remind you to do it? Maybe it's just me, but I'd sure as hell prefer a handpicked bouquet of dandelions given to me on some random Tuesday than the bells and whistles of yet *another* capitalistic expectation.

"But what about all of you? Are you buying into the grand illusion of candlelit dinners and heart-shaped tubs? Are you being fooled by the gestures of glittering jewelry that will no doubt turn your finger or neck green? What will you be doing, or not doing, tomorrow night or this weekend to celebrate? Let me know and give me a call at 1-800-844-5683. That's 1-800-UGH-LOVE."

Within seconds, the switchboard lit up like a Christmas tree. I cracked my knuckles and hit the button for the first caller. "Morning! You're on the air. So are you dialing in to defend the so-called magic of Valentine's Day, or do you also see it as a glorified cash grab?"

"Hi, am I on the air?" the voice asked, popping slightly through the line.

"Yes, this is Elliot West, and you're on *Love Is a Four-Letter Word.* What's your name and where are you calling from?"

"Melanie, calling from right outside Yonkers."

"Hi, Melanie from right outside Yonkers. So which is it? Magic? Or cash grab?"

"Definitely a cash grab," Melanie answered. "I mean, fifty bucks for a bouquet that'll be dead in three days? No thanks."

"Exactly! A thoughtful gesture shouldn't need to be wrapped in cellophane and bows. Sometimes it's the little things that mean the most. Am I right?"

"A hundred percent. I'd love it if my boyfriend would just make me my morning cup of tea without me having to ask or remind him how I take it."

"And you're worth that. It's never about the price, it's about the thought behind it. Valentine's Day, though . . . feels like it's turned thoughtfulness into a box to check, doesn't it. Thanks for calling,

Melanie." I pressed the next line. "Hello, you're on *Love Is a Four-Letter Word.* What's your name and where are you calling from?"

"This is Gwen calling from Jersey City."

"Hey, Gwen from JC! What's your take?"

"So I think I have to disagree with you. I actually like Valentine's Day. I mean, sure, it's commercial, but so are birthdays and Christmas. At least this holiday celebrates love."

"Yeah, I'll take my chances with birthdays. You can't always count on people, but you can *always* count on cake."

"Very true," Gwen giggled, "*buuuuut* can cake hold your hand in a crowd, wipe away your tears when you're sad, or cuddle up next to you on the couch while you're watching Netflix on a Saturday night?"

"*Guuurl,* if it could, I'd already be Mrs. Duncan Hines, that's for damn sure." I barked out a laugh and readjusted in my chair. "Thanks so much for dialing in." Glancing down at the switchboard, I pressed for the next line. "This is Elliot West, you're on the air."

"Hey, Elliot. This is Tia. Longtime listener, first-time caller."

"Love that! So tell me, Tia, how do you weigh in on this hot topic?"

"I have to agree with Gwen. Valentine's Day gets a bad rap, but I think it's kind of nice. I mean, I'm in a new relationship, and the guy actually planned something. Like, real effort. Dinner, a play, the whole thing. What's wrong with a day that reminds people to be a little extra thoughtful?"

I raised an eyebrow. "I don't know . . . maybe because you shouldn't need a calendar alarm to remind you to go the extra mile. Shouldn't that be, like, table stakes for a relationship?"

"But life can get really hectic, you know? Sometimes you need something like a holiday to snap you out of autopilot and make you stop and appreciate what you have. That shouldn't make the effort count any less, though."

"You make a fair point, but I still would argue that if you're only romantic when a holiday tells you to be, that's not love, that's seasonal programming. And if he needs Cupid to serve as his very own personal assistant, maybe it's time to think about whether or not you want to take this relationship any further. I speak from personal experience here, and trust me, better you figure that out now before you get in too deep." I glanced up at Ravi, who was giving me the signal to wrap it up. "Thanks, Tia, for calling in. We need to go to a quick commercial break. More *Love Is a Four-Letter Word* when we return."

Pushing the headphones back over my head, I sipped from my water bottle while the show's outro music played. Shuffling through the stack of ad copy, I pulled out the ones Ravi had earmarked for today's show. I cleared my throat with a quick cough, slipped the headphones back over my ears, and pulled the mic to my face.

"Today's episode is brought to you by Grubhub, the only thing in your life that shows up and *always* leaves you satisfied, and by Airbnb: Escape everything, including your bad decisions. Travel light and leave the emotional baggage behind. Be sure to use our promo code UGHLOVE, that's U-G-H-L-O-V-E, for an additional ten percent off your next stay."

Ravi brought his PROBABLY VODKA mug to his lips and, with a twirl of his finger, signaled we were back to the show.

"If you're just joining us on your morning commute, carpooling the kiddos to school, or tuning in during your Pilates workout, we're deep in debate over here about the 'virtues'—and yes, I am using air quotes—of Valentine's Day. Waste of time, or worth the hassle? Our last few callers seemed pro-Cupid, but let me throw some stats your way."

I flipped through the note cards until I found the one I was looking for. "Did you know that this year, consumers are expected to spend a record $27.5 billion on Valentine's Day? That's an average of $188.81 per person. And another study cited that a significant portion of Valentine's Day spending is driven by societal expectations, with forty-nine percent of consumers prioritizing cost when purchasing gifts. Prioritizing *cost.* Not thoughtfulness, or genuine oh-hey-this-random-thing-made-me-think-of-you vibes. Just how much was spent. Is that how we're measuring love these days? Isn't buying into this holiday saying *exactly* that? What do you think? Let's hear from . . ." I looked at Ravi and he held up a whiteboard with a scribbled name on it. "Maggie. Morning, Maggie, you're on the air with Elliot West. So let me have it, where do you stand in all this?"

"Hey, Elliot. I just wanted to share that my husband and I got married two years ago on Valentine's Day. Yes, we both realize it was a bit of a cliché, but why not fully embrace love on a day that's already dedicated to it? It felt like the perfect way to mark the beginning of our forever."

I read off the card I'd specifically prepared for this type of anecdote: "Did you know that couples who marry on Valentine's Day are eighteen to thirty-six percent more likely to divorce within five years compared to those who marry on any other date? I'm sure you'll beat those odds, but it does show just how many of us go into this day with our emotional blinders on, and I want all of you to have your eyes wide open to the possibility of disappointment."

Ravi set down his coffee mug, scribbled, "*Ooh*, nice!" on his little whiteboard, and flashed it at me with a huge thumbs-up.

There was silence on the other end of the line, and I was pretty sure Maggie had hung up until I heard, "I, um, I mean, stats are one thing, but I know what my husband and I have, and I'm not sure the fact that we chose February fourteenth as the day to mark our relationship changes anything."

"Look, I'm not here to rain on anyone's parade or crush romantic dreams. That's the last thing I want, but over the years, my listeners have come to count on me for honesty, and sometimes honesty stings a little. Actually, not gonna lie, sometimes it stings a lot. But I've come to think of myself as the big sister who tells you the things you don't necessarily want to hear but need to, because I truly care about you all. Trust me, love *is* a four-letter word and that word is *pain*. Because when it hits, it hits hard."

My throat seemed to tighten around the words, and my eyes filled with tears that I hurried to sniff back. I felt this raw and hadn't even told Maggie the worst part: that you never see it coming until it's too late. If you're smart, you learn to protect your heart or at least keep your expectations low. That was the only way to avoid the kind of heartbreak I'd barely survived.

I was just telling her what I wished I'd learned sooner. What hundreds of my callers wished they'd heard before they were cheated on, betrayed, belittled, or left devastated. Take your pick. Better they heard it from me than suffer it themselves when they were inevitably blindsided . . . like I had been.

For the next hour and a half, I fielded more calls, spread more of the gospel according to Elliot, cited a few more unsettling statistics, and comforted a few more members of the Lonely Hearts Club Band until Ravi queued up the show's final outro music and I saw the light in the booth switch from green to red.

Pulling off my headset, I wrapped my cards with a rubber band and filed them in my drawer with the rest of the week's show notes. The door swung open, and without looking up from where I was still rummaging through the desk, I said, "So what'd you think?"

"Another home run. The switchboard was going crazy. Fully illuminated the whole show. I sent a video clip to Greg at Sirius and Colleen at iHeart. They're gonna go nuts."

I stood up to retrieve my shoes from the other side of the room. "It's a ratings game. You know that as well as I do."

"Well, you've been playing the game like a pro lately, El. As of last week, *Love Is a Four-Letter Word* became the top-rated show in the metro area. Now Sirius and iHeartRadio are practically in a bidding war."

It was still hard to wrap my head around the idea that our little college radio show built on bad dating stories and no-holds-barred advice had morphed into a bit of a phenomenon with a devoted, cultlike following of women trying to navigate the treacherous world of modern love. Moving to either of those platforms would be a total leveling-up, taking my message from the metro area and pushing it into the stratosphere.

Not to mention that my agent managed to ride the wave of the recent buzz surrounding our show and negotiate a book deal with Simon & Schuster. *Love Is Dead, Let's Have Brunch* would be a sharp, quick-witted takedown of romance, packed with the wildest calls I'd gotten while hosting *Love Is a Four-Letter Word* over the years: cheating scandals so convoluted they belonged on a crime board, disastrous first dates that ended in emergency-room visits, and enough ghosting stories to put the notoriously haunted Eastern State Penitentiary to shame. The book would be part survival guide, part cautionary tale, and would entirely prove once and for all that love was nothing more than a beautifully packaged illusion.

This dream of mine was finally coming true. I had become the guiding light that I myself had so desperately needed in my own moments of emotional turbulence. The rational, detached, straight shooter who could move beyond feelings and just dish facts. What made it even more incredible was that my words seemed to really be resonating with people.

It was the confirmation I needed to know that walking away from Leo had been the right call, no matter how perfect our short time together this past summer had been. Because there was no such thing as perfect, not in love, not in life. "Perfect" was just a filter we placed over things to make them easier to believe in. And happiness that depended on someone else was too much of a gamble, one I wasn't willing to bet on, especially not when the odds were stacked against us all.

"Hey, don't you have that Galentine's Day speaking engagement thing later tonight?" Ravi asked. "Should provide some good fodder for Thursday's show."

"Yup," I said, scrolling through my phone to find the email from my agent about the event. "Rooftop Reds at the Brooklyn Navy Yard. I better get home so I can get myself together."

"And, um . . . change your pants?" Ravi joked, pointing to my cheeky undies flashing from beneath my jeans.

"What do you mean? Why? Not a cute look?" I joked, craning my neck over my shoulder to take a glance at just how bad the damage was.

Ravi smirked. "Just saying, might not be the *best* first impression."

I rolled my eyes, grabbing my coat. "Noted. I'll try to dress like a fully functioning adult."

"For once!" I heard him call out behind me as I hurried out the studio door.

Chapter Two

I pressed my apartment's intercom, holding it just long enough to hear my best friend Marin shout, "It's me! I'm in the lobby with a super-cranky Ethan, Sophia doing the potty dance, and a very fragile bottle of our favorite rosé. So please, El, let us in!"

Hitting the buzzer, I moved to the front door and pulled it open wide. Seconds later, the elevator chimed, and Sophia came barreling past me, not even pausing to say hello before making a beeline straight for the bathroom. Ethan followed right behind her, arms pumping, launching himself onto the couch like it was the finish line of an Olympic sprint.

"I was a total pushover and let Sophia order the venti-size Pink Drink," Marin said, setting down her bag and handing me a latte. "She's been needing to pee since 81st Street."

"You okay in there, Soph?" I called in the direction of the bathroom.

There was a flush, followed by the sound of the sink running. Finally, the door creaked open and Sophia toddled out, cheeks pink with relief. "Sorry, Auntie El. I shouldn't have drank that whole thing. Um, do you have any juice?"

"Yeah, juice!" Ethan called from the couch.

"No juice. You both just had big sugary drinks. Water," Marin said firmly.

"How about water with a side of cupcake?" I offered with a wink.

Marin sighed. "One cupcake . . . *to share.*"

"Deal." I looked at the kids, who instantly lit up. As their unofficial fairy godmother, I kinda loved that feeling. "And then maybe later you can give me a hand with Pickles. I got her a new ball to play in for when I need to freshen up her cage. Think you can help her test it out?"

"Yeahhhh!" they both squealed.

Ethan pulled a wrapper out from his pocket. "Can guinea pigs eat Fruit Roll-Ups?"

"Um . . . I don't think that'd be the best idea. But I appreciate you wanting to share your snack with her."

"Can we go say hello?" Sophia asked, already moving in the direction of Pickles's habitat tucked in the corner of the living room.

"Of course you can! She'll be so excited to see you. She's been asking about you all morning!" I replied to the backs of their heads.

Ethan burst out laughing. "Auntie El, guinea pigs can't talk!"

"You're so right! What was I thinking?" I joked back as I wandered into the kitchen to grab the cupcake I'd promised them.

From the living room where she was supervising with Pickles, Marin called out, "Hey, I actually managed to catch your *whole* show today."

Balancing two sippy cups and a plate in my hands, I came out and set them down on the table. "Yeah? And what'd you think?"

She paused, then said, "It was . . . informative."

"'Informative'?"

"All those stats about Valentine's Day and marriage and divorce rates. Scary, but informative."

"I used the stats to help prove my point, but you know the show's really more about the stories behind the numbers. All the women who have fallen prey to the trap of Valentine's Day."

"Women like me, you mean," Marin said with a raised brow.

"No! Of course not. You and Tyler aren't the rule. You're the exception. The happy, disgustingly well-adjusted exception."

Marin snorted. "Please. We argue about who left the sponge in the sink on a daily basis."

"No, I refuse to believe that any couple who made such perfect specimens"—I glanced over at the kids, who had made their way back to the table and were now licking frosting off the same cupcake—"could possibly fight about sponges."

She threw her head back and laughed. "Hardly perfect, but so damn cute it's hard not to see past their meltdowns and messes. Especially when they're tired. Which, speaking of, for all our benefit, I should put Ethan down for a short nap. He woke up at the crack of dawn and is moments away from going full Terminator. Can I put him in your room for a bit?"

"Of course, but let me do it. I'll hang with him until he falls asleep."

"You sure?"

"Please, it would be my pleasure." I made my way over to the TV and flipped it on with the remote. "You and Soph just go on snackin' and enjoy *Moana* for the hundredth time."

"Thousandth," Marin snarked as she tossed a handful of Chex Mix into her mouth.

"C'mon, dude, let's go rest in my room for a little while." I reached for Ethan's hand and pulled him off the couch.

"But I'm not tired," he whined, while his saggy posture told a completely different story. He rubbed his eye with a fist and yawned as if on cue.

"I know, but I am, and I was hoping you'd come keep me company while I take a short snooze. Would you mind?"

"I guess," he shrugged, and trudged beside me up the hall. "But don't play with Pickles without me, okay?"

"We would never," I promised. After I pulled the curtains closed, the room darkened, and I turned down the covers, lifted Ethan in my arms, and tossed him playfully into the mountain of throw pillows, his giggle like a wind chime as he plopped into the plush bedding.

"Auntie El, it's too dark in here."

"Not to worry, bud, I can put this on." I tapped my tableside lamp once, and it illuminated a light on its softest setting. "Better?"

"Yeah," he said through another yawn.

"Great." I pulled the blanket up and tucked it around his sides. "You snug?"

"As a bug in a rug," he said, repeating the line I'd taught him.

"Perfect. Okay, sweet dreams, little dude."

"I told you, I'm not sleepy."

"Yeah, I know. Let's just enjoy the quiet for a little while, and then we'll see how we feel," I hedged as I rubbed his back in circles.

"Ugh, fine," he said, but I could already feel his body relaxing under the weight of the thick coverlet. Turning his head toward the nightstand, the temporary quiet was broken with, "I like that picture of you."

"Huh? What picture?"

"That one. Under the lamp. Where is that?"

Craning my neck, I glanced at the picture in the frame, a five by seven of me on my study exchange in France during my sophomore year of college. I'd ended up staying for a few weeks after the program had ended, traveling around Paris and eating my body weight in croissants and fondue. Matty, my boyfriend and, really, best friend back then, had wanted to come for a visit, but with a pretty important internship he couldn't take a vacation from, it hadn't been possible. We survived on emails and texts and made it out on the other side, like I knew we would. I'd been convinced that if that time apart hadn't ended us, nothing would.

Turns out, I'd been very, very wrong about that.

"That's me in France at the Eiffel Tower, one of the most magical places in the whole wide world. I've only ever been to Paris that one time, but I've been dying to go back ever since. You wanna come with me, bud?"

"Only if I can take my mom. She'd miss me too much, I think," he said.

My cheek twinged with a smile that crept across my face in the dark. "I'm sure she would."

I thought of my own mother. How she'd get so wrapped up in her new boyfriends and relationships that she wouldn't have even noticed if I wasn't home some nights, let alone have missed me. And my father, who'd abandoned us both to start an entirely new family. What must it be like, I wondered, to grow up with two parents who loved you so fiercely and made you the center of their world so much that you never had to question your place in it?

Silence fell between us, and I was almost convinced he'd fallen asleep until his little voice squeaked, "Did you live there by yourself?"

"In Paris? Yeah, I sure did. Just me and a fridge full of cheese!" I joked. "Pure paradise."

"Oh," he said and fell quiet again. I rolled my head to the side to look at him, and as I did, he placed his pudgy hand on my cheek, and I melted under its warmth. He sighed. "Auntie El, I want you to meet someone, because I don't want you to be alone."

The comment caught me so off guard I wasn't sure whether to laugh or cry. Just shy of five years old, I was taken aback by his compassion and intuitiveness, seeming so wise beyond his years. "*Awww,* Ethan, I'm okay on my own. But why do you say that?"

"Well, if there's ever a fire, someone has to run in to get you out."

"A fire? What? Where did that come from?"

"Yeah, like in *The Greatest Showman,*" he announced, pronouncing *Showman* like show-*man.*

"Ohhh." I laughed. "Well, you don't have to worry about me, sweetheart. I have a brand-new up-to-code fire extinguisher right under my sink and a cutting-edge fire-blanket thingy Gigi Sonja proudly bought me from QVC. Now, get some sleep. If Mommy hears us chatting away in here, she's gonna have a cow!"

"Have a cow?!" Ethan barked out a laugh like the expression was the funniest thing he'd ever heard.

"Yes, a total cow!" I pressed, his giggle infectious. "So let's close our eyes, alright?"

"Okay, Auntie El. Love you," he said, rolling his head to the other side and burrowing deeper under the covers.

Love you.

The words made my chest tighten. It had been some time since I'd heard them directed at me. Yet here they were, and for a moment I was envious of Marin, who probably heard them unconditionally all day long, as natural to her as breathing.

It only took a matter of minutes, but when his snores soon became heavier and steady, I slunk out of the side of the bed and tiptoed out the door back to the living room, where Sophia was also passed out on the couch.

"He's finally asleep? Did he grill you with a million questions?" Marin asked, and followed me into the kitchen so we wouldn't disturb Sophia. "It's his new thing."

"Only a half million," I teased and picked through the Chex Mix for a few of the pumpernickel chips. "He did mention—and I quote—that he wants me to find someone because he doesn't want me to be alone. Apparently, he's afraid that if there's a house fire, Hugh Jackman or Zac Efron won't be available to run in to save me."

Marin slapped her hand to her forehead. "That damn movie. So great. And that soundtrack—amazing! But we watched it like a month ago, and it seems to have inspired a whole new phobia in this kid's life. He seriously insisted we needed to get a 'go bag' and put a few of his favorite stuffies in it 'just in case.'"

"No way this kid is five years old. He's a sixty-five-year-old man living in a little kid's body."

"You have no idea," Marin affirmed, pouring us each a bit more wine and taking a seat at the counter. "And besides, you aren't alone. I mean, yes, you *live* alone, but you have us."

I looked up at the ceiling. "Not to mention a smoke detector with fresh batteries. So don't you worry about me."

"El, I hope you don't take this the wrong way, but I always worry about you. I'm your best friend. It's my job. And your show today. I know it's a little bit hyperbolic, at least I hope it is, but I can't help but wonder how much of your schtick you've actually bought into."

"What do you mean? I *do* think love is a farce, and I'm happy with my life. No strings. No real family obligations," I said with a shrug.

Kind of hard to have family obligations when you don't have much of a relationship with your family to begin with, but I didn't say that part out loud. "I've got friends. You and Ravi. Your beautiful kids. The girls. Pickles. A great career. I'm good. Really. Girl Scout honor," I said, raising three fingers on my right hand.

"I love you, but Pickles isn't a substitute for genuine human connection," Marin said, crossing her arms as she leaned against the counter. I opened my mouth to argue, but she held up a hand, cutting me off. "You haven't dated anyone seriously since the Great Matty Disaster of '18. You've let that situation, and all your family stuff, tarnish your idea of love so much that you've convinced yourself you're better off alone. And that's not fair either."

I sighed. She just didn't get it. How could she? She was happily married with a unicorn of a husband and parents, not to mention unicorn in-laws who were more of a blessing than a burden. Marin didn't have to build walls. Unlike me, she had nothing she needed to constantly brace for. No letdowns, no sharp edges, just the familiar ease of a life that was steady enough to trust. That was exactly why I'd had to let things end with Leo in Mykonos this past summer. After all the heartache I'd endured, I'd managed to flip the script of my life, hardening my heart into something almost unbreakable, and I wasn't about to let him, or anyone, shatter it.

Sipping my wine, I reached for another handful of Chex Mix. "Anyway, my so-called cynicism is what has two hundred women paying good money for tickets to see me at a Galentine's Day event tonight. That mindset is what's now propelling me toward a potential spot with Sirius Radio and a big-time book deal."

"I just want your life to be what you decide it should be, not something you retreat into, that's all. Maybe see what's out there with an open mind and an open heart, and if after that you still feel like being on your own is what's best for you, then great, I'll happily throw you a 'Ringless Rager' or a 'Lone Wolf Luau' or whatever else you want."

I would always appreciate Marin looking out for me. Since our elementary-school days, she'd been the one dusting me off from every misstep and rooting me on to keep going. In a childhood filled with chaos and confusion, she was one of the few people I'd known I could always rely on and the reason I'd never felt completely alone in it all. But even so, I'd never told Marin about Leo or our time together. For as well as she knew me, she'd never understand why I'd chosen to walk away.

We polished off the bottle of wine, letting Ethan and Sophia get in a solid nap while I steered the conversation to more mundane things, like how the entire *Sex and the City* franchise had been ruined by the *And Just Like That* spin-off, especially without the character of Samantha holding all the other ladies accountable, all things Taylor and Travis, and hotly debated whether we were in the age demographic to consider a weighted vest for our morning walks in the park.

We came to no great resolutions on any of it. When the kids finally woke up, we played with Pickles, as promised, before I shuffled them out the door in enough time to get ready for my speaking event.

"See you at mah-jongg on Thursday. I'll grab those olives and that cheese you like from Murray's to bring."

"You don't have to, but I won't fight you either," Marin joked as she finished zipping up Ethan's coat and securing Sophia's hat onto her head. "Give Auntie El a big smooch before we go."

In tandem, they ran up to tackle me, and I allowed them to plow me onto the floor. Kissing them rapid fire on their chubby cheeks, I rolled them around in a fit of giggles before helping them to their feet and sending them on their way.

Chapter Three

The Uber slowed to a stop in front of a nondescript warehouse-type building tucked in the middle of the Brooklyn Navy Yard. I checked the map on my phone again, just to be sure this was actually the right address and not some setup for a sex-trafficking situation having to do with one of the ships docked just a few feet away.

The driver glanced at me in the rearview mirror, either sensing my hesitation or silently wondering whether I needed a minute to process my life choices.

"This is it?" I asked, my breath fogging up the cold window as I pressed my cheek against it, craning my neck to get a better look at my surroundings. "Rooftop Reds?"

"This is it," he confirmed, though he seemed less than comfortable letting me out somewhere so deserted. I appreciated his concern and lingered for an extra minute or so in the car, scanning the street for any indication we were in the right place. Then I spotted them: a pack of thirtysomething women marching up the sidewalk in their questionable-for-February stilettos, talking and laughing as they headed toward the same nondescript building.

"Yup, looks like this is it," I replied, but not before giving him a generous tip. I wrenched my coat closed against my chest and hurried toward the door to follow the line of ladies going inside. We piled into the elevator and relished the warmth emanating from being packed in so tightly. The woman closest to the front pressed for the top floor, and a few seconds later, we spilled out into a glass-enclosed atrium leading to an expansive rooftop vineyard, where attendees were already sipping from stem glasses, mingling under heat lamps inside the cozy tent.

By the registration area, they'd set up an easel holding a large poster of my headshot and a sign that read GUEST SPEAKER: ELLIOT WEST, HOST OF LOVE IS A FOUR-LETTER WORD.

"Hi there, do you have your QR code for your ticket?" a woman in a bright-red dress with even brighter red lipstick asked from behind the check-in table.

"Actually, I'm Elliot West, the speaker for tonight's—"

"Oh, yes, of course! Sorry about that, I should have realized. I mean, your face *is* right there." She chuckled as she gestured to the poster. "The event is completely sold out. You must have some truly stellar advice to share for us hopeless romantics."

"Sure, though I'd say my brand leans a little more toward cold hard reality than fairy tale."

She waited a beat, as if she thought I might be joking, and when she realized I wasn't, she cleared her throat and continued. "Well, anyway, here are your drink tickets. Six tastings are included. You can purchase bottles afterward. There are raffle baskets full of gift cards and goodies from over thirty local businesses. All proceeds are going toward the Brooklyn Food Pantry. Such a good cause. And then don't forget to check out our merch table and to sign up for a calligraphy name print or a head massage or a mini mani. So many great things to try."

I raised an eyebrow. "And, um . . . for my book reading? Where do you want me?"

"Right," she said, glancing toward the tent, where chairs were arranged in neat rows. "We've got the podium all set up and ready for you outside. Cassidy, our event coordinator, will meet you there."

I took the envelope, the red drink tickets poking out the top, and thanked her before heading over to the bar that was elaborately decorated in glittery pink hearts and other Valentine's Day decor. Finding some space at the end of the counter, I scanned the list of cleverly named tasting options displayed on an acrylic stand. And when a handsome man, wiping the fingerprints from a bell-shaped wineglass, came over to ask what I'd be having, I ordered the "Hello, Merlot" flight of three full-bodied reds.

"Here you go," the bartender said, setting out the three glasses. "Like any great relationship, these blends start light and get more intense as you go."

"As long as they remain *intense* and don't turn *toxic* like many *bad* relationships, I should be good."

"Touché," he said while he focused on pouring the exact amount for the tasting in each glass.

I glanced at my watch and knocked back all three samples in just a few gulps.

The bartender's eyes widened slightly. "Maybe I should have also mentioned that a good red is meant to be savored."

"I'll remember that next time . . . when I'm not the guest speaker," I said, motioning toward the tent, where some of the attendees were starting to find their seats.

"Oh, you're the one giving the talk? The radio host who totally trashes love and guys, right?"

"I don't *trash* love. I'm just very vocal on how much of a losing scheme the whole thing is."

He cocked his head to the side with clear skepticism. "Hmm . . . I hear your shtick is a bit more fiery than that. Think I'll need a security escort out of here? Armored car?"

"Well, I guess we'll see." I shrugged with a wink, tossed a few singles into his tip jar, grabbed my clutch and notes from the chair beside me, and headed outside. I'd made it about five steps onto the rooftop when a woman with a clipboard and a headset zeroed in on me.

"Elliot! There you are. I'm Cassidy, so nice to finally meet you. I've been a longtime fan. When we announced you were headlining our little Galentine's Day event, we were completely sold out in under an hour. A record," she gushed. "If there's anything you need, just wave me down. I have water set up on the stage for you next to your seat and a glass of our best cab. Your agent mentioned you like reds when we confirmed your booking."

I lifted my brows, impressed.

"It's a wine tasting, my dear. It'd be an actual sin if you didn't join in on the fun." Cassidy walked me to where they'd set up the seating in front of a small stage framed with twinkling lights. I took a seat in front of the crowd and sipped my water, excited to do what I did best: offer facts-first-feelings-later-style advice. It sometimes wasn't easy for women to hear, let alone accept, but that didn't make it any less true.

Cassidy stepped forward to introduce me. "Ladies, please help me welcome Elliot West to the stage." She glanced down to the phone in her hand as she read, "Ms. West rose to fame hosting the highest-rated collegiate radio show in history at Brown University before moving to our local airwaves, where she now hosts *Love Is a Four-Letter Word*, a no-holds-barred talk show that gives a sassy take on love in the modern world. Elliot just signed a six-figure deal with Simon & Schuster for her book *Love Is Dead, Let's Have Brunch*, which combines anecdotes from her own life, wild stories shared by listeners on her show, and her signature no-nonsense rules on dating—excerpts of which she'll be reading after some Q and A. Now, without any further ado, the maven of 'swipe left' wisdom, Elliot West!"

I stood up and gave a dramatic curtsy to Cassidy and a wave to the wide-eyed crowd. "What a wonderful introduction. Hello, everyone, and thank you for joining me on Galentine's Day. I applaud all of you for turning this holiday into a celebration of friendship and wine, two things you can *actually* depend on."

Titters and peals of laughter resounded from the audience.

"Like my radio show, I'd love to open up this first segment to Q and A from the audience." I glanced out into the sea of faces. "Who has a burning question about love, dating, or sex? I'm armed and ready," I said and lifted my glass of cab with a flourish.

A woman in the front row of the folding chairs shot her hand up like we were in a high school classroom.

I pointed to her with a grin. "Go ahead, you've got the floor."

"Hi, Elliot. I'm Lauren. Big-time fan, longtime listener," said the petite woman with prominent bangs that hung over her eyes.

"Hey, Lauren. Thanks so much for coming out tonight. So what have you got for me?"

"I was wondering, what are your thoughts on second chances?"

I scrunched my face. "I mean, are we talking about, *Hey, honey, you forgot to take out the garbage again*, or *Sure, Todd, of course, you can cheat on me for a* second *time?!*"

Laughter rippled through the crowd.

"Look," I continued, "I *do* believe in second chances . . . just not in relationships. Second chances are for restaurants with mediocre service and forgetting your grandmother's birthday, not for people who have already shown you who they are and how little they respect you. Once a cheater, always a cheater isn't a cliché for nuthin'. I mean, my Fifth Commandment clearly states *Thou shalt not chase what does not choose you.*"

Another hand shot up, and I pointed at a woman in a chic beret who was practically on the edge of her seat. "You, in the cute hat. Go ahead."

Pink Beret stood up. "What's the worst dating advice you've ever heard?"

"Oh, that's easy." I set my glass down to make air quotes as I said in a mocking voice, "'Just communicate.'"

The crowd reacted instantly with groans, laughter, even a dramatic gasp from somewhere in the back.

"No, really," I continued, holding up a hand. "I get it—in theory, communication is the key to any great relationship. But let's be honest, when a guy says, 'I'm just really bad at communicating,' what he actually means is, 'I don't like talking about feelings, and if you make me, I will shrivel up like an unwatered ficus.' And you all know Commandment Number Six states *Thou shalt not water dead plants.* Emotionally dead or otherwise!"

Laughter erupted around the space. Someone near the front clinked her wineglass against her friend's in solidarity.

Another woman near the back raised her hand as the chuckles ebbed, and I pointed to her to continue.

"Oh, me?" She popped out of her chair and said, "Hi, Elliot. I'm Kamila from Brooklyn Heights. I'm such a fan!"

"Hey, Kamila. Thank you so much for coming tonight. What's on your mind?"

She cleared her throat and spoke loudly from one of the last rows. "After all these years of listening to you, I have always wondered . . . Have you ever had *that* moment? You know, the moment of the relationship that makes you wonder how things might've turned out if you would have made a different choice? A lingering 'what if' that sneaks up on you late at night? A long-lost high school sweetheart? A missed connection? Maybe even a love-at-first-sight moment with a sexy stranger? So, do you have a story?"

I swallowed hard and my face warmed, feeling every ounce of those full-bodied reds now climbing up my neck and settling in the apples of my cheeks. The room swayed in a soft blur, and I wasn't sure whether it was the question or the wine that made it feel like I was suddenly on a rickety canoe in the middle of choppy water. "I . . . um . . ."

Leo's face, however, came into perfect focus. Eyes as blue as the Aegean Sea. Thick, dark hair and the bronze skin of a man who'd lived his whole life on the water out in the sun. His passable Greek mixed with a melodic South African accent as he ordered us drinks and dinner at the little taverna where no one spoke a word of English. The long fingers of his soft hands grazing my skin as he helped me into my cardigan, the sea breeze curling coolly off the water. A god by most people's standards. Just a fling while on a work trip to Mykonos this past summer. He'd been a dalliance and nothing else.

That is, until he became more.

"Um, sorry, what was the question?" I asked.

Cassidy leaned in to the mic. "She asked if, in spite of your more cynical take on love, you've ever had a missed connection or a love-at-first-sight moment?"

I forced a laugh, swirling the wine in my glass as if I could disappear into it. "Love at first sight? Oh, yeah. It happened the first time I saw a wine bottle with a twist-off cap. I knew we were meant to be."

Cassidy tilted her head and pursed her lips, clearly not satisfied. "Oh, no, we're not letting you off the hook that easily. Seems like you're dodging the question, which means there's gotta be more to the story," she said in a singsongy voice. "C'mon, it's just us girls here. You can dish!"

More to the story? More like a sweeping romance novel with an open ending that still keeps me up at night.

"Oh, y-you know, just one of those summer things," I stammered. And as I fumbled for the words, the memories crept in like an uninvited visitor, unsettling and relentless.

Last July, the radio station covered all my expenses for a two-week trip to Mykonos, famous for its singles' nightlife and party scene. If you were in your twenties, unattached, and looking for the opposite of love, chances were you'd find it somewhere on Super Paradise Beach. The plan was for me to conduct a series of on-the-street-style interviews, only in my case, they'd be on-the-beach interviews, further exploring the popular mantra "What happens on vacation stays on vacation."

The goal was to show that companionship, flirtation, and sex didn't necessarily have to lead to a relationship. That a good time didn't have to be anything more than just that. So I packed my cutest bikinis, my flowy sarongs, and my SPF and headed off for what had to be the easiest assignment anyone in the history of the world had ever been given.

On day six, I met Leo. He was surrounded by a group of good-looking guys reveling in the sun-soaked chaos of a stag party, kicking around a soccer ball, shirtless and carefree. I zeroed in on them immediately as the perfect subjects for my exposé, bachelors likely looking for nothing more than a weekend of harmless fun.

I went to the bar, ordered a round of Mythos, and carried the drinks over to the group as a way to break the ice. My approach worked, and it didn't take too long before the charming blokes visiting from

Johannesburg were regaling me with tales of their wild stag-do exploits. All except Leo, who remained absorbed in his pint and cell phone, barely registering that I was there at all.

After finishing the interviews, I thanked them and made my way back to the bar, laptop in hand, to transcribe my notes for the show. Leo followed, stepping up behind me to order another draft.

"You didn't want to interview me?" he asked in a low and sexy voice that practically knocked me off my stool.

I swiveled around and came face-to-face with one of the most striking men I'd ever seen. From far away he'd been good-looking, but up close, good Lord, he was damn near perfection. My stomach dipped and I struggled to produce enough saliva to swallow before I could speak. "Um . . . sorry?"

"You asked all my mates their views on love and dating, but not me."

"That's not true. I didn't bother you *or* the groom. *Him* for obvious reasons, and you because you didn't seem particularly interested." I shrugged and turned back to my computer.

"I was responding to a work email before, but if you're still looking for some additional content, I'm available now," he said, pulling up a stool. "What did you say your name was?"

"Elliot. West. And I think I'm all set. Your mates gave me *quite* an earful."

"Did they, now?" He lowered his voice. "You should know, that was mostly ego, not to mention that they were likely just trying to impress a beautiful woman."

"As opposed to your thinly veiled compliment probably meant to act as some sort of strategic charm offensive?" I squinted at him, not only to show my skepticism but because staring right at him was almost like looking directly into the sun. His chiseled bone structure and warm demeanor was making it hard to think straight.

He smirked, displaying the cutest creases around his eyes and highlighting the cleft in his chin. "Okay, you got me there." He pointed to my computer screen. "So why all the questions about relationships? Are you some sort of cultural anthropologist or something?"

An amused laugh tumbled past my lips. "*Pfft.* Hardly. I host a radio show that challenges the traditional notions of love."

He nodded in approval, and that's when I knew I'd reeled him in. A girl who hosted a show challenging the traditional norms of love? If that didn't scream vacay hookup, I wasn't sure what did. And so, in the name of research, I continued to charm and banter and laugh with this handsome stranger in the hope of tumbling into a little vacation fling myself.

Little did I know that over the next week, this small flirtation would erupt into an inferno, threatening everything I'd worked so hard to build: my radio persona as a cynic of love, my brand, and most terrifyingly, the walls I'd built to protect my heart from ever breaking . . . again.

Chapter Four

Those last few questions from the audience had hit a little too close to home, so I quickly wrapped up the Q and A and switched gears. I read an excerpt from my forthcoming book *Love Is Dead, Let's Have Brunch*, starting with my famous Ten Commandments of Love, a.k.a. rules very few follow, but that, in my opinion, everyone should. I covered the essentials, like why falling for someone who only communicates in memes and shared Instagram Reels was a guaranteed mistake, how bringing an ex back was like reviving Frankenstein's monster (a guaranteed horror movie plot), and the universal truth that love was a scam.

As I read, the Second Commandment jumped out differently than before: "Put thyself first. If you don't, no one else will. It's not selfish, it's survival. Oxygen masks, people." I paused, the words almost too sharp as they cut through the room. They echoed in my mind, taking me back again to last summer, back to Mykonos, back to Leo.

Leo finished out his stag-party obligations and, instead of flying home with his buddies, decided to switch his flight and stay in Greece for another week and a half to get to know me better as we spent our time sightseeing and drinking copious amounts of raki. Time flew by too fast as we took catamaran tours to Paxos and Rhenia Islands and did a Jeep excursion along the Houlakia coast to admire the Armenistis Lighthouse and the Monastery of Paleokastro.

We feasted on grilled octopus, marinated feta cheese, and fat, briny olives, spending far too many hours wrapped in one another's arms on a beach blanket, watching the sun slowly descend over the crystalline waters.

It had been the most perfect vacation distraction, fun and delightfully satisfying with no strings attached. That was, until we arrived at the Athens airport, ready to board separate planes bound for opposite sides of the globe. I'd firmly convinced myself that, regardless of how wonderful he was and how great I'd felt, this was all meant to be temporary. And that it was especially wonderful because it *was* temporary. That was the trick. To stay in something for only as long as the magic lasted.

But as we stood at the intersection where we had to set off to our different terminals, I couldn't seem to move my feet. Leo set down his bag and took me in his arms. My head told me to pull back, to cut ties as fast as I could before I fell too hard to walk away. But my heart silenced my inner skeptic, and I melted into him instead.

He smelled fresh and clean, a hint of sea salt lingering on his skin. I nuzzled against him, savoring the unfamiliar thrill of our undeniable connection and the startling realization that maybe he meant more to me than just a fleeting fling.

I have to let go. Now. Right now. Okay, though . . . now! Dammit, Elliot, let go! Turn around and head to your gate. This is not a drill!

Before I could untangle my arms from around him, he pulled away first, cupping my face in his hand and stroking my cheek with the soft pad of his thumb. "Okay, I have a crazy idea, but just hear me out." His voice was soft, as if he was afraid of shattering the moment . . . or maybe scaring me away. "I know we said this was just a fun vacation hookup, nothing else, but I think there could be more here, or at least I know I want there to be."

A lifetime of reasons I had cultivated on my own, witnessed through my parents' disastrous marriage, my own failed relationship that cut me to the bone, and my listeners' horror stories, reminded me why this could *never* work. They each fought for top billing, all perfectly honed weapons ready to fire.

I'd been training for this moment my whole life, right? The moment when love lurked around the corner and I knew better than to let it in. Instead, as a trained pro, I was supposed to booby-trap the house, to unleash every excuse, every justification, every scrap of evidence proving that we were a doomed voyage before we'd even set sail.

"Leo, but we—" I started to interject.

He cut me off, his voice gaining an exciting edge. "Did you ever see the movie *Before Sunrise*? You know, the one with Ethan Hawke and Julie Delpy? They meet on a train in Vienna, spend the night getting to know each other, and then here's the crazy part: They agree not to exchange any personal information. No numbers, no last names. They promise to meet one year later, at the same spot. No guarantees, just the hope that if it's meant to be, they'll find each other again."

"What are you saying? You want us to meet back in Mykonos next summer? After a year of not communicating? That's insane. Besides, I know your last name. And you know mine."

"You're right, no communication is way too nineties of a concept when most of us can't go twenty-four hours without social media, and a year is way too long. But what about December?"

"What about December?"

"I'll be in Paris most of December for work. We could meet there. It's a hell of a lot closer than South Africa or Greece for you. And think of it: Paris around the holidays. What could be more romantic?"

"Let me get this straight. You want us to agree to meet up in Paris in six months' time, based on . . . ? An old movie trope, a week of mind-blowing sex, and . . . what, exactly?"

He tilted his head, a knowing smile playing at the corner of his lips, aware that I was deliberately undermining the depth of what had passed between us. "Based on the fact that I'm falling head over heels for you. And I think you are for me too. We both know this week has been about more than just sex. But if we need more time to make sure this isn't just a rush of lust and strong Greek wine, let's keep it casual and take this next part of the year to see if we feel all those same feelings when we meet up again"—he looked down at the calendar on his phone—"on December twenty-fourth at the Eiffel Tower. Cliché, yes, but magical, also yes."

"I don't know, Leo. You don't understand. My radio show. My brand. It's all hinged on the idea that this . . . this feeling . . . this possibility . . . that *this*"—I gestured between us with a wave of my hand—"doesn't exist."

"But how can you deny what's standing right in front of you? It *does* exist. I know you feel it."

Suddenly the Athens airport intercom crackled with the final boarding call for my flight to New York.

"Shoot, I'm going to miss my plane if I don't . . ."

Leo stepped closer. "Tell me you'll meet me. December twenty-fourth. The Eiffel Tower. Promise me."

I picked up my bags and turned to leave. "I have to go."

He grabbed my hands and held them tightly. "Elliot, promise me," he repeated.

I looked into his eyes, feeling the weight of the moment, then gave a small, wistful smile. "Okay, I promise."

With my Q and A, book reading, and meet and greet now over, I milled around the rooftop space, glancing out onto the skyscrapers lighting the night instead of stars. Chatting with guests and peeking at the raffle basket goodies, like baking items, pricey bottles of booze, lottery tickets, and Yankees swag, I continued to sip the complimentary wine that Cassidy had made sure I was never without.

"Excuse me, dear, I just wanted to say how interesting I found your talk." A soft hand touched my shoulder, and I turned to see a striking woman who looked like she'd been waiting for me. She had jet-black hair and inviting gray eyes that seemed to hold the wisdom of centuries instead of decades. She was a bit (well, a lot) older than my usual demographic, but I was happy to see my message was universal.

"That's wonderful. So glad you enjoyed it," I said with a smile.

"I happen to be one of the entertainers hired for the event. Tarot readings. I just wrapped up for the night but was wondering if you'd like a turn before I leave, as a thank-you for your shared perspective this evening." She gestured to an open table as she already started to move to take a seat and shuffle a tarot deck in her weathered hands.

I watched her continue to maneuver the cards as if I'd already agreed. "Oh, um . . . sure, I guess," I stammered, and slid into the chair across from her. She trained her focus on me as she continued to rearrange the deck like a Vegas hustler. Cutting it in half, she distributed three face down and flipped them one at a time, nodding sagely as she delivered a generic-enough reading that included past heartache, present walls, and a future I refused to entertain.

And it wasn't lost on me that since she admitted to hearing most of my talk that she knew exactly what hot buttons to press and buzzwords to use to get me to buy into her act. I continued to play along and inwardly roll my eyes until she pulled one more card. As she drew it into her line of sight, she hesitated, squinting between me and the image she'd drawn. The candlelight flickered, casting shifting shadows over her face, but it wasn't just a trick of the light. Something in her also seemed to have shifted.

Her lips curved into a knowing smile as she tapped the card once, deliberate and firm.

"Hmm. You think love is a beautifully branded illusion, but I sense that there's been someone, a kindred spirit you met not long ago, who tested the mettle of your resolve," she murmured, her voice smooth and smoky. "He could see you, really see you, and you were too afraid to let him in. Maybe it's not love that needs to change, but the lens you've been viewing it through?"

A cold sweat prickled up the back of my neck. "Um, okay." My voice caught in my throat, and I was surprised at how strangely accurate her words were. In fact, they registered like she'd struck a gong in my chest, the reverberations moving like shock waves through me. "But I don't really understand. How am I supposed to change the way I see the world? How's a person just supposed to stop seeing life the way they, you know, see it? And how do I stop being afraid?" I hoped my tone didn't sound sarcastic because I was genuinely curious.

"All good questions. And I think I can help. How about you shake things up a bit with a little love spell, perhaps?"

I barked out a laugh and then bit it back when I realized she wasn't laughing too. Or even smiling. She remained as stoic as a storm, her stare fixed and focused.

I shifted in my seat, suddenly feeling too sober for this conversation. "Oh. You're serious."

"About magic? Always," she said, laying a single card she'd drawn down between us. The Lovers. My stomach did an uncomfortable little flip.

I cleared my throat. "Look, I appreciate the offer, but I don't think a love spell is really for me. I don't really believe in that sort of thing."

"Love, you mean?" she asked. "I know this. You've said as much."

"Well, no. I meant the spell. But yeah, also love."

"Isn't it worth, perhaps, taking the risk?" The woman leaned down, rustling through her bag until she found what she was looking for: a long red string. She knotted it three times and placed it in my palm. "This is your thread, the one that ties you to another," she explained. "You thought it was broken, but"—she closed my fingers around the thread—"some connections aren't so easily severed." And when I opened my palm again, the string was gone.

I blinked hard. "That's it? No abracadabra? No hocus-pocus?"

Now it was her turn to laugh. She reached for her deck and wiggled the cards back into their box before stuffing them into her bag. "For amateurs. Trust me, real magic doesn't require theatrics, just faith."

"Faith in what?"

"Faith in second chances, even the ones you didn't ask for."

I stared at the table, lost in thought. I never did meet Leo in Paris like we'd planned. There were so many reasons I'd convinced myself I couldn't go, and though I hated to admit it, so many nights I'd spent wondering whether by not going I'd made the biggest mistake of my life.

But that was all in the past. That door had closed, and I wasn't about to reopen it. Second chances were for hopeless romantics, for the naive. For people who believed in things like tarot cards and magic spells, fairy tales and happily ever afters, and I was none of those.

But even so, a small part of me couldn't help but wonder . . . what if?

Chapter Five

The next morning, the first thing I noticed was an unfamiliar warmth wrapped around me like a cashmere sweater. A steady, radiating heat pressed against my back, the weight of an arm slung over my waist like it belonged there. My breath hitched.

I didn't just *sleep* with people. Not anymore. Not for a long time.

My body stiffened as my brain caught up, heart hammering against my ribs, and I took shallow breaths, hoping not to wake the stranger next to me in my bed. The room smelled like clean linen and something deeper, something unmistakably familiar—faint cologne mixed with the natural scent of the sea—recognizable in a way that made my stomach lurch.

I swallowed hard and peeked through a squinted eye.

The bedroom was mine. My navy curtains, my cluttered dresser, the faint glow of the city at sunrise peeking through the blinds.

But my bed? My bed held a stranger. Someone I didn't remember bringing home. Someone whose presence should have jolted me awake and sent me straight toward the door. But instead, wrapped in his embrace, I felt an unusual sense of calm.

I moved as slowly as possible, peeling his arm off me inch by inch, my pulse pounding in my ears. He barely stirred, just let out a deep sigh and turned onto his back.

My stomach flipped. How in the ever-loving hell was Leo, South African Leo, Leo-from-halfway-around-the-world Leo, now in my bed?

Dark hair, a hint of stubble, lips parted in sleep. A strong jawline, the kind that looked carved for smirking. And beneath the covers, the outline of broad shoulders and a long, lean frame.

My mind reeled as I swung my legs off the bed and planted my feet on the hardwood. The room seemed to be tilting off its axis, and I was surprised my dresser wasn't sliding its way toward the windows.

I scanned the room, looking for any hint of what had happened. Why or how he was here.

And then I saw it.

A five-by-seven-framed selfie of Leo kissing my cheek in front of the lit-up Eiffel Tower, golden fireworks exploding in the background, now replaced the picture of me from my study abroad that had sat there before. In this photo, my face was flushed from the cold, my breath visible in the air, and Leo had his arm around me, our kitschy New Year's Eve glasses glittering in the flash.

The picture sat next to a mug of tea, the rare blend I always had to order online, steeped to the exact shade of caramel with a splash of milk, just how I liked it. All prepared in my favorite chipped mug, the one I always grabbed instinctively . . . But I *hadn't made tea.*

A shiver ran through me. My morning routine was muscle memory. I woke up, I made tea, I sat in bed for ten minutes before starting my day. But this had been done for me. Thoughtfully. Knowingly. Like it had been done a hundred times before.

I wrapped my hands around the mug, warmth seeping into my palms. This should've been comforting, and yet my skin buzzed with unease.

Am I losing my mind? Is this all just a dream?

I forced a breath and walked to the bathroom, bracing myself as I flicked on the light. My reflection looked the same. Messy hair, sleep-swollen eyes, last night's mascara smudged under one lid. But my toothbrush sat next to another one in the holder. An electric razor that wasn't mine rested on the sink.

I gripped the counter as my stomach twisted.

What the hell is happening?

I looked at myself in the mirror one more time. At the girl staring back at me. She didn't look lost or untethered. She looked . . . happy. The oversize T-shirt I had thrown on before bed wasn't one I recognized. It smelled like Leo. And my phone, charging on the bathroom counter, was already lighting up with notifications.

February 14.

Valentine's Day.

A picture on my lock screen . . . a picture I had no memory of taking, showed Leo and me standing in front of a Christmas-lit café, his arm around me, both of us smiling like we knew something no one else did. It was time-stamped December 24.

No. No, no, no.

But I never met him in Paris for Christmas. I'd never gone. I was *supposed* to meet him but changed my mind and instead spent Christmas exactly how I always did, rolling my eyes at Hallmark movies and drinking wine with my friends, insisting I didn't regret a thing.

Right?

His voice was thick with sleep, rough around the edges, and came from just outside the door. "El, you okay?" I jumped and turned off the light, as if the dark could hide me.

I needed air.

Now.

Fleeing out of the bathroom to the front door, I flung it open, sucked in a huge breath, grateful there was no one in the hallway at such an early hour, and tried to slow my racing heart. Each wheeze followed the last when I heard an all-too-familiar voice tinged with a smooth South African accent call out, "El, you grabbing the paper? I made you tea already before falling back to sleep."

I looked down to find a copy of *The Wall Street Journal* resting on my welcome mat. Only I didn't subscribe to *The Wall Street Journal*! I carefully grabbed the rolled-up newspaper between my thumb and forefinger, like it might explode, and glanced at the plastic cover, where the mailing label read LEO KINDELL.

What the hell? He lives here? Lives here enough to have his morning newspaper delivered here?

I slowly backed into the apartment, holding the paper a good arm's length from my body like it could potentially ignite, and scanned the space around me. All the art on the walls was now different, the furniture laid out all wrong. My eyes flitted over to Pickles to see if, with her keen animal instincts, she could sense whether we were in danger, but she was just happily munching away on some dried alfalfa. Apparently, I was the only one who felt like they'd stepped into a wormhole. I wanted to pinch myself hard enough to wake up, but a sinking feeling rooted inside me that this wasn't something I was going to be able to undo.

I made my way back to the room, peering around the doorframe to make sure he was really there. Leo was sitting up in bed now, the covers pooled low around his waist. He scrubbed a hand over his face before offering me a lopsided, still-waking-up smile.

"There you are," he said, voice still gravelly. "Thought you ran off on me."

"I have your . . . um . . . *Wall Street Journal*," was all I could manage to squeak out. I hovered in the doorway, not knowing what to say, what to do, where to put my hands. My brain felt stuck between two versions of reality, neither making sense.

He reached behind his pillow. "And I have your Valentine's gift. Why don't you come back to bed and open it."

"I'll just stay right here at a safe distance, if that's alright," I said, skirting the bed in a wide arc to reach the nightstand. My mug was there . . . something to soothe my Sahara-dry mouth . . . and, if necessary, a makeshift weapon, should things take a turn.

He laughed and patted the empty spot next to him. "Stop being such a goof and come snuggle."

My expression pinched like I'd sucked on a lemon. "I don't really love to, you know, snuggle."

"Since when? Last night you were more than happy to be the little spoon."

I choked on a sip of tea. The thought of being the little spoon and *enjoying* it was almost too much to bear. "Speaking of last night? Were you at the wine event? Is that where we reconnected?"

"Wine event? What are you talking about? Last night you passed out with your head in my lap, watching *The White Lotus*."

The White Lotus! Maybe there was a clue in that as to what timeline or reality I'd jumped to.

"Right, right. What season are we watching? Which hotel is it?"

His mouth twisted and he narrowed his eyes at me, his words coming slowly. "The one in Thailand? The one we talked about going to for our honeymoon someday. Are you okay?"

Honeymoon?! What the actual—

"But we're not . . . We didn't get . . ." My eyes zipped down to my left hand, which thankfully was devoid of any engagement ring. And then my eyes flashed to a long box in his hand, wrapped neatly with navy paper and a white silk ribbon, and I started to sweat again.

Leo held up the wrapped package and playfully shook it. "And don't worry," he said, as if reading my mind, "this isn't a ring either, but don't you want to climb back under these cozy covers and see what it is?"

Sensing there was going to be no way to dissuade him, I relented and crawled back under the blanket, doing my best to keep a comfortable distance.

"That's better." He sighed as he leaned over to kiss me lightly on the forehead and passed me the box. "Happy Valentine's Day, sweetheart. The past month has been the best of my life. Seeing you beneath the twinkling lights of the Eiffel Tower was unforgettable, and moving to New York to be with you was the best decision I've ever made."

"You moved to New York . . . for me?"

"You say that like it's a surprise," he teased, tucking a strand of hair behind my ear. "Of course I did. You know that."

"I . . . I do?"

His brows drew together as he turned on his side, his washboard stomach tightening with the movement. He motioned to the gift. "Now, are you going to open it or not?"

Unable to delay the moment any longer, I tugged on one side of the white silk ribbon while the other fell away. Carefully, I lifted the lid and my pulse quickened as I peeled back the tissue paper to reveal a framed picture of what appeared to be a map of the stars.

"A constellation?" I murmured.

"Not just any constellation. It's from the night we reunited in Paris. I really do believe that fate, timing, and something bigger than we can even understand brought us together once . . . and then back together again. And now we'll always have a piece of that moment with us."

It was romantic and poetic and everything the woman who met Leo under the lights of the Eiffel Tower would want to hear.

Only I wasn't that woman. I never went to Paris. I never met Leo.

None of it had happened.

So how the hell was he lying here next to me?

And then I remembered the spell. The freakin' love spell.

My stomach bottomed out and all my blood rushed to my ears. Suddenly lightheaded, I swayed in the bed, remembering the red string, knotted and pulled taut between the old woman's fingers, and the intricately illustrated tarot cards splayed out on the table. I tried to recall her words, something about connections that were not so easily severed and second chances, even ones you didn't ask for.

Had she somehow conjured Leo back into my life? Though positively preposterous, it was the only somewhat reasonable explanation I could come up with for any of what was happening.

In this parallel universe, I'd apparently met Leo in Paris in December just like we'd planned. We fell in love, and then he decided to move to

New York to be with me. If I opened my dresser drawer, I was pretty sure I'd find his boxers tossed haphazardly next to my Hanky Pankys.

The magic had worked. I'd somehow gotten zapped to an alternate timeline, and this was my life now! I gasped and my hands flew to cover my mouth.

Leo's eyes sparkled with delight. "I knew you'd love it. And"—his accent even more evident—"this is just the start of the Valentine's Day surprises. Tonight there's so much more waiting for you."

"More surprises?" I managed. "I truly am not sure how many more surprises I can take today."

He chuckled. "Just a few more. And you're going to love them. I promise. But first, I have to head into the office for a bit while you're meeting Sonja for brunch." He popped a kiss to my lips before rolling out of the sheets and off the side of the bed to lumber toward the bathroom.

"Who?"

He paused and spun around. "Sonja. Your mother. Are you feeling alright, sweetheart?"

"My mother? You know my mother?"

"I mean, does anyone really *know* your mother? She's a genuine live wire, that one."

I nodded slowly, thrown by the fact that he seemed to have met her. "Yeah . . . she is."

"Don't forget to meet me outside Madame Tussauds in Times Square at seven thirty EST, sharp. I mean it," he said with a playful grin. "That's seven thirty Eastern Standard Time, *not* Elliot Standard Time." And with that, he stepped into the bathroom and closed the door behind him.

Dammit, I guess he does know me well.

I sat frozen, marveling at the apartment that was both the same and not, listening to the sound of the shower and the man singing inside it, both a stranger and not. His presence was oddly familiar yet unsettlingly foreign, much like the song he was belting out at the top of his lungs. At first, it was just a jumble of sound, but then the melody began to take shape. Suddenly, it hit me. Journey. "Faithfully." A great song, actually . . . if not for the fact that it was being absolutely butchered in there.

While the muffled strains of the song carried through the apartment, I moved on autopilot, pulling on jeans, socks, boots. I found myself humming along before I even realized it.

What the hell am I doing?

This was madness. This wasn't my life. And yet the shower was running, steam curling under the door, and Leo's voice filled the space as if this really was his home. I grabbed my bag and keys with shaking hands.

I needed to get out of here.

Now.

Chapter Six

If I lived my life on Elliot Standard Time, it was because it was learned. My mother operated on her own version I affectionately referred to as Sonja's Schedule, which meant she'd arrive at an appointment anywhere between "fashionably late" and "I'll get there when I get there."

The café around the corner from my apartment was relatively empty, most of the rush-hour crowd already long tucked away behind their office cubicles. Only a few remained, likely students and remote employees, hunched over their laptops and sipping away on steamy lattes and cappuccinos.

Navigating my way in a stupor, I wove through the tables and displays and arrived at the counter with the automatic response of a thousand caffeine-deprived mornings.

My mind was still spinning with questions about Leo: where he came from and why he'd even shown up at all. I assumed it had something to do with the love spell, but that didn't make waking up next to him this morning any less surreal. If anything it made it more so.

"Oof, rough morning? I'm guessing you'll need a double today." Zadie had already started moving to grab a large cup and scribble my name on its side.

I held up three fingers.

"I gotcha."

Clasping my hands together in prayerlike gratitude, I dipped my head and said, "Bless you."

"Meeting your mom today?" she asked over the sound of the whistling pressure valve of the espresso machine, plumes of steam billowing from it like a locomotive.

I looked at my phone for the time. "Eventually. Or at least that was the plan."

Zadie chuckled as she wiped the handle on the milk frother with a cloth. "You can grab a table, I'll have Jenna bring the coffee over to you when it's ready."

I settled in at a small, out-of-the-way high top with a view to the street and watched for one of Mom's crazy caftans or a brightly colored, crochet poncho drifting up the sidewalk. Finally, about thirty minutes *after* we were supposed to meet, she breezed in, her hair a mess of platinum curls on top of her head in a lopsided bun and a bright rosy tint to her cheeks.

"Oh, honey, I can't even tell you what a great morning I've had. My therapy session with Dr. Lydel was next-level enlightening. Like someone turned on a light in a room I didn't even know was dark. We started out by talking about the recurring dream I have. You know the one where I'm stuck on that cruise ship that never docks, and somehow we ended up healing my inner child. I cried, I laughed, I forgave my mother. What could be better?"

What could be better?!

Maybe hopping in a cab or on the subway so that I didn't waste the last half hour waiting on her? Maybe having some consideration for someone else's time? Maybe acknowledging with an apology, or I'd even settle for a half-hearted hand gesture that showed she felt the tiniest bit guilty for assuming, as usual, the world would simply adjust to her very lax schedule.

And therapy? Since when has she been in therapy? She used to say it was for "people with too much money and not enough imagination." At least that's what she'd said to me when I casually mentioned I was considering going to see someone, which, of course, I never did based on her judgmental stance.

Mom was continuing to ramble on and barely came up for air when Jenna came by with two menus. She glanced over at Sonja and said, "Can I get you anything to drink?"

"Yes, hi, one hibiscus iced tea, but can you please confirm that the petals weren't exposed to any negative energy during transport? I can taste stress."

Jenna looked dumbfounded, as if she wouldn't even know who to ask about the energy exposure of their tea's hibiscus petals. And to be fair, who would?!

Mom peeked out from behind the menu she was now studying, her bejeweled readers perched at the end of her nose with the pastel beaded chains draped around her neck. "El, what's that *you're* drinking?"

"A latte with three shots of espresso."

"Oh, sweetie, don't you know what caffeine does to your sleep cycle?" She shook her head and sighed. "It must be why you look so exhausted. You know what, instead of the hibiscus, I think I'll have a green tea matcha latte with oat milk, but only if it's fair trade. You have no idea how vicious the underbelly of the oat-milk production has gotten. Just awful."

"Do you ladies know what you'd like to eat?"

"Hmm . . ." Mom continued to examine the menu. "Are your eggs caged?"

"Caged?"

"As in, do they come from hens kept in tiny metal cages their whole lives, or are they free range, wandering around and happy? Their emotional state greatly affects the overall taste, but more importantly, happy eggs have fewer free radicals."

Jenna glanced at me, almost as if to verify that Mom wasn't kidding, and when I shrugged, she eyed the kitchen. "I can check with the kitchen, if you'd like?"

Mom waved a hand. "That's okay. I'll just have the dry rye toast."

Jenna nodded, tapping the order into her tablet before turning to me.

"Three-egg omelet with cheddar and bacon and a side of wheat toast. Thanks so much," I said, handing back over the menu. "How's the semester going, Mom?" I quickly added, hoping to steer the conversation away from a full-on debate about my breakfast selection and whether my chakras could withstand the negative energy of a wheat shaft that had died stressed and unfulfilled.

She reached into her bag and opened her paper planner up on the table. "Great so far. A very engaged group. That reminds me, when do you think you can come and present to them?"

Mom was a Women's, Gender, and Sexuality Studies professor at Barnard College, and my radio show had proved to be the perfect counterpoint to her unit on how romance had been shaped by historical narratives, literature, and pop culture. Mom liked bringing in "real-world perspectives," which mostly meant letting her students interrogate me about my opinions while she played moderator.

"Just email me some dates and I'll see what I can do."

"Speaking of dates, what are you doing the week of March twelfth?"

"The whole week? Um . . . I'm not sure. Work, I guess. And probably some other stuff. Why?" I took another sip of my latte and readied myself for whatever obscure request I was certain was coming next.

She flipped through the pages of her planner until she reached the week in question and then looked up at me with big, excited eyes. "Well, Keith and I have decided on Belize. What do you think?"

I narrowed my stare and waited for a beat, not quite following. "For spring break?"

Mom laughed and slapped my arm like she thought I'd been making a joke. "No, silly. The wedding. I mean, yes, it *is* my spring break, but it also happens to be a good time for Keith to step away from work. But I need you to be there. Please say you can come."

"Mom! What are you even talking about? I've never even met this guy, and you've only been dating for like what, four months?"

"Elliot Rose West, you lower your voice. And it's been four and a half. We met on Halloween, remember?"

I don't know why I was surprised by her news. History clearly illustrated that I shouldn't have been. If she went through with it (always a big *if*), Keith would be Husband Number Four. Well, Three-and-a-Half, if you didn't count the quickie Vegas wedding, a drive-through ceremony that was annulled less than forty-eight hours later to what's-his-face.

For as averse as I was to love, Mom, fully in the other camp, was addicted. Or to the idea of it, anyway. Always chasing that cosmically aligned happily ever after with relentless optimism, only to end up in her divorce attorney's office a few months later when reality didn't match the fairy tale. I mean, wasn't it telling that she had her divorce attorney's number saved as one of her Favorites in her contacts?!

Dad, her first "Prince Charming," had turned out to be a lying, cheating frog. After a whirlwind romance during their grad-school days and an equally impetuous wedding, he'd walked out on her while she was eight months pregnant with me.

Dumbstruck, I stumbled through my thoughts until I could gather enough words to form a retort. "Oh, so sorry, you've known Keith four and *a half* months, *excuuuuse* me. Then by all means, don't walk, run down the aisle. Clearly, I'm the one being unreasonable here for thinking an engagement should last longer than a seasonal Starbucks drink!"

Mom shook her head, pursed her lips, and *tsked*. "You know, I would have thought Leo might have softened you a bit, but it seems to me you're as cynical as ever."

At the use of Leo's name, my brain scrambled as the threads of my life twisted together into a tangled knot. How did she know him? How well did she know him? It felt like too much to try to find out, my brain already reeling, so instead I bit back, "Don't bring him into this. You don't know anything about it!"

"Honey." She reached across the table to clasp my hands in hers. "It seems like you're getting very worked up. Take a deep breath with me, relax your jaw a bit, and tighten your pelvic floor. Close your eyes, and let's just mindfully breathe together for a moment, shall we?"

I yanked my hands back. "Can we please leave my pelvic floor out of this?! And I don't want to breathe, Mom! Just for once, I want you to be reasonable. The definition of insanity is doing the same thing over and over again and expecting a different outcome, and here we are . . . again. You, jumping into yet another marriage with another guy who's going to, no doubt, break your heart."

"No, El, Keith is different. Like how Leo's different from Matty."

Matty.

Just his name alone was enough to make my blood run cold and my hackles go right up. In the throes of my anger and frustration, I wanted to hit the pause button and ask her how exactly Leo was "different from Matty." But at this point, did it even matter? I'd closed that door years ago. Closed it, locked it, and tossed the key where I'd never have to find it again.

Luckily, Jenna suddenly appeared with our food, giving us both the perfect excuse to drop the topic altogether. So for the next half hour, Mom and I ate and made strained conversation, both of us careful not to step on another minefield and set off an explosion that would ruin brunch entirely.

After clearing our plates, Jenna dropped the bill on the table, and Mom and I both reached for it.

"I'm the mom," she said, which was a bit ironic, considering the number of times I'd had to pull her out of bed after yet another heartbreak, another failed relationship. How many times I'd had to get myself dressed and out the door to catch the bus for school alone because she'd been busy wallowing in a destruction of her own making.

"Yes, but I'm the one signing a big book deal in the next few weeks, not to mention the thing with Sirius," I teased, raising an eyebrow.

She nodded, held her hands up in retreat, and let me claim the check. After Jenna returned my credit card, Mom and I both stood to put on our coats.

Mom pulled me in for a surprisingly tight hug. "I really do hope you and Leo can come to the wedding. I can feel it in my bones. This one will be different."

"I'll let you know."

"The invitation's in the mail," was the last thing I heard before she wrapped a thick crocheted scarf around her neck, grabbed her tote, and bustled out into the biting February air.

After Mom left, I took a few more sips of my coffee, my mind racing between her latest dive headfirst into matrimonial chaos and the far more pressing issue: Leo, who was, in all likelihood, still in my apartment.

What if Leo had never actually been there at all? What if I hallucinated the whole thing? What would *that* mean? Sleep deprivation? Stress-induced delusion? Brain tumor?!

I wasn't ready to find out. Instead, like the well-practiced emotional escape artist I was, I gulped down the last of my politically incorrect espresso and was revived with a burst of caffeine and a ton of new ammunition for tomorrow's show script.

Thanks to Mom, I would deliver a blistering takedown of whirlwind romances, list the many, *many* dangers of impulsive life-altering decisions, and make a very strong case for why love spells should come with a surgeon general's warning.

Chapter Seven

I barely acknowledged Ravi as I rushed past him and into my office like a blur.

"Nice to see you too, El," he called after me.

Doubling back, I peeked my head out of the doorframe. "Sorry, Rav, you know, when inspiration strikes."

He shooed me away with his free hand and sipped from his coffee mug. "Say no more."

I kicked my shoes off, powered up my laptop, and clicked open a new Word document. Like a boxer preparing for a fight, I cracked my knuckles, shook out my fingers, and took a deep breath, rolling my neck with a satisfying *pop*, ready to type out a revised script for today's show, using the fodder from brunch to add in some hilarious material. And like a wrecking ball, out spun a full demolition of all the clichés of love and marriage, not to mention ridiculously over-the-top romantic gestures, like meeting a holiday hookup under the Eiffel Tower at Christmas, for good measure.

I was on fire!

I broke each thought into a new segment, as if they and my emotions were an open spigot pouring onto the page. Dozens of controversial questions I knew would light up the switchboard brighter than a fireworks display on the Fourth of July came flying out of my fingers. Today's show was going to be epic. Spice. Snark. And the kind of straightforward candor

I was known for. Not to mention giving my agent and the suits at Sirius exactly what I was sure they were looking for.

I saved it on my desktop as DEFCON1.docx and chuckled to myself before shooting this latest draft over to Ravi. As I snapped the laptop closed, my phone vibrated beside it on the desk. I turned it over and just about fell out of my chair when I saw a text from Leo.

Leo, who was apparently a saved contact in my phone. A saved contact complete with a photo of us lip-locked under the Arc de Triomphe. I guessed we'd ventured over there at some point when we'd reconnected in Paris?

But if it had really happened, then why couldn't I remember any of it?

When I closed my eyes, the images were there, like a dream, hazy around the edges. Sepia-toned photographs from an old-timey camera. Leo and I, hand in hand, walking along the Seine. Sipping café au laits in charming Parisian cafés. Us rummaging through knickknacks at an antique market in Le Marais.

An icy shiver zipped up my spine. I *had* met Leo in Paris, or at least some version of me had. A record scratch that didn't just interrupt the song but changed it entirely. It seemed that, as planned, six months after we stood together in the Athens airport saying our goodbyes, we reunited, and apparently, all the sparks were still there?

Despite my reservations, my doubts, my career . . . I'd actually taken a chance on love?

No. I hadn't. I know I hadn't.

I'd called it off a few weeks before I was supposed to leave for Charles de Gaulle Airport. As much as I may have thought a fun tryst in Paris would be momentarily exciting, to meet Leo there would have indicated I was interested in more between us, and I wasn't. I couldn't be. So I decided it was better to just end it before either of us pictured it going somewhere it never should.

But then how was he here?! And why?!

The weathered face of the tarot reader from last night flashed through my mind again, and I almost laughed at how ridiculous it all was. But on the other hand, Leo *had* appeared in my bed out of nowhere. So what did that mean? It was actually magic? A love spell? A plot twist straight out of a Disney movie? Was I supposed to expect talking armoires next? Dancing candelabras? The idea that her spell had actually worked was completely bonkers. But if it wasn't that . . . then how did any of this make sense?

I needed answers or for her to reverse it or whatever she needed to do to put my life and my sanity back in working order. Before opening the text from Leo, I googled the number for Rooftop Reds and sat back in my chair as the phone rang.

"Rooftop Reds," a woman on the other end cooed.

"Yeah, hi, I'm Elliot West and I was the speaker at your event last night. I was wondering—"

"Speaker? Last night? We didn't have a speaker at our event last night."

"Of course you did. It was me."

"No. No, we didn't. Are you sure you're calling the right place, hon?"

"The Galentine's Day thing?"

"We held a Galentine's Day event here, yes," she replied with her voice going up on the word *yes* like she was trying to be polite though certain I was mistaken.

"Then I don't underst—" Right. Of course. In this multiverse version of my life, I wasn't the headliner at Rooftop Reds last evening. Instead, I'd apparently fallen asleep last night with my head in Leo's lap while we watched *The White Lotus*. "You know what? I must be mixing up my calendar. Sorry. Anyway, if you could just give me the contact information for the tarot reader you hired as one of the entertainers? I'd love to book a private reading."

"The who?" she huffed, now clearly annoyed with my confounding questions.

"The mystic. The tarot lady. Jet-black hair. A little older. You know, the one shuffling the deck like a card shark?" I joked.

A beat of silence. "We . . . we didn't have a tarot reader at the event last night either. We were *supposed* to," she sighed, "but the company had a double booking and couldn't get anyone to fill in, so we hired a calligraphist instead."

"Perhaps there was a last-minute availability with the company, and they sent one that you aren't aware of? Because I know for a fact there was a tarot reader at your event last night, and I really need to speak with her," I pressed.

"There's nobody else to ask. I was the one who checked in all the vendors and entertainers, and no one came to do tarot readings. Unless maybe it was just an enthusiastic guest who decided to set up her own fun. You know how those Brooklyn hipsters can be!" She laughed at her own joke, but when she didn't hear me join in, she cleared her throat. "I'm so sorry, but I don't think I can help you out. I s'pose I could give you the name of the company we usually use, but they aren't, like, *legit*. They advertise themselves more as comedic entertainment. They're not actually psychics. But I have heard about this one lady in Queens who apparently can—"

"No, no. It's okay. I'm just . . . Never mind. Thanks anyway," I managed, even though my brain was racing.

Who was the tarot card reader, then?!

I sighed, more confused than ever, the notification of Leo's unread text still lingering on my screen. I clicked on it and opened the GIF of Colin Firth warbling through the song "Our Last Summer" from *Mamma Mia!*

Underneath it said:

Leo: I can still recall . . . Happy Valentine's Day 😍

Was he serious?

Ravi poked his head into my office. "You ready? I need you in the studio in five for a sound check."

"Ready . . . and maybe a little *too* keyed up," I said, trying to shake off the text and the strange conversation about the tarot reader. I slipped my phone back into my pocket, grabbed a fresh printout of today's show copy, and followed him out the door.

"Great, keyed up is what boosts ratings," he said with a wink.

I settled into my seat and ran through a series of sound checks with the engineer before Ravi gave me the thirty-second cue. Slipping my headphones over my ears, I tapped the microphone one last time and waited for a final nod from the booth.

Ironically, I'd decided days ago that I'd kick off the show by talking about Commandment Number Seven from my Ten Commandments of Love and Dating: *Thou shalt not resurrect an ex.* Since Leo had suddenly reappeared in my bed this morning, no topic could've felt more on the nose or painfully relevant.

I took a breath, steadied my voice, and with one final nod from Ravi launched into my opening. "Hey there, loyal listeners. Elliot West here, your favorite voice of reason, coming at you from Midtown Manhattan. Though I know many of you may be celebrating Valentine's Day today . . . *bleh*"—I fake-vomited into my mic—"I think we've all spent enough time rooting through the pros and cons, but mostly cons, of such a stupid holiday, and honestly, I don't want to give it any more of a spotlight than it already gets. So instead, today we're talking all about the EX Factor. You know, that one guy who seemed perfect on paper and had you totally hooked but you knew deep in your bones the spark would fade faster than New Year's resolutions by January third. So don't go anywhere, because we're going to be tackling the ultimate relationship pitfall and probably the most sacred of all my commandments: *Thou shalt not resurrect an ex*, today, on *Love Is a Four-Letter Word.*"

Ravi turned up the intro music and gave me a thumbs-up before cuing me to jump back in.

"Ladies, it's time that we're honest with ourselves. They're our exes for a reason, right? Probably because they weren't just yesterday's news—they're the headline nobody wants to read twice. But in those moments of weakness, we convince ourselves to hit rewind, like a bad reality show on its seventeenth season. Why do we do it? Is it nostalgia? Loneliness? Or just plain old hope that this time it'll be different? Let's take our first caller." I pressed the illuminated button on the board. "Hi, you're on the air with Elliot West. What's your name and where are you calling from?"

"This is Linda from Montauk."

"Hey, Linda from Montauk. What's your take? Why, like clueless moths to a dwindling flame, do we keep getting pulled back to our exes?"

"I know with me and my ex, there's this undeniable chemistry. It's like this electric energy between us I just can't seem to shake. Maybe it's his pheromones or something, or the way he smells. *Ugghhh,*" she groaned. "It just gets me every time."

"Here's the deal: That magnetic pull? It's not fate or destiny. It's just your brain getting played. And pheromones? Pheromones make us no better than animals in heat. Do you really want to be a lioness chasing the same deadbeat tomcat? No. You don't. Trust me. Okay, let's take our next caller," I said, switching lines. "You're on *Love Is a Four-Letter Word* with Elliot West. What's your name and where are you calling from?"

"This is Adrienne from Forest Hills."

"Give it to me straight, Adrienne. How do the men we've kicked to the curb keep sneaking back into our hearts and, let's be honest, our beds?"

Just as I said the word *bed,* I glanced up and there was Leo, standing behind Ravi in the sound booth, clutching a take-out bag from my favorite sandwich shop down the street and giving me a small, shy wave.

Shit, what is he doing here?

Adrienne had already answered me, but in the blur of unexpectedly seeing Leo like a goddamned jack-in-the-box, I totally missed what she'd said.

"I . . . uh . . . sorry, Adrienne, can you repeat that? Bad connection on my end."

"Sure, I was just saying that sometimes it's not even about the guy, the ex. Sometimes it's timing, or careers, or just life pulling you in different directions. You're simply not on the same page. But then weeks, months, or even years later, things shift . . . and suddenly, you realize maybe you were meant to come back together after all."

At that, Leo's whole face brightened, obviously thinking of our relationship. But none of it was real. We hadn't come back together of our own accord. This was something else entirely. Something forced, something unnatural. Something masquerading as fate but scripted by some kind of dark magic.

I cleared my throat and charged ahead. "No. Returning to an ex is like trying to put toothpaste back in the tube. Messy, pointless, and guaranteed to leave you frustrated and with no more in there than you started with. If you weren't in the same place then, chances are you're both still reading different maps. Which makes this the perfect moment to remind our listening audience of Commandment Number Nine: *Thou shalt not confuse being wanted with being valued.* And Commandment Number Ten: *Thou shalt know thy worth—and add tax.*" I lifted my eyes to Leo and continued, "You know yourself better than anyone else. Don't let a little nostalgia convince you anything has changed just because they suddenly show up with flowers and a jawline sharp enough to cut through your common sense. Okay, next caller."

For the next forty-five minutes, I continued my sermon on exes, red flags, rebound traps, and the delusions we dress up as destiny, all the while Leo watched me from behind a wall of glass. I was honestly surprised he didn't hightail it out of there, but instead, he was still waiting for me when the show finally ended.

I pushed open the studio door and stepped into the sound booth. Ravi raised his hand for a high five. "You were on fire, El. Killer set."

I slapped his palm. "Thanks." Then I turned to Leo. "Hi. What, uh . . . what are you doing here?"

He handed me the takeout and said, "You rushed out of the apartment so fast this morning, you forgot your lunch. I thought I'd surprise you with a pastrami on rye from Katz's Deli. Your favorite. Besides, it gave me the perfect excuse to swing by."

I looked down at the bag, the foil-wrapped sandwich nestled in a handful of white paper napkins and packets of mustard. Katz's was all the way on the Lower East Side. Completely on the other side of the universe from the studio as far as New York City geography went. Not to mention the enormous peak lunchtime crowd he probably battled just to bring me something special. "Wow. Um. Thank you."

He motioned toward the studio with his thumb. "That was . . . that was really something."

I raised my shoulders. "That's *me*. That's what I do. Remember when we met in Mykonos, I was on assignment, talking to people about casual vacation flings? My brand is all about the pitfalls of love." I hoped the blunt truth might somehow jar him into realizing this current version of us was nothing like the one *I* remembered.

He pulled me into his chest with strong arms. He smelled great, like cedar and santal, and I suddenly understood completely what Linda had been saying about pheromones. "Exactly, it's your brand. Who you are on the radio. But that's not who you *are*. I know you, El."

I backed out of his arms and deadpanned. Not joking in the least. "Yes. It most certainly is who I am." But he barely registered the severity in my tone, the coldness in my reaction, as he pulled me back into a sweet bear hug I couldn't wriggle out of.

Dammit, he smelled so good it made my knees a little weak.

"I should probably get back to work. Ravi likes to do a postshow rundown," I said, squeezing out from under his arm.

He glanced down at his watch. "Oh yeah. Me too. I've got to get back to the office. But I'll see you tonight."

"Tonight?"

"Valentine's Day? Our date? Madame Tussauds? Seven thirty?"

Madame Tussauds? Ah yes. Because who wouldn't want to spend Valentine's Day surrounded by a bunch of dead-eyed wax figures of celebrities no one cares about? Regardless of what he thought, this guy clearly didn't know me at all. It was more than evident that whatever decision I'd made back in Paris had been a huge mistake.

And the sooner I let him know, the better. I'd break it off at the museum. Shut it down. Go back to normal.

So I nodded. "Right. Yes, of course, see you tonight."

Chapter Eight

I pushed my way through the throngs of tourists and street performers in Times Square, and there was Leo, holding a small potted succulent in front of Madame Tussauds, waiting for me.

"Right on time." He grinned. "I had the under/over at fifteen minutes. Elliot Standard Time, right?"

"Look, Leo, I—"

"Here, this is for you," he said, handing me the desert plant.

"Um. Thank you? But, *uhh*, why are you giving this to me exactly?"

"I'm well acquainted with your argument that," he said, clearing his throat dramatically and raising his hands as if to make air quotes, "'the gift of flowers is a pox on our overly capitalistic society.' So instead I chose something more practical. A cactus. It requires little care, little water, and they say having greenery in your office can be beneficial."

"Beneficial for whom? Never mind. Listen, you seem like a really nice guy and everything, but I can't . . ."

Just as I was about to finish the rest of my sentence ending whatever *this* was between us, a taxi came speeding around the corner, and in the blink of an eye, Leo pulled me in close so I didn't get splashed when the car hit a flooded pothole right next to where I'd been standing. Pressed up to his chest, I sucked in a quick breath.

Whoa. Why did he smell so damn amazing?! A fresh and clean contrast to the rank odors that saturated this overcrowded part of Midtown. His biceps were flexed as he held me upright, and it was almost like I'd forgotten the way his touch could ground me, even in the chaos of the city. Like it had in Greece.

"Are you okay?" he asked, easing me back just enough to scan my face. "The cab didn't get you, did it?"

I turned my head to examine my coat. "No, I don't think so."

"What do you say then?" he said, offering the crook of his elbow. "Shall we?"

Reluctantly, I slipped my arm through his and followed him farther down the sidewalk, surprised when we didn't turn into Madame Tussauds and instead kept walking.

"But I thought—"

"What? That I was taking you to Madame Tussauds for Valentine's Day?" He laughed. "I think I know you a little better than that. I just needed a meeting spot to throw you off track, and it seems like my evil plan worked."

He looked so proud of himself. It almost would have been downright adorable if this was a real Valentine's Day date, which, of course, it wasn't.

"*Okaaay*, so then, where *are* we going?" I asked.

"You'll see, my dancing queen."

"Your what?"

"Patience, young grasshoppah," he said as he spun me around with an impromptu move. Though caught off guard, my feet seemed to know what to do, and I twirled easily under his outstretched arm as an actual giggle escaped past my lips.

"How was brunch with your mother?" he asked, pulling me back to his side.

Before I could stop myself, the unrestrained truth fell out of my mouth. "How it always is with her, stressful and disappointing."

Though logic told me to keep my distance since he was practically a stranger, something deeper kept nudging me to open up, to let him see more than I usually allowed.

"Why disappointing?" Leo asked.

Another question. I fought to swallow down the words of everything pressing on me, but all the frustrations I'd been biting back came pouring out. "Three different husbands, and every single one cheated, walked away, and left her as a shell of her former self, and now she wants to take her chances with number four after knowing him for less than six months?!"

"Look at us, though? You and I only knew each other for what, like two weeks before we agreed to meet up again in Paris. I have to admit I wasn't sure you'd come. But then when I saw you coming through the crowd that day in December, my heart practically exploded out of my chest. When you find a connection like ours, you'll move heaven and earth, and even all the way from South Africa to Manhattan, to chase it. Protect it. Make sure it doesn't slip through your fingers. And now look at us."

But why, in this new timeline or whatever the hell this was, had I taken the chance on him?

Maybe, though, by coercing him even further down memory lane, he could help me piece together what actually had happened?

"Yes, that's all true," I faux-conceded in an attempted fishing expedition. "It was quite the whirlwind. Sometimes I can barely recall the exact details . . ."

"Really? 'Cause I remember it all so vividly. You telling me that before we met, you thought love was nothing more than an illusion. That you'd convinced yourself it wasn't real, that it was just a fairy tale people told themselves to fill the emptiness in their life."

"That sounds like me."

"Then you told me I was your safe harbor. That I made love feel possible again, like something you could finally believe in."

I blinked. "Well, that does not sound like me at all."

Leo studied me with a puzzled expression. For a second, I thought he might push the issue, but instead, he just shook his head and kept walking until he abruptly stopped in front of Studio 54, the legendary 1970s discotheque, transformed into a Broadway theater sometime in the nineties, and said, "Here we are. End of the line. Hope you're ready for your Valentine's Day surprise."

I stared up at the marquee, but my mind was already thousands of miles away, back on the island of Mykonos, to the night Leo and I had our first real date. Through a mix of persistence and undeniable charm, he eventually convinced me to give him a chance.

I suggested we meet at a neon foam party thrown by Le Ciroc on Super Paradise Beach, an event I'd been invited to by the brand. I still needed to grab a few last interviews for the show and figured it was the perfect place to blend work with a little fun. Dressed in a Day-Glo tangerine crochet dress with a black bikini underneath, I met up with him at the bustling beachside bar.

He looked incredible in fitted white linen pants and a matching button-down, the top few buttons undone to reveal his toned chest. The crisp whiteness of the fabric only further emphasized his rich tan and striking light eyes.

Between collecting interviews and sound bites, I found myself being surprisingly drawn back to Leo, who shared bits of personal history between sips of ouzo. He was the youngest of four, raised by older sisters who treated him like their personal dress-up doll and involuntary guinea pig for their homemade DIY beauty treatments.

He worked in private equity, consulting for McKinsey, specializing in advising investors on major deals, a detail he'd clarified after catching my confused expression when he'd given his job title. He explained that though the hours were relentless, he thrived on the constant movement and the way no two days ever looked the same.

His parents, married for over forty years, had recently retired to Pringle Bay, a quiet coastal village near Cape Town, where he'd grown up. As for him, the nature of his job meant relationships rarely had time to take root, but he confessed that, whether it was the overwhelming influence of his sisters, or his parents, who still ogled each other and snuck in pinches, pokes, and other playful reminders of their unrelenting love, Leo was a hopeless romantic at heart.

His revelation had stopped me dead in my tracks. Until that moment, he'd been the ultimate vacation fantasy. No strings, no expectations, just the thrill of the moment. Besides, weren't we all forever chasing the high of a fun flirtation in a foreign city? That's what this had been . . . at least for me. But after spending more and more time together, I wasn't so sure whether Leo and I were on the same page.

However, before I could process it any further, the DJ kicked up the energy, spinning electrifying mash-ups of eighties classics with current-day hits. The sound of Wham!'s "Wake Me Up Before You Go-Go" collided with Chappell Roan's "Pink Pony Club," making it nearly impossible to hear Leo above the beat. My body rocked to the rhythm, and I allowed myself to be taken away for a moment by the swell of the music, the neon lights, and the saccharine smell of the fog machine.

"Hey," Leo called out to me. "What do you say we go somewhere where we can actually hear ourselves think?"

"Why would we want to do that when *not* thinking is so much more fun?" I twirled in place, spotting a Le Ciroc brand rep circulating with shots of their newest vodka. Grabbing one off her tray, I punctuated my point to Leo by throwing it right down the hatch before snagging another shot for good measure.

I offered it to him, but he shook his head and gestured for me to go for it. So I did and then, after handing the glass back to the server, I tugged Leo by the hand onto the dance floor. Pulling him up against me, his hips swaying in time with mine, I relished in the delirium, in the muggy warmth that blurred the edges of the moment, and in the way his hands roamed up and down my body until they settled around my waist.

And then I knew I wanted him to kiss me. *Needed* him to kiss me. I pressed up on my toes and arched my neck as an invitation. Threading my fingers through his hair, I drew him closer and closed my eyes in anticipation.

Finally, his lips swept over mine. Gently, almost chastely, which was sweet but not exactly what I was aiming for. I leaned in harder, pressing myself forward to let him know it was okay to amp things up a bit.

"Hey, now," he said, stepping back to put some space between us. "Why don't we take a beat here."

I narrowed my gaze, studying him like an endangered species at the zoo. Never in the history of men had a guy "taken a beat" when situated in the fast lane to getting lucky. "What do you mean?" was the first thing that came to me amid my obvious puzzlement.

"I mean, I'd like the opportunity to woo you a bit first."

"That's sweet, but in this case really unnecessary."

"It's not unnecessary to me," he countered.

"Look, don't misunderstand me. I'm not the kind of girl who sleeps around, but I'm also not the kind of girl who's naively expecting any more to come out of something we both know is temporary. So you don't have to worry about the woo? Let's just enjoy the night for what it is."

"I've told you a bit about who I am. Now I want to get to know *you* better. And I'd rather not have a relentless bass line competing for my attention. C'mon, let's get out of here. I know the perfect spot."

The words *let's get out of here*, at least in New York singles lingo, had always been a euphemism for "Your place or mine?" But Leo seemed to genuinely mean it in its most literal sense. He wanted to leave the chaos of the party behind and go somewhere we could have an actual conversation.

I didn't know if it was the earnest look in his expression or the fact that, out of the corner of my eye, I could see the DJ getting ready to spray the entire crowd with a tsunami of neon foam, but I found myself nodding and taking his strong hand as he led me through the crowd and into a taxi that had just dropped off a group of partygoers.

"Little Venice," Leo called out to the driver, holding the door open as I slid into the back seat. He followed, pulling it shut behind him. The driver nodded and set off down the dark, winding roads of Mykonos.

About fifteen minutes later, the cab dropped us at a narrow maze of whitewashed streets, where couples strolled hand in hand through charming little boutiques and tavernas under scalloped fairy lights. I glanced down at my outfit, slightly mortified by my Day-Glo tangerine crochet dress and matching bikini.

"Leo, I don't think I can walk around like this."

He gave me a knowing grin, as if he found the situation more endearing than anything else, and pointed to a shop a little farther down the way, its bright-blue doors framing an array of delicately embroidered clothes on display outside.

I riffled through the racks, loading Leo's arms up with flowy white skirts, dresses, and blouses, before heading inside. Leo made himself comfortable on a small bench covered with dainty pillows while I tried on the different outfits, making a game of coming out to model each one for him.

He held up his fingers like a scoreboard, finally flashing both hands in the air when I emerged in a one-shoulder maxi dress that hugged me in all the right places yet flowed with the effortless ease of a classic toga. I spun around, letting the fabric skim and drape just right, then turned to the salesgirl. "Can I wear it out of the store?"

She nodded and I followed her up to the counter. Before I could even fish my credit card out of my wallet, Leo was already signing the receipt.

"Thank you. But you really didn't have to do that," I said, tucking my card back in my bag.

"I know. But remember how I mentioned I'm trying to woo you?" he said as we stepped out of the store and back onto the bustling street. It was almost 10:00 p.m., but the alleyways and shops were as busy as if it were midday.

"I get it, but I wasn't expecting a scene straight out of *Pretty Woman*," I said with a teasing smile.

Though I'd made it pretty clear that he didn't need to roll out the red carpet for me to be on board with a little summer fling, he stopped walking and turned to me, his gaze searching. "I know we only just met, but there was something between us right from the start. And I think you felt it too. So tell me why you seem so hell bent on pushing me away?"

His comment stopped me cold. "I . . . I'm not. I just don't know what exactly you want from me. I mean, we're both thousands of miles from home. We don't have to pretend this is going to be anything more than it is."

"Why do you keep saying that?"

I narrowed my eyes at him, a challenge to the man who for some reason could see me without really even knowing me. And regardless of the butterflies turning my stomach into soup, his intuition was more than a little unnerving. "Okay, well, what if I told you I don't believe in love. Like categorically don't believe in it."

"I'd say that some men would interpret that as some sort of challenge."

"But not you?"

"No. In my experience, love isn't a puzzle to solve or a prize to win."

I swallowed, caught off guard by his certainty. "Then what is it?"

"It's a risk. A chance." His voice was quiet but firm. "One you're either willing to take, or you're not."

"And you'd be willing to take that kind of chance on someone you barely even know? Someone you just met a few days ago?"

He tilted his head slightly. "I think I already have."

The memory of his words that night in Mykonos hung in the air, but just as quickly as it'd come, the vibrant neon lights of Studio 54 snapped me back to the present. New York City's familiar soundtrack of taxis honking and the chatter of dozens of people conversing all at once filled my ears, and above me, the marquee flashed in bold, glittering letters: MAMMA MIA! THE IMMERSIVE EXPERIENCE!

"You've got to be joking!" An involuntary squeal burst out of my lungs, half in disbelief, half in delight.

Leo grinned, stepping beside me. "A theatrical dining experience that transports guests to the Greek island of Skopelos for a night of dancing and debauchery." He nudged me playfully. "I remembered how you mentioned once that you wanted to go. And Greece *is* kind of our thing."

I turned to him, my pulse still unsteady, though now for an entirely different reason. "You actually listened?"

His smile deepened. "Of course I did. Now, are you ready to embrace your inner dancing queen or what?"

I swallowed a laugh, staring up at the doors, then back at him. "Are you?" I challenged.

Leo didn't hesitate. Instead, he tightened his grip on my hand and said, "Oh, I'm ready. I just don't know if the rest of the audience is quite ready for me hittin' those high notes."

I rolled my eyes but couldn't fight the smile tugging at my lips as I followed him into the theater, the familiar beat of "Waterloo" blasting through the lobby speakers as we were swept inside with the crowd.

Chapter Nine

Leo held the door for me, his hand resting on the small of my back, a touch both gentle and intentional. As we walked through the dark, narrow hallway of the transformed club, the space unfolded into something almost unrecognizable. It looked more like the Plaka in Athens than a New York discotheque, with whitewashed walls, flickering lanterns, and vines of bougainvillea hanging from archways.

A shimmering, mirrored ball spun overhead, casting flashes of silver and gold across the dance floor, reflecting off sequined-clad revelers who swirled and swayed like something out of a dream. Inside, the lights were bright, almost blinding. But through the haze of the smoke machines, there was Leo. Steady beside me in the sea of chaos, as if he belonged here. As if this night were just another chapter in the story of us.

The one where I'd chosen to meet him this past Christmas in Paris.

A bell-bottom-clad server swung by, holding a tray of Voulez-Vous Vodka Sours, and Leo grabbed two without hesitation. "For the lady," he said with an exaggerated flourish.

I raised an eyebrow. "You're really leaning into this, huh?"

He shrugged, handing me the drink with a grin that was as knowing as the one before. "You once said that for you, *Mamma Mia!* was 'the cinematic equivalent of a warm hug.' And I figured, after brunch with your mom, you could use one."

I blinked, taken aback. I *had* said that exact thing after seeing the movie years ago, and every time I fired it up on Netflix since. How did he know that? The love spell's meddling now hummed at the back of my mind, like a tune I couldn't shake, tangled with the pulsing beats of ABBA echoing through the venue.

We were led to a table near the dance floor as a cast of actors in spandex and platform heels wove through the crowd, belting out "Super Trouper" like they were auditioning for Broadway.

The waiter appeared, as though summoned by the absurdity of it all, carrying two plates of something suspiciously orange and cheesy. "Here we are! Two orders of Take a Chance on Me Mac and Cheese. The table next to you sent them over. Said something about a bet?"

I whipped around to see a group of women, probably in their fifties, waggling their eyebrows at me from across the room. "You're the radio girl! Right? Elliot West?" one of them called out. "We heard yesterday's show all about your Valentine's Day cynicism! So we just wanted to see if you're actually having fun or what?"

Leo laughed, leaning in toward me with a mischievous glint in his eyes. "Oh, she's having fun. She just may not be ready to admit it yet."

But here's the thing . . . I *was* having fun. And it wasn't just because of the ridiculousness of it all. Not because of the sparkles, or the costumes, or the music that made it feel so right. It was the way Leo effortlessly disarmed me, like he knew exactly how to tug at my heartstrings without pulling too hard. The way he read me, like sheet music, like some melody I couldn't quite name but couldn't help but hum along to. He didn't pressure me to feel a certain way, but somehow, he made me want to jump in with both feet.

And *that* was a dangerous kind of charm.

I didn't fully understand it until that first night in Little Venice in Mykonos, when after my declaration about not believing in love, Leo led me through the labyrinth of small streets that opened up to the waterfront. The Aegean Sea lapped against stone foundations, where people strolled past holding hands. It was there that I first realized just how easily he could pull me in.

We found a small taverna where we picked our fish from a display, and the octopus was so fresh it looked like it had just crawled out of the ocean. The waiter recommended a bottle of Santorini Assyrtiko, explaining that its crisp, citrusy notes would pair perfectly with the seafood.

Tourists and locals crowded the tables, their voices blending into a melodic hum of Greek, Italian, French, and scattered bits of English, floating on the very breeze that seemed to be turning the iconic windmills in the distance. The air was rich with the scents of grilled cod, briny feta, and fresh oregano, mingling with the sharp tang of ouzo and the honeyed sweetness of baklava cooling on trays nearby.

Little Venice at night was an intoxicating collision of chaos and charm. And as I gazed out at the dark horizon, where the lights danced across the water like scattered stars, I felt caught in the space between reality and something far more enchanting.

We settled in, and I became aware of the way the humidity had brought out the texture in my hair, now curling freely around my face, wild and untamed. Leo reached over, his hands brushing my cheek as he tucked a strand behind my ear.

"It's really beautiful. Thank you for bringing me here," I said, the warmth of his fingers like fire against my skin.

"*You're* really beautiful."

I shook my head. "I keep telling you, you don't have to worry about the woo."

"Is that like a saying from your radio show or something?"

"No, but maybe it should be," I said, pulling out my phone to quickly add it to my Notes app.

He scrubbed his chin, studying me. "I can't quite work you out."

"Really? And I thought I'd made myself pretty clear," I replied playfully.

Crossing his arms over his chest, he responded, "That's right, the girl who categorically doesn't believe in love." He sipped the wine and I watched the golden liquid touch his lips before it seemed to drip lazily down the sides of the glass. "Have you ever heard the Greek myth of Atalanta and Meleager?"

I shook my head. "No, I don't think so."

"Atalanta was a fierce huntress who swore she'd never marry. The only way she'd even consider a suitor was if he could beat her in a footrace."

"A race? That's a bit extreme . . . and random."

"It was. And she was faster than anyone. No man had ever beaten her. But Meleager . . . he didn't try to outrun her." Leo met my eyes. "He ran with her. He kept pace, just to be near her, to understand her. He wasn't trying to win. He just wanted to show her he was there, right alongside her."

Something about the way he told the story made my pulse quicken. But I refused to get caught up in the moment. "If you think I'm going to fall for you by the end of this dinner, then you're a bigger hopeless romantic than I feared."

"Of course not by the end of this dinner, don't be silly." He casually plucked a fat green olive from the small ceramic bowl in the middle of the table and popped it into his mouth. "How much longer are you staying in Mykonos?"

I rested my chin in my hands. "Another week and a half or so. Why? What exactly do you have in mind?"

"Like I told you, I have the good fortune of being able to work from practically anywhere. So what if I extended my trip too?"

"You know I'm not going to fall any more in love with you over the next seven to ten days, right? In fact, it's actually more likely that somewhere in that time we realize we have nothing in common, aren't even remotely attracted to each other, and are now trapped in this ridiculous trip, counting down the days till it's over."

"Well, despite *that* glowing review, I still think it's a great idea. So what does that say about me? Look, I didn't have a lot of time for sightseeing while on our stag do, but I would like to explore the island a bit. And I'd like to do it with you." He paused a beat, rolling the olive pit on his tongue, and sighed. "You might be right, and this could just be a fleeting moment on a rock in the middle of the Mediterranean Sea. But what if it's more? Elliot, I'm not asking you to slow down, I'm just asking if I can run alongside you."

For the next week and a half, he did.

Together, we snorkeled at a secret swimming spot near Fokos Beach, enjoyed a private wine tasting in Ano Mera, explored the lighthouse at Armenistis, wandered through hidden alleyways in Mykonos Town searching for the best loukoumades, and watched the sunset most nights from a quiet, tucked-away cove only the locals seemed to know about.

Throughout it all, I did my best to tell myself I wasn't falling for him. It was easy, at first, to just dismiss it as nothing more than a summer indulgence with a very clear, very imminent expiration date. But with each passing day, each heated glance, each lingering touch, a chink in my armor let in just enough light to make me wonder whether I was fighting a battle I'd already lost.

And clearly I had lost, because here I was, sitting across from him in the electric hum of Studio 54. Only now, Leo wasn't just a passing thrill. Apparently, he was my actual boyfriend.

The music changed to the rhythmic melody of "Dancing Queen," and without hesitation, I let him pull me to my feet. My heart was beating too loudly, but he was already twirling me into the flashing lights, letting loose like it was the easiest thing in the world.

I thought for sure I'd stumble, but he was there, steady, matching every move, every word of the song. His voice, off-key and loud just as he'd promised, was the only thing I could hear as we sang together, laughing and spinning, unembarrassed and free.

By the time we collapsed back into our seats, breathless, hoarse, and desperately in need of some water, the stage had shifted. In the center of the room, a spotlight captured the actress playing Sophie as she began singing "Lay All Your Love on Me" with the actor playing Sky.

"That scene looks eerily familiar," Leo remarked.

I turned to him. "What do you mean?"

"Really? A hopelessly lovestruck guy desperately trying to win over his girl on the shores of a Greek island beach?" He lifted his eyebrows at me, and through his cheeky grin, I caught a flash of amusement.

It was all too much. The adoring way he was looking at me. The intensity in his eyes. And most of all, the fact that I didn't have the first clue as to how we'd gotten here. Yes, Leo had managed to pierce my stone heart in Mykonos. Even that day in the Athens airport when we made our plan to meet up six months later, I was so swept up in the moment I actually thought I might . . . And then, time passed.

We'd talked and texted, and he was just as funny, sweet, and charming from afar, but the radio show was really starting to take off, and then the book offer came in, all based on my brand of believing that love was a fleeting illusion. I convinced myself that what we'd had over the summer was lightning in a bottle and that the man I was planning to meet under the Eiffel Tower would never, could never, live up to the foolish fantasy so many women fell victim to.

And *I* refused to fall because I knew better.

All the messy history with my parents . . . and then with Matty . . .

Yeah, I knew better.

So I stayed in New York and buried all my feelings for Leo beneath logic and ambition until whatever magic, enchantment, or cosmic chaos had happened on Galentine's Day brought him crashing back into my life.

I shook the thought away as a line of dancers sashayed through a side door, waving white linen napkins in the air to the percussive upbeat music. Leo grabbed his and mimicked their motions along with everyone else at the table. Watching him intently, his bright smile and genuine enthusiasm was just as captivating as the show itself.

I blinked, trying to reconcile the reality in front of me with the version of myself who would have scoffed at all this just a few months ago. No, just *yesterday*! Me? Getting swept up in a *Mamma Mia!*–themed disco extravaganza? Laughing and singing along as strangers in elaborate costumes twirled napkins overhead like we were extras in *My Big Fat Greek Wedding*? It felt upside down. I was supposed to be the one with my arms crossed, making snarky, cynical comments about how this was all just one big ploy to sell overpriced Voulez-Vous Vodka Sours.

But instead, here I was, leaning into the moment and into *him*.

Leo glanced over, catching me watching him, his grin widening. "What?" he mouthed, amusement dancing in his gaze.

I shook my head, feeling my cheeks flush. *Nothing,* is what I wanted to say. Except it wasn't nothing. It was everything. The way his energy drew me in, the way he made it so damn easy to let my guard down. I wasn't supposed to feel this much. Or feel this free. Not after heartbreak had kicked my ass one too many times, leaving me with nothing but disappointment and another strong justification for writing off love for good.

And yet, I did feel fantastically free.

For a girl who prided herself on keeping her feet firmly planted on the ground, I was starting to feel dangerously close to floating.

Thankfully, the moment was broken and I was off the hook from answering when one of Donna and the Dynamos, the actress playing Tanya, left the conga line and kick-ball-changed over to our table, pulling Leo from the crowd just as the music changed to "Does Your Mother Know," the number in the musical where she flirts with all the younger men on the beach.

Leo looked slightly uncomfortable as she gyrated, teased, and danced in circles around him. But being a good sport, he played along, the audience cheering and urging him on more with every pelvic thrust.

And when "Tanya" shimmied his shirt right off him, his broad shoulders and still-bronze skin evoking whistles and whoops from the ladies in the audience, he turned the same color as the actress's candy-apple lipstick, and my face flushed with secondhand embarrassment.

The music flowed into a new melody as she gave Leo a quick peck on the cheek, ruffled his hair, and tossed him his clothes. He tugged his shirt back over his head, his smile never faltering, and she danced him back over to our table as I patted the chair next to me, but instead, Leo held out his arms as an invitation to join him on the dance floor.

I shook my head no, but he remained undeterred. "C'mon, Elliot, what've you got to lose?"

With the song "Take a Chance on Me" now pulsing at full volume and his hand extended toward me, my pulse skipped in time with the music. Despite every instinct that usually kept me firmly on the sidelines, the thought of taking this chance suddenly felt less like a risk and more like the only thing I wanted.

And as colorful confetti rained down on us both like we were standing in the middle of Times Square at the stroke of midnight on New Year's Eve, I did.

Chapter Ten

Ravi looked shocked when he walked off the elevator to find me already in the office, reviewing my notes for the epic post–Valentine's Day show. I'd snuck out of the apartment early while Leo was still sound asleep. The two of us had danced until Studio 54 turned on its lights and kicked us out. By the time we made it home, we were too exhausted to do anything but crawl beneath the covers, where he held me until I bolted awake this morning, heart racing, just to check that he was still there beside me and it hadn't all just been a dream.

Yes, I was wildly attracted to him. That was never the problem. And yes, we'd had a magical night, dancing until dawn. My raccoon eyes and throbbing feet were proof of that! But I wasn't ready for a sexual kind of intimacy yet. What had happened between us in Greece had been spontaneous, a whirlwind caught up in sun-soaked days and wine-drenched nights, where reality, regardless of what we said, felt a million miles away.

But this? This was different. Waking up next to him this morning, with two months of my life missing and my heart teetering between confusion and curiosity . . . I needed to catch up to the version of me that had lived those days before I could even consider anything physical happening between us. The version of me that apparently trusted this man enough to invite him to move in, and sleep next to me, and build a life I wasn't even sure I was ready for.

So I left Leo a note saying I had to be at the studio early, and for the first time, maybe ever, beat Ravi into work.

He tapped lightly on the door, this time clutching his And Yet Despite That Look on My Face You Are Still Talking mug. "My, my, Elliot West, as I live and breathe," Ravi teased in a dramatic Southern drawl, fanning himself with his hand.

"Stop, it's not like I'm *always* late."

Mom was always late. I was just more, let's say, "strategic" about my arrival times.

"Well, we don't refer to it as Elliot Standard Time around here for nothing."

Leo had used that exact expression yesterday: Elliot Standard Time. He'd dropped it so casually, like he was already in on the joke my friends never let me live down. Like he was a part of my inner circle. But if that were true, then why hadn't it occurred to me that Ravi, or any of my friends for that matter, might be able to help me piece together the last two months of missing memories?

"Ha. True. Good one. Elliot Standard Time. Yesterday, Leo ribbed me about that too. You like him, right? I mean, as far as, um, boyfriends go?" I shot a glance up at Ravi and paused, waiting for him to throw out a clue . . . any clue at all.

Ravi eyed me quizzically. "Leo?" He took a deliberate sip of his coffee and shrugged. "Well, sure, I had my concerns at first, of course. But overall he seems like a good dude."

I ran my hand through my hair and feigned coolness (probably doing a terrible job), plopping my elbows onto the desk and resting my chin in my hands. "Huh . . . really? Concerns? Interesting? Like, um, what kind of concerns?"

His face contorted like he was holding back something he wasn't sure he should say. "I guess not really so much about him as it is about you."

I pulled back and sat up a bit straighter, now on high alert. "About me? What does that mean?"

He scooted some papers aside on the desk and rested his hip against it, settling in. "Meaning, you've built your brand on the idea that love is an illusion, so when you returned from your trip to Paris and announced to the office you'd fallen head over heels, I admit I was worried. Worried for the Sirius deal, for your book offer, for your brand, all of it. It felt like overnight, you might unravel everything we've worked so damn hard for. And for a guy of all things?! It was like a kung-pow kick of irony straight to the gut."

Dread settled in my chest, a slow, tightening vise. "But it hasn't, um, changed me or any of that . . . has it?"

Now Ravi was looking at me like I'd really gone off the rails, his squinted eyes so narrow I could barely see his irises. "No . . . Thankfully, you've been as cynical as ever. But should I be concerned? Are you having some kind of amnesiac episode or a stroke or something? Why are you acting like this is all headline news?"

Relief washed over me. Thank God, I hadn't done anything to jeopardize my career. I hadn't let myself get swept away, hadn't made any rash decisions that could undermine everything I'd worked for.

But the spell? Had it rewritten my past or just inserted Leo into my present? Had it somehow made me choose to meet him in Paris back in December, setting everything in motion? Or had it instead just dropped him into my life now and stitched together a false history to make it all feel real?

The truth was I had no freakin' idea, and trying to untangle the complexities of multiverse theory was giving me a migraine, not to mention a full-blown existential crisis.

"Amnesia? Um . . . I don't think so. I'm okay, just tired from last night."

"Oh, right, Valentine's Day. Do me a favor and go for the jugular today, regardless of how swoony your evening with your new beau may have been. Keep reminding yourself about all the needless spending. All those crusty boxes of overpriced chocolates. All the public PDA. You have *years* of stories and material. You can't let a guy you've known for a few months soften your edge."

I couldn't even believe we were having this conversation. "You're worried about me waxing poetic?" I said, shuffling my notes, "I'm primed and ready for this postgame V-day takedown. Trust."

Ravi took a sip of his coffee, nodding thoughtfully before turning on his heels, his sneakers squawking on the linoleum floor as he made his way to the sound room to get ready for the show.

This, ladies and gentlemen, was my Super Bowl. I could almost hear the *Rocky* theme echoing in my mind as I took a deep breath, cracked my neck, and rolled my shoulders back. With one last glance at my notes, I was ready. I marched from my office into the studio, flopped down onto my seat, and pushed a pair of headphones over my ears. Leaning into the microphone, I murmured my usual, "Test one, two, test," until Ravi gave me a thumbs-up.

"You're on in thirty seconds," he said. "Knock 'em dead."

"That's the plan. Love is a battlefield, and I, my friend, am a mothereffin' sharpshooter."

Ravi laughed, leaned into his mic, and let out a dramatic *kaboom* before cuing up the familiar intro music. The overhead red light flashed three times before turning green, and I was off to the races.

"Good morning, heartbreakers, hopefuls, and anyone currently drowning in post–Valentine's Day regret," I purred, my voice sliding into that familiar mix of warmth and wickedness my listeners had come to expect. "It's your resident love cynic, Elliot West, here to support you like a sister through the aftermath of Cupid's latest carnage. Did you wake up next to Mr. Right . . . or Mr. Just for Last Night? Did the flowers he bought you yesterday wilt before your first cup of coffee this morning? Or are you still picking stray glitter from that heartfelt, handmade card that felt more like a Pinterest cry for help? If so, you're in the right place. For the next two hours I will do my very best to cure your love hangover on this post–Valentine's Day morning. I want to hear from you! Everything from your V-day horror stories to you gloating about your evening with Prince Charming, I want to hear it all. So hit me up at 1-800-844-5683. That's 1-800-UGH-LOVE. Just be warned, I am armed with sarcasm and amped up on righteous indignation this morning, so don't expect any mercy."

I glanced over at the switchboard, which was already aglow with incoming calls. I pressed down to answer the first in the queue.

"You're on *Love Is a Four-Letter Word* with Elliot West. What's your name and where are you calling from?"

"This is Charlotte calling from Stamford."

"Hey, Charlotte from Stamford. How was your Valentine's Day?"

"So, there's this guy I've been sort of seeing these last couple of months."

"Whoa, I'm going to stop you right there. What do you mean, 'sort of seeing'?"

"Well, we hang out sometimes, mostly at his house because he's got all the sports channels. I cut the cord on cable a while ago. Anyway, last night he invited me over."

"Wait . . . he invited you over *for* Valentine's? Or last night he just so happened to invite you over? Those are two very different things."

"What do you mean?"

"Well, if it's the first one, you were a priority. If it's the second, you were an afterthought."

Charlotte hesitated. "I'm trying to remember . . ."

"Sweetheart, if you don't remember, it's because there is nothing to remember. You were just a last-minute 'I'm lonely on Valentine's Day' backup. ESPN or not, you need to be the 'main event' in his life. Love Commandment Number Three states: *Thou shalt not put all thy eggs in one emotionally unavailable basket*, and it sounds to me like you've got a whole dozen in there. The price of eggs these days ain't cheap, and yours shouldn't be either. Next caller!"

Ravi coughed to stifle a laugh, but I was in the zone now, the cadence of the show unfolding effortlessly. I clicked over to the next person on the line.

"This is Elliot West, you're on the air."

"Hi, Elliot. Longtime listener, first-time caller. So excited to get through! This is Moira from Manhasset."

"*Ooh*, I'm lovin' that alliteration. Whatcha got for me, Moira from Manhasset?"

"Last night, my bestie hosted a Lonely Hearts Club dinner, where each guest brought an ex to set up with someone else."

"Hmm, 'cause there aren't a million different ways *that* could go sideways. But continue . . ."

"It didn't just go sideways, it went off the rails, into a ditch, and burst into flames! I drank way too much wine and ended up hooking up with my ex, who I don't even like or respect, in my bestie's front hall coat closet, because I was feeling a little bit sad about being single on Valentine's Day, and now even worse, he won't stop texting me."

"You must have missed my show yesterday. This is why the Seventh Love Commandment clearly states"—I punctuated *clear-ly-states* with an audible tap of my finger to the desktop—"*Thou shalt not resurrect an ex.* Bringing back an ex is like reviving Frankenstein's monster: messy, terrifying, and bound to destroy everything in its path. We gotta let the dead stay dead. Not to mention, Moira, that you have beautifully illustrated my exact point. This stupid Hallmark holiday made you feel vulnerable. Less than. A failure. A random date on a calendar that some greedy corporate goon probably invented to line his pockets or score a date, turning your choice to be single into some sort of personality flaw. No, ma'am! Next caller."

The phone lines were blowing up. Now I knew how Rocky Balboa must have felt before knocking out Apollo Creed. I stretched my arms out and cracked my knuckles before pressing the next lit-up phone line. "You're on *Love Is a Four-Letter Word* with Elliot West. What's your name and where are you calling from?"

"Is this really Elliot West? Holy shit, I'm such a fan. Oh, shit, can I say shit? Ahh, shit, sorry!"

I couldn't help but laugh audibly. "Don't worry. FCC fines only apply if I say it. So tell me, who do I have the pleasure of speaking with on this fine February morning?"

"This is Dina calling from Queens. I can't believe I got through!"

"Well, believe it, Dina. You're live. Talk to me, Queens. What's on your mind?"

"Well, actually, this is kind of funny," she said, a nervous laugh in her voice. "I saw you last night. When I was out with my girlfriends."

That caught my attention and a sharp pang of panic jabbed under my ribs. "Oh?"

"At the *Mamma Mia!* immersive thing," she added quickly. "It looked like you were on . . . on a date?"

My brain flashed to last night and the swirl of disco lights, the ABBA soundtrack, and the group of older women who'd practically cornered me, wanting to know if I was having a good time.

Sweet mother of Meryl Streep.

I sloughed off my panic and proceeded with caution, my guard already up. "Oh yeah, so much fun. I've had 'Dancing Queen' stuck in my head all morning. For those of you like me who love glitter and wildly enthusiastic choreography, I can't recommend *Mamma Mia!: The Immersive Experience* enough," I said, leaning into an over-the-top plug for the show in a desperate attempt to change the subject. "Not very demure, but oh-so-very sequined. So did you gals have a good time?"

"Yeah, I just . . . I was wondering. How can you say all this stuff about love being one long con job when you were out there looking like you were living your very own rom-com?"

My heart dropped into my stomach. "I'm sorry, what?"

"Oh, come on!" Her voice was playful but sharp. "You were *beaming*," she went on, her words coming faster now, like a freight train barreling toward me. "And dancing. With that gorgeous guy. What is it you always say? That love is a scam? Well, it sure looked like you bought the deluxe package, honey."

My throat went bone dry as my mind scrambled, grasping for a lifeline.

"*Okaaaay*, just hold on there a minute," I said, forcing a laugh that sounded about as natural as a politician's apology. "About that . . . I can totally explain how it probably looked like we—"

"Explain what? That you're kind of a hypocrite?" She said it as a joke, but it clearly was not.

Ravi's eyes shot up to lock with mine, horror-struck and frozen in place, as a noticeable hush fell over the studio.

"I wouldn't call it hypocrisy," I started, aiming for calm but hitting somewhere closer to manic. "I mean, yes, I *was* there. And yes, I *may* have been . . . enjoying myself, but that doesn't really mean—"

"'Enjoying yourself'?" she barked. "Girl, you looked like you were auditioning to be the fifth member of ABBA!"

Jesus. What, did she take notes?

"Look, I . . . It's complicated, okay? I was doing research . . . for the show . . . a secret segment sort of thing . . ."

"On what? How to fall head over heels while singing 'Gimme! Gimme! Gimme!' at the top of your lungs?" The caller's taunt was a biting, playful jab . . . and she wasn't relenting.

My pulse pounded in my ears. "It's not what it looked like," I blurted, now in a full panic. "I wasn't—I mean, we were just—"

"We? So there *is* a 'we'?"

Oh.

No.

"I didn't say that!" I practically shouted.

"You kind of did."

My cheeks burned. "Okay, but—"

"So, Elliot . . ." Her tone went syrupy sweet, the one-two punch of the final knockout. "Care to explain how that fits into your anti-love manifesto?"

A choked noise escaped me. I opened my mouth, but no sound came out.

The air went dead.

And I was flatlining.

Chapter Eleven

"Go on, we're all listening," Dina, the relentless caller, prodded, still hanging on the line, as the ON AIR light blinked tauntingly on the desk.

I took a breath, doing my best to recompose myself, even though sweat was starting to trickle down my armpits.

Calm down, Elliot. This doesn't have to be a big deal.

All I had to do was downplay everything with a sort of vague indifference, which shouldn't be too hard, considering that was basically how I felt about Leo anyway.

Vaguely indifferent.

. . . Didn't I?

I exhaled sharply, letting my shoulders drop. "Okay, fine, you caught me." I threw my hands in the air in surrender even though Dina couldn't see me through the phone line. Sighing, I began, "I was out on a kind-of date with a guy I met over the summer who, by some strange twist of fate, suddenly reappeared in my life, as if by magic. But that's a story for another day. And yes, maybe I was beaming—your words, not mine—but I can assure you, it isn't that serious. Sure, Leo's ridiculously charming and, let's be honest, very easy on the eyes. And I have to give him credit for planning such a fun and out-of-the-box evening, knowing how obsessed I am with *Mamma Mia!* Not to mention the fact that we met in Greece, so his thoughtfulness was impressive. But it's not like I've suddenly abandoned all my beliefs just because some guy managed to exceed my expectations for *one night*. Even if I did have a good time. Like a surprisingly good time. I mean . . . well, I'm not sure what that even means. Except, I guess, maybe, I'd have to admit that Valentine's Day isn't always a total scam. I suppose, with the right person, it can even be sorta nice."

As the words fell out of my mouth, I froze and glanced up at Ravi in the sound booth, whose eyes were as wide as saucers. He held up his WHAT THE ACTUAL F coffee mug to the glass partition as he shook his head in disbelief.

"Anyway, it's been great speaking to you, Dina," I quickly stammered. "Now, let's take a brief pause to hear from our sponsors." I queued up the outro music, signaling our commercial break, before Ravi stormed into the studio.

"I . . . I . . ." Ravi stammered, flustered and frantic. "What the hell was that, Elliot?"

"What? What's wrong?" I blurted defensively, even though I knew very well what he meant.

He held up his fingers to make air quotes. "'Valentine's Day isn't always a total scam. I suppose, with the right person, it can even be sorta nice.'"

"Oh, that?" I waved a dismissive hand at him, despite the fact that my heart was pounding out of my chest. "I don't know. It just . . . just came out. Anyway, you need to do a better job screening the callers. I don't appreciate being put on the spot like that."

I knew I wasn't being fair. Ravi had been my biggest champion (not to mention one of my closest friends) since we'd met at college in the booth of Brown's small radio studio. Curmudgeonly, yes, but also steadfastly supportive. And talented as hell. He was the one who'd sent tapes of the show to the top talent agencies in NY and LA. The one who convinced me we could take this thing to the next level, never once wavering in his belief that our show would be a success.

"On the spot? You're the one who got caught out on a romantic date," he countered.

"It wasn't a romantic date. Leo surprised me. I didn't have any say in our plans."

"Uh-huh. I'm sure you were *SOS*-ing for a way out the whole time."

I dramatically dropped my jaw in shock. "Rav, did you just use an ABBA pun?"

"*Soooo* not the point. Look, you swore this relationship wouldn't change you or your hard stance on love."

"I did? Right, I did. It hasn't and it won't."

"It better not. Sirius is"—he pinched his thumb and forefinger together—"this close to making the offer. Everything we've worked for is right there and about to pay off. Are you really prepared to throw it all away for what, a charming distraction?"

Before I even opened my mouth to answer, he turned on the heels of his Nike high-tops, returned to the booth to give some sort of instruction to the sound engineer, and then stomped out the studio door toward his office. He never left during a live show. Not to take a break. Not to pee. Never.

Shocked, I looked back down at the switchboard, which was brightly lit up with callers, all of whom were probably ready to pounce on my seemingly sudden change of heart. Rather than dig myself into a potentially deeper hole, I decided to move away from the dial-in portion of the show and launched into one of my more popular segments: "Ghost Stories," where listeners emailed in their most brutal ghosting experiences, and I would deliver a hilarious eulogy. It was perfectly pre-scripted, with no chance of any other unexpected questions derailing my vibe.

About halfway through the segment, my eyes caught a flash of Ravi as he reentered the studio to take his usual seat. His coloring had readjusted back to his usual shade of caramel, less flushed than he'd been when he stalked out, and I was relieved to see that after a few minutes, he was actually snickering and nodding right along with the bit.

Then he held up his wrist and tapped on his watch, signaling the end of the show. Normally, we'd head straight into his office for a "postgame" recap, but I already knew his feedback, and since I agreed with all of it, I figured, what was the point? *Love Is a Four-Letter Word* was the one area in my life where my confidence never faltered, and yet I'd let Leo somehow unsettle me.

That couldn't happen again. Ravi was right. I'd worked too hard, built my brand from the ground up. I'd gone from a college disc jockey to making a real name for myself in the industry, and I wasn't about to let Mr. Magically Shows Up Out of Nowhere cost me everything.

I grabbed my things quickly, no lingering glances, no unnecessary words. Without a goodbye, I made my way out the door, heading straight to Marin's place and the familiar comfort of our weekly ladies' mah-jongg game.

I held the box of cheeses and olives from Murray's in one hand and lightly knocked on the door before pushing it open with the other, knowing Marin always left it ajar on the afternoons we played.

"Mar, it's me," I called into the living room.

"I'm just wiping up the floor from Ethan's shower so none of you slip and kill yourselves in here," she called back. "I swear more water ends up out of the tub than in it. Give me one second."

I set my bag down beside the coatrack, hung my jacket on an empty hook, and wandered over to the snack table where Marin had laid out the best of Trader Joe's snacks, things like hummus dips, crispy pita chips, and dark-chocolate peanut butter cups. I added my goodies to the spread before snagging a handful of trail mix and wandering over to the fridge to grab a seltzer.

I made my way back into the living room, and a moment later, Marin stepped out of the bathroom, smoothing her damp hands down her leggings. "Hi, love," she said, kissing me lightly on the cheek. "Sorry, I'm such a mess."

Aside from the water marks on her knees, she was immaculate, as always.

"Stella and Jada are on their way," she said, then added, "Shoot, let me grab the bubbly and OJ from the fridge."

I sat down at the bridge table and placed a rack in front of each of the four chairs. Almost without thinking, I began flipping over the tiles and building my wall. Mah-jongg, once a game I'd dismissed as something only old ladies played, was apparently having a revival among Gen Zers. Marin had convinced me to sign up for lessons at the 92nd Street Y with her, and I was hooked from the start.

Even though I rarely won, there was something about creating order from chaos, spotting patterns in the unpredictable, that spoke to me. It was the way the game forced me to stay on guard, watching every move, reading between the lines, always figuring out how to shield myself from what might come next.

I'd been doing *that* my whole life.

Marin set the drinks down, took the seat beside me, and began stacking a neat row of thirty-eight tiles in front of her. "Sorry, I didn't get a chance to listen to the show this morning. It was absolute mayhem around here."

"Don't worry about it. It wasn't one of my best anyway. Actually, 'not one of my best' is a bit of an understatement."

Marin looked up from her tiles, her brows knit with concern. "Why? What happened?"

I was just about to dive in when the door swung open and Stella and Jada walked in. Marin stood to greet them and took their coats. "Snacks are up," she called over her shoulder as she tossed their things on her bed and grabbed a handful of carrots from the counter before settling back into her seat.

Stella slid into the chair beside me and gently covered my hand with hers. "Oh, honey, we heard the show. Are you okay? That caller was a total B. You should've just hung up on her."

"Who's a total B? What did I miss?" Marin asked, continuing to arrange her tiles.

"I'll explain later. I just want to try to forget all about it for a little bit."

Marin gave me a knowing look. "Fine. Consider it deferred, but you're not off the hook. So . . . how was everyone's Valentine's Day?"

Jada huffed and said, "Marcus and I had the most disappointing dinner last night at Pappardelle's. Their holiday prix fixe menu? What a joke. A total rip-off. The options were super limited, and did I really need to pay $100 a head for a small box of off-brand chocolates they handed us at the end with our check? Ugh, we should've just stayed in, ordered takeout, and caught up on *The White Lotus*."

She popped a grape and a cube of cheese in her mouth and looked over at me. "What about you, El? Sounds like you and Leo had a fabulous time. I remember when Marcus and I were in that new-relationship phase and he felt like he had to go the extra mile, not just make reservations at the restaurant down the block."

"Oh, that's right. Mr. Wonderful, as always, knocked it out of the park." Marin lined up four champagne flutes, expertly removed the foil, and popped the cork without ever breaking eye contact.

I was temporarily stunned. They all knew Leo. Like *knew* him, knew him. The way my mom and Ravi apparently knew him as some sort of fixture in my life. We'd probably gone out on a handful of double dates, and I'd even venture to guess at this point they very likely knew more about him than I did.

Wait a second . . . They very likely knew more about him than I did.

A light bulb went off. Ravi hadn't been all that helpful in filling in the missing gaps about Leo, but four women, chatting away over a mah-jongg game, sipping mimosas? That was a whole different story.

And I was fairly certain I'd finally be able to crack The Case of the Reappearing Summer Fling wide open, one ivory tile at a time.

Chapter Twelve

An hour and four hands later, only three of which resulted in a mah-jongg (for everyone but me), I managed to learn that Leo hadn't actually moved across the world for me but had requested a six-month secondment to his company's New York office. As he apparently told Marin on one of our two double dates, he wanted to "see where our relationship could go without the long distance," and I was, it seemed, all too happy to let him.

From Stella, I discovered that I hadn't come to mah-jongg much in January since Leo and I were too busy "hibernating in our love nest," and Jada let me in on the most humbling nugget of all, my adorable nickname for him was . . . *Snugglebug*.

I stared at them, certain they were joking, but their amused expressions told me they were most certainly not. I did my best to absorb every nauseating detail, quietly piecing together the missing parts of my life like a puzzle. And when they finished, I could see it clearly, the full image of a couple who had gone from a fleeting connection in Mykonos to a full-blown relationship in Manhattan.

Evidently, we were the kind of twosome that liked to spend Sunday mornings at the farmers' markets in the Lower East Side, stocking up on what we needed for the week. The kind that just signed up for a Thai cooking class. A pair who, on rainy weekend afternoons, could be found wandering the Antiquities galleries at the Met. Leo and I were everything I had railed against. Everything I believed didn't exist outside of a nineties rom-com. We were the kind of love story I'd spent years convincing others wasn't real.

And that was precisely the problem.

If we were only a few months in and I was already stumbling live on air and whistling a completely different tune than what I'd built my brand to be, then Ravi was right, this was a one-way ticket to career self-destruction.

But even more than just my brand, wasn't this core philosophy about men and dating and relationships part of my identity? I'd spent my formative years despising my father, who'd left us to shack up with a hotter new model, and reminding myself that I didn't need anyone. Relying on someone else for happiness was dangerous, like handing over the keys to your emotional well-being and hoping they didn't crush it.

Marin glanced down at her watch. "What do you say? One more game? I have to pick up the twins from my parents at four."

"Rack 'em up," Stella said, twirling her finger in the air before restacking the tiles. "Elliot, I was listening to the show the other day, and thank God Brian wasn't home, because I nearly had to baptize myself after that one caller."

Jada practically choked on her mimosa. "OMG! I know exactly what you're referring to. That segment was unhinged."

"Hey, what are you guys talking about? I want in on the joke," Marin said, looking between them.

I was too busy trying to hold my mimosa in my cheeks to keep it from bursting past my lips. "Oh, God, yes. From my 'Textual Tensions' segment," I said after a desperate attempt to swallow as the bubbles burned my nostrils. "This listener wrote in to share a line she claimed to be so steamy, so naughty, so irresistible, that it is one hundred percent guaranteed to make your boyfriend or husband want to jump your bones immediately."

Marin flailed her hands, gesturing wildly with her champagne flute to continue as it splashed about. "*Ooh*, okay, okay, so what's the line? You can't leave me hanging."

Jada, pressed a hand over her mouth to keep from laughing. "You tell her, El. I don't think I can say it with a straight face."

Casting a glance from Jada to Stella and then back to Marin, I sighed and relented, "Okay, but don't say I didn't warn you. So apparently, if you say the words, 'I want to feel you grow in my mouth,' your significant other will literally short-circuit and be singularly focused on that one thing until you make good on your offer," I said with a shrug.

"OH MY GOD! WHO IS SAYING THAT?! Stop it right now!" Marin's shock was visible from her bulging eyes that seemed to shrink her forehead to mere centimeters, and her mouth fell comically to the floor.

Stella, with tears in her eyes from laughing so hard, grabbed her phone and waved it at us as she said, "Actually, I've been thinking about it since it aired, and I kinda think we should test the theory. Might even make for some good follow-up content for your show, El." She waggled her eyebrows at me.

I stopped maneuvering my tiles and considered, kinda forgetting altogether that I was included as part of her "we." "What did you have in mind?"

Stella continued, "How about this? Everyone will text their significant other the magic phrase, and we'll clock their responses, see how spot-on the gal from your show was with her claim."

"No. No way. Tyler would die of a heart attack if I sent him that!" Marin cried, her face already flushing a whole new shade of vino, somewhere between a cab franc and a Syrah. "He'll think my phone got hacked!"

Stella was already texting away, her lightning fingers flying over the keyboard like they were on fire. "Brian will *definitely* know it's me. No doubt about it! He'll probably respond with a dick pic and a drooling emoji or something equally crass."

Jada took her phone out of her bag and started typing too. "Marcus is gonna think I've been kidnapped and it's a code to signal for help or something." She was giggling as she typed. "Okay, if we're doing this, then we're *all* doing this? Agreed?"

No. Wait, what? No way. I could never—would never—text that to Leo, especially after knowing him for like a minute and a half!

"Okay, everyone hold up your phones and show the text," she ordered.

Ugh, but this was *my* bit, from *my* radio show, and I didn't see a way to bow out. I suppose I could use the excuse that Leo and I were in a newer relationship, but to be honest, wasn't that precisely the time when you'd send these kinds of risqué texts? Early on, when the passion flame burned brightest.

They all finished typing out the phrase and then held up their phones as proof, waiting for me to do the same. Reluctantly, I keyed in the X-rated sentence, I want to feel you grow in my mouth, lifted the screen to show them I was willing to take one for the team, and hit send.

Within seconds, incoming texts started bouncing around the room like an eighties arcade. The familiar ring of a FaceTime call resounded loudly from Marin's cell amid the sea of *ding*s and *ping*s, causing us all to practically fall to the floor in stitches.

Marin, tears pricking in the corners of her eyes, flipped open the screen with her finger to accept the video call.

"Holy shit, Tyler! Put your pants back on! What the hell are you doing? It's like three in the afternoon!" Marin howled into the phone as she scurried out of the room to deal with the call, shielding her naked husband from sight.

At this point, we were barely holding on to life. Cackling and gasping, with little squeaks punctuating the silence, sending us further into an absolute fit.

Another text alert sounded and Jada shrieked in horror, clasping her hand to her wide-open mouth. "Marcus just texted that Isla has the family iPad that all our messages are linked to, and now apparently our six-year-old is asking him what 'grow in my mouth' means? Oh my God, kill me." She buried her face in her hands, pretending to cry between genuine fits of laughter, spurred on by the rest of us, including Marin, who'd just tossed poor Tyler off the video call. We were doubled over and wheezing when Jada's phone pinged again and she peeked a trepidatious eyeball through her fingers to check her messages once more.

"That son of a bitch!" she barked out, slapping her hand to the table before laughing even harder.

She flashed the phone in our direction, the words JUST KIDDING ABOUT ISLA in big letters from her husband on the screen.

Jada dramatically grabbed for a handful of napkins and playfully patted her brow, panting in relief. "Sweet baby Jesus, thank God! I wasn't sure how I was going to dig myself out of that one! Not to mention afford all the therapy Isla would undoubtedly need." Still laughing at the close call, she clutched her chest and texted him back, a wide grin lighting up her face.

Another chime. This time, it was Stella's husband, Brian, responding with the old reliable . . . dick pic. She flashed us all a quick peek before tossing her phone onto the table with a smug, "Told you so. Do I know my man or what? How about you, El? What's Leo have to say for himself?"

I'd been so distracted by the chaos of the last few minutes I had almost forgotten there was likely an equally unhinged response waiting for me. Sure enough, the icon showed one new text. I clicked it open, held my breath, and read his reply.

Leo: You're trouble. You know that, right? I was already thinking about you, and now I don't think I'll ever get you out of my head. Come home soon. I miss you.

I was in shock. His message wasn't vulgar or crude. Cocky or cliché. It was sweet. Playful. Romantic, even.

Goddamnit.

"C'mon, I see that look on your face. Spill. What dirty talk did he hit you with?" Stella poked.

I held the phone out for them to see, Stella taking the lead to read it aloud. "'You're trouble. You know that, right? I was already thinking about you, and now I don't think I'll ever get you out of my head.

Come home soon. I miss you.'" After pausing dramatically, she burst out, "Are you freakin' kidding me?! I got a dick pic—in terrible lighting, no less!—and you got . . . that? Actual prose and a kissy-face emoji!"

Marin jumped in. "You know that response right there is proof positive that you won the boyfriend lottery. Forget Greece. Forget Paris. That, ladies and gentlemen, is the real gold standard."

I knew they were right. Leo had exceeded my expectations, though to be fair, they weren't particularly high to begin with. It was still early days, and he was on his best behavior. But that wouldn't last. His true colors would surface soon enough. They always did.

However, walking away wasn't as easy as it should have been. For once, the usual impulse to cut and run felt . . . off. But that didn't change the facts. This had to end. For the radio show, for my career, for everything I'd built. No question, I had to make a clean break *today*. Then Leo would go back to South Africa or whatever magical realm he'd appeared from, and I could go on with my regularly scheduled life.

Marin pushed back her chair, still catching her breath. "*Oof*, my ribs hurt from laughing so hard. Sorry, but I have to kick you guys outta here. Quick cleanup, then I need to go grab the kids." She stood, stretching and shaking off the last bits of energy from her laugh attack.

"Oh, wow, I didn't realize how late it was getting. I should go too, then. The nanny leaves at four on the dot," Jada said, already packing up the racks and mah-jongg tiles with practiced precision.

"What about you, Elliot?" Stella asked with a sly grin. "Oh, never mind. You've got Mr. Wonderful waiting at your apartment, just itching for you to make good on that text." She bounced her eyebrows provocatively and offered a not-so-sly grin.

Jada and Stella collected their things and left together, while I lingered behind to help Marin clean up.

"You can head out," Marin said. "I'm just going to toss the rest of this into containers."

"I don't mind helping. I'm not really in a hurry," I replied.

Marin paused, mid–Tupperware burp, and eyed me skeptically. "Why not? No disrespect to Tyler, but had I been the one who had gotten that swoon-worthy text from Leo, you'd see my outline imprinted on the wall like in one of those old Road Runner cartoons." She snapped closed one of the plastic lids on the peanut butter cups and turned to me. "You doing okay? I know opening up yourself . . . your life to someone has been a big change for you."

There it was. A flicker of recognition, like Marin could still make out the person I used to be. The one I was before Leo had mysteriously materialized.

"I can see . . . *anyone* can see, he's a good guy. But that doesn't mean he's right for me. You don't understand. Now is not the time to let my feelings cloud my judgment. I can't afford to lose myself right now. Everything I've worked so hard for is at risk of slipping through my fingers."

"Is that another way of saying 'everything you've built to protect yourself from getting hurt?'"

"What does that mean?" My defensiveness taking on more of a biting tone.

"Elliot, I know you. You can put on a brave face for everyone else, but I see the pain Matty left behind."

Matty.

The scar that kept splitting open, no matter how many times I tried to stitch it shut.

Matty and I grew up side by side. As the son of my mother's best friend, Izzy, he and I had been thrown together since we were in diapers. Like most boy-girl friendships, ours went through all the phases. We started off inseparable, then hit that awkward the-opposite-sex-is-gross stage around twelve.

Everything shifted again at thirteen, when Matty kissed me during a game of spin the bottle at Marin's apartment. We didn't speak for about six months after that, paralyzed by mutual embarrassment. But by the time we both ended up at the same high school a year later, we managed to find our way back to each other.

It wasn't until junior year, at Mom's third wedding, that anything romantic really happened between Matty and me. This one was small, just her closest circle. Izzy, of course, and Matty. We all crammed into a narrow back room at a restaurant in Little Italy where the waiters sang opera between courses and the house Chianti came in wicker-bottomed bottles.

By the time dessert rolled around, cannoli cake, Mom stood up to give a toast. She called Vic the love of her life and said she finally understood what real partnership looked like. Everyone clapped. Except for me. I just couldn't pretend.

I grabbed a bottle of wine off the table and slipped away, down the long staircase to the kitchen and out into the alley behind the restaurant. That's where Matty found me a few minutes later.

Even from outside, we could hear Antonio, our singing waiter, serenading the newlyweds with "*Che Gelida Manina*," the famous love song from *La Bohème*, which I only knew because my mother's second husband thought himself to be an opera aficionado.

"I love this one. I wish I knew what they were saying, though," Matty had said softly, his eyes closed as he took in the song.

"If I'm remembering right, I think Rodolfo is telling Mimi about his love for her, how he dreams of their life together," I'd told him.

It was then that Matty asked me if I'd ever thought of him as more than a friend, something I'd wondered about countless times but had never been brave enough to risk. He was solid, dependable, a steady presence, the exact opposite of the revolving door of men in my mom's life, not to mention my own father, who had never really been around with any consistency. I'd never wanted to jeopardize what we had.

But then, that night in the alley under the big, glowing full moon, Matty had kissed me, and everything had changed. We fell in love. A passionate, all-consuming kind of love, like Mimi and Rodolfo. For as much as I had been trained from my youth to see love as fleeting, I truly believed he was my forever.

Until a few years later, when he betrayed me in the worst way possible.

Marin's voice broke the silence, pulling me back to the present. "You're still carrying Matty with you, aren't you?"

"No. Of course not. That's all in the past."

"I hope so. I really do. You know, when you think about it, relationships really aren't that different from mah-jongg. You have to discard a tile to be able to draw a new one. And you, my friend, have got a really great new tile waiting for you at home, complete with a sexy accent. I just don't want you to let the past keep you from . . . playing the game. Know what I mean?"

I pulled Marin in for a hug. I understood what she was trying to say. And maybe, in another time, her words would've shifted something. But right now, I couldn't shake the certainty that I had to walk away from Leo. For all the reasons I'd told myself were true: my career, my reputation, the deals I'd fought so hard to land—my book, Sirius, everything.

Chapter Thirteen

I rehearsed my speech the entire cab ride home.

Leo, this has been amazing, but I think we got caught up in something that wasn't supposed to last.

Lame.

You're incredible, but . . .

No. Ugh. Too cliché.

Sure, we had a moment, but maybe that's all it was meant to be.

Ooh, better.

By the time I climbed the stairs to my apartment, my game face was on and I was ready to set the record straight. Clear the air. Free us both from whatever this was before it went *too* far.

But when I pushed open the door, I was not met with the quiet sanctuary I'd been counting on for the clean break I'd meticulously plotted out.

Instead, I stood paralyzed, my mind racing but my body immobile.

Sitting on my couch, comfortably sipping tea like they hadn't just materialized out of thin air, were my dad and stepmom.

"Elliot!" Dad's booming voice filled the room, his face lighting up like we weren't as close to estranged as neighbors who'd barely nod in passing.

"Surprise!" his wife chirped, her smile so wide I thought her tight face might crack in two.

I blinked. My brain was misfiring left and right, like a circuit board sparking and smoking before complete combustion.

What. The. Hell.

We were never close. Not the kind of father and daughter who called just to catch up or even remembered birthdays. After he left Mom and me to build a new life, she broke down and I hardened. I saw him now and then, but never because I wanted to. When he remarried a few years after the divorce, after making it clear he was gone for good, something in me closed off. That's when I started keeping people at a distance. Love, too. It felt safer not to need anyone at all.

Behind me, I felt Leo step up, his presence warm at my back. He took one look at my expression, then glanced at them and then back at me. His brows puckered just enough to silently ask: *Should we make a run for it? Or should I get some popcorn?*

I gave him a look that screamed, *Please tell me this is a hallucination.*

His lips twitched, but to his credit, he recovered quickly. "Uh . . . does anyone need more tea? Or . . . maybe, should I grab something stronger?"

"Gin!" Dad and I said in unison.

Dad cleared his throat and scratched at his forehead. "I know we should've called, but we were in the neighborhood and thought . . . why not pop in?"

"Pop in?" I echoed, my voice a little too high-pitched to be convincing. We didn't do popping in. He knew it. What exactly was he playing at?

As Leo slid past me to head toward the kitchen, he stepped in close and murmured under his breath, just loud enough for me to hear, "Blink twice if I need to fake a gas leak."

My eyes caught his, and he gave me a barely perceptible wink and assuring smile, the kind that said, *I've got you.*

And before I could overthink it, Leo's hand brushed lightly against the small of my back, as if to steady me as I navigated whatever fresh hell this was, and he continued to the kitchen. I expelled a heavy breath, feeling a little bit lighter and more assured with him in my corner. On my side.

"So . . ." I drew out the word, dropping my bag onto the counter like I wasn't silently eyeing the door to bolt. "What brings you guys to *my* neck of the woods?"

My stepmom, Shira, beamed. "Oh, we've got news!"

I could practically feel Leo's curiosity spike from where he was hovering by the fridge, but all I could think was . . . *Please, for the love of God, don't let this be an MLM pitch. She's absolutely the type. Oh God. Is she pregnant again? No, no way. She's too old for that. Right? My stepsiblings are already teenagers.*

Leo cleared his throat, stepping in like the seasoned social buffer he apparently was. "Here we are . . ." he said as he passed around a mystery drink I could only hope was *something* and gin in my mismatched crystal tumblers. Because if life had taught me anything, it was that surprises in the West family rarely came with good news.

"I hope you made mine a double," I muttered, flashing him a grateful glance before turning back to the lovebirds on my couch, bracing myself for whatever bombshell they were about to drop. I took a long, desperate pull from the cold glass, the burn of piney bitterness sliding down my chest like dragon fire. "Thank you," I mouthed to Leo, and I felt his fingers snake around mine.

"Big news, you say? Okay, so let's hear it," I said in a tone that I hoped concealed my uneasiness. My palms felt like they were prickling with sweat, but if they were, Leo showed no signs of it bothering him in the least.

Dad leaned forward, lacing his hands together like he was about to deliver a TED Talk, not the catastrophe I was already bracing for. Beside him, my stepmother (though I still practically choked on the word) smiled like a Stepford wife . . . like this was all perfectly normal.

"Well," Dad said, letting out that dramatic sigh he always used when he thought something was earth shattering but wanted to act chill about it. "Your mother and I have been talking."

"Nana?"

"No. Not your grandmother. Your actual mother. You know, the one who raised you and still texts in all caps."

I gasped mid-sip, the heavy pour of gin searing my throat and stinging my nostrils until my eyes watered. "You . . . and Mom?"

"Yes."

"Wait, like *my* mom? Mom? Sonja?"

"Yes," he repeated.

My voice was growing louder, as if maybe he wasn't hearing me correctly. "Like your former wife?"

"Yes. Her. That's the one. The only mom you've got," he answered, clearly unsure whether we were doing some sort of bit that he hadn't been made aware of.

"Tell me you're joking. What the hell are you doing talking to her? What could the two of you possibly have to say to one another after all these years? I can't even imagine!"

"Well, since she and Keith got engaged, we've been reflecting on things. And we realized that we're both happy now, and that's something to celebrate. No more tension, no more history weighing us down. You know, she and I *used* to love each other and cheer each other on. Before we were married, we were the very best of friends."

"I'm sorry." I gestured wildly with a wave to stop him from continuing his stream of lies. "But was that before or after you cheated and left us? Please remind me where in this fantastical past you're clocking your infidelity. You know, the one that tore our family apart, not to mention made mincemeat of the woman you so boldly stand there and claim you loved. Like, what are you even talking about right now?!"

Shira leaned forward. "Now, wait just a second, Elliot. It wasn't as black and white as all that."

Dad rubbed her knee. "Shira, it's okay, you don't have to." His lips drew into a thin slash mark, slightly downturned on his face. "I'm sorry you feel that way, honey, but people change."

"Well, I don't think I can." I snapped the words out before I could stop them.

Leo shifted beside me, his thumb tracing a light, steadying pattern against my hand. I hadn't even realized I was still gripping on to him.

Dad stood from his chair, and his trusty sidekick followed suit. Popping up to her full height before he'd even straightened, she'd clearly been eagerly awaiting her exit cue.

He fiddled with the buttons on his sleeve and fixed the hem of his shirt. "I just wanted to tell you in person, so our showing up in Belize on your mother's big day wouldn't catch you by surprise."

Now it was my turn to jump to my feet. "Wait, what? Are you kidding?! Tell me you're kidding." I turned to Leo. "He's kidding, right?" I dramatically spun around to Cruella McStepface. "He's kidding, right?!"

Dad sighed, the patience in his voice faltering. "Elliot, can we stop with the theatrics and just have a conversation about this? Your mother invited us to her wedding. We thought since you'd be going, it'd be a wonderful way for us to finally put the past to bed and celebrate embracing the new instead of holding on to old wounds. I called the hotel, and they said you hadn't reserved a room yet, so I used my miles to book you and Leo into one of the waterfront Coconut Villas. It's their nicest room. It even has a swim-up pool."

He looked at me as if I should be grateful. One generous gesture does not a reconciliation make! Not when he'd been absent for most of my life.

"Wow. Lovely. The Coconut Villa. That sounds . . . exotic," Leo said, trying his best to break the tension.

"Thanks," I spat, making sure to add, "I'm not even sure we're going to the wedding."

"Well, the room's there if you decide to. And you should. For your mother. Plus, Keith's a really decent guy."

I was dumbstruck as he and Shira gathered their things, exchanged pleasantries with Leo, and strolled to the door like they hadn't just dropped a plot twist M. Night Shyamalan would envy.

The second the door clicked shut behind them, I sagged into the couch.

Leo let out a low whistle. "Well, that was certainly something."

I groaned. "This is a nightmare."

He nudged the glass back toward me. "More gin?"

I stared blankly, unable to respond.

Leo plopped down next to me and placed a reassuring hand on my thigh. "Do you want to talk about it?"

Tears of frustration stung the corners of my eyes, and I kept my head back against the couch, not able to look at him. "What? Talk about the fact that my practically nonexistent father and witch of a stepmother showed up out of nowhere and dropped an emotional bombshell? Oh, yeah, totally, let's unpack that dysfunctional suitcase, give you some more insight into why I'm a train wreck in relationships. Maybe after we can make vision boards and trauma-bond over chamomile tea."

"I'll take that as a no." He turned to me. "How about this? While you finish your drink, I'll go run you a warm bubble bath, light some candles, put on some Enya. You'll have no choice but to stop bracing like a piano's about to fall on your head."

"Isn't it, though?" I sighed and rolled my head on the cushion to face him, the tears I'd been holding back now streaming down my cheeks. "When you've spent your whole life dodging pianos, relaxing starts to feel like negligence. You forget what it's like to breathe without bracing."

He wiped the tear with his thumb and looked up to the ceiling. "Nah, the forecast isn't calling for falling Steinways. Not tonight anyway." He took me by the hand. "C'mon, let's go convince your nervous system it isn't under siege."

Leo led me down the hall to the bathroom, where he knelt and turned on the faucet, holding his hand under the stream until he seemed satisfied with the temperature. Then he carefully scooped in two generous handfuls of my lavender sea salt, followed by a swirl of bubbly soap. While the bath filled, he stood up and lit a few of my vanilla sandalwood candles, setting them on the edge of the tub.

Leo tilted his head toward the door. "I'll go grab some music and refresh your drink. Do you want a book or anything? That one from your nightstand, maybe?"

"No, this is, um . . . great. Thank you."

He smiled, clearly proud of his "boyfriend" skills, as he went in search of the Alexa.

The water was hot when I climbed in, the kind of heat that stung at first but promised to soothe as my body adjusted. I sank in slowly, my skin prickling with goose bumps as I submerged, the foamy white bubbles covering the surface like little bursts of breath. The candles flickered and their shadows danced on the walls as the scent of eucalyptus and lavender wrapped around me like a soft command to just let go.

But I couldn't. The fact I'd come home tonight with every intention of breaking things off with Leo still weighed on me. I had rehearsed my speech, crafted it with clean logic and the kind of brutal efficiency I normally reserved for on-air takedowns.

But then my dad and his glow stick of a wife showed up like we were on an HBO drama, and Leo . . . Leo didn't flinch. He didn't hightail it out the front door. He didn't stand there like a deer in headlights. He held the space for me, quietly, calmly, like a guy who knew how to craft chaos into comfort.

Now here I was, water lapping gently against my shoulders, the bathroom tiles aglow with dancing firelight, and I couldn't do it. I couldn't pull the pin on something that, despite all my better judgment, felt this safe. Then again, what was safety compared to all the other *things* at stake? My career. The show. The book. My reputation.

No, romance was but a blip on the radar. A momentary refuge. A fleeting illusion.

I had to tell him. When he came back in here, I would end it.

But moments later, with Enya's "Only Time" cooing out of the Alexa he set down on the vanity, he slipped off his clothes and climbed into the tub, pulling me back into his arms, wrapping them around me, and my resolve faltered. My body, traitorous and tired, settled into his as he held me.

And the words that had been there to end it between us . . . right on the tip of my tongue . . . evaporated with the steam curling off the water's surface, thin and elusive as smoke.

Bubbles pop. Candles snuff out. And hot water eventually turns cold. Of that much I was certain.

As for the rest . . . all I knew was that he ran me a bath. And we were still sitting in it, cozy and warm and together.

And that had to mean something, didn't it?

I guess I was about to find out whether staying with Leo was a risk worth taking, or if it would be the gamble that cost me everything.

Chapter Fourteen

Leo climbed out of the tub first, his body slick with suds and glowing in the golden candlelight. I was in awe. *Daaaaamn.* He was undeniably gorgeous. How had I forgotten he looked like that?! Perfect golden skin, even in February. A thick head of dark hair that had a soft wave at its ends. And the perfect amount of stubble to accentuate his rugged good looks.

Droplets of water clung to his skin before sliding away, causing rivulets to curve and wind along the dips in his lower back. I literally had to pick my mouth up out of the tub when my brain decided to rejoin my body. Reaching for a towel, Leo ruffled it through his hair before tying it (low!) around his waist. Then grabbing for another, he snapped it open and extended the fluffy plush to its full width, an invitation to be wrapped up. To continue to be cared for.

I stood, the water splashing as I modestly positioned my back to him and allowed him to drape the soft cloth around me. Spinning me around, Leo offered his hand as I stepped out of the tub and then rubbed my biceps up and down, to warm me. He was remarkably gentle and intent, his focus never wavering.

We changed into warm pajamas and settled onto the couch in the living room. Outside, a light February flurry had started. Nothing that would shut down New York City, but enough to at least slow it for a while. Leo pulled up the shades for a better view, the streetlights catching each flake as it drifted past.

"I think this weather calls for hot cocoa," Leo said.

"There's a bag of mini marshmallows in the cupboard right next to—"

"—the box of Rice Krispies, I know," he answered, looking confused by my direction.

Of course he knows where the mini marshmallows are . . . He's been living here for months.

A few minutes later, he returned from the kitchen with two steaming mugs piled high with whipped cream. "For you," he said, passing one over.

I took a sip, and the drink was rich and velvety and delicious.

"The secret is a hint of chili. It gives it a little kick," he said with a wink. "My dad's recipe. Speaking of dads, are you doing okay?" Leo set down his mug, lifted Pickles out of her cage, placing her in his lap, and curled next to me on the sofa.

"I'm sorry you had to bear witness to all that. It's complicated with me and my dad. He hasn't been around for most of my life. Moved on to his new family. Seems me and Mom were just the warm-up act before the main event."

"As if you could ever be that. Anyway, I kinda figured he wasn't really in your life since you don't talk about him much. For the few times I've met Sonja, I've never heard you mention more than a word or two about your dad. Especially not that he lived within 'drop by' distance to your flat. But he seems to want to be involved now? Trying to make some kind of amends with your mom? It sure sounded like he does?"

As if almost instinctually knowing Pickles had become my support animal, Leo passed her over to me. With big round eyes and her nose twitching with curiosity, she slowly inched up my chest, finally nestling herself in her favorite spot, squarely between my boobs.

"Who even knows with my father? He seems to flit in and out when it's convenient or interesting to him, no real permanence or dependability. His attention span is even shorter than his list of excuses, so sure, today he wants to make things all hunky-dory with Mom, but tomorrow, he'll probably go back to referring to her as Secondhand Stevie Nicks."

He laughed at my joke and said, "But what if they really did put their differences behind them?"

"Then what? We'd somehow fool everyone into believing we're the picture-perfect, dysfunctional-functional family? Hard pass. Putting us all in one place is more combustible than a *Real Housewives* reunion, which is just one of the *maaaannny* reasons I will not be attending Sonja's fourth wedding."

Leo got off the couch, clutching his mug of cocoa, and walked over to the window. "I hope you'll reconsider your decision. I've always believed that it's important to show up for the people we love, *even if* they make it incredibly difficult to love them back."

He stared out into the dark, the wind tossing thick flakes to and fro against the glass. His gaze tracked their descent as he watched in amazement, like a little boy catching his first glimpse of winter's magic, afraid to even blink in case it disappeared.

"As you can imagine, we don't get much snow in South Africa," he said softly, leaning closer to the pane. "It still gets me every time. There's just something about how it looks, how it falls, you know?"

I crossed my legs under me on the couch and reached for a blanket from the armrest.

"Tell me more about South Africa. Cape Town. What's it like there?"

He crossed back to the sofa, and I opened the blanket as an invitation to join me. He snuggled in and sighed. "Like nowhere else, really. Table Mountain towers over the city—its flat top gets covered by clouds every morning. Us locals call it the 'tablecloth.' You've got Camps Bay with its white, sandy beaches and palm trees, perfect for watching the sunset. And during whale season, you can sometimes spot humpbacks breaching just off the coast. It's incredible, like the ocean itself comes alive."

"*You* come alive just talking about it. Sounds breathtaking."

"Most special place in the world. And trust me, I've seen enough of it to know. Though I'd never been to Mykonos before last summer. I'm glad you were the one I got to experience it with. In truth, I'm grateful for all the moments I've gotten to experience with you, especially since I moved here."

His voice trailed off, and for the first time, it hit me. More than Ravi or Marin or any of my other friends, Leo was the one who could help me piece together the missing months of our relationship. Why exactly *did* he leave Cape Town and his family behind and move to New York? What transpired in Paris between us to make him take that kind of leap of faith? It was time to slap on my Nancy Drew detective hat and do a little digging.

"So . . . it must've been a pretty big deal for you, leaving everything and everyone back in Cape Town and traveling practically around the world . . . just for . . . me?" I glanced up at him, eyes wide, hoping the question wouldn't expose how little I really understood about the situation.

"Choosing you? Easiest decision I've ever made," he said, tucking a loose, damp curl behind my ear. "I mean, you couldn't just leave your radio show behind. My job was fine with me working out of the New York office. And now, here we are."

I sat up a little straighter on the couch, Pickles shooting me a look of annoyance that I had disrupted her slumber. I picked her up, gave her furry head a little smooch, and set her back in her cage before rejoining him on the sofa. "Right. Now, here we are. Living here. Together. All these months. Together. And you were just that sure it would all work out this way. That leaving everything behind . . . would be worth it?"

"Until now, my career has been the most important thing in my life. Do you know how many countries I've traveled to for work? Over thirty. Do you know how many places I've actually taken the time to explore or truly experience? Almost none. When I met you that day at the beach, it was like . . . I don't know, maybe it was your moxie or something? The way you carried yourself with so much confidence? And *then* you talked to every single one of my mates but not me, and if I'm being honest here, I think that made me jealous without you even trying." Leo shrugged with a shy smile. "I know I acted like I'd extended a million work trips before, all cool and confident, but honestly, I'd never done that in my life. But I wanted to get to know Mykonos better, not to mention the girl who claimed she categorically did not believe in love. I wanted to get to know *you*."

"Leo, that wasn't just some line I threw out as a challenge or anything, I really do mean . . ." Then, remembering we were sitting in the alternate version of our relationship and not mine, I chose my words more carefully. "I really . . . I really *meant* it."

"If I'm being honest, I don't know if I truly believed in love either. I mean, I'd seen my parents' relationship. Forty years plus together and they're disgustingly in love and completely obsessed with each other. So of course, I knew it was possible. I just wasn't sure it would happen for me. Not with the way I was dedicating so much of my time to work over relationships. Before I met you, I had a series of failed ones. I prioritized my career and my independence, being able to travel anywhere I was staffed, but I was alone. I had no one to share it all with. And then you came along like a breath of fresh air, and I had the most fun exploring Greece with you that I'd had in . . . well, I can't even remember how long. And the harder you insisted we were just a summer fling, the more I realized I wanted us to be something more, something real. So I threw down that stupid Paris gauntlet, hoping it would keep us both open to the possibility of love . . . and thank God it did."

My mind kept echoing my own words like a Ping-Pong game: *But I categorically do not believe in love. Howeveeeeer*, the possibility of love? The one that seemed to be staring me right in the face, nestled beside me on the couch, sipping hot cocoa with a sexy whipped-cream mustache as the snow continued to fall outside? Why was I pushing so hard against whatever this was that the universe was trying to show me? Why was I denying myself what I knew could feel so good?

So when he leaned over and his fingers lifted my chin to draw my mouth to his, I kissed him back, with no reservations and no hesitation. The sweep of his tongue against mine caused all the blood in my body to rush to my head, and I felt lighter and dizzy with every sensation. Every wall I had built between us softened beneath the heat of his lips, every reason I'd told myself to keep him at a distance dissolving into the taste of him. The need was intoxicating, electric, curling through me until it was impossible to imagine letting go.

So why was I fighting it? I guess that even though this glitch-in-the-matrix version of me had known Leo for months now, *real* me had only been with him for what amounted to a couple of weeks. And honestly, I wasn't sure what the ethics of sleeping with someone who might be an apparition were. However, when he deepened the kiss, all thoughts of propriety or resistance completely evaporated, and I ran my hands through his hair to settle around his neck to pull him even closer. He stood, scooping me effortlessly into his arms, and I expelled a breathless laugh against his cheek. Without breaking the contact of his mouth on mine, he carried me down the hall, the quiet thud of our bedroom door snapping closed behind us, sealing the choice I'd already made.

Chapter Fifteen

In the two weeks leading up to Mom's wedding, which I'd reluctantly agreed to attend after not-so-subtle prodding from Leo and a barrage of pushy emails and nonstop texts from my parents (a motherfreakin' ambush, if you ask me), I walked a tightrope between giving in to my growing connection with him and trying to keep it all from affecting the radio show.

Was it getting harder to rail against love when I was spending sun-filled Sunday mornings with Leo at the Lower East Side farmers' market, taste-testing lemon-thyme infused honeys and locally sourced organic vegetables?

Maybe.

Was I struggling to deliver my typical rants of antiromance after spending the last two rainy weekends wandering through the Antiquities galleries at the Met hand in hand with Leo while quietly sharing earbuds for the museum's audio tour?

Perhaps.

The truth was, Leo and I were starting to be everything I'd once mocked with fierce derision in segments like "Couples Who Brunch in Matching Outfits, and Other Things That Should Be Outlawed," and now here I was, brunching, cooking, slow-dancing through the Greek and Roman wing like I hadn't once called love, and I quote, "a farce that fell somewhere between a grand illusion and a cheesy marketing scam."

But I was still damn good at my job, and while *Love Is a Four-Letter Word maaaaay* have dulled its claws just the tiniest bit, professionally speaking? I still felt razor sharp.

I shimmied myself from underneath the comforter and carefully nudged the blanket aside, trying to slip out of bed without waking Leo. Dangling my legs off the edge, I stretched my arms overhead and reached for the small mound of jewelry on the nightstand. But Leo, it seemed, had other plans. His arms wrapped around me with surprising speed for someone half asleep as he gently rolled and pulled me back into the fortress of sheets with a mischievous little growl.

"And where, might I ask, are you running off to?" he murmured, his accent thick, even thicker in his sleepy grumble.

I closed my eyes and breathed him in. Like his scent could convince me to toss aside my to-do list and stay. "I have that appearance on *Good Day, Manhattan* this afternoon, remember? And I was going to make it to SoulCycle before that."

He waved a hand toward the window. "But it's pouring outside. Stay in bed with me a little longer." Scooting even closer, he draped an arm around my waist and pressed his smooth lips to my shoulder.

"It's just drizzling," I said, but didn't move. Not a breath. Not even a muscle.

Pressing his face into the crook of my neck, his body was warm against my skin. "You can't go. You're sugar. You'll melt." He licked my earlobe and gave it a playful nibble as white-hot bolts of electricity jolted straight to my nether region.

"And you're an absolute liability to my self-control."

Though it took every fiber of my being not to roll over and pin him underneath me, smother him with kisses, and allow us to fall into something neither of us would want to stop, I really did have to get moving if I was going to make it to the gym and still have time for hair and makeup before I was live on air.

"Hmm . . . I could say the same, that you're a liability too. In the very best way, of course." His baby-blue eyes pierced straight through me, and I found it hard to breathe, let alone move. I had to leave. Now. Right now.

Get out of the effin' bed, Elliot!

But instead, I stayed wrapped in his embrace, pretending the world didn't exist outside this room. Pretending my career wasn't on the line, my brand wasn't slowly unraveling thread by thread. Pretending I wasn't standing dead center in the very mess I always vehemently told my listeners to avoid.

But eventually, the inevitable won out, and I peeled myself from the cocoon of Leo's arms and forced myself upright. "I gotta go," I muttered, pulling on whatever jeans and hoodie were within reach.

"Don't forget about tonight," Leo called to me from inside the bedroom.

"Tonight? What's tonight?" I yelled back.

He stepped into the living room, his pajama pants slung low on his waist, and leaned into the doorframe. "Our eight-month anniversary. I knew you'd forgotten."

Apparently we were those people? The kind who celebrated month milestones?

"No way! I didn't forget!" I said, pretending like I wasn't secretly googling same-day-delivery anniversary gift ideas.

"Just be home by six."

"Yes. Six. Anniversary date. Got it."

Leo shook his head with a knowing smile, turned on his heel, and walked back toward the bedroom, his soft chuckle barely audible as he disappeared down the hall.

After a kick-ass Taylor Swift–themed spin class and a quick shower, I hurried into the studio entrance and was surprised to find Ravi waiting for me in the lobby. He'd clearly been pacing, and as soon as I walked in, he took me by the crook of the elbow and hurried me in the direction of the greenroom.

"What . . . what are you doing here?" I asked, barely keeping up with his long stride. I tried to feign excitement at seeing him, but confusion colored my delivery. I honestly couldn't even remember a time when Ravi had ever shown up at an appearance outside the station, not to mention addressed me in such an admonishing tone.

"I came to prep you for the segment since you didn't respond to a single one of my messages all weekend."

Oops.

"I was busy," I clapped back.

"Oh, I know. Instagram kept me fully updated."

Without even waiting for a response, he turned the knob of the greenroom, pushing it open, and I followed like a kid being led to the principal's office.

"Listen, Ravi, I—"

The moment the door shut behind me, he whirled around, dark clouds in his stare.

"No, you listen. I tried to warn you. I trusted you to be able to handle it. And maybe it's my fault for giving you more leeway than I should have these last few weeks. But your edge is gone. Your rants are watered down. Your punch lines? Flat. You're hedging like you're more concerned about your romance than our ratings. Like your heart isn't really in it anymore."

"That's not fair. I'm not—"

"You are. And people have noticed. Sirius higher-ups have noticed. The advertisers have noticed. It seems everyone with ears has noticed but you!"

I crossed my arms, defensive but silent.

"You used to go for the jugular. Now it's all . . . vague sentiments and barely there snark. You think you're balancing it all, but you're not. You need to get your head on straight and deliver a grand slam this morning. This segment is a huge opportunity for you to plug our show and your book and the brand, and I can't have you all wishy-washy when this can really launch things in the right direction and get things back on course. Do you hear what I'm saying?"

"Okay, okay, I got it," I grunted. As if on cue, a production assistant knocked to call me in for hair and makeup.

"Go," Ravi said. "But remember what I said. Bark *and* bite. Don't forget what's at stake . . . for all of us."

I nodded and followed the PA down the corridor. As the glam team filed in and started brushing, buffing, and curling, I tried to pretend like I wasn't silently unraveling. I stared into the mirror, fire slowly replacing the shock.

Vague sentiments and barely there snark, my ass.

I was about to give Ravi so much snark he'd be drowning in it and begging for a life raft.

As the show's third-hour guest, the spot usually reserved for local celebrities and fluff pieces, I'd be doing a segment they were calling "Romance, RIP?" where we were going to discuss the death of romance in the age of ghosting, swipe culture, and dating apps.

This was my wheelhouse. My domain. I'd show Ravi and the rest of my listening audience that I could tackle the death of romance with the same sharp humor and no-nonsense truth that had made me a staple on the airwaves.

And I did.

As soon as the show lights came up and I was introduced, I was in my element again. Game face on and taking no prisoners. Dripping with wit and oozing with bravado, I hit the show's cohosts, Chelsea and Carson, with so much charisma they barely knew what to do with themselves.

I was on fire . . . that is, until the conversation veered away from my well-rehearsed anecdotes about other people's unfortunate love lives to my own when Chelsea asked me a point-blank question about the most romantic thing a partner had ever done for me.

And like a deer in headlights, I completely froze up.

I barked out a laugh and tried to punt the conversation out of personal territory. "Define *romantic*. Are we counting grand gestures or just when he didn't interrupt me midsentence?"

With a calculated flick of her stiff blond news-anchor helmet of hair, Chelsea said, "C'mon, Elliot. Our viewers want to know. Your *listeners* want to know! You've been in relationships, right? Dish, girl. What's the most romantic thing a partner's ever done for you? There has to be something. I find it hard to believe there hasn't been at least one good apple in the bunch."

"I mean, romance is such a vague concept. Like, what even qualifies as romance? Who decides that?" I stalled.

Chelsea angled toward Carson. "I think romance is . . . is sacrifice, don't you agree, Car? At its core, it's someone putting someone else's needs ahead of your own." She shifted back in my direction. "Surely you've experienced that in your life with a significant other? You must've?"

They both looked at me expectantly, as if the answer should be obvious. This was live TV, and unfortunately, I didn't have time to deflect or talk my way out. As if my blunder on the post–Valentine's Day episode hadn't taught me a thing about lying under pressure, I stepped right into it . . . again.

"I mean . . . a few weeks ago, my boyfriend ran me a bath after a rough day. Lit a few candles. Played Enya, of all things." I gave a small, awkward laugh. "He didn't say a word. Just sat behind me and held me. And for once, I didn't feel like I had to perform or protect anything. I just . . . was."

Carson and Chelsea stared at me, frozen in identical masks of wide-eyed disbelief, mouths slightly agape, like I'd just announced I believed in mermaids or that the earth was flat.

I blinked, suddenly aware of the silence my admission had created. Out of the corner of my eye, I could see all the color drain from Ravi's face behind the camera.

"I, uh . . ." I cleared my throat, fumbling for my footing. "I mean, it's not like he does that sort of thing *every* night. Though, yes, he is very thoughtful."

Too late. The moment was already spiraling, and I knew it. I'd cracked the veneer. And they'd seen everything.

"Boyfriend?! So you *do* have a boyfriend?" Carson squealed like he'd caught a kid with their hand in the cookie jar. "I thought you'd be the last person on earth taking bubble baths with their beau!"

Chelsea, sensing blood in the water, poised like a hyena to attack and quickly joined in on the razzing. "What happened to 'Love is a capitalist construct designed to sell diamonds and disappointment'?" she teased, her glossy lips curving into a smirk.

I forced a laugh, the kind that didn't quite make it to my eyes. "Okay, fine, I admit. I crumbled. I'd had a hell of a day and wasn't even thinking. The call of the bathtub was too enticing to ignore. But I maintain it was a *very* temporary lapse in judgment."

Carson leaned forward, practically vibrating with glee. "Oh, come on, Elliot. You can't drop an Enya-size bath bomb and *not* give us more details. Let's call him! Your boyfriend!"

"What?!" I shrieked, my eyes darting to Ravi in the wings, pacing again. But even he couldn't save me from what was coming.

"Such a fantastic idea," Chelsea squealed. "Yes, let's get him on the air. I'm sure our audience would love to hear from the man who managed to chip away at your stone-cold heart."

"I don't know if that's really such a great . . ." But before I could finish protesting, one of the production assistants was already holding out their palm for my phone. I tried to swat him away, but like the eager gnat that he was, he continued to grab for it. In the throes of resisting, I caught a glimpse of Ravi, who looked like a fully steamed kettle ready to blow, and lost focus on the PA with the quick hands. He snagged it from my grip, and seemingly the breath from my lungs with it. He jotted down Leo's number and passed the paper over to Carson, who made a dramatic show of waving it around before dialing.

"I'm sure he's busy working. He may not even answer," I muttered, only to have Leo pick up on the second ring.

"This is Leo," he said, his voice low and just a little rough, like he'd been caught off guard, which of course he had.

"Leo! Hey, this is Carson and Chelsea from *Good Day, Manhattan*! We're sitting here with your *girlfriend*, Elliot West, who's currently regaling us with stories of your grand romantic gestures, including a candlelit bubble bath." Carson grinned into the mic. "So tell us, what is it like dating the woman who's built an entire career convincing people that love is complete BS?"

"Um." Leo cleared his throat, like he was unsure how to answer. "I would just say her public and private persona are very different. She's . . . not exactly the person you all think she is."

Shit.

At that, Ravi's top had completely boiled over, and I watched him stalk off the soundstage without looking back.

The very last thing I needed was for Leo to make me sound vulnerable or fake. Nothing alienated listeners more than a phony. This interview was sinking faster than a ship with a hole in its hull, and I knew I had to turn it around before I lost absolutely everything in the wreckage.

"Look," I jumped in, "Leo's a nice guy, but it's nothing serious. We met in Mykonos on Paradise Beach, so you can imagine how casual it all was." I turned to the audience, flashing a bright, confident smile. "It's a fling, because, ladies, we all deserve a bit of fun without needing to call it love, right? We've only been dating a little while, and the truth is, he doesn't really even know me or honestly mean all that much to me."

"Leo, do you hear that?" Carson smirked. "Guess no matter how many bubble baths and Enya playlists you throw at her, some things . . . and people . . . just can't change."

I forced a laugh, light and breezy, the kind that had gotten me through hundreds of segments. "Well, if he thought he could *fix* me, that's on him. I'm not a rescue dog. I didn't come with a sad Sarah McLachlan montage and a promise to love him forever."

There was a deafening silence on the line. A full beat. Two, actually.

"Wow," Leo said flatly. "Okay."

There was a long pause. Carson and Chelsea blinked at each other, deciding whether to dive into action, sussing out if the dead air was a disaster or just enough of a dramatic pause that would cause the ratings to blow the roof off the studio.

Finally, Leo's voice came through the line quieter, distant, and something else, something harder to place. "Right. I guess some things can't change," he muttered.

Then the line clicked, cutting off sharply.

"Well, that's all the time we have," Chelsea chimed in as she wrapped up the show. "Let's thank our guests, the incredibly talented Jason Isaacs, musical guest Gracie Abrams, and host of *Love Is a Four-Letter Word*, Elliot West."

The cameras cut, and the PA moved to unmic me, but I barely noticed, Ravi's words about having to choose between Leo and my career from earlier still echoing in my mind. And I had chosen. Publicly. In a way that no doubt hurt and humiliated Leo.

I checked my phone, the empty screen mocking me. No message. No sign of him.

"Great show, Elliot," Carson said, clapping me on the back with a grin. "We'll have you back when that book of yours hits the *New York Times* bestseller list."

I forced a smile, but it felt like a mask slipping off. The words came easily, but my mind was still back on TV, replaying the moment I'd dismissed Leo, making him sound like he didn't matter to me at all.

Another glance at my phone. Still nothing.

It was okay. I'd be okay. I did what I thought was necessary for my career. For Ravi's career. I did what I *had* to do.

But then the doubt hit like a wave, crashing over me, and with it came the heavy realization: I might have just thrown away the possibility of everything.

My phone buzzed in my hand and my heart leaped. I flipped it over in hopes of seeing a message from him but instead was met by a flood of notifications on my socials, most likely reactions to the segment. I couldn't even bear to look at what they said. My stomach fell to my feet.

Ravi: What. The actual. Hell.

Ravi: You torched the segment *and* Leo. On air. In real time.

Ravi: Come to the greenroom. Now.

I sat there, staring at the text thread like it had just punched me in the gut. My mouth still wore the fake smile I'd plastered on for Chelsea and Carson, but inside, my organs were staging a full-on revolt.

Leo hung up. On air.

I'd embarrassed him—*on air.*

My legs moved automatically, carrying me through the hallways with all the grace of a crash test dummy. I barely registered the intern offering me a refill of coffee. Just waved them off like I was swatting at smoke and begrudgingly stepped into the greenroom, where Ravi was waiting for me.

"You want to tell me what the hell that was?" he shouted.

"They put me on the spot, and I did my best to turn it into a bit," I said weakly. "It . . . it just got away from me."

"A *bit*? Elliot, that was a PR disaster in real time. People now think your love life is a joke. You know who doesn't find that funny? Our sponsors. Corporate. Sirius execs, who'll have real money on the line. And me. I *do not* find this funny."

Tears were welling in my eyes, from frustration, from shame for what I'd just done to Leo, for this undeniable guilt I couldn't stop feeling, "This is my life. My personal life!"

Ravi was unfazed by my tears or my plea. "Not when you make it live on air, it's not. Not when you *are* your brand. You think you can keep these worlds separate. That's impossible. I could have told you months ago that they'd bleed together like cheap dye in a washing machine. And guess what? You're the one throwing in the red sock. This is about me too, El. You're taking me down with you. Everyone who has worked to get you to this point."

My mouth was as dry as cotton, and I struggled to swallow. "So, what? You want me to break up with him and then share all the gory details in some flashy segment? Issue a press release about my emotional availability?"

He fired off the final shot, unfiltered and unapologetic. "You can't have it both ways, El. You want to be in love? Then *be* in love. You want to be this brand? Then *be* this brand. But the middle-of-the-road thing you're doing? It's going to kill the show and leave you with absolutely nothing. You need to choose. Him or the mic."

His words stung like an actual slap. Ravi had been my producer since my radio show at Brown. He knew me better than almost anyone. He'd been there for the whole breakup with Matty. He knew what it did to me. How it was the final blow to my belief in anything lasting. He watched me harness all that pain into becoming hard-edged radio personality Elliot West, who wore sarcasm like a shield and kept everyone at arm's length. He was one of my best friends, and to hear this unflinching and merciless review cut me to the core.

I opened my mouth to answer but didn't know what to say.

"Figure out your shit, Elliot. I mean it. There are millions of dollars on the line. Our careers are on the line. All the deals we have in the cooker and everything that matters. All of it will disappear in the blink of an eye. You're walking a tightrope and pretending you're on solid ground. Either your career matters to you or it doesn't. But if it does? You can't keep playing both sides. Not like this. Not like today. Not ever again."

With everything I'd fought so hard to reach hanging in the balance, despite the unrelenting ache in my heart, the choice became painfully clear. And this time, I couldn't let myself be swayed.

I knew what I had to do.

Chapter Sixteen

After wresting my keys from the lock, I opened the front door of my apartment and the scent that met me at the threshold practically knocked me off my feet: Buttery garlic and sizzling rosemary. A hint of lemon zest? I froze in the doorway, taking it in like a bloodhound in some Michelin-star kitchen.

A low light glowed from the hallway, and a hum emanated from deeper in the apartment. Music played low from the speaker, something bluesy and sultry, and felt altogether scandalous for a Monday evening. The dining table, typically buried under a graveyard of unopened mail and promotional show merch, was fully set. Tablecloth. Real plates. (I'd forgotten I'd even had those!) Cloth napkins?! Where on earth—

But then I saw Leo in the kitchen . . . scraping scraps into the waste bin and stuffing pans of uneaten food into Tupperware containers. Wearing the navy button-down that made the turquoise of his blue eyes even more brilliant, his sleeves rolled to his elbows, and hair still damp from a shower, he kept his back to me, even though I knew he'd heard me jangling the keys in the door.

He had flour on his pants and heartbreak inscribed in his posture. Like his hurt and disappointment had settled into his shoulders and they couldn't quite fake ease anymore. Leo continued loading the dishwasher and kept his eyes focused on the wet plates in his hands, refusing to meet my eyes.

Finally, after what seemed like a lifetime, he spoke. "I figured you'd had a hell of a few days, and it would be nice for you to come home and we wouldn't talk about work. You'd eat. You'd relax. And we'd toast to our anniversary. But so much for that plan."

He wiped his hands on a dish towel, balled it up, and tossed it into the sink. "I thought you'd let someone take care of you for once. But apparently, you're not a 'rescue dog in a sad Sarah McLachlan montage.'" The dishes clanged as he gripped the edge of the counter, as if anchoring himself. "You made me sound like a joke, El. While I was planning dinner, you were busy serving punch lines. I thought I was showing up for you, proving that not all men are stereotypes. Meanwhile, you turned me into a sound bite. I can't believe I've been so stupid."

His voice cracked a little, and it almost broke me. He didn't raise it. He didn't turn to look in my direction. But every word landed with pinpoint precision, soft and lethal, like a sprinkle of salt against an open wound.

Turning to face me with hurt in his eyes, he asked, "Why did you meet me in Paris, Elliot? Why?" His voice dropped to a whisper. "If you knew you'd never be willing to let me in, then why'd you come?"

But I *hadn't* come. I'd picked my career. Months ago, I'd made the choice. Clean, deliberate, and final. I wasn't supposed to be here. I wasn't supposed to care. So why was I here now, standing in my kitchen, buckling under the weight of a decision I'd already made?

"I'm sorry, Leo, but I can't be the girl you want. That's the truth. Besides, none of this is real!" I shouted, gesturing wildly, not sure if I was referencing the magic spell, the whole idea of love, or both.

I could see the muscle twitching in his jaw, the way his knuckles tightened slightly around the fork in his hand. "Look around you. The life we're starting to build together. If none of this is real, what is it, then?"

I stood there, heart pounding, working to breathe through the chaos in my head and trying desperately to come up with an answer to his question.

He leaned back against the countertop, arms crossed against his chest, his jaw clenching tighter with each second that passed.

I shook my head, heat rising up my neck. "I can't do this. I can't let myself believe in something that's just going to fall apart. Not again. I'm just trying to stay upright here, and I'm sorry, but my default is to lean on the only thing that's been steady in my life: my career, my brand, the stability I built for myself. It's what's gotten me through *everything*."

"No, you're looking for a reason to run. So just say that. Don't burn down the room and then go and blame the match."

And just then, I wanted to tell him this was actually about *more* than just my career. I wanted to tell him about Matty. How there had been a time when I was naive and wide-eyed, and even though my parents had broken apart in ways I still couldn't completely wrap my head around, I'd still believed things could be different for me.

It took all I had not to admit right then and there that it wasn't just the show that kept me from jumping into love with both feet, it was the way Matty had shattered my trust, leaving me with a fragile heart I wasn't sure I could risk again. I wanted to say all of that, but instead, I stayed silent, which seemed to say a lot more to Leo than my words ever could.

I surveyed the table. The tapers flickered, and the bubbles in our Vinho Verde had completely fizzled out. Leo sat down, resting his head in his hands. He closed his eyes and exhaled.

"You know, you told me who you were. From day one, you told me. I just didn't want to hear it. Didn't want to believe it." He looked up and into my eyes. "So I suppose I gave you no choice but to shout it at me. I could've done without the on-air part. I don't think I deserved that kind of public humiliation, but in fairness, you did try to warn me." He paused and let out a sigh. "I guess when I saw you waiting for me at the Eiffel Tower, I thought it meant we wanted the same thing."

How could I possibly know why the alternate timeline version of me showed up that day in Paris, because that girl *wasn't me*! But looking into Leo's expression, all softness and surrender, I could only assume what she must have been thinking. "I imagine what she wanted . . . I mean, what *I* wanted, was to be with you."

"But not anymore?" he asked.

I didn't know. I wasn't sure if the magic spell was meant to show me what could've been if I'd taken a different road *or* if it was meant to reaffirm the choices I'd already made. I didn't have the first freakin' clue what fate was trying to tell me. Only that it had led me here. To this moment. And even with everything I'd experienced, everything I felt, I still had no idea how to answer his question.

What I did know was I needed a little distance from him and from work. To take a breather and to figure it all out. And I guess he did too, because before I could suggest it, Leo said, "I think we need some space. Why don't you go ahead to Belize without me? Spend time with your family. Spend time getting clear on what you really want. I'll try to meet you there for the wedding. Things with work are pretty busy for me anyway. I could use the time here to sort some stuff out too."

"Leo—"

"I'm not perfect, Elliot. This isn't a Nancy Meyers rom-com. I might hurt you. In fact, I probably will because that's what happens in real relationships. Not intentionally, but people hurt each other and forgive each other, and they try again. And if you're looking for a version of love where the person always says the right thing or never makes a mess of it . . . that's not me. But I'll always show up for you. Real, honest, and fully in it, because I don't know us any other way." He leaned back in his seat and shrugged. "I'm not so sure about you, though."

"What do you mean?"

"Who *is* the real Elliot West? The woman who rails against romance on the radio, or the one who shares with me her sadness and her joys and lets me cradle her in my arms? You need to decide what you want. Who it is you want to be. You see, love, I've learned, doesn't survive in halves. Eventually, it needs a whole heart." He stood up, his chair scraping against the wood floor. "And I'm offering up mine. Maybe take the next few days and decide if you'll ever trust me with yours."

Love doesn't survive in halves.

The words echoed like a verdict. After years spent dissecting other people's heartbreaks, I was standing in a pile of rubble of my own making. The clarity I once wielded like a scalpel had vanished, and when I looked up, so had Leo, the front door clicking shut behind him.

He spent the next three nights on the couch, leaving for work before I was even awake and coming home long after I'd gone to bed. We became shadows under the same roof, carefully avoiding each other, like silence was safer than saying the wrong thing.

Before I left for Mom's wedding in Belize, I reminded Ravi I'd be out of town for a few days. He didn't look up, just gave a short nod and muttered, "Good. Maybe you'll have things figured out by the time you get back."

No warmth. No curiosity. Just quiet disappointment wrapped in clipped professionalism. And honestly, with everything I'd put in jeopardy for our show, I couldn't blame him.

The morning of my flight, I set my alarm for just before six, hoping to catch Leo still asleep on the couch. Hoping for something? A goodbye, even? But when I stepped into the living room, the pillows were stacked, the blankets folded, and he was already gone.

Chapter Seventeen

Nobody mentioned the puddle jumper to Belize. Not Mom. Not Dad. Not Leo. Nobody. Not a single soul mentioned that the only way to get to Ambergris Caye was via a sardine can with wings, a plane that rattled, groaned, and climbed through the sky like it was held together with hope and duct tape. One strong gust of wind and I was certain they'd be picking pieces of our fuselage out of the Caribbean.

I knew nobody told me, because if they had, I would have certainly used it as an *actual* excuse to skip Mom's wedding altogether. But even without the fear of plummeting to my death in some wind-up toy sky scooter, I still had enough reservations to rethink the whole thing. First, there was the fact that Dad and Shira would still be attending. My estranged parents, who for most of my life couldn't stand to be within a mile of each other, had somehow agreed to spend a long weekend at a resort the size of a small parking lot.

Then there was Mom and her impulsive decision to marry Keith, a guy she'd known for fewer days than a Sephora return window, and whose mess I would no doubt be cleaning up come Fourth of July. And to add insult to injury, there was everything going on with Leo. Leo, who'd appeared out of nowhere, had somehow managed to become a fixture in my life and turned everything I was so sure about right on its head.

While my heart and mind raced with thoughts of our plane careening out of the sky, surprisingly enough, all I wanted was his hand in mine instead of Marin's well-moisturized death grip. Though I was incredibly grateful to my best friend, who'd heard the sheer desperation in my voice when I'd called her in a panic about attending the wedding alone and without hesitation agreed to be my plus-one to this shit show.

"Jesus, El, you're going to snap my fingers in half," Marin cried, yanking hers out from under mine and swatting me with the issue of *The Sophisticate* she'd been reading.

Suddenly, the pilot came on the loudspeaker. "Alright folks, we're just about to start our descent into Ambergris Caye. Please make sure your seat belts are securely fastened and your tray tables are up. Keep an eye out for the beautiful turquoise waters, and try not to panic if the plane feels like it's taking a few extra dives, that's just us trying to give y'all a better view. We'll have you on the ground in no time."

I tried to take comfort in the fact he said *ground*, not *ocean*, but even still, I couldn't help but wish for Leo's strong arms to be wrapped around me as we glided down through the clouds and over the scattering of small islands and reefs that made up Belize. I leaned over Marin and peeked out the window. The aqua-blue water and whitewashed buildings reminded me of Mykonos, and as we (thankfully) touched down on the narrow runway of Ambergris Caye, my thoughts once again drifted to Leo and Greece. Without thinking, I turned on my phone and shot off a quick text to let him know I'd, by the grace of God, landed safely.

After twenty-five minutes in an open-air jeep, Marin and I finally arrived at the Tide-Kissed Resort and Spa. The boutique hotel was charming and sun soaked and tastefully bohemian, but also quite small. Like there was no-avoiding-anyone type small. Just a main, hacienda-style building and a handful of villas along the water. As we pulled up, a bellhop met us at the main entrance, took our bags from the car, and pointed to the check-in area.

We followed him into the bright, airy lobby, where glass doors opened directly onto the beach, framing a spectacular view of the ocean. A warm breeze drifted in off the sea, soft and salt-sweet, and for just a moment, I was glad to be there. But at the sound of Mom's voice echoing off the polished tile and glass walls, the moment ended as quickly as it'd come.

"Ellie Belly, you're here!" she squealed, her bangle bracelets jangling as she waved her hands in the air. "And Marin, what a wonderful surprise. Keith and I were so moved to hear that you wanted to be a part of our celebrations."

Marin didn't miss a beat and wholeheartedly entertained Mom's spiel. "So happy I was able to come, Sonja. This place is beautiful."

"Mom, hey," I said, trying for casual, as I leaned in to give her a kiss on the cheek. "You didn't want to mention the little puddle jumper of death?"

"Of course not," she said breezily. "I knew if I did, you'd chicken out and miss all the fun."

"Ms. West, we have you all checked into the Coconut Villa for the next four nights," the front desk agent said, handing me back my passport. "Is Mr. Kindell with you?"

"No, he should be joining me later in the week. Maybe?"

"Wait, Leo isn't here?" Mom asked, her concern visible in the deep *V* that formed between her brows.

With a dismissive shrug, I said, "He had a work thing come up last minute, but hopefully, he'll be here in time for the wedding."

Mom popped out her bottom lip and tutted. "What a shame. We have so many activities booked through the hotel—zip-lining, paddleboarding, scuba diving. Your dad and Shira are really keen on that one. Did you know Shira is a PADI-certified scuba diver?"

No, I did not know that Shira was a PADI-certified scuba diver. Considering my mother had spent most of my life referring to her as She Who Shall Not Be Named up until a few days ago, I hadn't even been positive Mom knew Shira's real name let alone be well versed in her extracurricular activities.

"Throw your bags in the room, get freshened up, and then come meet me, Keith, Cannon, and Allegra for sunset yoga," Mom said.

Cannon and Allegra? Dad's kids with Shira. Mom was doing beachside yoga with Cannon and Allegra? Had I just stepped into *The Twilight Zone*? Did that little plane rocket me into some alternate universe? *Orrr* . . . maybe that tin can went down, I'm dead, and this is hell?!

"You know . . . uh, the effects of the Xanax I had to pop on that ridiculous plane haven't quite worn off yet, so I might just take a little siesta, grab a shower, and meet you guys for dinner," I responded.

"Sure, honey. But you'll be missing *ouuuut*," she cooed. "How about you, Marin? Wanna join us?"

"Actually, a good stretch and some calm breathing sounds just perfect after that very nerve-racking flight where your daughter tried to claw me to pieces with her bare hands," Marin joked.

"Wonderful. Let's head down there to get a good spot. Oh, El, don't forget to check through the itinerary I sent you. Tonight is our Lover's Luau. You'll find a grass skirt, coconut bra, and other goodies waiting in your room. Festive attire is very much encouraged!"

My soul briefly left my body at the words "coconut bra," and I momentarily considered throwing myself into the sea. Instead, perhaps as a Pavlovian response, I nodded slowly and mentally calculated how many drinks it would take to make any of this feel normal.

Cool, can't wait to process my childhood trauma in synthetic palm fronds.

I let out a weak "Sounds good" over my shoulder as Mom and Marin took off for the beach, and I zigzagged through the maze of garden paths, scanning the room numbers like a countdown to my refuge. And then, just as I walked past the pool, Dad's booming voice called out to me from a pineapple-shaped raft in the middle of the crystalline water.

"Looking for your room, El?" he called. "You're down a little that way in the villa *riiiiight* next to Shira and me. Cannon and Allegra are doing beachside yoga with Mom, if you're interested."

Did he just say "with Mom"? With Mom?! As if he hadn't spent most of my life referring to her as my "Incense-Loving Forest Goblin of a Mother"?

"Thanks, I'm good. Gonna grab a nap. Catch you guys in a bit."

"We'll be here," he said, splashing Shira with his feet.

I turned on my heel before he could say anything else, before he somehow drove another nail into this hellscape of a coffin.

The winding path toward the villas curved through manicured palms and sandstone steps, my sandals slapping against the wet tiles, my pulse thrumming louder than the waves crashing beyond the trees. I just needed to make it to my room. Just a few more steps. Just past the hibiscus bush, then a left at the ridiculous wooden sign that said STAY SALTY, BEACHES.

The second my hand closed around the villa's brass doorknob, I let out a shaky breath. In my mind, I was already face-first on the bed, buried in overpriced throw pillows, maybe screaming into the upholstery and pretending I didn't care how much mascara I'd get all over it.

But then I saw him and couldn't believe my eyes.

Farther down the lush green path, framed in golden afternoon light and swaying palms, he was just . . . there. Towel slung over his shoulder, sunglasses and a bottle of suntan lotion loose in his hand. Completely unaware.

He didn't see me. But I saw him. And my heart didn't just drop . . . it plummeted. Like it had fallen out of my chest, slammed into every rock on the way down, and landed in the sand in bloody little pieces.

Matty.

What the hell . . . What the actual hell . . . was he doing in Belize?

Chapter Eighteen

"Maaattheeeew," a voice called out from the path between the villas. It was his mother, Izzy. I'd expected *her* to be at the wedding. After all, she'd been Mom's best friend since they were kids. But Matty? He hadn't been at Mom's last wedding. Why would he show up to this one?

As he turned toward Izzy, I hurriedly fumbled with my key card, praying for the lock to flash green so I could slip into my room before he saw me. Once safely inside, I slammed the door closed and slid down the back of it, falling like a marionette with its strings cut.

I crawled over to the large glass slider that led to the patio and peeked through the slatted blinds. There Matty was, standing in the sun, deep in conversation with Izzy. Was he real? Was this more magic? Had that witch of a fortune teller, or whatever she was, conjured him back into my life too?

No. No. No.

I hadn't seen him in, what was it now, at least five years? Maybe a little more? I'd worked hard to avoid anywhere I thought he might be. Places we used to go. People we knew in common. I had erased Matty from my life, so what on God's green earth was he doing here? And if he'd been invited, wouldn't it have been at least a little humane for Mom to give me some kind of a heads-up?!

Just the sight of him knocked the breath out of me, like my body still hadn't forgiven him. Well, because it hadn't. How could it? A betrayal like that stays with you like a wound that never fully closes, its rawness always just beneath the surface.

And suddenly, I was back there, in our senior year of college, me at Brown, him just a few hours away at Boston University. We'd defied the odds, staying together through the ups and downs of undergrad life, and even my brief stint abroad. Despite my rocky childhood, my parents who were never exactly role models, and all my doubts about conventional happily ever afters, I'd believed in Matty. I'd believed in what we had.

I may have doubted everything else—marriage, commitment, whether love could be enough. But not him.

Not for one second, him.

If anything, the distance between our schools served to strengthen us. Sure, I missed out on some typical college experiences: frat parties, late-night gossip sessions with my roommates, and weekends spent cramming in the library with a study group, because I was spending the weekends with Matty in Boston.

But it was worth it. Matty was my best friend, my confidant, my future. And I loved him. I loved him so much that when he called to say he had the flu and couldn't make it to my a cappella group, The Brown Soundwaves', big showcase, I skipped the after-party and rushed over to check on him right after the performance. I remembered how it was pouring rain the whole drive into the city. Even so, I made a quick detour to his favorite delicatessen in Brookline to pick up his beloved navy bean soup and their famed roasted chicken and cranberry salad.

I had circled his apartment building half a dozen times before I could even find a parking spot within a reasonable distance, one that would let me dash from my car to the entrance without getting completely soaked. Shoving the bag of takeout under my raincoat, I was relieved when Matty's nighttime doorman, who was just settling in for his shift, recognized me and motioned me into the lobby.

"Hey, Lou," I said, shaking the rain off my jacket, droplets scattering across the floor.

He looked up from his newspaper. "Miss West? Is Mr. Adler expecting you?"

"No, but he's down for the count with the flu. I come bearing soup and TLC. Actually, would you mind giving me the key? He might be asleep, and I'd rather not wake him just to open up the door."

"Course not," he said, unlatching the wooden cabinet behind the desk, pulling Matty's spare key off one of the hooks, and handing it to me.

I thanked him and pressed the elevator button, riding it up to the eleventh floor. I lowered the bag of soup and bread to the ground, then quietly eased the key into his lock. Inside, the apartment was dim, lit only by a thin strip of light spilling from his bedroom. I crept toward it, careful to muffle my steps as I reached to close the door without disturbing him.

But suddenly in the deafening silence, I heard a giggle. A woman's giggle, followed by a low murmur and the unmistakable rustle of sheets. My stomach dropped and my entire body froze in horror, my hand still hovering near the doorknob. The rhythmic creak of the mattress, a breathy laugh, and then Matty moaning a name over and over again.

Hannah.

Hannah.

Hannah.

I wanted to turn and run, but I couldn't. I was all lead and glass. Too heavy to move, but too fragile, I feared, to survive it if I tried. Then, without meaning to, without even realizing what I was doing, I started backing away, the wooden floorboard creaking underneath my feet.

I heard Hannah say, "What the fuck was that?"

After, Matty's voice, sharp and alarmed, said, "I heard it too. Shit, is someone in the apartment?"

Then feet thudded across the floor, and his bedroom door flung open so that Matty and I were standing face-to-face.

"Christ, Elliot, what are you doing here?" he shouted.

"You . . . you said you were sick. I came to, um, to check on you . . . to bring you soup," I managed to squeak out.

Behind Matty, the girl, Hannah, was next to his bed, scrambling to get dressed, like she'd been caught mid-crime, which she kinda had.

His eyes darted between me and Hannah, his face a mix of shock and guilt. "I didn't expect . . ."

The air, tight in my lungs, was a pressure cooker expanding in my chest. I held up a hand, cutting him off. "Don't. Just . . . don't."

What could he possibly say to make this okay? Absolutely nothing. Not one damn thing. He'd betrayed me. Lied, cheated, and shattered every promise we'd made. The one person I believed would never hurt me had just broken me in the most intimate way . . . and I'd never even seen it coming.

"Please, El, let's talk. I'll ask . . ." He paused, maybe realizing that saying her name would make her real.

"Hannah," I supplied.

He turned an even more pronounced shade of crimson. "I'll ask Hannah to go."

"No, please, don't get rid of her on my account. Just tell me one thing: How long? How long has this been going on?"

He didn't need to answer. The look on his face told me everything I needed to know, that it hadn't been going on long enough for me to catch the signs, but long enough for him to think I was blind to them.

But now my eyes were wide open and staring at the truth, ugly and undeniable. Matty had become the living embodiment of everything I feared most about love. That it could make you vulnerable and powerless, so much so that you found yourself standing in the hallway of your boyfriend's apartment, clutching his get-well soup, wondering how the hell you ended up here.

And at that moment, I vowed I would never wind up in this place again. I wouldn't ever allow myself to be that gullible or unguarded. That naive or that trusting.

That open.

So I closed off my heart, reinforcing it with walls of skepticism and a fortress of emotional distance. And when Monday rolled around, instead of the usual disc-jockeying and dishing I typically served up on my college radio show, *Go West*, I launched into a diatribe on the deceptions of love, so sharp, so vitriolic, that the number of calls flooding into our phone bank nearly crashed the whole system.

I'd harnessed all my hurt and sadness into a far more productive emotion: rage. It radiated from me, oozing from every inch, every pore, and blasted out full force over the airwaves. But instead of turning off my listeners, it seemed to ignite them. We were unified in our common experience of heartbreak and the messy, glorious aftermath of survival.

Suddenly, I was inundated with interest from people who, like me, had their souls shattered in one way or another by love. Through word of mouth, *Go West* took off like gangbusters. Eventually, at Ravi's suggestion, it was rebranded as *Love Is a Four-Letter Word*—a title he felt better captured the show's new tone, rawness, and depth.

And just like that, the entire trajectory of my life changed. After Ravi sent over a reel of my best segments, a top New York agent reached out with an offer of talent representation and negotiated my deal with WNYC, where my show quickly became the highest-rated one on the air. I put Matty in the rearview mirror, only revisiting that wound when I needed new fuel or a hit of the righteous rage that started it all.

Only now here he was. In Belize. Just four villas down from me.

As I crawled around on the ground like an adrenaline-fueled Roomba, I told myself I was fine. Repeated the mantra over and over as a way perhaps to convince myself that the Matty thing was a chapter closed, a ship that had sunk to the bottom of the sea with a Do Not Resuscitate tag zip-tied to its hull. But all it took was one unexpected glimpse of him, bare chested, suntanned, and comfortably joking with his mom, for my insides to short-circuit as if he'd spilled battery acid into my central nervous system.

I grabbed my phone to text Marin and typed:

Me: ARE YOU DONE WITH YOUR DOWNWARD DOG YET?! S.O.S. EMOTIONAL DEFCON 1. COME TO MY VILLA STAT!!!

Ten minutes later, she burst into the room, her beachy braid unraveling as she tumbled in. "What? What happened?" Marin panted, not even bothering with a hello.

And before I could stop myself, I launched into it. "Matty's here. I saw him. Like, saw him, saw him. He was *tanned*, Marin. And happy. And barefoot. Like, why would my mother not mention anything to me about inviting him, or worse, that he'd decided to attend?! I thought she was just dippy, but maybe she's actually diabolical. Like seriously, what. the. hell?!"

Marin winced. "Girl, I don't even know how to emotionally triage all of that. I'm gonna need flash cards or a whiteboard or something."

I flopped onto the bed. "Jesus, I thought I was over this. No. I *am* over this."

That was an outright lie. I knew I wasn't. Not completely, but I'd stuffed my feelings down so deep that even I'd almost made myself believe they weren't there anymore.

And maybe that was the scariest part. Because if I could still unravel this easily over Matty, then what did that say about me now?

Marin sat beside me and nudged my shoulder with her own, pulling me out of my thoughts. "So we keep you occupied. Strategic avoidance. We're talking packing your schedule so full that you physically can't spiral unless you pencil it in. Beach massages. Snorkeling. Dramatic sun-hat brunches. Obviously, lots of mimosas. Maybe even that mezcal tasting you said sounded pretentious." Her voice lifted with well-meaning encouragement, which only made my panic feel sharper, more unreachable.

"I'm serious, Marin. I never got closure. I just . . . converted my trauma into a brand and built a career on my new personality. What if I see him again and I just, like . . . combust? What if I punch him?" I gasped with the realization of a whole new caliber of horror. With my hand over my mouth, I cried, "What if he tries to talk to me, and I ugly-cry in the hotel lobby while Cannon and Allegra live stream my self-destruction on their TikToks as they sip their virgin piña coladas?"

She took my face in her hands to slow my tirade and smiled gently. "Then I'll dramatically fake a medical emergency, and we'll blame it on bad ceviche. Or I can just wrap you in a towel like a beach burrito and heroically fireman-carry you out of there. I mean, I've been really kicking some ass at CrossFit lately. I think I totally could."

Finally, she cracked my hard veneer of worry, and a tiny, almost involuntary smile tugged at my lips. Grateful for my best friend wasn't even close to a good enough descriptor. I was overwhelmed by her support.

"Full Matty Containment Protocol. FMCP," she confirmed. "You'll only see him when absolutely necessary, like during the wedding ceremony Saturday, or like if he's choking and you're the only one around who knows the Heimlich."

I gave a weak laugh. "Meh, even then, I'd have to think about it."

She laughed and nudged me again. "Good, a joke. That feels like progress. Hey, you'll be okay. It'll be okay." She raised her hand, her fist closed and her pinkie hooked out for me to clasp with my own. "Whatever it takes, we keep him away from you. Far away from you. Promise."

Chapter Nineteen

Marin's plan worked great . . . for the next three hours, anyway, until the Lover's Luau, where I and my coconut bra accidentally bounced straight into Matty at the poke bowl station, his back to me as he reached for a second helping of ahi tuna.

"Sorry, ma'am. I didn't mean to—" His eyes widened, then softened, his whole face brightening at the sight of me. "Elliot. Hi. I've been looking for you everywhere. Waiting and hoping to run into you. I must've walked the length of the resort at least ten times today."

"I didn't realize you were here, or I would have started on the other buffet line," I said, trying for cool even though my stomach bottomed out as we stood face-to-face.

"You look . . . Well, you always look . . . like you. You look like you. Just as beautiful as I remember."

I wanted to tell him he still looked like him too. The floppy hair a little more professional, more trimmed. A few more creases around his eyes but still boyishly handsome, only with stronger features now, a sharper jawline, slightly hollowed cheeks, and a light stubble that added a more rugged edge. But instead, I straightened—tight, rigid, and silent.

"So how are you?" he asked, like it'd only been a few days since I last saw him. Not an entire lifetime.

"What the hell are you doing here, Matty?"

Before he could answer, Marin swooped in like an FMCP superhero in a grass skirt, ready to save the day but with zero chill. "Elliot!

Good! Here you are. I've been looking everywhere for you." She paused and eyed him from head to toe, not hiding the disdain morphing her features into a snarl. "Matthew."

"Hi, Marin," he said. "Good to see you too."

She made a very audible vomiting sound. "Ugh! Don't." Squeezing between us to box him out, she continued, "Anyway, I saved us two seats *wayyyy* over there, let's go." And without waiting for a response, she grabbed my arm, sending the baja shrimp on my plate hurtling to the ground, leaving Matty in the proverbial dust.

On the way, we zoomed past Mom, Keith, and a couple of teenagers I could only assume were his kids. We passed Uncle Ted and his latest trophy wife, then Matty, who had settled under a nearby palm tree with his plate.

We'd made it only a few more steps when I felt a gentle tug on my arm. I spun around to see Izzy, who pulled me into a quick hug. "Hey, Marin," she said, and gave her a kiss on the cheek. "Can I steal El for just a moment, to grab a drink real quick?"

Marin eyed me first, like a good best friend, to check for a green light, and when I gave a small nod, she reached to take the small buffet plate from my hands. "Sure, of course. I'll find us some seats."

Izzy wove her arm through mine as we sidled through the outdoor space. "So, my girl, how are you holding up? I'm so sorry you didn't know Matthew was coming. Your mother said she wanted to be the one to tell you."

"And, of course, she was too self-absorbed to have remembered. And I was blindsided. Some kind of heads-up, or at least a choice in attending, would have been nice."

I didn't mean to get snippy with Izzy. After all, it wasn't really her fault that my mother didn't even think to give me any warning.

"I at least want to apologize, then. I thought Matty had said things with you two were improving, and I couldn't help but hope you two might finally patch things up. Selfishly, I miss our trips and our outings together. They haven't been the same."

"He told you things were okay between us? Well, *someone* certainly practices revisionist history. He and I haven't said so much as a word to one another in over five years. He tried to reach out early on, a few times, but I'm not interested in rehashing it all."

She paused, her lips set in a thin line. "I know I promised never to get involved, but, El, five years is a long time. He knows what he did was wrong."

I shook my head, feeling my chest tighten. "Wrong? No. It was so much bigger than that. *Wrong* doesn't even begin to cover it."

She studied me for a long moment, then let out a quiet sigh. "You know, holding on to that kind of anger . . . it's not healthy and it has a way of leaking into everything else. Of course I'd love to see you and Matthew be able to move past it and go back to being at least friends again, but really, I'm saying this for you. I just don't want to see *you* carrying around that weight forever."

"Izzy, please, enough. I can't do that with Matty. I just . . . can't." I shook my head, feeling the sting of tears starting to rise. Forcing a lighter note into my voice, I tried to steer us away from the conversation. "What I *can* do, though, is hunt down those drinks. Come with me?"

"Fine, but only if you're buying," she joked, putting her arm around me.

"It's an all-inclusive," I reminded her.

"That's right." Izzy laughed, giving me a little squeeze as we made our way over to the bar, where a harried bartender was juggling orders and pouring rum punches two at a time. Izzy ordered a glass of white wine for herself, then glanced at me with a raised eyebrow.

"A margarita, please," I said, the anticipation of the tart lime and tequila almost sharp enough to cut through the knot in my chest.

"Salted rim," Izzy added on my behalf, because of course she knew how I liked mine best.

A few minutes later, drinks in hand, we wove back through the crowd to the long table where Marin was waiting, saving me a seat next to where Dad, Shira, Allegra, and Cannon were locked in a heated debate about which season of *The White Lotus* was the best.

"The first one. No question. Set the stage for the rest," Allegra argued.

"Yeah, but this last season? Come on. It was so much more emotionally raw and visceral than the others," Dad countered.

"It has to be the second season. Sicily. What a setting! I swear, every episode was like travel porn. I was ready to pack up my suitcase and get on a plane each week. Wasn't even sure I should keep watching, I was so worried I actually might. Right, honey?" Shira said, rubbing her hand over Dad's.

Dad looked up from his plate. "What about you, Elliot? Which season did you like best?"

I set my food down on the table and climbed onto the bench. "I didn't really . . . you know, watch. Just a few episodes here and there."

"See," Cannon said from across the table. "Way overhyped, right? Everyone acted like it was the second coming of TV or something. More like rich people whining in exotic locales. Bor-ing. I'm totally with you, Elliot."

I looked over at my half brother, who had to be, what . . . twenty? I tried to do the dysfunctional family math. Let's see, I was about two when Dad left Mom and me for his secretary, who promptly ended it when she realized he wasn't as much fun in real life as when he was an office fling. He then went through a series of girlfriends—if you could even call them that, more like weekend experiments—before he met Shira, also his secretary but with better staying power, when I was about five. About a year later they got married, then a year after that had Cannon, followed shortly by Allegra.

And the sad truth was, I didn't really know either of my siblings. Not well, anyway. It always seemed to me that Dad moved on with his new family, showing them both the kind of warmth I never saw from him, and I suppose I resented them for it, even though looking at them now with an adult perspective, I knew deep down none of that was any of their fault.

"Glad to know I have an ally somewhere in the West family," I said, tipping my margarita glass toward Cannon in a loose toast.

"What do you mean by that?" Dad asked, frowning like I had just accused him of a crime. "I've always been on your side, haven't I, El?"

"Sure, when you bothered to show up."

The atmosphere at the table started to shift at my comment, Allegra taking a dramatic sip of her drink and Shira resting a supportive hand on Dad's forearm.

"That's not exactly fair," he started. "I tried. I did. But your moth—"

Before he could finish, Keith clinked his glass and stood up.

"I just wanted to take this opportunity to thank all of you for making the trip to Ambergris Caye to be here for our wedding. I know that little plane is really something," Keith said with a chuckle. "But hey, we made it! It's so wonderful to look out into this sea of faces: family, old friends, new friends, all here to celebrate with us. It means more than I can put into words."

The space was closing in on me: Keith and his professions of eternal love for my mother, Dad and Shira canoodling like they were on their second honeymoon, everyone awkwardly pretending we were all one big happy family, and just a few tables away, Matty, looking maddeningly at ease, like none of this was out of the ordinary.

How the hell had they all managed to move on, when I was still picking up the pieces from the fallout that thus far had been my life? Dad didn't come to my high school graduation because my "bog troll" of a mother would be there.

His words.

Mom, similarly, refused to come to my senior a cappella showcase at Brown because she felt his "toxic aura was contagious." And now they were toasting one another and making merry, like the past twenty-nine years hadn't been one long, miserable standoff with me playing sheriff square in the middle of the fray.

I felt like I was going mad. Like I'd stepped through the looking glass or into a Norman Rockwell painting where families did things like talk about what season of *The White Lotus* they enjoyed most over thick cuts of prime rib instead of TV dinners eaten alone for decades, none of them present or there for me in any way that mattered.

The air, squeezing me like I was being vacuum-sealed in my own skin, was making it almost impossible to breathe. As my vision blurred around its edges, I grabbed Marin's hand and managed a quick, "I'll be right back," before discreetly standing up and maneuvering around the space toward an exit.

I wasn't sure where I was going, but I needed a minute to pull myself together, all the moments of the day dragging me out to sea like a riptide. Then the soothing, rhythmic sound of the ocean crashing onto the shoreline called to me. I made my way down the beach, where the sunset was peeking behind thick clouds low on the horizon, casting the most beautiful purple and navy hues across a darkening sky. I hiked my dress up to my knees and waded a few feet into the water, fully aware that this was prime shark-feeding hour, but I reasoned that maybe that was a better alternative than returning to dinner.

"Hey, stranger," Matty said, and somehow, just his voice made me feel like the sand was shifting under my feet.

I turned to him. Foamy white crests were lapping against his ankles, the cuffs of his pants rolled up to mid-calf. "You don't even like the ocean, remember? Ever since your mom said we weren't allowed to watch *Jaws* because it would scare us, but we did it anyway."

"That's right. How old were we?"

"Eight. I slept over at your apartment," I answered.

"Pretty racy for eight."

"Strictly PG. We stayed in our respective sleeping bags all night."

"Not true. As *I* recall, you were actually the one who had the nightmare about the movie. Made me scoot over so you could sleep next to me," he joked.

"I don't remember that."

"I do. I remember everything about us," he said, so quietly I almost missed it.

"Really, Matty, why are you here? We haven't seen each other or even talked in—"

"Five years, thirty-seven weeks, and twenty-two days," he said without missing a beat. "Not that I've been counting or anything."

I advanced on him, closing the space between us, and crossed my arms over my chest. "That's the thing, why *have* you been counting? What do you want from me?"

"I miss you. I miss having you in my life. Which I know I have no right to say, but there it is. We've been friends since we were in diapers. Thanksgivings. Christmases. Easters. Birthdays. Mom *still* hasn't forgiven me for ruining things so badly that our families can't spend the holidays together anymore. So when she mentioned she was going to Sonja's wedding, I asked if I could tag along. Maybe I knew it was the only chance I'd have of trying to fix things between us."

I shook my head. "So you come here and corner me? Force a conversation I'm not ready to have. May never be ready to have. What are you doing?"

He ran a hand through his hair and blew out a heavy breath. "I know you don't owe me anything. I understand that. But we're unfinished business, you and me. I'd like to exist somewhere in your orbit again, even if I can't be part of your universe anymore. I'm not asking for much, just a chance. A chance for you to see me as something more than the villain in your story."

White-hot anger churned in my gut, thick and molten, rising faster than I could contain it. It bubbled under my skin, roiling with every flash of our memories together, the good and the bad. With my fists clenched and my jaw tight, my whole body practically vibrated with the effort of holding it all back.

"Not asking for much? You're asking for everything! I gave you everything. Every damn piece of me. The parts I locked away from the rest of the world. You had those. And now you think you can waltz back in with a charming smile and that look and expect me to forget?"

He shifted his weight and rubbed at his jaw. "I'm . . . I'm not expecting us to go back to what we were, but one mistake made shouldn't destroy everything we had and everything we *can* have."

One mistake?! That mistake devastated me, reinforced everything I feared most about trust and relationships. My chest heaved, breath coming fast and shallow. "You didn't just break my heart, Matty. You broke me!" I shouted at a volume so loud even I was taken aback.

He opened his mouth to speak, but I was already shaking my head, laughter sharp and cutting. "You're the fucking storm, Matty! The category five hurricane! I survived you once, but I'm not stupid enough to stand in your path again."

And, as if on cue, like we were in the climactic scene of a Hollywood movie, dark storm clouds suddenly rolled in and a light rain began to fall, getting heavier until we were soaked to the bone, but still, neither of us moved. Wet clothes clung to our skin as we both stood there, stuck in a stalemate. Him trying to absorb the weight of everything I'd just laid bare, and me feeling the relief at having vented it all, not to some faceless audience out on the airwaves, but to the one man I needed to hear me.

He was silent, the roll of the waves paired with the hard rain like static in the otherwise tense quiet between us. Rubbing his neck, his face taut and pale, he looked anguished, as if I'd knocked something loose in him.

And then a surge of lightning flashed across the sky.

He glanced up toward the clouds swirling overhead and then back at me. "We should get inside. It's dangerous to be out here and exposed like this."

There was no undoing it now. The words were out. The silence was broken. And Matty was back in my life, like it or not.

"Yeah," I said, turning away. "It is."

Chapter Twenty

The next morning, I picked half-heartedly at a limp slice of papaya on my breakfast plate while Marin sat across from me, radiating the frantic energy of someone trying to defuse a ticking bomb with a plastic spoon.

"Okay," she said in a low, conspiratorial voice, glancing around the outdoor terrace like someone might be eavesdropping. "I gave the whole FMCP a lot of thought when I got back to my room last night."

"The what?"

"Full Matty Containment Protocol! C'mon, El, get your head in the game," she replied, like it was as common an acronym as CPR or LOL.

I set down my coffee mug. "Right. Yes. FMCP. Continue, please."

"Did a little digging this morning at seaside yoga with your fam. Word is, Matthew and Izzy are locked in for the catamaran tour. So if you stick to literally any other activity on today's wedding itinerary, you should be in the clear."

I nodded mutely, stabbing a cube of cantaloupe so hard it rocketed off my plate.

Marin leaned across the table. "Hey, you okay?"

"Sure, yeah, just fine. Everything's fine. Living the dream: eating mushy fruit in a tropical dystopia, trapped with all the headliners from my therapy sessions." I chased an errant strawberry around my plate with a fork jab, sending another piece of fruit flying, nearly toppling my mimosa in the process.

"You know, that would actually make a killer title for your future memoir: *Headliners from My Therapy Sessions.* I would tell you to file that one away if you'd ever actually *gone* to therapy." She clapped her hand over my forearm and gave it a supportive squeeze. "But it's fine. You're gonna be okay. We'll get you through this together, like we always do."

My eyes lifted to hers, and I was so grateful she was sitting across from me, even though I couldn't help but think of Leo and what he was doing at that exact moment.

We'd exchanged a few texts since I arrived in Belize, and in true Leo fashion, he always replied promptly and said all the right things. But I could feel him holding back, perhaps trying to give me the space he thought I needed, or maybe he was reverting back to old habits, burying himself in his work as a way to avoid getting in too deep. I still didn't know whether he was even coming to the wedding in a few days. He hadn't brought it up, and since I was too afraid to ask, neither had I.

Not to mention, seeing Matty had stirred something deep in my core, reminding me why I'd put up so many walls and drawn so many boundaries in the first place. And though Leo had defied a lot of expectations, it wouldn't be long before he let me down too. Maybe it would be better to just let the relationship fizzle out like it was supposed to after Greece.

Like I'd decided before.

Then why did a small part of me miss him? Like this morning, when I took a walk on the beach and there was the most incredible sunrise after the storm. The sky was streaked with gorgeous shades of yellow and orange, like a sherbet dream. I snapped a picture and sent it to him, but not before deleting the words Wish you were here from the text.

Maybe it was all the rum punch I sucked down after my tangle with Matty and the flood of memories dredged up during our fight, but when I returned to my villa last night, my bed felt empty. I craved the warmth of Leo's arms wrapped around me, the comfort of his solid presence, and the calm he'd somehow pressed into my bones when he'd pull me close.

But more than just his physical being, it was the way he always made the world feel a little less sharp and threatening, like a wizard who could slow the chaos just enough that I could regain my footing. Without him, the night had stretched out long and restless, the silence wearing me down like water on stone, carving out the parts I believed had been so solid. Tossing and turning, I cursed myself for how easily the old wounds had reopened at the sight of Matty.

Over these last few weeks, Leo'd made me believe I could be someone braver. Someone softer. Someone who didn't have to build a fortress around her heart just to survive. But Leo wasn't here. And the longer I sat with that ache, the more I wondered if maybe I was fooling myself all over again.

No. This was ridiculous. Even without Matty reappearing in my life, my career was still teetering on unstable ground. My brand, diluted. Leo was a risk I couldn't afford to take, not now. Personally or professionally, it was all the same. All one had to do was look around Family Dysfunctional Island to see the inevitable wreckage of putting love ahead of reason.

Reason *had* to win. I'd come too far. Sacrificed too much for it to not.

Marin opened the day's itinerary. "The catamaran's clearly out of the running, so what are you thinking? Mindful meditation with your mom or zip-lining with Keith? You know my thing about heights, so I think I'll give deep breathing with Sonja a go. Worst-case scenario, I'll close my eyes and fall asleep. I haven't had a proper nap since before the twins were born."

"Speaking of, any update on how they're doing with Pickles?"

"Tyler checks the cage every morning and night, and the kids texted me a picture of them 'snuggling' with her and feeding her carrot sticks. I'm tellin' you, that guinea pig is living her best life right now. She's having her own little holiday and being spoiled completely rotten. Hope you don't mind."

"Mind?! Are you kidding? I'm jealous! Next time they text, tell them Auntie El says 'thank you for watching her baby and to give

Pickles extra kisses.'" I glanced back down at the itinerary again. "Well, I think it goes without saying that the last thing I would find relaxing is sitting in forced silence with my mother, so I guess swinging from the trees it is."

"Good. I think that'll be a great chance for you to try to get to know Keith a little better," Marin urged.

I curled my lip in objection. "Why?"

"Um, because he's marrying your mother and de facto becoming your stepfather?"

"Stepfather? Please, I give their marriage six months. And that's being generous."

Marin cocked her head to the side and pursed her lips in disapproval. "I was chatting with him a bit yesterday by the pool, and he seems like a really decent guy. Did you know that before he became a data solutions architect he was a Navy SEAL?"

My head shot up. A Navy SEAL?! Navy Walrus, maybe? His dad bod and the way he lumbered around the pool didn't exactly scream elite Special Forces. "Navy SEAL? Really?"

"Yeah. And he's got some pretty wild stories from back then."

"Wow, I didn't realize I'd been replaced as your best friend. Just how long did you two kiki for anyway?"

She shot me a look. "He's nice, El. Different from the others. Like how Leo's different from the others."

Hard as I tried, I couldn't hide the shift in my expression when she mentioned Leo.

"What? What'd I say?" Marin pressed.

"I wasn't totally honest with you about Leo when I asked you to be my plus-one and play defense with my family. Leo does have to work, but we also had a fight a few nights before I was supposed to leave for the wedding. He thought we needed to take some space from each other."

She sighed, her frustration apparent in the rigid bend in her posture as she flung her hands in the air. "I knew you'd do this."

"Do what?"

"Throw away something this good with both hands."

"That's kind of unfair, isn't it?"

"Is it? You know, I used to think your whole radio schtick was a persona, like how, I don't know, Howard Stern is a jerk on the air but supposedly actually a nice guy in real life. But the longer it's gone on, the more I'm starting to wonder how much is an act and how much is just who you really are now."

Crossing my arms over my chest, I planted my feet, standing my ground. "I'm the same me I've always been. Brutally honest. Sharp and unfiltered."

"No. This isn't just about Leo. I saw it in your face the second Matty arrived. It's your fear of letting love in, of being vulnerable again. So you pushed him away, guarding against pain you've already decided is inevitable. If you keep at this game, one day it'll be just you and that stupid hamster because you'll have driven the rest of us off in the name of self-preservation."

"Pickles is a guinea pig! And what, you're my therapist now?" The words came out harsher than I meant, but it was easier to charge at her than admit she was right.

"No. I'm your friend. Your best friend."

"I know, and I'm sorry I bit your head off. It's just that Matty being here, on top of my mom *and* dad . . . and everyone else, it's, it's a lot. I'm not handling it as well as I could be, I know that."

"It doesn't have to be this way. You *could* have another ally. You know, the best thing about letting people in is it means you don't have to handle everything on your own."

I knew she was talking about Leo, and I didn't want to hear any more about it. My head was already swimming. "I should get going. According to the itinerary, the bus for the ropes course leaves in ten."

I stuffed some sneakers, a water bottle, and a few other things into my backpack, and just as I was turning to leave, Marin called to me.

"Promise me you'll give Keith a fair shot, okay? Remember what I said about letting people in."

"I will," I mumbled half-heartedly.

"Elliot Rose West," she said, arching her right eyebrow.

"Okay, okay, I'll try. How 'bout that?"

She rolled her eyes, shook her head, and muttered, "Close enough."

Chapter Twenty-One

Stuffed in the back of a sweaty bus, its sad excuse for an air conditioner poorly circulated around a barely there draft, I clutched my backpack in my lap like it contained state secrets and a live grenade instead of just my water bottle, a granola bar, SPF 70, and a half-charged power bank. The windows had been flung open in a hopeful attempt to combat the heat, but all they really did was invite in a syrupy breeze that stuck to the back of my throat like hot honey.

With my eyes cast forward, I was trying to breathe through the humidity and the unease churning in my gut when a few more resort guests boarded the shuttle. I scanned them quickly—no familiar faces. Relief. For about two seconds. Then Keith climbed up the steps, followed by a couple of his family members with the same receding hairlines and distinct chins, and then finally . . . *Matty.*

AHHH! No!!!

I wasn't sure whether I should duck behind the seat and attempt to crawl into my own handbag or fake diarrhea and bail, but before I could do any of those things, the bus driver sealed the doors behind Matty and lurched us into motion with a groaning grind of gears.

Why was he here?! He was supposed to be on a catamaran, sipping rum punch and making poor choices to a Bob Marley soundtrack. He shouldn't be here. Not on this bus. Not effortlessly breezy with his headphones dangling and his legs stretched confidently into the aisle like a man who looked like he'd just escaped from a *GQ* cover shoot.

The blood drained from my face, pooling somewhere around my ankles, and I sank lower in the seat, out of sight, and tried to figure out whether I could will myself into another dimension or at least into the luggage compartment below. I planned to make myself as travel-size as possible during the ride, hang toward the back of the crowd as we exited the bus, and just hope to God Matty was so far up front and ahead on the course that I'd get by with him never even knowing I was here.

The next forty minutes were a slow, vibrating crawl down a jungle road, the heat doing nothing to dull the awareness of him just a few seats away. I spent the whole ride trying not to be sick in my own lap or accidentally make eye contact. Both, I feared, would end me.

When we finally rattled to a stop at the ropes course and zip-lining grounds deep in the Belizean jungle, our guide, a woman with the shoulders of a linebacker and the calm authority of someone who could and maybe had wrestled a crocodile before breakfast, stepped in front of us and clapped.

"Alright, folks, listen up! We're short a couple of guides today, so you'll need to partner up. Two people per zip. Double the fun, right?"

Panic surged. I scanned the crowd. Most of the families and couples already paired off, chatting and laughing like extras in a travel brochure. And then, of course, I caught Matty's eye. His face lit with excitement and he half lifted a hand, like he was about to wave me over, while every cell in my body screamed, *Absolutely the fuck not!*

I sidestepped Matty's gaze so fast I nearly sprained something, and pivoting hard, found myself facing the only other unpaired person in sight.

Keith.

Awesome.

I glanced between Matty and Keith, Matty and Keith—gah! dammit! But when Matty advanced toward me, instinct took over and I made a beeline for Keith, whose eyes brightened as he spotted me approaching.

"Hey, partner!" he chirped, way too brightly. "Didn't see your name on the roster until this morning. Kinda thought you were more of a rum punch on the open water kind of a gal?"

"Then clearly you don't understand the chaos I'm capable of when emotionally compromised," I snarked, trying for jovial but coming out a bit sharper than I'd intended. He chuckled, which caught me off guard, and gestured for me to lead the way through the path over to where thick ropes and neon harnesses were set out along a massive tree line.

While we were getting strapped into gear that looked better suited for a mission to Mars, Keith checked his straps and buckles with the casual confidence of someone who'd done this before, which according to Marin, he had back in his Navy SEAL days. All while I stood there, trying not to get distracted by the sensation of Matty's eyes on me.

I shifted my attention to survey what I was getting myself into, and suddenly my chest grew tighter against the straps of the harness. Desperately, I tried not to hyperventilate. The vibrant greens of the expanse started to swirl together like an oil spill, my pulse warbling in my ears. I glanced up. The first platform looked . . . fine. Manageable. But each was secured progressively higher, and somewhere around station four, I officially lost the plot.

I swallowed past my nerves and hiked with the group up a short trail to where the ropes course began, an obstacle gauntlet strung through the branches like some deranged jungle gym designed by Tarzan himself.

Keith moved through each phase with practiced ease, calling out an occasional, "Watch your footing here," or "Left rope's more stable than the right," like he'd done this a thousand times. Meanwhile, I was clinging to every cable and narrow wooden plank as I was suspended thirty feet in the air, sweating through my tank top, and reevaluating every life decision that had led me to this moment.

The wood creaked under my sneakers. My palms slipped. At one point, a monkey darted across the line in front of me, and I screamed, nearly drop-kicking it into outer space.

Keith glanced back. "You good?"

"Totally!" I wheezed. "Just communing with nature. At great heights. With primates. Over the void."

He chuckled but didn't tease. Just waited patiently until I made my way across, step by agonizing step. Finally, we reached the launch platform for the zip line, and that's when my body gave out. I stood frozen, heart racing, the canopy below a sea of leafy doom. My hands trembled as I reached for the cable, then pulled back. I couldn't do it.

Keith stepped beside me, his tone calm. "You okay?"

"Nope. Not okay. Not even a little okay," I managed, breath shallow.

He didn't laugh. Didn't downplay the feeling. Instead, he bent over a little to meet my eyes. "You're scared because your brain's doing its job," he said gently. "It sees a drop and says, 'Nope, danger, abort.' But the thing is, fear isn't always accurate. Fear doesn't know you're suspended by gear rated for thousands of pounds and checked by someone trained for it."

I blinked at him. "Fear might not be accurate, but damn, is it convincing."

He smiled. "Sorry. Force of habit. Navy SEAL training. We had this phrase: 'Calm is a choice.' You don't fight fear by pretending it's not there. You breathe through it to give it less power."

I stared at him, this man I'd written off as a generic ex-military Dad Type with a corny laugh and a suspiciously easy smile. And here he was, grounding me like some kind of Zen master.

"I . . . I don't trust the cable," I muttered.

"Don't have to trust the cable. Trust yourself," he said, his voice low and kind. "You won't fall."

I swallowed hard but nodded. Clipping us in, he double-checked the gear with slow, steady hands, and when he wrapped an arm around me to brace us for takeoff, it wasn't intrusive. It felt solid. Safe.

The platform swayed underneath me, and my stomach dropped, my eyes slamming shut. But Keith continued to coax me quite literally off the ledge. "Just breathe. You're doing great. Look out at the horizon and enjoy this incredible view! You ready?"

And before I knew it, we stepped off the platform and into the open expanse, together. The wind roared around us, and somewhere between trees blurring beneath me and Keith's calm voice in my ear, I realized I wasn't panicking anymore.

I was flying.

By the time we landed on the other side, my legs were jelly but I was laughing, like actually laughing, the sound echoing through the trees, unfamiliar and wild, like it had been hiding in my chest for years.

Keith grinned. "Told you you'd crush it."

"Thanks," I said, quieter now. "For . . . getting me through that."

Keith gave a small shrug, adjusting the straps on his harness with a forceful yank. "You did the hard part. I was just here for support."

I studied him in profile as we continued on the course and he turned to help a little girl behind us adjust her helmet. There was something weathered but gentle in the way he moved. The kind of man who'd seen a lot, maybe more than he'd ever say out loud, but didn't need to make a show of it. Not flashy, not slick.

Just present.

Keith clipped me in for the next obstacle and offered me a warm smile of encouragement. I gripped the rope and took a breath, surer this time.

Not perfect. But thanks to Keith, a bit more steady.

Chapter Twenty-Two

I slumped against a mahogany tree, sweat dripping down my neck and soaking into my shirt. Pouring some water from my canteen over my head, I let it run through my scalp and trickle down my back. The course was mostly behind me, with just one last zip line left to conquer. It stretched out like a giant silver ribbon over the mangroves and the turquoise ocean below. Three stories up, but Keith and the guide kept insisting it'd be worth it.

"Hey, any space over there for me?" Matty asked, nodding at the patch of ground to my left.

I looked around, almost incredulous. "Are you sure one of the other millions of trees doesn't look more appealing? I mean, that one *waaaay* over there looks like a beaut."

He didn't even hesitate, disregarding my very persuasive argument for literally any other tree, and dropped down next to me. "Are you planning to avoid me this whole trip, or just today?"

"You're not supposed to be here. You're *supposed* to be lounging on a catamaran right now." I kept my attention forward, aiming for indifference.

"I switched when I saw you'd signed up for the ropes course. I figured, with any luck, we'd get tethered together and you'd have no choice but to talk to me," he said with a smile that might have seemed charming to any other girl, but I knew better.

I stood up, brushing dirt from my legs. "Talk to you about what? I said everything I had to say to you last night."

He flashed an easy grin. "Right, when you affectionately referred to me as Hurricane Matthew."

"Consider yourself lucky. That was the mildest insult I had on hand."

"I'm a regular listener of your radio show. Believe me, I know full well you were going easy on me."

My head shot up. "Wait, you listen to my show?"

He shrugged. "I guess I realized it was the only way I'd get to hear your voice and kinda, you know, keep you in my life on a regular basis."

I stared at him. I couldn't believe it. Matty listened to *Love Is a Four-Letter Word.*

All this time, I'd been sending my heartbreak out into the airwaves, railing about love, railing about betrayal, spinning clever little monologues that were really just armor. And all that time, he was out there, tuning in. He knew exactly how I felt about him. He'd heard every word and come to Belize anyway.

The ropes instructor clapped her hands together. "We're going to start harnessing up for the final part of the excursion, our zip-line grand finale, if you will. This one is also a tandem ride, so try to find a new partner and hop over to the line when you're ready."

I popped up on my toes, scanning the crowd for Keith even though it defied the instructor's directive, but ever the rule follower, Keith was already suiting up with his nephew.

I turned, desperately looking for someone, *anyone*, who wasn't Matty.

Like Noah's Ark, though, it appeared as if everyone had already paired off two by two.

Shit.

Matty raised his eyebrows and gave a little shrug, gesturing between us, like, *Well, here we are, the last ones remaining.*

"I don't think I'm going to do it," I said, backing a step away from the harness station. "That one is really high up there, much higher than the last zip line, and I'm not feeling as brave as I was."

"You? Not feeling brave?" he said, stepping closer. "You're the bravest woman I know. Have been since we were kids. Remember when we wanted to see that band Vampire Weekend play? But it was at that sketchy warehouse in Bushwick. How old were we? Fourteen? I was ready to chicken out, but you navigated us through three subway transfers and a guy peeing in a shopping cart like it was nothing. Even though we were way underage, you walked inside like we owned the place, and the bouncer didn't even blink."

"That wasn't bravery. That was a padded push-up bra and Ruby Woo Red Lipstick."

He blushed, and glanced down. "No, you were brave. I used to be so in awe of you. I still am."

The instructor's voice cut in, calm and steady. "Okay, everyone, we're going to start our climb up the ridge. Once we're at the top, we'll get you harnessed in for the zip line. For now, keep an eye on your footing. It's a bit steep."

As soon as we reached the top, the instructor shoved Matty and me together, tightening the straps of our harnesses with a determined efficiency that left no space for hesitation. Suddenly face-to-face, we were so close I could feel his breath on my cheek, warm against the cooler air. Our feet fumbled for balance, the rigging locking us chest to chest, no room to turn, no chance to look away.

I couldn't help but notice that his frame felt different. More solid. Muscular. Like a man. Not a boy. He smelled the same, though, like Tom Ford Oud Wood. I remember when he picked out the cologne at the big Macy's in Herald Square. I told him I liked that scent best, and he bought it without a second thought.

"You know, you smell the same. Like vanilla. Like the way you always did when we'd hug and you never wanted to be the one to let go first," he said.

I'd forgotten that. Now I was the girl who always let go first. Who pushed people away, who left before *she* could be left.

"Alright, you two, step up onto the platform," the instructor called, tugging on our shared harness one last time. "I'll give you the countdown, and then you push off together, hard. Got it?"

Matty and I stood with the toes of our sneakers touching, our feet edging the side of the platform. My eyes locked on his, and a cold fear washed through me. "I . . . I'm not sure I want to—"

"Three . . . two . . . one!" she called.

Before I even knew what was happening, the guide gave us a little shove as Matty pushed us off with both feet, and suddenly we were flying, air whipping hair into our faces. His chest was warm against me, and for a split second, it felt like nothing had ever gone wrong between us.

But then, we started slowing . . . maybe a hundred yards shy of the landing platform. The world tilted slightly, and the zip line jerked to a stop, leaving us dangling in the open air over the jungle below.

"Matty! What did you do?" I shrieked.

"Nothing. I didn't do anything," he said, his voice tinged with defensiveness.

"Oh, c'mon. Isn't this exactly what you wanted? For me to be stuck here, alone with you? I mean, it's why you didn't go on the catamaran, isn't it?"

"You're the one who wouldn't help us push off. We probably didn't have enough momentum to make it all the way across."

"Well, now what happens?"

"Wrap your legs around me. Maybe we can swing and get this thing started again."

Reluctantly, I complied. We rocked back and forth like two amateurs on a broken carnival ride.

Nothing.

"I don't think this is working," he grunted, still trying.

"Oh no? What was your first clue? The total lack of movement or the fact that we look like a pair of horny koalas mid-coitus?"

Suddenly, a voice called up from down below. "Try not to panic. This happens at least once a month. We just need to get the tow line from the shed and find another instructor to help out. Don't go anywhere."

"Don't go anywhere?! Where does she think we're going?" Matty mumbled.

And I couldn't be sure if it was the altitude or the adrenaline, but suddenly the absurdity of the entire situation, me tandem-harnessed to my ex, stuck on a zip line at least one hundred feet off the ground, struck me as ridiculously funny, and I burst out laughing.

"What could you possibly find funny about our current predicament?" he asked.

"This . . . you and me . . . stuck like this. I mean, I swore I would never speak to you again in my life, and now here I am, tethered to you like . . . like . . . we're in a rom-com written by someone who hates me almost as much as I hate you."

He pulled back as if my words had slapped him, the mention of me hating him seemed to hit him harder than the whiplash of the zip line's jolt.

He drew in a breath, his eyes contrite when they met mine. "I messed up. Big-time. And I know I broke your heart. But I didn't think . . . I didn't think you hated me. I mean, I wasn't in our relationship alone, El. You have to admit that a part of you was always waiting for the other shoe to drop. Our whole future was standing right in front of us, and I couldn't get you to meet me there. And I—"

"Oh, so this is somehow my fault now?" I snapped, my voice sharp enough to cut through the humid air. "You cheated, Matty. You lied. And now you're saying what, that I somehow pushed you into it? Made you fuck . . . what was her name? Hannah? Because I didn't trust you enough?"

He didn't answer right away, but I could feel the tension radiating off him like heat from the steel cable we were suspended on. "Don't," I said, shaking my head. "Don't try to rewrite history just because you suddenly feel bad about how it ended. You don't get to call my walls the problem when you were the one who proved I needed them in the first place."

"Hey, up there!" a voice called from far below, breaking the moment like a pin to a balloon. "We've got the tow line and should have you moving again in two shakes!"

Neither of us responded.

I looked out over the canopy, the view blurring with unshed tears I refused to let fall. Part of me wanted to scream at him. Another part wanted to vanish completely. But mostly, I just didn't want to be here, suspended in midair, in every sense of the word.

Stuck.

With Matty.

With the ache of who I used to be. The vulnerable version of me I thought I'd long left behind, but who had apparently just been waiting for the right moment to resurface.

Chapter Twenty-Three

After an exhausting morning in the jungle, I was more than ready for a hot shower and a nap in my dark and air-conditioned room. I reached into my backpack for the key card, and as my fingers wrapped around the edge of the plastic, Izzy's voice floated down the path behind me.

"Elliot! Yoo-hoo!"

I closed my eyes for half a second and then turned around to greet her. "Oh, hey, Izzy. How was the catamaran?"

"So fantastic. We snorkeled at Coral Garden Reef. I never knew your dad and Shira were such expert divers. They basically led the whole group. If you get the opportunity, you should really get out on the water with them."

"Yeah, maybe," I said, shrugging.

"So, I'm glad I caught you. I wanted to know what time to be ready later."

"Ready for what?"

"Sonja's bachelorette party, of course."

I yanked the wedding weekend itinerary from the front pocket of my backpack. "Bachelorette party? There's nothing on the schedule for tonight?" I said, scanning the page again.

"Exactly. She left tonight *wiiiiide* open for whatever it is you're planning."

"Whatever *I'm* planning? She thinks I'm throwing her a bachelorette party? Has Mom completely lost her mind?"

"Well . . . you *are* her maid of honor," she joked.

"Since when?!"

Izzy looked flustered by my confusion. "Since always. Didn't she ask you?"

"Ask me? When has she ever consulted me on anything?"

"True, but maybe she thought it was just assumed?"

My eyes almost rolled right out of my head. "C'mon, Izzy, this is her fourth wedding. Do we really need to go through the stupid pomp and circumstance of it all again?"

Izzy sighed and crossed her arms over her chest, her boobs now threatening to pop out the top of her bathing suit. "I get it. I do. But it's different this time."

"It's different every time." I threw my hands in the air. "Ugh! Fine. What did she have in mind? Penis hats and a 'kiss the bride' sash?! Or can we just do like some dinner, throw back a handful of tequila shots, and call it a night?"

"How about I get an official head count and arrange the dinner plans—at least take that off your plate—and you just figure out the nighttime fun. You're a hell of a lot younger than me and probably can find lots more things to do using those apps and whatever," Izzy offered.

I glanced at the time on my cell and groaned. "I'll go to the concierge, see what I can figure out."

"Your mother'll be thrilled." Izzy kissed me on the cheek. "I'll text you the head count as soon as I have it."

"Great, and I'll see if the gift shop has anything shaped like male genitalia?" This wasn't my first rodeo, and probably wouldn't be the last.

After Izzy left, I swiftly recruited Marin to help me, and by sunset, we'd managed to wrangle a plan that felt festive-ish: predinner at the beachside restaurant with cocktails and embarrassing stories, dinner wherever Izzy managed to find us such a last-minute reservation, followed by a "spontaneous" game of wedding-themed charades in the villa. Marin even managed to round up some dollar-store accessories at a nearby bodega: plastic tiaras, novelty sunglasses, and one feather boa that had clearly seen better days.

Sonja, though, to her eternal credit, was overwhelmed with appreciation and acted like we'd flown in Beyoncé for her big night.

"Oh, El, this is just what I wanted, something casual and meaningful!" she cooed, teetering slightly in heels I was 80 percent sure she borrowed from the 2006 section of her closet.

"*Meaningful* was definitely what I was going for," I said, sipping my cocktail and wondering how the hell I'd become so proficient in acting like the adult in our relationship.

After a few rounds of necessary shots, a surprisingly cutthroat dirty charades game, and a toast that involved tears (hers) and reluctant tenderness (mine), we drifted down to our final party stop, karaoke. The festivities were already in full swing, evident from the cacophony of voices floating out into the night from the resort's open-air lounge, fighting to stay on pitch.

"Mom, I can't believe you're still going strong. Are you sure you don't want to just call it a night? Get that very important beauty rest for this weekend?" I murmured to her as we walked arm in arm under string lights.

"I'm getting married in forty-eight hours!" she squealed, her eyes gleaming. "This is one of my last nights as a free woman."

I barked out a laugh. "A free woman? Four marriages later, I'm pretty sure you haven't been a free woman since the Clinton administration."

One sharp glance from Marin was enough to tell me I'd better ease up on my jabs before the night went south. I relented with a smile and said, "Okay, who's ready for some karaoke?"

"I'm sorry to do this to you, babe, but I'm gonna head back to my villa and FaceTime with the kids before they go to bed. Will you be alright if I duck out?" Marin asked, leaning into me with a quick hug.

"Um, no. You know Mom's gonna wanna pull me into one of her *Mamma Mia!* routines," I whispered.

"Just tell her you're on strict vocal rest. Doctor's orders," she said with a cheeky grin as she headed in the direction of her villa.

After Marin left, the rest of us stepped into the bar just as someone murdered their way through a rendition of "Total Eclipse of the Heart." Mom spotted Keith, his family and friends, and other wedding attendees at a cluster of tables near the stage.

She gave me a big kiss on the cheek, completely disregarding my dig, and scurried off to surprise him from behind. I watched him brighten when he spotted her, and the delight in her expression as he swept her into his arms for a kiss to much raucous clapping and hollering from the crowd.

The lights in the lounge were low, all palm-frond shadows and lanterns strung like drunken constellations. In Honor of Sonja and Keith, Love Songs Only! a sign declared in bold, glittery lettering, which stood beside a makeshift stage set up next to a festive tiki bar.

I stood near the back, nursing a watered-down margarita, the condensation beading against my palm. Every table was filled. Laughter, clapping, even a few drunk resort guests belting out Elton John like they'd just discovered sassy hips and vibrato.

Lounging with a group of half-familiar faces, head thrown back in laughter, I heard Matty before I'd spotted him. Our conversation high above the treetops still reverberated in my bones, leaving me unsettled and on edge.

"Next up," the enthusiastic emcee boomed, "Matthew Adler!"

Matty gave a casual salute, and his table mates cheered him on as he started walking toward the stage. Naturally, I assumed he'd pick something ironic. A throwback. Maybe something from Queen or Blink-182 or One Direction.

"Thought I'd go with a classic, because you know, nothing says 'vacation vibes' quite like some public humiliation," he said, earnest and annoyingly charming. Shuffling a hand through his hair, he grabbed the mic as the DJ cued up the song. "And I guess when I think of a love song, this is the only one that ever comes to mind."

Then . . . the first haunting notes of Meat Loaf's "I'd Do Anything for Love" began to play. A song we used to sing on every road trip and sometimes off his apartment fire escape at the top of our lungs when we were feeling particularly angsty. Matty'd shake out his curly hair, taking Meatloaf's part, of course, and then I'd come in, doing my best to imitate the unforgettable rasp of so many nineties female rock artists, usually to the detriment of my vocal cords.

Seriously? He picked *this*? I didn't care how nostalgic it was, didn't he realize a twelve-minute anthem was a little ridiculous? Karaoke songs should be, like, three to four minutes, tops.

His self-indulgence was nothing short of astounding.

Then he started to sing, quietly, sincerely. It wasn't a joke. It was a full-on performance. When the chorus hit, he scanned the crowd and found me with the precision of someone who'd never stopped knowing exactly where I was.

And then I couldn't help but remember the way I used to hang on every word he sang in this song. The lyrics. The promises. Back then, I'd believed he'd move mountains and cross oceans for me, until his betrayal spoke louder than every vow he ever made.

Oh, you'd do anything for love, Matty? Guess fidelity didn't quite make the cut.

But really, this wasn't about Meatloaf's banger. It wasn't about Matty's desire to serenade the crowd with a monster ballad. Apparently, this was about me. His 'Big Gesture.' A rom-com moment. As if a song could erase all that had shattered us.

Spoiler alert: It could not.

Seething, I focused on the drink in my hand, my fingers gripping the glass so tightly I half expected it to shatter. Then came my cue, the part I always used to jump in for. He looked right at me, eyes twinkling like we were sharing some private joke, and extended the second mic in my direction.

"Come on, Els," he said, his voice booming over the song that continued to pulse behind him, "you know you want to."

I slid off my stool and crossed the room . . . right past him without even so much as a second glance.

Chapter Twenty-Four

By the time his final note rang out, the crowd was on their feet, clapping, whooping, and cheering. All except me. I was over by the bar waving my arms, trying like hell to flag down the bartender for the drink I so desperately needed. Of course, though, he was buried under a sea of people using Matty's twelve-minute number as some sort of karaoke drink intermission.

I pushed up on my toes and waved a twenty-dollar bill in the air, hoping that might do the trick. No such luck. Instead, the bartender nodded vaguely in my direction while serving the next ten people in line.

"Hey," Matty called, weaving through the crowd of drunk people in Hawaiian shirts and cargo shorts. "You left me hanging up there. Not to mention I can't believe you passed up the part where you always steal the show."

"Yeah, well, I don't really feel like dueting with you anymore," I mumbled and turned back to the bar.

He sidled up to me. "But we always sounded better together."

I pounded my fists on the counter, practically flinging a piña colada into some poor stranger's lap, and spun around to face him. "You know what that performance was? Weaponized sentimentality. The kind of throwback that leaves actual bruises. God, that song. *That* song. Do you even know what it means?"

He smirked, a boyishly charming-type grin. "Nobody knows what it means. That's what makes it so iconic. What's the thing Meatloaf won't do? Your guess is as good as mine," he answered, missing my point entirely. "Look, El, I was aiming for . . . I don't know . . . poetic? Poignant? One of those big gestures where everyone claps and cheers us on as we reunite."

"Matty," I huffed.

"I'm hoping, perhaps in vain, you'll give me . . . give us . . . another chance. That you might be able to forgive me." His eyes were locked on mine, catching the glowing light of the tiki torches swaying in the shadows.

"Another chance?! Do you have sunstroke or depleted electrolytes or something, because those are the *only* actual reasons you'd think it's even fair to ask that!"

"Ellie Belly!" Mom appeared out of nowhere, clearly tipsy from too many Bahama Mamas as her drink sloshed out of her glass. "Ellie Belly, me and Izzy need you to be our third Dynamo for 'Super Trouper!'"

"Mom, I really don't feel like—"

"You know, your energy is really throwing off my chi! C'mon, we've done this number at every single one of my bachelorette parties. Okay, maybe not the first one, before I married your father. Well, actually . . ." She paused, squinting and pointing at her stomach. "Come to think of it, you *were* there." She reached out to try to pry me from my seat.

I folded my arms over my chest. "Seriously, Mom, I'm not in the mood. See if Aunt Kitty will play your Julie Walters."

She waved her hand dismissively, sending more of her drink flying out of her cup. "She can't, her gout is flaring. Besides, I want you. So get in the mood because the DJ already has it all cued up."

Izzy shot me a look like I was stomping all over their vibe. And maybe I was. But her timing was, as usual, completely (and expertly) inconvenient. Then, the bright notes of ABBA spilled from the speakers. Mom grabbed my hand and yanked me up to the stage, where she and Izzy snapped into their poses.

"Ellie." Mom nudged my elbow with a wide grin. "Put your mic up in the air!"

Begrudgingly, I lifted the microphone to half-heartedly get into position as Mom whispered, “Don’t forget, you’ve got harmony with Iz. I’ll take the lead.”

How could I forget I was her backup singer . . . her backup everything, for as long as I could remember? The one who made sure she got up and out the door when another breakup left her too numb to move. The one who bought groceries because she was out most nights, forgetting I needed to eat dinner too. The one who stayed up waiting, just to lock the door behind her.

And as we bounced around the stage, stumbling through the loose (and I do mean *loose*) choreography, I was momentarily blinded by the white glare of the spotlight. Then during the bridge when Izzy swung me around in an off-balance twirl, suddenly the crowd came into sharp focus, and I could see all their faces staring up at me.

Dad. Shira. Allegra. Cannon. Keith. Matty.

Though he wasn’t there, Leo’s face suddenly flashed in my mind too, along with our Valentine’s Day date at *Mamma Mia!: The Immersive Experience*, waving napkins overhead and belting out “Dancing Queen.” And I suddenly realized I wished he really was somewhere in this audience, his encouraging smile and gentle eyes cheering me on.

Then there was a rush of sound and another flash, the bright spotlight catching me in the eyes. When I blinked, the world shifted, and suddenly, I was no longer singing karaoke in Belize. I was at the Moulin Rouge in Paris with Leo, the same stage lights bright and warm, sipping champagne as we watched a flurry of can-can girls high-kicking and spinning in unison. We stumbled out at the end of the night into the snow-kissed streets of Montmartre, and we kissed under the glow of a wrought-iron streetlamp, fat flakes falling like powdered sugar through a sifter.

It was a new memory, no doubt, but as real and vivid as any I’d ever had. My brain was scrambling, trying to make sense of it all. My feelings about being up here with Mom at yet another one of her bachelorette parties, the sight of my family in the audience, Matty’s impromptu performance, and, most of all, Leo.

This vision of us together in Paris, happy. In love. Leo, who had appeared back in my life like magic.

My brain was spinning so fast I couldn't land on a single thought, let alone a lyric, and so I stopped singing. Mom, of course, noticed and gave me a little nudge, not playful, not even in rhythm. More like a reminder. *Come on. Smile. Be part of the fun.*

"Elliot," Mom whispered. "Hey. What's going on?"

"Nothing."

"Then, 'Sing out, Louise!'" she joked, quoting the famous line from *Gypsy*.

"Super Trouper" was coming to an end, and Mom and Izzy landed impressive splits on the ground, throwing jazz hands in the air as the crowd, now on its feet, called for an encore.

Mom turned to me. "What do you say? Should we do 'Waterloo' next?"

"I think I've had enough for tonight."

I handed her my mic and started to hurry off the stage when Mom caught my arm and said, "C'mon, just one more song. *Pleeease*, it's my bachelorette party!"

"Really, I'm tired. It was a long day of zip-lining, and it's like a thousand degrees out here. I just want to take a cold shower and get a good night's sleep. You guys stay and keep the party going."

Her forehead creased with confusion. "But you and Keith got along today. He told me all about it. Said you had a wonderful time."

"Yeah, he seems like a really decent guy."

She put her hands on her hips. "Then why are you being like this?"

"Like what?"

"Like how you always are. Why can't you celebrate with me? Be happy for me for once?"

"It's not always about you, Mom. I have a lot going on right now with my own life. Did it seriously not register that Matty's here? *Matty*, who I've spent the last five years actively avoiding? And you just . . . what? Pretend that's not a big deal? On top of everything else this weekend? Do you have any idea how hard this all is for me?"

She actually had the nerve to roll her eyes as she huffed, "Is *that* what this is about?" Sipping the drink in her hand through a bendy straw with an indifferent *sluuuurp*, she licked her lips and shrugged. "Why should Matty even matter? You're with Leo now."

"Of course that's how you would keep score. I'm with Leo, so I should be able to just move on, replace one guy with the next, right?" I pinched the bridge of my nose between my thumb and index fingers, hard. "Look, let's not do this tonight, okay? I'm just asking to be dismissed from my maid of honor–ly duties for the rest of the evening so I can take a breather. Please." My exasperation fell out in a whoosh, and Mom looked offended but resigned.

Her shoulders dropped, voice lowering. "Fine. Go."

The music from the speakers was already shifting into the opening chords of "Waterloo." Mom hopped back onstage, lifted the mic with a forced grin pasted on her face, and started to sway with Izzy like nothing had happened between us.

I stepped down carefully, feeling the lights and heat and noise dim behind me as I moved farther and farther away, through the lounge and past clusters of people buzzing with energy. I was halfway down the path toward my villa when I heard my name. Once. Then again. I didn't turn, but the footsteps behind me picked up, and within moments, Matty closed the gap between us. I whipped around to face him.

"Jesus, what?! What is it you want from me?!"

He stepped forward and shrugged, his arms cast open, not demanding, just waiting.

I looked away, afraid that if I met his eyes, I'd fall apart.

"Nothing. I just . . . You seemed like . . . you know, you might have needed a friend. I know you. I know how upset you can get when you've had it out with your mom."

It was true. He had been there for every fight, every argument, every clash, every standoff for most of the first two decades of my life.

It was Matty and Izzy's apartment I'd run to when Mom's latest crash-and-burn relationship had sent my world spinning again. I could always count on Matty to cheer me up. Or at the very least, to suggest a plan so absurd it would distract me from whatever she'd done that had me fuming.

"Tell me what I can do to help turn this night around?" he asked. "I can walk you to your villa, of course. Just make sure you get back okay. Or we can go to the Salty Pineapple and throw back shots until we forget our names, birthdays, and basic motor skills. *Orrrrr*, we can pull a Bonnie and Clyde and leave this whole place in a cloud of dust as we watch it disappear in the rearview of our Ford V8. I realize I'll have to somehow get ahold of a Ford V8, but I'll do it for you . . . anything for you. You know that."

And deep down, I did know that. That the Matty who'd been my childhood savior was still somewhere deep inside him, ready to jump to my rescue without a second's hesitation.

"Didn't Clyde have a mustache? I feel like he had a mustache," I managed to joke as I sniffled and wiped my nose with my sleeve.

"I can grow a mustache."

I actually snorted out a laugh. "No, you can't! Don't you remember when you tried back in high school and you looked like . . . well, a little like . . . Frida Kahlo. A handsome Frida Kahlo, but yeah, I'm sticking with my answer."

"Frida Kahlo?! You've got to give me one of the Mario brothers, at the very least."

"Okay, fine. I'll give you Luigi, *before* he hit puberty."

"Hey!" He poked me playfully. Instinctually, I folded, the ticklish sensation causing me to wriggle against him. When he stopped and my laughing slowed, we were only inches away, face-to-face, his quick breath warming my cheek.

"You know, El, I've never stopped . . ." he whispered, but the rest of his sentence got lost in the galloping of my pulse in my ears.

And then—

A voice shouted in the distance. Followed by laughter. Music. Someone calling for a group photo. The world came rushing back in, loud and bright and real.

Maybe Matty had never stopped feeling love between us, but I had.

I had to.

But this feeling of not hating him as much as I did even an hour ago, that was something new.

"I should get back to my villa." He took a step forward to escort me, but I held up my hand. "Don't. I mean, thank you, but it's okay, you don't have to. I can walk myself. Good night, Matty."

I turned before he could answer, before I could let him back in. The night air brushed my skin with calm, but my mind couldn't quiet. Tonight I'd already given Matty more than I meant to: not forgiveness, of course, but the smallest crack in the wall I'd built, and even that felt a little too risky.

Chapter Twenty-Five

The sunlight streamed through the thin linen curtains and swayed in the salty breeze. After the chaos, overstimulation, and complete storm surge of unresolved tension with pretty much every person in a two-mile radius, sleep had been a weighted blanket, pinning me to Earth. I squinted against the light and listened to my own breathing. The steady pattern of each inhale and exhale.

Wait.

I focused harder, and from behind me, I heard a mirroring of my breath, deeper and more sound, a slight growl beneath it. *My* inhalation. *Other* inhalation. *My* exhalation. *Other* exhalation. I felt it on my shoulder as real as my own.

Oh.

My.

God.

Not Matty. Not Matty. Pleeeease, *not Matty.*

But sweet Jesus, if it's not Matty, then who the fuck else would it be?

I rolled over, ready to punt whoever it was straight out of bed, when—

Leo.

Leo?!

Hair mussed, mouth slack in sleep, one arm thrown over his head like he'd been reaching for me in a dream. A faint line creased his cheek where it had pressed into the sheet, and his skin almost glowed in the cast of the morning light.

For a second, my brain couldn't compute what my eyes were seeing. Like I'd conjured him out of sheer need, like my body had sent up a flare into the universe and he'd followed the smoke all the way to me.

Relief hit first. Not the quiet kind, but the sob-in-your-throat, knees-give-out variety that moved through me like a tidal wave. It didn't make sense. Him being there. How relieved it made me feel. And how much I realized I'd needed him. None of it made any sense at all.

And maybe that was exactly the point. I hadn't been aware of how tightly I'd been coiling all the muscles in my body, like a lion ready to strike . . . until I saw him. In that instant, every last one of my defenses unclenched. Not because I decided to. Because my body did. On instinct. Because it finally felt safe.

But I still couldn't wrap my brain around how Leo was here, lying next to me after everything that happened last night. In fact, it seemed so implausible that maybe he wasn't really here at all and this was just a sleep-deprived, stressed-out, half-hungover manifestation. I blinked at him, examining how the soft hair on his muscular forearm blew in the stream of each heavy exhalation, and slowly poked a rigid finger into his chest. As my fingertip pressed into the firm muscle under his shirt, he stirred to reposition himself, but his eyes remained closed.

I poked again. Harder.

His lids fluttered, and the faintest smile tugged at the corner of his mouth. "If this is your idea of foreplay, we've got to work on your technique," he murmured, voice thick with sleep.

"You're really here." It came out more like a question than a statement.

He opened his eyes, gaze still a little hazy through thick lashes, but unmistakably warm. "Of course I'm here. I got in very late last night, and since you were sleeping like a stone, I didn't want to wake you."

I sat up, trying to untangle myself from the bedsheets. "But . . . after last week. The fight. The infrequent texts. The way I left. You saying you needed space. I guess . . . I just thought . . ."

Leo pushed up onto one elbow. "We had an argument. That's all it was. A real one, yeah, but still, it was just a fight. I needed a minute, not a lifetime. I'll be honest and say there was a moment where it felt easier to fall back into old patterns and bury myself in my work. But you mean too much to me. *This* means too much to me. So I decided there was no choice but to get on that plane. Though, I wish I had known it was a glorified wind-up toy. I white-knuckled it the whole time, and I fly a lot."

A lump formed in my throat. "I really didn't think you were coming," I managed. "I figured you'd probably had enough. That I pushed you away too hard this time."

His eyes softened, and he reached out to caress my cheek with his thumb. "There's no such thing, Elliot. We're adults. In a real, grown-up relationship. And I understand now that when you love someone, you show up."

His words almost split me in two. So simple, so uncomplicated, yet powerful enough to steal the air from my lungs.

Showing up. Staying.

Table stakes in most relationships. But uncharted territory for me. Trust had always felt like a gamble . . . one I kept losing. So I started folding early, protecting whatever pieces of myself I had left.

Emotion rose, sharp and sudden, in my throat. I bit my lip, nodded, and leaned into his shoulder, letting my forehead rest there, his solidity as sure as gravity. He *was* here. He *had* come.

So why couldn't I just believe this was real? That he wasn't going to be one more hand I'd misplayed? Why couldn't I just give in to the moment?

Because.

Because I knew how much it could hurt to be wrong. Because being around Matty last night reminded me what it was like to have it all fall apart, and I'm not the type who falls apart anymore. I'm the one who helps other women put themselves back together.

Leo swung his legs around the bed, pushed up, and stretched, muscles rippling down his back. He turned his head toward me, a teasing spark in his eye. "I'm heading into the shower. Care to join me?"

His offer was tempting. I mean, I was only human after all. And yet for all the reasons I was desperately trying to convince myself were true, I couldn't shake the idea that taking the leap would end up costing me everything. "I promised Marin I'd take a beach walk with her this morning. We like to get our ten thousand steps in before noon. Helps offset the afternoon cocktails. How about I meet you at breakfast?"

He smiled. "Breakfast it is. See you there."

"Leo!" Marin's voice rang out across the resort restaurant as she bounded over to where he was standing in line at the omelet station. "You came! I knew you would." She flung her arms around his neck, then turned to me, one brow raised and a satisfied smirk on her face.

"How was your sunrise walk?" Leo asked.

"Great. Just enough cardio for me to be able to justify that stack of pancakes over there," Marin said, pointing to the buffet table. "And after I polish those babies off, I'm heading straight back to my room for a little Nappuccino."

Leo blinked. "A what?"

"My tried-and-true vacation hack. You consume your favorite caffeinated beverage, in my case, a cappuccino, then take a short twenty- to thirty-minute power nap." She clapped her hands together. "You wake up and—bam!—both the caffeine and the nap have kicked in, and you are ready to rock and roll. Scientifically proven and totally life-changing."

"I'll have to try that sometime," Leo said, sounding almost convinced.

I quickly interjected, "I have tried it, and all that happened was that I woke up sweaty, heart racing, and convinced it was 2007."

"Then you must not have done it right." Marin shrugged, already turning toward the buffet. "Like I said, scientifically proven. So yeah, Nappuccino, and then I was thinking of trying surfing. Kinda always wanted to give it a shot, and the instructor is an absolute babe."

I eyed her, and she threw her hands up in immediate defense. "I took an oath of marriage, not a vow of blindness! Just because I'm married doesn't mean I can't enjoy the local scenery. Oh, look, they just brought out a fresh tray of pancakes. Sorry, not sorry," she said, and beelined in the direction of the already forming line.

Leo looked straight at me as he reached up to brush a stray hair from my face after she'd gone. "If you'd told me how absolutely beautiful this place was, I wouldn't have dragged my feet getting here." He gave me a slow smile and pressed a kiss to my cheek. "But honestly, it's nothing compared to you," he whispered in my ear as he pulled away. "Oh, and you might want to stick with coffee or just a light breakfast. I planned a little something special, if you're up for it, and I think you'll want to save some room."

Intrigued, I nodded, already scanning for a latte to take on the road, when I spotted Matty lingering at the fruit buffet, weighing his options. Matty, who Leo knew nothing about because I'd never told him. I hadn't been willing to crack that door open, to let the pain spill out and ruin the act I'd been perfecting for years. Strange, but in all the chaos of the last few days, it had never once occurred to me that if Leo did actually show up for the wedding, he'd be standing face-to-face with my ex and the past I'd worked so hard to bury.

And now, here Matty was, frozen midsentence with one of the servers, holding a toothpick spearing a wedge of pineapple. His eyes flicked between me and Leo, the recognition of what he was seeing unfolding on his face. No smirk. No mask. Just a slow blink and a look that made it painfully clear that it wasn't just the alcohol talking last night. His heart had been on full display.

"I'm going to grab some more coffee," Leo said, leaning in, completely oblivious to the awkwardness firing between me and Matty from across the solarium. "Want anything?"

"I think I'm good. Thanks," I responded before watching him disappear into the sea of other guests queuing for their breakfast items.

"Leo!" Dad clapped a hand on his shoulder as Leo returned, almost spilling the fresh coffee in his grip. "Glad you made it."

Bracing the hold on his cup to minimize the spillage, Leo dabbed at his wet fingers with a napkin. "Wouldn't have missed it, sir."

"Good lad," Dad said, nodding with approval. "Do you scuba dive? We're headed to an incredible spot, the Great Blue Hole. It's supposed to be one of the best dive sites in the world."

"Thanks for the invite, Mr. West. It sounds brilliant, but unfortunately, I don't. Besides," Leo said, turning to me, "I was hoping to spend the day just Elliot and me. I wanted to check out the town, and the guy at the front desk told me about this hidden beach on the far side of the island. I thought maybe we could go there for a picnic. Of course, only if you want to?"

I caught sight of Matty across the room again. Part of me wanted to go over and introduce him to Leo, just to get it over with and see whether there was any chance the two of us could ever find solid ground again. But I already felt too exposed, even after the little softness I'd let slip last night, breaking maybe the most important commandment I'd written in Sharpie across my heart: *Put thyself first. If you don't, no one else will.*

I was Elliot-freakin'-West, forged by fire, and every time, I'd had to rise from the ashes when everything else burned. And thankfully, right now, Matty, today's fire, was politely staying out of my way. I didn't have to face the past. I could just pretend I was on some glorious tropical vacation (instead of whatever version of hell this was) and go with Leo on this little adventure.

I nodded. "Alright, let's see this hidden beach of yours."

No promises. No expectations.

Just one day. On my own terms.

Exactly how I liked it.

Chapter Twenty-Six

In the town of San Pedro, Belize, where vendors were setting up stands packed with ripe bananas, mangoes, and colorful citrus piled high, the cobblestone streets shimmered in the heat, the stones slick from an earlier burst of rain that had since burned off beneath the punishing Caribbean sun. Golf carts rolled down the unpaved roads, weaving through streets already bustling with tourists and locals seeking out charming cafés and brightly painted juice bars.

Leo parked the moped he'd rented for the day on a narrow side street, and I unclipped my helmet and handed it to him.

He took my hand as we slipped into the flow of the morning crowd.

"I thought we'd spend a little time in town before heading to the other side of the island. The front desk clerk told me about some great spots he said we should check out."

"*Ooh*, sounds great. So where to first?" I asked.

"You'll see."

I followed him through the bustle of people heading in every direction: some toward the beach, some to the pier, some settling into beachside restaurants. We stopped in front of a handmade sign that read Tomas's Taste Bud Trek.

Before I could ask, Leo clarified, "The concierge helped me arrange a private food tour so that we can take in the sights, smells, and flavors as we explore. Thought it would be a fun way to experience the town. And apparently, Tomas is like *the* local authority on all things Belize."

Just as we were scoping out the entrance and where exactly to find our guide, out strode Tomas with the swagger of a man who'd never worn sunscreen a day in his life and probably never needed to. He wore a battered straw hat decorated with a pin that said WILL WORK FOR GARNACHES, and his floral button-down was unbuttoned just enough to suggest he either had no shame or a deep love affair with humidity.

"Buenos dias, new friends! So happy you could join me today for this tasty adventure. Are you ready to get started?" He looked at his watch and then up to the sky, as if to verify with the position of the sun. "Let's get going. This way, fellow food pilgrims!" He marched in front and led us down an alleyway until he flourished an arm toward a shaded corner stall tucked between two souvenir shops selling things like wooden turtles and surfboards. "You haven't *really* tasted Belize until you've had the ceviche from Doña Marta's. This is where we'll officially start our tour."

A woman with silver hair and weathered skin scooped fresh shrimp from a gleaming stainless bowl, dousing it with lime juice and folding in diced tomatoes, onions, and bright-green cilantro. The vegetables sparkled like sunlight caught in a net of glass. She handed me a tiny paper plate with a crisp plantain chip overflowing with the mixture.

Leo grinned beside me, crunching his own chip. "This might actually be better than the gyros we ordered in Mykonos from that little stand I swore deserved its own food documentary."

I elbowed him, laughing, and Tomas clapped with delight. "And just think, we are only getting started, lovebirds! Come, come, this way, I have much more to show you!"

He led us onward, weaving through narrow streets where the smells changed like the pages of a pop-up book: sizzling masa, stewed meat, roasted chilies. We stopped at a rickety stand with a cast iron griddle where a teenage boy flipped Pirishpak Mayan eggs, cracking them over a blend of crushed tomatoes, habaneros, and ground pumpkin seeds.

The heat hit my throat like a surprise party with a flamethrower, but the spice danced beautifully with the richness of the yolk. I coughed, grabbed Leo's lemonade, and Tomas patted my back with delighted approval. "Yes! You feel it in your corazón! That's how you know it is authentico."

At the next stop, we devoured Salbutes, puffed corn tortillas topped with shredded turkey, pickled onions, and cabbage slaw so tangy my whole soul felt refreshed. The street buzzed around us with clinking bikes, bursts of music from open windows, and a nearby group of kids chasing a soccer ball barefoot across the sand-packed road.

Leo brushed a fleck of pickled onion off my lip with a gentle thumb. "I love the way you're always willing to throw yourself so completely into new places and experiences. I think that's a lot of the reason why I fell in love with you in Greece. Just how open you are to the world," he murmured, and I grinned at him, swiping at the sauce on my chin with a crumpled napkin.

I was caught by surprise to hear him describe me that way when usually people considered me to be so closed off. Placing my hand on his cheek, I met his eyes and marveled at the way he looked at me. "That's very sweet. And here I thought you'd only decided to approach me because I was wearing that cute little neon bikini," I joked.

A smile split across his face and he chuckled. "Obviously, of course, you were the most beautiful woman I'd ever seen. But there was something more, something magnetic, about you, and I couldn't keep myself from wanting to get to know you better. And then once I *actually* did, I mean, well, then I was a total goner."

By the time we reached the Garnache cart, I wasn't sure I could handle another bite, but then the aroma hit me. Charred corn, refried beans, and crumbled Dutch cheese layered onto a crunchy tostada. A tiny firecracker of a woman handed them out like she was dealing joy.

"Okay," I said, biting into it and groaning in delight. "This. This here is my new religion."

Tomas laughed appreciatively and wiped his forehead with a red bandanna he withdrew from his back pocket. "Ah, but we are saving the best for last. We now begin the sacred chocolate pilgrimage. Hold on to your sombreros, amigos, because the factory is just ahead."

We followed him down a winding stone path shaded by banana trees. The air changed, cooler, thicker with the scent of cacao pods, earth, and something nostalgic and ancient I couldn't quite name. My hand found Leo's without thinking. He squeezed it once, a quiet tether between us.

We arrived at the Belize Chocolate Company, a charming little shop where the windows were lined with truffles and other chocolate-dipped confections.

"This, my friends, is where I leave you. But before I go, would you like me to take a picture of you two lovebirds as a memento?"

"Oh yes, that would be great. Thank you," Leo said as he pulled out his phone and handed it to Tomas, who snapped a quick selfie first and then chuckled to himself before turning the camera to us.

Leo pulled me close, and I tightened my arm around his waist, inhaling the fresh scent of his shirt and the musk of his warm skin. The moment was dizzying and delightful, and I was suddenly overwhelmed with gratitude.

Tomas handed Leo's phone back to him. "I hope you have enjoyed a tasty afternoon, relishing in all the amazing flavors of my hometown. You will be in good hands here, I assure you. And please don't forget to leave me a review on Yelp if you feel so inclined."

Leo shook Tomas's hand, slipping a fifty-dollar bill into his palm as he did, thanking him for the wonderful experience. Tomas's eyes widened at the generous tip, and he slid it into his pocket and then clapped Leo on the back. "Gracias, amigo. Be sure to come back and visit the next time you find yourself in Belize."

"Oh, we will," I answered and watched Tomas head off down the road in the opposite direction.

Gesturing to the shop's front door, Leo ushered me in, and I was immediately hit with the deliciously sweet smell of cocoa butter and caramelized sugar.

"Leo, I don't think I can fit one more bite into my stomach."

"That's okay, we're here to make the chocolate, not taste it. I signed us up for the Bean-to-Bar Experience."

"Go on," I said, raising an eyebrow. "I'm intrigued."

"Honestly, I don't know much more than that. The hotel concierge said it was not to be missed."

Just then, a minibus that looked straight out of the 1970s with its rusty muffler expelling thick exhaust rumbled to a stop, and we stepped back out into the heat to meet it. The faded words THE BELIZE CHOCOLATE COMPANY were barely visible on its side.

The accordion bus doors groaned open and out shuffled a young woman with jet-black hair and an adorably round face. "Hello, hello, chocolate lovers! So happy you could join us today for the famous Cacao Quest Tour, where we will learn how our wonderful local chocolate goes from growing as beans on the trees in our fields to lining the walls of our shop as beautiful solid bars, like works of art. I am Malina and will be your guide for the tour today. Please line up in front of me, so I can check you in as you board, and then we will be on our way!"

"On our way to where, exactly?" I whispered to Leo.

He shrugged. "I'm not really sure. I assumed we'd be in the back of the store in their kitchens or wherever they make the candy. I didn't know the experience included a bus trip off the premises. But hey, I'm game for an adventure if you are?"

I looked into Leo's eyes, his contagious enthusiasm almost palpable. "Lead on. Let's add another adventure to our growing collection."

After about a dozen tourists wearing tropical shirts and bucket hats climbed up the bus steps and took their seats, the doors creaked closed and Malina climbed behind the wheel. She jerked the gearshift into drive, the wheels lurched forward, and we rumbled out of the small parking lot. As soon as the bus turned onto the main road, Malina grabbed for a microphone headset and adjusted it in front of her mouth. "Can everyone hear me back there?"

When her question was met with a handful of whoops and cheers, she continued, "You are all in store for a fun and informational experience where you will see firsthand how we harvest the sacred cacao bean. Then we will return to the shop, and using the very same techniques as the Mayan artisans did centuries ago, we'll craft some chocolate treats.

"But at the Belize Chocolate Factory, we believe in zero waste, so we utilize every part of the cacao bean. For instance, the husks are used to make our own brand of tea, and pressed cocoa butter is the main ingredient in our body products. In just a few moments, we'll be arriving at the Peini Cacao Plantation in Punta Gorda, one of many farms in the region dedicated to preserving our traditional local practices. Enjoy the scenery as we make our way. We should arrive in about fifteen minutes."

The bus didn't have air-conditioning, so Leo stood up to reach over me and, using all his weight, yank down the stubborn window. "That's better," he said as the wind whipped through, making it feel at least a few degrees cooler. "Who knew we'd be riding in such *style*?"

Right as he said that, the bus hit a bump hard enough to send me airborne, landing squarely in Leo's lap. He looked down at me, a slow grin spreading across his face. "Never mind. As far as I'm concerned, this just became a five-star ride."

With a devilish smirk, I rolled off him and settled back into my seat, a quiet smile playing at my lips.

Leo leaned closer to be heard over the sound of the growling engine and the whistling wind. "Jokes aside, I really hope you're having a good time. After what happened in New York, I wanted to remind you of us. Of the fun, yes, but more than that, of the good. The kind of good that makes the spats and rough patches worth it."

I looked into his warm face, so familiar, so steady. "I *had* started to forget . . . but it's coming back to me."

The bus rolled to a complete stop, and all twelve of us (sweaty and sticky from the ride) unloaded, grateful to be in the cool shade. Malina led us down a steep trail. "These here are Criollo and Trinitario cacao trees," she explained, "native to the region and grown without any chemicals. The pods take six months to ripen, and each one holds thirty to fifty precious seeds."

She reached up and gently twisted a sun-bronzed pod from a tree, splitting it open with a practiced tap of a machete. The inside looked like a mess of wet, pale garlic cloves.

"Go on, taste it," she encouraged, handing it to Leo.

He looked alarmed. "This looks like an alien egg."

"You eat the slimy coating," Malina instructed, "and then spit out the bean."

His eyes widened. "Whoa," he said. "It's sour . . . like mango and lemon had a baby."

I took one, expecting bitterness, but was surprised by the tart, floral burst. The texture was a little horrifying, but oddly addictive.

As we continued on, Malina explained each part of the fermentation process, demonstrating how the pods were dried in the sun, then roasted and ground by hand. In a small open-air workshop, the scent was intoxicating—rich, earthy, and slightly smoky, thick with the aroma of freshly warmed cacao. Malina lifted a handful of dried beans and let them fall through her fingers. "What makes Belizean cacao so special," she said, "is the terroir, the unique mix of our soil, our climate, even the sea breeze. You can taste the land in every bite. It's what gives our chocolate its soul."

An older woman in a bright-pink shirt and camera secured around her neck piped up, "Oh, my husband and I learned all about terroir on a winery trip we took in France last year." Her eyes were wide with excitement as she spoke to the group. "If you haven't had a chance to visit Château Adelaïse in Maubec, one of the best vineyards in the country, we highly recommend!"

"Hmm," Leo whispered. "Maybe a French wine tour will be our next trip," before leaning in to watch the local woman demonstrate the grinding process, his curiosity genuine. His easy way with people, his attentiveness, and his sincere interest made me ache in the best way.

He glanced over and caught me watching. "What?"

"Nothing," I said, feeling a smile tug at my lips.

Leo walked over with a small wooden spoon of thick, unsweetened chocolate. "It's gritty, bitter as hell, and basically is the consistency of mud. Want some?"

"Hmm, tempting," I joked, but in spite of myself, I bent at the waist to tilt toward the utensil in his outstretched hand.

I pinched my face immediately, my taste buds almost ready to file a formal complaint.

Through a distinct grimace, I managed, "Delicious. I've always wanted to taste sidewalk chalk."

We started to laugh, the kind that bubbles up without effort. That held something more than flirtation or humor. Perhaps ease? I didn't know if that meant it was love. But I knew what it wasn't.

It wasn't what I'd ever had with Matty. And for the first time, I could see that. Clearly and without hesitation. It was its own completely new thing, something fragile, unfamiliar, but quietly promising.

Chapter Twenty-Seven

We stumbled out of the Belize Chocolate Factory carrying a bag of confections (and with the kind of sugar coma that could level a small city). The sunshine hit me like an instant defrost button after the freezer-level AC that had been blasting inside the shop.

Leo glanced at his watch. "Time for the next stop on our itinerary," he said. A short ride on the moped later, we pulled up to a desolate stretch of road that seemed to lead nowhere at all. The hotel desk clerk hadn't exaggerated when he called this place a *hidden* beach—there wasn't a trace of shoreline in sight.

Leo grabbed the snacks and wine we'd picked up on our food tour from the back of the bike and led the way through what could best be described as someone's overgrown backyard. We ducked beneath a weathered No Trespassing sign (the same one the hotel clerk had instructed it was okay to ignore) and followed a narrow, rocky trail for another five minutes, the sound of waves drawing us forward. The trees finally opened, and white sand stretched out before us.

The untouched beach went on for what seemed like miles, turquoise water lapping gently at the shore like it had all the time in the world. The sand was soft as sifted sugar, and the only sounds were the hush of the tide and the occasional call of seabirds overhead. It reminded me of some of the spots we'd visited in Mykonos last summer, except this place was quieter and far more secluded, and it seemed to remind Leo too, because he said,

"Doesn't this look a lot like that cove near Agios Sostis? The one we had to hike down to barefoot because it was so slippery?"

I remembered.

I remembered how we'd grabbed a bottle of crisp white wine, a mix of dips like tzatziki and hummus, and warm pita bread from a taverna on the way. We packed them up, and Leo did his best to traverse the steep hill without dropping any of our precious cargo. We spent the rest of the day swimming, snacking, and sunbathing, and it ended up being one of the best of my life.

"Since we didn't bring an umbrella, what do you think of that spot over there," Leo said, pointing to a clearing of the beach shaded by a few large palms.

I nodded. "Lead the way."

We settled beneath the leafy trees, Leo laying out two brightly striped towels he'd borrowed from the hotel, side by side. I kicked off my sandals, slipped out of my cover-up, and stretched out on the sand.

Digging around his bag, he said, "I brought thirty or fifty," and held up a bottle of sunscreen in each hand.

"Fifty, I think. This Caribbean sun is no joke, and the only thing that could add to the circus-level chaos of a wedding is me showing up sun-blistered and molting like a lizard."

"Good choice," Leo confirmed, tossing the thirty back into the bag. He flipped the cap and squeezed a thick dollop into his hand, the lotion smelling of coconuts and lime. "Let me get your back."

Before I could protest, his warm palms smoothed over my shoulders, dragging his thumbs slowly down the line of my spine. His touch was firm, practiced, the glide of lotion leaving behind a cool sheen that contrasted deliciously with the heat of his skin. Every deliberate stroke lingered a fraction too long, his fingers brushing just beneath the strap of my suit, teasing as though he was daring me to stop him.

I closed my eyes, aware of the shiver that ran through me, the kind that had nothing to do with the ocean breeze, as I relished the way his hands felt, mapping my body like he was memorizing me.

"Turn," he directed, pulling me from my almost catatonic state of bliss, and I spun around to face him.

He squeezed another little pearl of cream into his hands and warmed it between his palms before cupping my face. His thumbs swept gently along my cheekbones, tracing the delicate skin beneath my eyes with a tenderness that made me almost forget my own name.

His fingers skimmed down to my jaw, sliding slow and sure, until he smoothed the lotion into my neck with a careful, almost reverent touch.

"You're glowing already," he teased softly, though the heat sparking in his gaze had nothing to do with the Caribbean sun.

I cleared my throat, desperate for something to ground me, and snatched the bottle from his hand. "Your turn."

He smiled and scooted closer, squaring his shoulders and sitting tall, and I squeezed a bit of lotion onto my fingers. My hands spread across the firm planes of his chest, slicking the cream over muscles I was appreciating maybe a little more than I should have. His skin was soft beneath my palms, and the scent of the sunscreen mingling with the salt air was almost dizzying. I dragged my fingertips deliberately, slow enough to make him suck in a breath.

"Careful," he murmured. His eyes had fallen closed, and his voice rumbled low, "You're enjoying this."

I smirked, rubbing in another sweep down his rippling abs. "Maybe I am. Sun protection is serious business."

He chuckled, and as soon as we were both sufficiently lubed up, we lay down next to one another, just close enough that our arms nearly touched, but not quite.

We stayed like that for a while, soaking up the sun in easy silence, when Leo turned to me, pushed his sunglasses down to the bridge of his nose, and said, "I packed some snorkeling gear I picked up at the beach shop. Wanna give it a go?" He pulled a pair of flippers and a mask from his small duffel and held them out.

"Let's do it," I responded as I slipped the mask on and carried the flippers to the shoreline. At the foamy edge of the surf, I grabbed the crook of his elbow for balance and leaned into him to slide my feet into fin-shaped shoes.

We waded in, side by side, the water so clear it felt like walking into glass. Tropical fish darted beneath the surface like moving confetti, and when I dipped my face below, I gasped through the snorkel at the sudden explosion of coral and color. Leo pointed at a school of yellow tangs and blue angelfish, then at a curious sea turtle that hovered near a rock like it was eavesdropping on us. The Aegean Sea had been beautiful and crystal clear but didn't have anywhere near the variety of colorful sea life as in the Caribbean.

Time slipped away underwater as we allowed the gentle current to pull us along the coastline. When my fingers were sufficiently prune-y and my mouth tasted like a salt lick, we drifted back to shore, our limbs loose and heavy. We collapsed on our towels with a collective sigh, like the ocean had rinsed us clean of all our stress and worries. I stared up at the sky, letting the sun dry the droplets on my skin. *This* . . . this peace, this weightlessness wasn't what I was used to, and the calm of it felt liberating.

I looked down the beach where the shoreline sparkled with pastel-colored shells as far as the eye could see. Even though Mom and I hadn't mended fences after our argument last night, I knew they'd look beautiful decorating the tables at her wedding reception. I emptied the contents of my tote, brushed the sand from my knees, and told Leo I was going for a walk. I'd barely made it a quarter of the way down the beach when a sharp pang sliced through the taut flesh of my foot.

"Shit!" The cry escaped before I could stop it.

A jagged edge of glass or coral, I couldn't tell which, bit into my skin. Blood was already pooling from the cut, and I stumbled backward, landing hard on my ass. Within seconds Leo was jogging toward me like a character on *Baywatch* . . . minus the bright-red bathing suit.

"Elliot! What happened?" He dropped to his knees beside me, scanning the sand before zeroing in on the gash.

"I'm fine," I lied, gritting my teeth as the sting bloomed sharp and white hot.

"You're bleeding. That's not fine." His tone was firm but not harsh, the kind of voice that didn't invite argument. Without hesitation, he scooped me up, just lifted me as if it was nothing, and carried me toward a large flat rock tucked just past the shoreline.

"You really don't have to do this. I can hobble," I muttered half-heartedly, suddenly acutely aware of my arms around his neck, the thud of his heartbeat against my own chest, the way he held me so protectively.

"Just relax, I'm not trying to hijack your independence or anything. I'm simply doing my best to keep the sand out of the open cut. Now, hold still."

He grabbed his water bottle and poured a slow stream over the gash, the blood swirling with the clear liquid like smoke curls before dripping into the sand. The coolness was a relief, but what really undid me was the way his hands worked, confident, gentle, and precise. He ripped a strip from his shirt—his actual shirt—exposing his impressive stomach, and wrapped the material clean around my arch. I watched him work in silence, the pain already dulling beneath the tide of something else. Something warmer. Something softer.

"There," Leo said, satisfied with the makeshift bandage and seeing that my foot had stopped bleeding. "Let's just make sure to get some disinfectant and a clean bandage when we're back at the hotel."

"You didn't really have to do all that, but thank you. It already feels a lot better." I glanced down at my wrapped foot, then looked back up at him. "Have you ever thought about how people dealt with cuts and scrapes like this . . . say, in the seventeenth century? Must've been brutal without anything like antiseptic. Something as simple as a foot gash could have been the literal end of you."

Leo laughed. "That's funny you said that. I seriously think about that sort of thing all the time. Like a few years ago, I had to have an emergency root canal from an infected abscess. Would've taken me out in a heartbeat if I'd been born back then."

"Exactly. Something like swimmer's ear could have been your ultimate demise. Pink eye? An ingrown toenail? Thank God for antibiotics and penicillin. And that we were born in the twentieth century."

"Right? Imagine the words on your gravestone reading, 'Here lies Leo. He died of a paper cut.'" He smiled with a cool easiness that swept over me, almost completely distracting me from the throbbing in my foot. "Well, in this case, I think you'll live," he said, smoothing over the bandage one last time. "So tell me, what did I miss these past few days? What's been going on with the wedding?"

The questions were casual, but they invited so much more than an easy answer. And more than that, getting into all the family and Matty drama would most certainly pop this blissful bubble of a day I was having. "Oh, you know, nothing much. Just the usual craziness that surrounds all of Sonja's nuptials. Really, I should be used to it by now."

"Nothing much? That guy eyeing you at breakfast like a boy who'd lost his puppy didn't seem like 'nothing much.'" Leo leaned back on his elbows, the rock beneath us still warm in the midday sun.

So he *had* noticed Matty tracking me in the dining room.

"Oh, Matty. Matt. My mom's best friend Izzy's son. We . . . we grew up together."

He ran a hand across his jaw, a slight smile on his face, and said, "And let me guess, he was madly in love with you, as all the boys must've been."

"Actually, we were madly in love with each other." The words slipped out before I could stop them.

He sat up. "Did you date?"

I popped up next to him. "Yes. And it ended . . . spectacularly badly. About five years ago."

Leo was quiet for a beat, then asked, "So is he the reason?"

"The reason?"

"For the rules. The radio show. Your armor?"

My breath hitched. The question landed . . . a bull's-eye. It was like he had a sniper's scope on my softest spot, and instead of holding fire, he'd unknowingly pulled the trigger.

Was Matty the reason?

I mean, I started *Love Is a Four-Letter Word* after I caught him cheating. So many of my commandments came directly from the wreckage of that relationship, the pitfalls, the blind spots I'd ignored, the red flags I'd waved away like they weren't burning right in front of me.

But was he the sole reason?

No.

I was the product of a thousand little heartbreaks. Some mine, some inherited, some observed.

Matty was just the last straw.

"Matty didn't just break my heart, he broke my trust, my belief in something real. He was my boyfriend, yes, but also my best friend. He knew my history. He'd watched me clean up every mess, understood that I was the one holding it all together every time my mom's heart got broken, how her pain always landed in my lap. And still, he did the one thing I thought he never would. So when he cheated, it wasn't just a betrayal, it was the final blow. Like the floor dropped out from under me."

"So then what's he doing here?"

"We haven't spoken, not a single word, since we broke up. He said he wanted to apologize and explain himself. But I'll never move past it. I mean, how do you get over something like that? You don't. You can't."

He nodded along as I spoke, like he was taking it all in and giving it full consideration. "I don't believe that there's one right way," he said gently. "But maybe forgiveness starts with realizing you're not the same person you were back then. And neither is he. People screw up, but that doesn't always mean they're beyond redemption. And even if it does, sometimes it's not even about them anymore. It's about you. You, being able to finally let go of the hurt you've been carrying around like . . . like a suitcase you never set down."

I swallowed, feeling that familiar instinct to run, to shut down the rest of the conversation before it got even more real. But over these past few weeks, brick by painful brick, Leo'd managed to break through more of my walls than anyone had in years. He was getting dangerously close to my heart now, but I didn't move. I didn't want to. And for as much as it scared me, he was right—I wasn't the same person I used to be.

This version of me, the one who had taken the leap, seized the chance, gone to Paris—all those decisions had been guiding me here to Leo and this moment in Belize. And for the first time in a very long time, it felt like I was exactly where I was supposed to be.

Pulling him back down, I snuggled in close next to him with my head on his chest, dozing off to the sound of his heartbeat thudding under my ear. The breeze was cooling as the sun dipped lower in the sky. Leo checked his watch. "We better get going if we want to make it back in time for the rehearsal dinner."

"Can we stay here? Just a little bit longer?" I pulled his arms around me like a blanket. "Just like this?"

He blinked, surprised, then drew me closer without hesitation. "Yeah, just like this. As long as you want."

Chapter Twenty-Eight

Upon returning to the villa from the hidden beach, our skin glowing from the sun and our hair stiff with salt, Leo slipped into the bathroom to shower so we could get ready for the rehearsal dinner. I kicked the sandals off my feet and sank into the corner of the bed when, without warning, a sharp feeling of déjà vu hit me.

Suddenly, I wasn't in Belize anymore, I was in a softly lit hotel room in Paris, slipping off a towering pair of scarlet Christian Louboutins, wincing as I rubbed my aching arches. Without warning, Leo's warm hands slid around me from behind, his lips tracing slow kisses along my neck, sending a shiver down my body straight to my cramped toes.

I blinked, and somehow without moving even a single inch, I was now back in the villa, the ocean breeze drifting through the screen doors that opened onto the lanai. The shower ran in the bathroom, Leo's off-key singing of Journey echoing at the top of his lungs.

Shaking off the feeling of reliving a moment I couldn't quite place, I reached for my toiletry bag on the nightstand. Carefully, I unwrapped the makeshift bandage, poured cool water over the wound, and smeared on a thin layer of Neosporin before sealing it with a wide Band-Aid. When it was done, I set my foot down. But instead of the villa's wooden floor, it met the velvety carpet of our Paris hotel room, where the windows framed a perfect postcard view of the city's Haussmann-style buildings.

What the—

My eyes flicked up, and suddenly Leo was in front of me, unbuttoning my shirt with that slow, deliberate focus that made it hard to breathe. His knuckles brushed my skin with every button undone, leaving a trail of heat in their wake. Electricity fired between us with each careful maneuver, like the crackle before an impending storm, and I dizzied at the feel of his broad hands sliding across my skin.

I reached for him, inching closer across the cool sheets. My hand found the warmth of his shoulder. I leaned in, the space between us narrowing, ready for the kiss—

But the world tipped.

I tumbled off the bed, landing hard on the mahogany floor with a dull thud that knocked the breath out of me.

A beat of silence. Then from the bathroom, Leo's voice (very real and very off-key) rose above the rush of the shower, still belting out "Don't Stop Believin'."

And I wasn't in Paris anymore. I was back in Belize again. In our quiet villa. Apparently losing my damn mind.

What was happening to me? Sunstroke? Maybe we'd been out at the private beach too long. Dehydration?

Leo's voice floated in from the shower. "You coming in here, or do I have to sing the whole setlist alone?"

I walked into the bathroom. "Only if you promise not to hit the high note in 'Faithfully' again."

He stuck two fingers out from behind the glass door. "Scout's honor."

"Do they even have Scouts in South Africa?"

He peeked his head out and scoffed. "Do they *have* Scouts in South Africa? For the record, yes. And I have a sash full of badges to prove it."

"What were they for? Loudest singing? Most dramatic shower performances?"

"They should have been, but no. Mostly knot-tying and first aid. Speaking of, how's the foot?"

"Thanks to you, I don't think it'll be the cause of my untimely end."

I watched him, water running down his broad chest in rivulets across his washboard stomach. Soap bubbles clung to his shoulders and settled at the nape of his neck. That familiar, unexpected stir of intimacy from before flared inside me. The memory of his hands on my skin, his lips brushing my neck in Paris. The ache settled deep, pulling me closer.

I slipped out of my clothes, dropping them to the cold tile bathroom floor and letting them pool at my feet before I stepped into the forceful stream of hot water, the steam billowing around us like a cloud.

Facing him, my breasts pressed against his chest, droplets still sparkling in the curls of his soft chest hair, and my arms wrapped around his waist. I smiled up at him. "Hi, you."

"Hi, you," he returned, his soapy hands making their way down my sides to settle on my hips.

He bent down to kiss me as I pressed up on my toes to meet him halfway, the sensation of his body on mine and his tongue sweeping across my lips caught like wildfire. Never relinquishing the pressure of his mouth on mine, his body tightened against me, responding to every nibble and peck I pressed to his wet skin. I couldn't seem to get enough. I didn't realize how hungry I was for the touch of someone whom I was starting to really fall for. I was ravenous, and once the floodgates had finally opened, there was no stopping us.

The passion of our kisses intensified, and with wet hair and wet bodies, he turned the water off and lifted me out of the shower with such little effort I gasped into his mouth. Kissing and giggling with each step, we flopped down into the cloud of tangled sheets, his weight pinning me to the mattress as each touch caused me to melt farther and farther into the soft down of the bed. We were naked and panting and more full of desire than I'd ever remembered feeling for anyone . . . ever. It wasn't a matter of wanting him . . . I needed him.

He settled between my thighs, hovering over me as if waiting for permission. When I wrapped my arms around his neck and pulled him closer, he took the cue and pushed inside with a satisfyingly deep thrust, a cry rising from somewhere deep within me, one I barely recognized.

The steady rhythm of his rocking against me as my hands moved through his hair and down his back grounded me in the moment, allowing the rest of the world to fall away. No more wedding nonsense. No more Matty bullshit. No more overwhelming anxiety. Just the two of us, wrapped up in a moment that was completely ours, thoroughly enjoying the steadiness of one another, and I was certain I would be content to live like this for the rest of my life.

I mean, why had I been fighting him so hard? What was I so afraid of? Relishing how good this felt, his body, the closeness, the way everything else just disappeared. It was hard to even remember what I had been trying to protect myself from.

He breathed hard into my neck with an irrefutable groan of pleasure and my head rolled back into my pillow as I enjoyed every sensation of him, the push, the pull, the ultimate release, and finally the merging of everything I'd kept at arm's length for too long. Breathing heavily and indescribably sated, I sat up and reached for the sheet, wrapping it around myself.

Leo, also winded, propped himself up on a pillow, the smile on his face warm and satisfied. "You know, the way the light's falling across your face . . . it reminds me of how you looked when the sun streamed into our hotel room in Paris. That image lives in my mind like a sepia photograph," he said, his words tender and sincere.

I wanted to say, "I'm sorry, but I don't remember . . . any of it." But that wasn't entirely true anymore.

Ever since he'd come back into my life, I'd been catching flashes of that timeline . . . at karaoke, in certain glances, in the way his hand brushed mine, earlier in the villa . . . moments so vivid they felt like actual memories. They had to be.

And yet, logic whispered on repeat: *You never went to Paris.*

You chose your brand, your staunch beliefs, your carefully constructed fortress. You didn't choose Leo.

A sharp knock broke me from my thoughts.

"*Yoo-hoo*, Ellie Belly, are you there?" Izzy's voice carried through the door to accompany her knocking.

"Who's that?" Leo asked.

"My mom's best friend, Izzy." I grabbed a robe off a hook on the bathroom wall, tying it around myself as I went to let her in.

"Oh, hey, so glad I caught you," Izzy said, stepping inside with her usual breezy confidence.

"I'm just getting ready for tonight. What's up?"

"Look at your tan! I'm so jealous. I just skip right past golden and go straight to lobster. Anyway, I thought maybe we could compare toasts . . ."

"Toasts?" For some reason my brain went instantly to the morning's breakfast selection, wondering why the hell she would need a consultation on Belizean bread. Until she clocked my blank expression as confusion.

"For tonight. The rehearsal dinner. Your speech? I think your mom wants you to give a toast tonight at the dinner and then another at the wedding tomorrow."

"Excuse me?!" She had to be kidding. This had to be some kind of joke. But when she met me with the same look of disbelief, perfectly mirroring my own shock, I had no choice but to confess. "Um . . . I didn't write a toast. Let alone toasts *plural.*"

Izzy blinked. "But . . . you're her maid of honor."

Leo suddenly came up behind me and, like a well-timed and well-trained Jedi master of defusing tension, placed his hand on my shoulder in an effort to neutralize me before I went nuclear.

"Hi, I'm Leo. I don't think we've met," he said, extending his hand toward her.

"Izzy." She gave him a lingering once-over, eyes narrowing slightly as if putting a face to the name, sizing him up. Maybe she was even comparing him to Matty? "El, your mother is going to be crushed if you don't say even a few words . . . or at least offer her and Keith some well wishes."

"The bachelorette party was one thing. Some phallic balloons and naughty games. But you can't expect me to stand up in front of everyone and pretend that I think this wedding is a good idea."

Izzy frowned. "I thought you liked Keith. He said you two really hit it off at zip-lining."

My jaw clenched at the thought of cleaning up another one of Mom's messes. "Jesus Christ, this isn't about Keith. It's about her! About Mom, making yet another mistake with no regard for the consequences. Following her heart, not her head. Who's going to make sure she gets up and goes to teach her classes on time when he walks out on her in a month or a year? When it inevitably crashes and burns, who's going to make sure her rent gets paid or that there's food in the fridge when she's too heartbroken to even get out of bed? I'll be the one helping clean up her mess. And I've accepted that. But you can't ask me to stand up there and cheer her on while she ruins her life . . . again."

Izzy pressed her lips together and tilted her head slightly. "You're scared she's going to get hurt again, and you want to protect her. I do too. But sometimes . . . loving someone isn't about standing in judgment or stopping them. It's about showing up, even when you know they might stumble, and hoping they learn to stand on their own."

My frustration took the form of tears stinging the corners of my eyes. "I'm tired of being the one who holds everything together when she falls apart."

"Please, El, just be there. It's that simple. Stand tall, raise a glass, fake a smile if you have to. That's all I'm asking."

"Oh, that's *all*?" My sarcasm wasn't even remotely veiled. "Don't you think that's a lot?"

"For your mom? No, I'm sorry, but I don't think it is. I'll see you tonight." Izzy's eyes softened. She gave me a small nod and started walking away, leaving me staring after her, gritting my teeth at the unfairness of it.

Stand tall. Fake a smile. That's all I'm asking.

As soon as I closed the villa door, I cried, "FUUUUUCK! GAH! We're just supposed to pretend next year won't be the same damn mess with a different guy in some other tropical location? Like she won't be left heartbroken and crushed again by yet another man and another relationship she's putting on a pedestal, like it'll finally fix everything. It never has. Not a single 'this is the one' relationship has ever brought her the happiness she's chasing. I just can't. I can't pretend anymore to celebrate this . . . this . . . train wreck!"

"Okay, just hear me out," Leo said, voice calm. "Maybe Izzy's not wrong. Maybe it's less about celebrating their marriage and more about just . . . being there for your mom. And yeah, maybe she's foolishly following her heart, but can you really blame her for that? Love doesn't always make sense. We know that. Look at us. I'm from South Africa, you're from New York. We met in Greece. Now we're in Belize. You couldn't script this if you tried."

"We should start getting ready. I think I'll go take a shower for real this time," I said.

"I could help wash your back. No funny business, I promise," he said, in what seemed to be a desperate attempt to try to get us back on the same page.

"That's okay," I said, forcing a smile as I turned away. "I've got it."

I didn't wait for a response. Just grabbed my things, walked toward the bathroom, and closed the door behind me.

Chapter Twenty-Nine

The wedding was set to take place on the hotel's dock, followed by a reception on the beach. But for the rehearsal dinner, Mom and Keith had rented out a small seafood restaurant just up the road from the hotel, famous for its grilled lobster, rum punch, and incredible sunset views. By the time Leo and I arrived, most of the guests were already out on the dance floor, swaying to the rhythm of a local Caribbean band.

Keith spotted us from across the patio and pointed over to the seating chart: a black net draped over a driftwood frame, the words FIND YOUR PORT OF CALL stenciled in white letters across the back.

"Let's see where we're headed," Leo said, scanning the fishing hooks to find our names. "Here we are, Table Seven: Ship Happens."

He raised his eyebrows and led me through the maze of tables until we landed at ours. I was relieved to find we were seated with Marin plus a handful of Mom's colleagues, professors from the women's studies department at Barnard she'd worked with forever. I hadn't even realized how many had come for the wedding. I threw out a few friendly waves and then scanned the room for Matty. He was on the far opposite side of the space deep in conversation with Shira.

Leo set his suit jacket on a chair. "Can I get you ladies a drink?"

Marin shook her head and glanced down at her phone. "Not yet, thank you."

"I'll take one," I said quickly.

"Wine? . . . Or something stronger?"

I eyed him with a look that said everything I didn't.

"Gin, got it. Be right back," he said and left to make his way toward the bar.

Marin turned to me. "I thought after a day with Leo you'd be a little lighter. So why does your face look like that?"

"What's wrong with my face?" I deadpanned.

"You mean, aside from the fact that you look more like you're at a funeral than a wedding?"

"I'm . . . I'm just taking it all in," I responded with a shrug.

"My ass! You're pouting. If anyone can recognize the Elliot silent treatment, it's me. Remember that one time in sixth grade? *Gurrrl,* I thought you were gonna be mad at me forever."

"Yeah, well, that's what you get for convincing me you knew how to cut bangs," I said, only half joking.

"Seriously, though, what's wrong? Did you have a shit time with Leo today?" Marin asked and sipped her water.

"No, not at all. That's the thing, we had an amazing time. And then Izzy showed up at my villa, reminding me I'm supposed to give some stupid toast tonight, and suddenly I'm spiraling. If my mother's past has taught me anything, it's not to let things get too serious. Keep it light, fun, and most of all, temporary. Like, what am I even doing here in Belize with Leo? And now, on top of everything, there's this—" I motioned toward the hibiscus flowers, the coconuts with the initials S and K carved into them, the flickering candlelight. "This? This whole scene? It's all a goddamn joke."

Marin's eyes widened as she glanced around. "Can you keep your voice down? You might think this is all ridiculous, but this is what she thinks is going to make her happy. How can you fault anyone for chasing joy? In a world this harsh and exhausting, isn't it brave, hell, almost defiant, to keep running toward love, even after it's knocked you flat on your ass again and again? Life's messy, but having someone to go through it with? Pretty f-ing amazing. You would know that if you ever stopped overthinking everything.

You're so busy running through the what-ifs, you never think about the what-could-bes. Maybe your mom's just brave enough to go after what she wants. Either way, at least she's trying. What are you doing?"

"Excuse me?"

"You and Leo have something rare. You found someone who really sees you, who shows up for you. Anyone can see you're happy with him. What I can't understand is why you're fighting it so damn hard."

I went to open my mouth to respond, but my voice caught, tight and raw in my throat. Instead, I glanced at the dance floor. There was Matty, light and laughing, spinning Izzy in a way I used to know all too well. Then my gaze wandered over to the entrance, and I spotted my mother, hovering at the door, her eyes finding mine instantly through the swarm of hugs and hellos from the other guests. She looked almost surprised to see me, like after our fight at karaoke last night, she hadn't really expected me to come.

Snaking through the sea of greetings, she made her way over to us just as Leo returned with our drinks. Mom extended a limp hand in his direction like some sort of duchess. "Leo, you made it! I knew you would."

"Wouldn't have missed it," he said. "Congratulations, Mrs. West."

"Mrs. Banner in a few hours," she corrected. "And really, I keep telling you, just call me Sonja."

"Wait? You're changing your name?" I asked, surprised. "In all these marriages, you've *never* changed your name."

She hesitated, smoothing the front of her dress. "It's important to Keith, so . . ."

"So?" I cut in. "So what? You're giving up your name for his ego?"

"It's not about ego, Elliot. Keith isn't asking me to change who I am. Just to commit to our partnership. And I think . . . I think that's a really lovely thing. It's what I want too."

"Yeah, for now," I muttered.

For a moment, she stood there stunned before she straightened her shoulders and forced a smile. "Nice to see you, Leo. Don't miss the buffet. The lobster's absolutely divine."

After she left, I sat, swirling my gin tumbler in slow circles, the condensation puddling into the white linen like little Rorschach tests. The music from the band floated up into the gauzy Caribbean night, a lazy steel-drum version of something retro and harmless. Around me, everyone seemed flushed with sun-kissed skin and boozy glows, their laughter easy, their shoulders loose.

I glanced up to the dance floor again, watching it all like an outsider looking in.

My father stood near the edge, Allegra's hand in his, their hips swaying in tandem. He twirled her and she threw her head back with a giggle, moving like they had been doing it for years. They probably had.

The comfort between them wasn't just biological. It was more than him just being her father. It was the easy, practiced way that came from years of being really known. Allegra was, what, seventeen? Eighteen? Barefoot in a sundress, hair knotted on top of her head, eyes full of light. And he was the kind of dad I used to pretend I had when I'd lie to my teachers about why he wasn't at my soccer games. Or the science fair. Or anywhere.

Next to me, Marin raised an eyebrow at the scene. "Cute," she murmured, and took a sip from her spritz.

I forced a smile. "Yeah."

Leo leaned in, his voice low. "You okay?"

"Fine," I said too quickly. "I just didn't know he could dance like that." My eyes were fixed across the room. "Or laugh like that. Or . . . be like that." I nodded toward them.

They spun again, and I caught an unrecognizable flash of something in his face. Pure joy. The kind of joy I never remembered him having when I was little. It was silly, I knew that. Years had passed. People change. But as he tucked a stray curl behind Allegra's ear and whispered something that made her beam, I couldn't help the pang that lodged deep in my chest.

"He's the dad I used to imagine having," I murmured, "when I'd try to pretend he hadn't left."

Neither of them said anything. They didn't have to. I didn't mean it as a dig. Not really. It was just the truth. Marin busied herself with her drink. Leo gave my hand a gentle squeeze, grounding me in the moment, but the ache lingered.

The band changed songs, and I finally looked away. But even with my back turned, I could still feel the sharp sting of absence, the unfairness of watching someone else get the version of my father that I never got. Somewhere off to the right, someone tapped a fork against a glass and called for toasts.

Perfect.

A few heads turned, and the murmurs of the party died down as the DJ dimmed the music. I straightened in my chair and reached for my note card. The words I'd quickly scribbled down after Izzy left the villa suddenly felt foreign in my hand. Like I'd written them for someone else entirely.

Standing, I cleared my throat and raised my glass, trying like hell to smile, but its tightness felt forced and uncomfortable. "Hi, everyone. For those of you who don't know me, I'm Elliot, Sonja's daughter and, apparently, her maid of honor, though I'm still not quite sure how that happened."

A light chuckle worked its way through the crowd.

"Tonight, we're here to celebrate love. Again."

A smattering of a few more chuckles, but this time, I paused and caught Dad's eye. He smirked but looked increasingly uncomfortable.

But I didn't relent. Instead, I lifted my glass and continued, "To new beginnings. Fresh starts. And finding that one person who doesn't just *get* you but . . . sticks around. Through thick and thin, highs and lows, the good times and the not-so-good times."

I offered another smile, more forced this time, as my eyes darted straight to Matty. Now it was his turn to fidget.

"Well, Keith, welcome to the family. You've already survived a week with us in paradise, so I guess that's a promising start. And Mom . . ."

I took a breath, holding the pause like a hostage and hoping like hell the words would come out softer than the cynic in me would deliver them.

"You look . . . happy. I hope that's exactly what this chapter brings you. Sincerely, I really do. Happiness. Stability. And someone who finally keeps their promises."

Dad again shifted in his chair, and I noticed Shira take his arm and rub it supportively.

"So let's raise a toast to second chances. May these two finally stick the landing."

I sipped from my raised glass to the sound of a few sparse claps and a room full of even more puzzled looks.

I set my flute down a little too hard, the dull *thunk* of it against the linen-draped table louder than intended. Marin leaned toward me, tight lipped, her eyes scanning mine for signs of a deeper unraveling.

I offered her a vague shrug, then excused myself with a mumbled, "I need some air."

Leo's hand brushed my arm as I pushed my chair back. "You want me to come with you?"

I shook my head. "I just need a minute. I'll be right back."

I wandered toward the edge of the garden, the beat of the band's bass still pulsing faintly through the ground, and leaned against a whitewashed column that framed the patio. Inside, laughter and clinking glasses painted a much cheerier picture than the one looping in my head.

I hadn't even heard the footsteps behind me until Matty's voice broke the silence.

"You okay?"

I turned sharply. "Seriously?"

He held up his hands. "Just asking. You looked—"

"Stop, just stop! Jesus, Matty, what do you want from me?" I snapped, crossing my arms tightly across my chest.

"Nothing. I just want to make sure you're okay. That's it. I just didn't want you to be alone, not if you didn't want to be."

I opened my mouth, ready to hurl something sharp and cutting back at him about how he didn't get to play the good guy now, but I stopped when I saw Leo approaching through the open patio doors.

Leo's brow furrowed as he stepped into the circle of light. "Everything okay out here?"

Matty glanced at me. "Yeah, great. I was just leaving. El, I'll be inside if you want to talk."

He turned and disappeared into the shadows without waiting for a reply.

Leo watched him go, then looked back at me. "Elliot, please, talk to me. About your mom. Your dad. About . . . Matt. About any of it. All of it. I get that you're hurting, but don't shut me out."

"I'm not shutting you out," I snapped. "I'm protecting what's left of me."

He shook his head slowly and took a few steps closer. "Do you remember that myth I told you in Mykonos? About Atalanta and Meleager? Atalanta, the fierce huntress who swore she'd never marry. Said she'd only consider a man who could beat her in a footrace. But Meleager, he didn't try to outrun her. He ran with her. Matched her stride for stride. Not to win, just to show her he was there. That he understood her. That he wasn't going anywhere." He looked at me, quiet and steady. "That's all I want to do, Elliot. Run beside you. But you won't let me. You won't let anyone even get close enough to try."

"When we met, I told you who I was. I told you I didn't believe in love. That wasn't some dare or gauntlet I threw down for you to overcome. It was the truth."

"Then why? Why did you meet me in Paris?"

"I didn't meet you in Paris! I chose my career. My future. I chose myself!" I shouted with a forcefulness that surprised us both.

"What are you talking about?" he said, his voice low but certain. "You stood with me under the lights of the Eiffel Tower and let the world fall away. Just for a moment, it was only us. Don't rewrite it all now because you're afraid. Afraid of getting hurt. Of letting someone in."

"You're the one trying to rewrite history. You show up out of nowhere, completely scrambling my compass, making me question all the things that I've always known to be true, and suddenly I'm supposed to forget every single thing I believe? All the rules I set to keep myself safe?"

"Fuck the rules." He took my chin between his thumb and forefinger, lifting my gaze to his. "You think this is about Paris or Mykonos or whatever city you can neatly file me under, but this isn't about geography, Elliot. This is about *you*. You keep telling yourself that you're not capable of love, but it's not true. You've just built your whole life around not needing anyone, and now someone shows up who makes you feel something and you're scrambling to convince yourself that it's not real. That *I'm* not real."

I looked away, pulling my face from his hands as my heart hammered against my ribs. "You don't know me, Leo."

"That's where you're wrong. I do know you. And it scares the hell out of you. I know you sit in the center of your world like it's a fortress, and all your sarcasm and commandments are your armor. I know you'd rather be right than happy. And I know you think pushing me away will protect you. But it won't. It just leaves you alone."

"Alone is safe," I whispered.

"No, alone is familiar. Don't confuse the two."

The stinging that burned behind my eyes felt like a fire my tears were threatening to extinguish. "You don't understand what it's been like, watching my mom fall apart over and over again, watching my dad start a new family like his old one never even mattered. Having the last man I trusted make me feel safe . . . and then betray me like it meant nothing. All I've ever been was collateral damage. Why the hell would I put myself in a position to be shattered like that again?"

He stepped in close, his voice barely above a whisper. "Because maybe for once, you won't be the girl left holding the broken pieces. Maybe this time you're the one who gets to be held."

He reached out like he'd done so many times before, but I pulled away. "Don't, Leo. I . . . I can't."

"Can't or won't?"

"What difference does it make?"

"All the difference in the world, actually."

"Well, I guess there isn't much more to say, then, is there?" I managed before turning away from him and making my way back inside the restaurant. Though Leo followed behind me, we kept to separate corners, allowing the steam from our heated argument to continue to simmer under the surface.

Catching a cab home and still not speaking, we both fell into bed without another word, the silence like a towering barricade between us.

Chapter Thirty

I woke to the sound of gulls cawing and waves crashing, sunlight already pooling across the villa's tile floor. The spot beside me in bed was empty, the sheets cool. The mattress didn't seem to have any trace of an indent left by his sleeping body.

Leo ran most mornings, usually before sunrise, claiming it helped clear his head, and after last night's fight, I was certain that's where he must have gone. I stretched, stiff from the tension of all the shit that had hit the fan during our argument, and reached for my phone: 8:47 a.m.

We were supposed to meet Marin for breakfast at nine. Whatever he was up to, I assumed he'd just find us there.

I brushed my teeth and pulled my hair into a knot, hoping the salt air would pass for styling product, and tried not to replay the argument over and over. We'd both said things we didn't mean, or at least things I hoped he didn't mean. I'd been sharp, defensive, and tired of being asked to open doors I'd long since locked. Still, we'd gone to bed not speaking, backs turned, and that silence felt deafening now.

I checked my phone for a text from him, but there was nothing.

Walking across the resort, the sun was already hot on my skin. My eyes scanned the pool deck, the beach chairs, the bar. No Leo. At the restaurant's entrance, I spotted Marin waving from a corner table, sunglasses atop her head, mimosa already in hand.

I slid into the seat across from her and glanced around one more time.

"Hey," I said, trying to sound casual. "Has Leo been by?"

Marin took a sip from her flute and blinked. "Who?"

I gave a little laugh, unsure if she was messing with me. "Very funny. Leo. Leo! Leo?!"

Her brow creased. "Elliot, who are you talking about?"

I waited for the punch line, for the glimmer of recognition, for the slow dawning that this was a poorly timed joke. But Marin just tilted her head, puzzled, not a flicker of familiarity in her expression.

My mouth went dry. "Leo, my wedding date? My boyfriend? South African? He was at the rehearsal dinner! How do you not know who I'm talking about?!"

"I . . ." She shrugged and let out a small awkward laugh, sipping her drink again. Perhaps to fill the uncomfortable beat of silence that fell between us. "Are you sure you're okay, El? I mean, you were pretty out of it last night. Maybe it was a dream? And you? A boyfriend?"

I stared at her. "A dream? Are you kidding me right now? No. Marin, he's real. He's . . . He *was* here. You *know* him. Whatever it is you're playing at right now, it's not funny."

I pushed back from the table, heart pounding, and turned in a slow circle, scanning every face in the dining room. I moved quickly through the restaurant toward the front desk.

"Hi," I said breathlessly. "Can you check if Leo Kindell is still checked in? He's in Villa 9B with me. My name is Elliot West."

The concierge tapped a few keys on his computer and then blinked, politely confused. "I'm sorry, ma'am, there's no record of any guest with that name staying here."

My vision tilted. "Of course there is. He's . . . he's my boyfriend and he's been staying with me. He's on my reservation, arrived yesterday." My pulse was racing, and I could barely get the words out before I finally managed, "Please check again."

He not so stealthily eyed his colleague before reentering the information as requested and then turned the monitor to face me. "You see, no one here by that name, nor has there been over the past thirty days." He pointed to the search fields to clarify. The words: No Guest Found emblazoned on the screen like a verdict.

"But I . . . I don't understand," I stammered, still staring at the blinking cursor next to the words.

Another voice behind me called, "El, oh good, there you are."

I turned to see Mom fanning herself with a spa pamphlet. "I wanted to tell you that hair and makeup will be coming this afternoon, so you have the morning to do what you like. Just be sure to be at the bridal suite by four o'clock. And real four, not Elliot Standard Time four."

Dismissing the jab—because *really*, who was she to talk?!—I grabbed her arm, tears threatening in the corners of my eyes. "Have you seen Leo anywhere?"

Her face twisted slightly, confused and gentle, the way you look at someone who's just lost their footing. "Um . . . who? Oh, is that the name of the cute bartender you were chatting it up with the other day?"

"No, Mom! Leo? The man I've been dating?"

Mom practically laughed out loud. "Leo? I—no, honey. I don't think I've ever met him. And you didn't mention you were dating anyone . . . not seriously. I would have offered you a plus-one. Anyway, I'm off for a day of bridal pampering with Izzy. I'd have asked you to join us, but after last night? I got the message loud and clear."

With that, she turned on her espadrille and headed in the direction of the hotel spa.

So last night did happen? The rehearsal dinner, the passive-aggressive toast . . . every bit of it real, and yet somehow, none of it with Leo?

My breath turned shallow. The world moved, spinning in dizzying circles. The noise around me felt suddenly too loud, the colors too bright, like I was seeing it all from underwater.

I stumbled back, clutching the edge of the concierge desk for support. A buzz of fear filled my ears as I panic-scrolled through my phone's camera roll.

No pictures of Leo. At least, not any recent ones that I could find. Not from our adventure on the chocolate tour. The selfie Leo had sent from his phone, the one Tomas had taken of us in front of the shop, was gone. There was nothing from the *Mamma Mia!* show we'd gone to. Not a single piece of evidence of any of it from the past few weeks anywhere to be found.

Just the Mykonos photos from the summer, more than six months ago. But how? HOW?!

No one remembered him.

No one remembered *us*.

And somehow, the space he'd filled felt even heavier now that it was empty.

"Miss, can I help you book any excursions for the day? You could rent a moped, maybe, to explore the island? There's this charming little chocolate shop in town where you can make your own confections from scratch. And a hidden beach I absolutely recommend, but don't tell anyone I was the one who told you about it. I only share it with our most special guests," he added in a whisper.

"Thanks, but I'm okay. I was just . . . I'm going to . . ."

I'm going to what? Stay at the hotel and search for evidence of my missing, magical boyfriend? Try to act like any of this is remotely okay? That I'm okay?

"Morning, El." Dad's voice came in from the front entrance as the glass doors drew open. "I was hoping I'd catch you at breakfast, but this is even better."

"Good morning, sir," the front desk clerk offered with equal enthusiasm.

Dad gave a little wave and turned to me. "Hope you didn't schedule anything for the day just yet because I booked a private fishing excursion and was hoping you and Marin would want to join us. I was coming here to confirm our reservation," he said, eyeing the man behind the counter, who picked up on the request and was already typing away on his keyboard.

"Yes, sir, a party of six is scheduled to leave the dock at ten thirty a.m. Does that sound correct?"

"It does. Leaves us plenty of time to get back, relax a bit, and get ready for the ceremony. So what do you say? You in?"

"I don't really think I'm in the right headspace for—"

"But it's mahi-mahi! And what better way to clear your head than an afternoon on the open water? Fresh air, tropical blue sea, it doesn't get any better than that. Besides, we haven't gotten a chance to spend any real time together." He crossed his arms over his chest. "I'm not taking no for an answer."

"Thanks, it sounds like fun, but really, I—"

Just as I was scouring my brain for a reason not to go that Dad would accept, Marin came into the lobby looking for me.

"Sheesh, woman, where did you go? I grabbed you a stack of pancakes off the buffet, but they're like hockey pucks now. You okay?"

"Perfect timing," Dad said to Marin. "I was just inviting you and El to join us on a family fishing trip today."

I looked at Marin with a face that expressed in no uncertain terms that she was supposed to help me with an excuse to get out of it. One of the best things about a lifelong friend is the ability to say everything with just a glance and no words at all.

But Marin, ever the peacemaker, grinned and said, "Actually, I think that sounds lovely. El and I haven't had a chance to enjoy the water much, and I hear they serve some killer rum punch on board."

I shot her a glare that all but shouted *Traitor!* and forced a smile.

"Wonderful! See you ladies on the dock at ten thirty, sharp."

Chapter Thirty-One

The irony of the name stenciled on the side of the fishing boat, *Knot Enough*, wasn't lost on me. Sure, it pointed to the fact that the boat was a bit of an eyesore, but it also summed up just about everything there was to say about my relationship with my father. He wasn't a bad guy, just absent for more of my life than he was present.

It was a picture-perfect morning. And I hated it.

Not just because of the trip itself, which, of course, would be torturous, stuck bobbing in the middle of the ocean with my father's second family. No, I hated it because the world had the audacity to keep spinning when mine had tipped completely off its axis.

Leo was gone.

Not left-me-at-the-airport gone. Not I'm-just-not-ready-for-this gone.

Gone.

Like he'd been plucked from the narrative entirely. Deleted. Forgotten. By everyone except me. And I couldn't make sense of any of it.

Over the sputtering engine, the captain shouted, "We're gonna motor about four miles past the reef line into the Caribbean, where the big ones are really biting, while Kai, my first mate, mixes up some of the best spiced rum punch this side of the Placencia Peninsula."

Marin frowned. "Shit, did he say we're going *into* the Caribbean?"

"It's mahi-mahi fishing. Of course we're heading out into open water." Dad laughed, slipping off his flip-flops and handing them to Kai before climbing aboard.

I leaned into Marin. "What's wrong?"

"I thought we'd be staying near the reef. I've just been known to get a little seasick, but only in choppy water. I'm sure this'll be fine. Let's give it a shot. I'm not bailing on you to fly solo with your dad and his kids." She reached for Kai's hand as he aided her onto the deck from the dock.

"I don't want you to get sick. It'll ruin your whole day. I'll be fine," I told her, even though I wasn't exactly sure that was true.

"Gurl, haven't I told you, I'm your ride or die. Or should I say boat or die? On second thought, how about we not say 'die' when we're heading out onto the open sea."

With a snort, I slung an arm around her shoulders and gave her a squeeze. "You're a really good friend, Marin, in case I haven't told you lately."

After a quick safety demonstration from the captain, Kai got to work on his legendary rum punch, and a deckhand passed out rods, offering help with baiting the lines. Shira and Allegra, happy to enjoy the boat ride but morally opposed to harming any and all marine life, headed to the front to sunbathe, leaving Dad, Cannon, Marin, and me to fish.

The sun beat down from a cloudless sky, the horizon bleeding into the shimmering sea like a watercolor left too long in the rain. The boat rocked gently beneath us, the occasional squawk of a gull overhead the only sound above the slap of waves against the hull.

I sat near the stern, sunglasses hiding my eyes, a rod in my hands I hadn't bothered to bait. My dad was up front, fiddling with Cannon's life jacket, while Shira slathered sunscreen on Allegra's shoulders and pointed out something in the distance, another reef maybe, or a pelican dive-bombing for fish. Marin lounged beside me, her baseball cap pulled low and a can of La Croix at her feet.

At first, the sea was calm, like a glass-bottomed pool. The water was so clear you could almost see all the way down to the reef. But as we crossed from the shallow turquoise into deeper blue-green, the waves started to swell. And once we hit the navy depths, they really began to roll.

I glanced over at Marin, who had taken on a pale, olive cast and was gripping the railing so hard her knuckles had gone white.

"*Oof*, you don't look so hot," I said gently.

"I don't feel so hot."

I brought her a bottle of cold water, rubbed her back, and asked, "What do you need? What can I get you?"

"Nothing. I'll be fine. I took some Dramamine, so I'm just waiting for it to kick in. Once it does, though, it may knock me out, which could be for the best. Just didn't want you to think I croaked."

The captain dropped anchor and announced we'd reached a good spot for catching mahi-mahi. I lifted my rod to cast, but it was heavier than I expected, nothing like the one I'd used the time I had gone fly-fishing with Dad. I'd been just about twelve. Mom was off honeymooning in Spain with husband number three, and Dad had agreed to watch me for the week. Cannon and Allegra were at art camp somewhere in the Adirondacks, and Shira couldn't leave her yoga studio, so Dad took me to Wyoming on his annual fishing trip.

I don't think we exchanged more than a handful of sentences that whole week. Even so, out on the river with the current tugging at our legs, Dad carefully showed me how to thread the line and flick the rod, and for once, we were in sync. And maybe for the first time ever, I felt a little bit close to my father.

But then, near the end of the trip, as we packed up the gear, he glanced over and said something like, "Not bad for a tagalong week." He meant it as a joke, but it stuck with me, the idea that I would always be an unplanned invitee, an afterthought. Because the truth was, I didn't really fit into his new life, or Mom's either.

It was then that I started building one of my own. And the thing no one tells you is, once you get used to moving through the world in a way that doesn't include anyone else, it gets so comfortable, so predictably safe that it only gets harder to make room for someone else. Something that had become painfully clear in the way I couldn't make room for Leo.

A couple of bigger swells hit the boat, and Marin suddenly went from pale khaki to army green.

"I think I'm gonna go . . . *hic* . . . and have a lie down in the cabin . . . *hic*." She held a clenched fist in front of her mouth, as if desperately holding back whatever was threatening to come up.

"Want me to go with you?" I asked, feeling terrible that she'd even attempted this trip, now seeing her look more like a pimento olive than my best friend.

"No, I'd like to . . . *hic* . . . maintain my image of resilience and not have you see me . . . *hic* . . . curled up in a fetal position begging Poseidon for mercy," Marin said and shuffled off to her self-imposed exile belowdecks.

"You know, she should really have stayed out here in the open air," Dad murmured after Marin had already left. "She's only going to feel worse inside. Do you need any help baiting your line?"

"No, I've got it."

I skewered a slimy chunk of sardine onto the hook and cast it into the water. Cannon meandered off to the back of the boat, texting and completely oblivious to the gorgeous view, leaving Dad and me alone.

We gripped our poles side by side, the silence broken only by the sharp smack of water against the boat's fiberglass hull. Like in Wyoming, we fished in peace and quiet, just a handful of words traded, nothing anyone would mistake for real conversation.

He reeled in and recast, then glanced at me sideways, finally breaking the awkwardness with, "So . . . have you been having a good time?"

The question echoed in my mind, dull and distant, like someone tapping on glass underwater.

Had I been having a good time?

The easy answer was no. Not after everything. Not with the tension with Mom. Or the fact Matty was in Belize trying to get back into my good graces. And especially not with Leo gone, vanished in the most impossible way, leaving behind only the imprint of his presence. I could still feel him, somehow. The warmth of his hand at the small of my back, the shape of him next to me in bed, the way he always seemed to know what I needed before I said it.

And yet, it was like he'd never existed. No one remembered. Not Marin. Not Mom. Not even me, if I wasn't careful. The details were already starting to feel slippery, like a dream I couldn't quite hold on to.

And on top of that, there was the wedding itself. My parents, their tangled histories, my own resentment and exhaustion, all of it had bubbled up and out, like a pot left on the stove too long.

I wanted to scream, to cry, to laugh at the absurdity of it all. But mostly, I just wanted to go back to that hidden beach and feel the sun on my skin with Leo beside me, making dumb jokes about pirate treasure and eating our melted bars of Belizean chocolate.

Instead, I was here.

I wrapped my hands tighter around the fishing pole and swallowed the salty air thick in the back of my throat.

"Have I been having a good time?" I repeated, finally returning to his question. "Um . . . some parts," I said. "The rest . . . I'm still trying to make sense of."

Dad looked at me as if he expected me to continue.

"It's complicated," I exhaled.

"Complicated how?"

"Just complicated. Dad, can I ask you a question?"

"Course you can."

"Why are you here?"

"You know I love to fish."

"No, not *here* here," I said, turning to face him. "Like here in Belize. Why after years of avoiding Mom would you come to her wedding?"

"I told you. We've buried the hatchet. We've both moved on, and honestly, we're in good places now. And I've come to realize that there's really no point holding on to old baggage when there's room for something lighter . . . like, I don't know, mutual respect and maybe even a bit of joy for one another. Before everything got so messy, your mom and I were real friends. The kind who rooted for each other no matter what. I think after all these years, we've finally found our way back to that place. Certainly sooner would have been more ideal, but better late than never."

"And what about me? Where did I ever fit into any of that? Because honestly, it never felt like I did."

Dad puffed out an audible breath and set his pole in the holster. "It's my fault that you had to deal with a hell of a lot more than a kid should've. But I thought I was doing the right thing at the time. I told myself staying would just make things worse for you."

"But you didn't fight for me," I said, the words slipping out before I could stop them. "You started over. New wife. New kids. You were just . . . gone. And I was the one left picking Mom up off the floor."

"I didn't know how bad it got for you," he said. "Not until much later. And by then . . . I didn't think you'd want my help."

"Maybe I didn't. But it doesn't mean I didn't need you to try. To offer it. To at least feign the illusion that you were there for me."

His jaw tightened. He looked like he wanted to reach out to touch my arm, but he didn't. "I'm so sorry, El. And I know saying that now doesn't fix anything, but it's the truth. You deserved a better dad."

The ocean stretched out before us, indifferent and infinite, and something about it made my chest ache. Looking down at my hands on the pole, my knuckles had gone white. I opened my mouth, then closed it. I didn't know how to respond to his confession.

Yeah, I sure as shit deserved a better dad! I deserved the version Allegra and Cannon knew.

But firing shots now wouldn't change anything about anything. And this was the most we'd ever spoken about it . . . ever, and it felt like something had shifted between us.

"You want to know why things are hard for me, Dad?" I asked. Now with the gates thrown open, I couldn't seem to keep my feelings at bay. "Because every time anyone gets close, I brace for impact. I'm so afraid to let anyone really see me. To need anyone."

"You know, your mom and I, we listen to your radio show. And . . . I want to phrase this the right way because, of course, we're proud of your success, but the hurt you wear so boldly on your sleeve and the hard time you have letting anyone close, we know we've both had a hand in forging that armor. And we thought maybe, just maybe, if we came here as a bit more of a united front, we could show you that it doesn't have to be all or nothing," he said. "That relationships, like people, are complicated. Flawed. But they're not worthless because of those things."

I was speechless. Dad and his family showing up wasn't a thoughtless, selfish act, but an intentional attempt to reach me, to convey that in spite of our past, we could have some semblance of a better relationship in the future.

Just then my rod snapped taut, and I knew I had something on the line.

Dad leaned over the railing to see. "Looks like you got a live one there."

My pole bent sharply, the reel whining in protest, and I leaped into motion to grasp the handle with both hands, and braced for the struggle.

"Don't yank it," he said quickly, maneuvering himself behind me. His voice snapped into something calm and steady. "Let it run for a second. That's a strong pull. You've got a real fighter."

The line zipped out, the pole bucking like it was being shocked to life. My heart pounded, part adrenaline, part panic.

"Okay, now ease it back toward you and keep the tip up," he coached. Dad stepped in closer, one hand hovering near mine on the rod, not touching, just ready. "Short pulls. Reel as you lower. You got this."

I tightened my grip with renewed focus, my arms straining. The fish jerked and yanked with surprising strength, but I countered, feeling it tire with each crank of the reel. Dad leaned over the railing again to try to get a better view and let out a long, impressed whistle.

"She's right there, El. Right at the surface. Just don't let her dive under the boat, it's what instinct will tell her to do," he instructed.

"I'm . . . trying," I grunted, wrenching the rod back and forth against whatever was on the line.

Though he stood close, he still kept his hands back, allowing me to earn each inch gained on my own. Beads of sweat rolled down my forehead and moistened my neck, but I wouldn't forfeit even a centimeter to swipe them away.

Then when it seemed Moby Dick and I were destined to be permanently locked in a stalemate of wills, my muscles screaming in opposition, Dad stepped forward to offer help. I gave a small nod, and he came in behind me, his arms circling mine, his hands gently covering my own. My pulse thundered in my ears, but it wasn't just the fish causing it.

It was the strange feeling of support. Of not being alone in the fight.

"Keep the pressure on," he instructed. "We've almost got 'em."

Together, we gave the pole a few hearty heaves and finally, a glint of silver-green broke through the surface with a splash. The fish thrashed wildly, water spraying up like a fountain. A flash of gold shimmered in the sun, bright and brilliant.

With one last heave, we brought it up and over the side of the boat, the fish landing in the bucket with a thud that felt almost symbolic. I collapsed back against the railing, my arms shaking, laughter bubbling up in my throat.

"Well, look at us," Dad said, a huge smile forming on his face.

I turned toward him, brushing hair off my damp forehead. "Yeah, look at us. Thanks, I don't think I could've reeled it up on my own."

"No way, that fish fought like hell. It was a two-person job, no question."

Just as Dad was freeing the fish from the line, Shira and Allegra appeared from the front of the boat.

"We heard all the excitement and wanted to see what was happening back here?" Shira said.

Dad proudly held up the mahi-mahi. "We caught ourselves a sea monster." He dug in his pocket for his phone. "Can you take a picture of us? I'll want to remember this day." Passing it to Shira, he pulled me in close for a side hug and held the fish out like it was the catch of the century.

"Okay, you two. On the count of three," Shira said, counting down till she snapped the shot. "I got it. Now that you're done with the photo op, think we can toss her back, so she can live out her best fish life?"

Dad passed me the mahi-mahi. I leaned out, waited for a swell, and gave her a careful shove back into the sea, her tail splashing as she disappeared beneath the waves. We fished a bit longer, our lines casting lazy arcs across the cerulean water, but nothing else bit. We sat in silence, but it wasn't awkward anymore. This time, it was the kind of quiet that comes after a long and very overdue conversation.

The air turned sticky and bright as the sun climbed higher in the clear blue sky, and by the time we anchored back at the hotel pier, Marin climbed out of the boat's galley like she'd only been slightly run over by a freight train.

"Come on, lady," I said, threading my arm through hers as we stepped onto the dock. "Let's get you some good meds and a dark air-conditioned room."

She managed a weak smile. "If I die, tell my kids I love them."

About ten minutes after I'd tucked Marin in with a bottle of ginger ale, some antinausea medicine, and a cool compress, she slipped into a deep, peaceful sleep. I stayed by her side for a while, watching the steady rise and fall of her chest. When a sudden, loud snore broke the silence, confirming she was out like a light, I left a note on her bedside table, grabbed my laptop, and quietly slipped out the door.

Chapter Thirty-Two

The beach was quiet and relatively empty, with most of the hotel guests out on excursions around the island. I spotted a lounge chair with an umbrella already set up and eased into it, letting the ocean breeze wash over me as I popped open my laptop.

I cracked my knuckles and dug in for some cybersleuthing. I needed to know how much of Leo had been real. The photos from our time in Greece were still on my phone, so that part at least was solid. But everything else from the past few months had vanished without a trace.

I typed his name into Google, and a handful of hits popped up. I clicked the first one. His LinkedIn profile. The picture was a professional headshot, but it was definitely Leo. His résumé backed up what he'd told me when we first met: He was a consultant working at the firm McKinsey, based in Johannesburg.

Next, I opened his Instagram account. I scrolled, faster at first, then slower, until I landed on what I was looking for, the photos from this past summer. Us in Mykonos: swimming, hiking, camping. Our bright-white smiles made brighter by sunburned noses and deep tans.

Then I tapped through his most recent pictures. One was even dated yesterday, the location tagged as Marrakech, Morocco. Leo stood in the desert beside a camel, a brilliant sunset of red and orange blazing behind him. He looked so happy . . . and impossibly far away.

There was no trace of Belize. No hint of a time he'd lived in New York City with me. Just image after image of Leo roaming the globe solo, like he had no one to miss.

My heart sank as I realized this was all the proof I needed to know I hadn't met him in Paris. That part of the story had never been real. I'd stuck to my guns and beliefs, and our lives kept moving on, separately. Time had ticked by, and now he probably just thought of me as nothing more than the girl he met on a summer holiday. The one who broke his heart by not showing up to meet him.

The ache of knowing what might have been was almost enough to swallow me whole, but what could I do about it now? Whatever fairy dust had been sprinkled on us had only given me a glimpse of a possible life. But that magic was gone.

And so was Leo.

The realization struck me hard and lethal, like a blade between my ribs.

I closed his Instagram and opened my emails. With all the madness of the past few days, I hadn't had the chance to check in and was worried I may have missed something important from my agent or Ravi.

Most were the usual messages from fans of the show, looking for love advice or sharing a funny dating anecdote. Two were from Ravi, asking for my outline for next week's episode so he could start his preproduction prep, and one was from my editor at Simon & Schuster with the latest round of notes on my book, *Love Is Dead, Let's Have Brunch*.

I clicked open the file she'd sent and was immediately met by a terrifying tangle of red lines and suggestions in the margins of my manuscript. There were so many comments I couldn't tell where my words started and the edits began. Already overwhelmed, I immediately closed it. Maybe I'd tackle edits later, when I wasn't still a little fuzzy from the glass of Kai's famous rum punch I'd polished off on the boat ride back to the resort.

Instead, I opened a blank document to begin an outline for Tuesday's show. My original angle was all about the absurdity of destination weddings. A true takedown of the entire practice of asking people to give up *their* own vacation time (not to mention hundreds, if not thousands of dollars) to celebrate a union that probably wouldn't even last as long as the trip.

The idea of forcing friends and family, most of whom probably didn't even like each other, to spend days in super close proximity, participating in activities and pretending to be thrilled about it, was the kind of material that usually killed on *Love Is a Four-Letter Word.*

But the words weren't coming as easily as they should have been. It was hard to summon full outrage after such an oddly cathartic boat trip with Dad. Just as I was about to set my fingers down on the keyboard, Izzy's voice called out to me from across the sand.

"El, hey, we've been looking all over for you! We need a fourth for mah-jongg. Your mom and Shira want to play. You in?"

Mom and I hadn't really spoken since our spat at karaoke, and I assumed my not-so-subtle toast had gotten her horns completely twisted. I wasn't in the mood to deal with either her passive-aggressive silence or the risk of another blowup if one of us said the wrong thing.

"I just sat down to do some work. Maybe later?" I yelled back.

Izzy readjusted her bag over her shoulder and headed in the direction of my lounge chair, like a woman on a mission. "C'mon, El, after the lackluster toast you gave last night, you need to try to smooth things out with her before later. I know it sometimes feels like you're the parent and she's the child."

I looked up at her. "Sometimes?"

"She's really been working on herself. But you'd have to let her in, just even a little bit, to see it. Sure, it doesn't make up for every misstep. Not even close. But it shows she's trying, and sometimes, trying is the first step toward something better."

Izzy always had a way of cutting through my bullshit with surgical precision. When I was ten and had come home from a particularly rough day at school where some girl had called my shoes "tragic," Izzy was the one who took me to get ice cream and told me how she'd once worn neon leg warmers to a first date in 1986 and still managed to get a second one.

When I got my period at a sleepover and cried in the bathroom for an hour when I got home, she was the one who slipped me a chocolate bar under the door and told me it was just the beginning of becoming a woman and a lifelong grudge against white shorts.

She wasn't just my mom's best friend. She'd been there. Really there. Like a second mother, sometimes even like a first. So yeah, maybe she had every right to call me out when I acted like a brat. Especially when it came to Mom. Especially now.

I glanced at the blank screen of my laptop, the cursor the only thing on the white page, taunting me as it blinked. Closing my computer, I shoved it in my tote and stood up with a dramatic grunt of surrender, sand clinging to the backs of my calves as I hurried to catch up with Izzy across the patio.

"Ugh, fine," I hollered. "But if bamboo tiles start flying at my head, I'm blaming you."

Izzy barked out a chuckle and playfully rolled her eyes. "Well, I'm sure you'd deserve it."

Izzy shuffled the tiles on the table, the click of the plastic squares punctuating the silence. When she finished, we racked them into four neat walls, and Shira dealt us each our thirteen to begin the Charleston, a series of tile exchanges meant to improve your position in the game. Sometimes that's exactly what happened and things began to shift in your favor, but other times, especially when you couldn't see the hand at the start, you'd end up worse off than before.

Part luck, part skill, part piecing together a puzzle with missing edges, that's what made the game of mah-jongg so challenging. Ultimately, you had to accept the tiles you were given and somehow try to make the best of it.

We sat at a weathered teak table under a generous straw umbrella, just a few steps from the beach, where the tide lazily lapped against the sand and retreated in soft, rhythmic sighs. Izzy barefoot, one leg tucked under her as she studied her mah-jongg card. Shira, humming to herself, adjusted her sunglasses as she inspected her hand, the picture of vacation ease.

And then there was my mother.

She carefully aligned her rack with her perfectly manicured fingers stiff with precision. She didn't speak right away, but I could feel the uneasiness between us still lingering in the air.

"You remember the rules?" she asked without looking at me, her tone light but edged.

Reaching for my tiles, I gave her a half-hearted smile. "I'm good."

A beat passed, taut and crackling with static energy.

"I'm East, I'll start," Izzy said brightly, breaking the tension with the practiced calm of someone who'd refereed one too many of our squabbles. She reached over to the wall, picked up a tile, and then quickly tossed it into the center of the table face up. "Three Dot."

"Call," I said, picking up Izzy's discarded tile.

"You do know if you call for it, then you have to show the meld. And there's no going back once you show your hand," Mom said, like I should've known better than to commit so early into the game.

I mean, if anyone should know that . . .

I set my pieces face up on the rack. "I am fully aware, thank you."

It was Mom's turn next. She reached for a tile, studied it like it held all the answers to the universe, then after what felt like forever, finally tossed it away.

If only she put that much thought into all her life decisions . . .

The game dragged on like that for a while, Mom and me making passive-aggressive digs at one another all while Izzy and Shira did their best to keep things light and easygoing.

"Uh, guys? I think I'm ready to call mah-jongg," Mom said after picking up the tile she'd apparently been waiting for all game.

"Let's see, Sonja," Shira said, sliding closer to her chair.

Mom spread her tiles out and pointed to the line on the card she'd completed.

Izzy leaned over to inspect the hand more closely. "Look at that, you nailed it. What does everyone think? Shall we play another round?"

"You know what?" I said slowly, evenly. "I think I'm getting a bit warm. Maybe I'll go for a dip in the pool."

Mom tilted her head, tight-lipped. "Well, that tracks."

I looked up sharply. "Excuse me?"

Shira stiffened. Izzy froze, mid-reach.

Mom sat back and folded her arms. "It means this is what you do. You pull away the second things stop being light and easy. The moment there's the tiniest bit of friction, you bolt."

A long silence settled between us. The waves crashed a little harder in the distance, as if they could sense what was coming.

"Can you two excuse us a minute?" Mom asked, eyes still locked on mine.

Exchanging a glance, they stood, Shira reaching for her half-full mai tai before she shuffled away.

Izzy grabbed her rum punch and leaned in close to the table. "Am I okay to leave you two?"

Neither of us replied.

"I think this needs to happen . . . for both of you. But remember, no matter what's said, deep down, you love each other. Oh, and also, the people on the beach didn't come here for your emotional fireworks, so try not to disturb their margarita naps."

As soon as she was gone, I leaned forward, jaw tight, trying to keep in mind what Izzy had said about keeping things to a reasonable decibel. "You want to talk about pulling away? You want to talk about leaving? I mean, you and Dad basically wrote the manual on that."

She blinked. "Elliot—"

"So, what? You get to air it all out, but if I do the same, suddenly I'm the one who's out of line?"

"Oh, I think you do plenty of airing out," Mom said.

"What's that supposed to mean?"

"You mean, *aside* from that very pointed toast you gave last night in front of all our guests? Or how about every morning when you go on your show and turn on that mic and tell the world exactly how Dad and I screwed you up . . . like it's . . . like it's entertainment or something," she replied, her voice catching slightly.

"Well, if the shoe or *show* fits."

"That's not fair," she murmured, swallowing hard. "We did the best we knew how."

"If that was your best, then I guess thanks for the material."

The look on her face made it clear I'd gone a step too far, and I immediately regretted it.

"Do you know why you never win at mah-jongg, El?"

I shrugged. "Why don't you go ahead and enlighten me."

"It's because you don't play to win."

"Well, that clears it all up. Thanks, Mom."

"You play defensively. Always watching everyone else's moves, worrying about how their choices will mess up yours."

I let out a short laugh. "So? Isn't that the point of the game?"

Mom shook her head. "No. The point is to build *your* hand. Play *your* game. To take risks. But you're too busy protecting yourself to ever go after what you really want." She sighed, took my hands into hers and looked me square in the eyes. "I knew, I mean, of course I knew from what you shared on the air that you were angry, but I guess I never realized you were *this* angry," she said.

"I'm not angry, Mom. I think I've just learned to put up walls. It's how I keep myself from completely falling apart. When Matty cheated, it wrecked me, but it didn't sink me. You know why? Because somewhere deep in my gut, I expected it. I *expected* to be let down. Dad left us, *both* of us. And you . . . you were always chasing after happiness in someone else, like I wasn't enough."

Her lower lip trembled, but I couldn't stop now. A tear slid down her cheek, and she swiped it away, shaking her head. "I didn't know you felt that way."

"Because you never *asked*. You were so wrapped up in your own pain that you never saw mine."

"I didn't know how to be happy," she finally said. "Not on my own. And definitely not after your dad left. I'd put so much of myself into building our life together and our little family that I didn't know who or what I was once he was gone. I was twenty-two, Elliot. With a kid and rent due and this . . . crushing silence that filled the house every time I walked in. And it reminded me so much of my own childhood, I could barely breathe."

I glanced up at her. I'd never heard that part before.

She took a sip of her lemonade and expelled a long breath before continuing. "My mom—your grandma—suffered from depression for most of my life. I'd come in from school and the TV would be on, a pot of something boiling over, and she'd be sitting in the dark like she was just watching the shadows move across the walls. I told myself, *swore* to myself, I'd never feel that kind of emptiness again. But then I did. After your father left."

I swallowed hard, her words hitting like a stone dropped in my stomach.

"So I looked for something . . . anything to fill that space. Attention, affection, men who made promises they had no business making. I didn't know how to show up the way you needed me to." She paused, her voice shaking and lashes wet. "And I'm so sorry. I'm so damn sorry I couldn't be the perfect mother for you."

"I didn't need perfect," I finally managed. "I just needed to know I mattered."

Her tears spilled down her cheeks, and she quickly blotted them away with the linen napkin on her lap. "You did. You *do* matter. I'm sorry I didn't put you first. I didn't know how. I was too busy looking for someone to fix me. When I met Keith, I wasn't looking for someone to save me. Not anymore. I was looking for love. The right kind of love. The kind that respects who you are and your boundaries. The kind that's patient, encouraging, and unconditional. The kind that doesn't ask you to shrink or hide parts of yourself. That's what I want now. For me, and I want that for you too, my darling."

I tried to swallow past the lump in my throat, but the emotion sat there, solid and unyielding. "Keith's nice, Mom," I managed. "We were partnered up at zip-lining, and you're right, he's different from the others. I didn't expect to like him, but I actually do."

Relief softened her expression. "Really?"

"Yeah."

She hesitated, then said, "El, I'm sorry I wasn't more sensitive to what you were going through with Matty being here. You put up such a good front, but I should've known it was just that . . . a front. I let myself believe that meant you were okay."

"I've been anything but okay," I said. "But I didn't know how to ask for help. I just . . . I wanted you to see me without me having to say it."

Her voice cracked. "I didn't. And I'm sorry. But I see you now. I do."

I reached across the table, and she met me halfway, her fingers curling tightly around mine before she pulled me into a hug that felt like both an apology and a promise.

Izzy and Shira ambled into sight up the beach, and I waved them over, cuing it was safe to return. Putting the tiles back into the set's hard case, I gave Izzy a quick look implying that Mom and I were okay, and she slid on her flip-flops that were still kicked under the table.

"We should start heading back so we have time to freshen up before the wedding," Izzy said as she slung the mah-jongg bag over her shoulder.

"Izzy's right, Mom. You're the bride. And you're marrying a great guy. You deserve to feel amazing tonight."

Mom met my gaze and linked her arm with mine as we started walking back toward the hotel, the salty air wrapping around us like the promise of a new beginning.

Chapter Thirty-Three

The dock, all decorated for the wedding, looked enchanted with votive candles lining the sides, their glow creating ribbons of light across the wooden planks. At the end stood a canopy of white gauze, draped with tropical flowers that cascaded to the sand below. The sunset was the most perfect backdrop of lavender and turquoise brushstrokes sweeping across the sky.

Guests had kicked off their heels and loafers by the sign at the edge of the beach that read LEAVE YOUR WORRIES, AND YOUR SHOES, HERE, AND STEP INTO THE MOMENT. Rows of white foldout chairs were filling quickly, the soft murmur of excitement blending with the gentle crash of waves.

Izzy and I wore similar-style periwinkle dresses that matched the sky almost perfectly. My hair was pulled back just enough in a delicate braid to keep stray strands from falling into my face. Mom's dress was a simple yet stunning white silk slip gown. Her hair was loose and tousled, the ocean's humidity coaxing it into the kind of perfect beachy waves people pay hundreds to re-create in salons.

I glanced toward Keith, already waiting on the dock for his bride. His hands were folded in front of him, and he looked sharp in a crisp white linen suit, his tie the same soft lavender as our dresses, and a smile that practically lit up the whole beach. At the cue of the officiant, the Caribbean band off to the side started playing a soulful rendition of Bob Marley's "Is This Love."

The wedding planner handed Izzy a fresh bouquet of elegant gardenias, peach-colored roses, and leafy fresh ferns, and together she and Keith's oldest son began their procession down the sandy, candle-lined aisle to the canopy.

When they were about halfway, I turned to Mom, gently lowered her veil, and tucked a defiant tendril back behind her ear.

"You know," she whispered, "at every other one of my weddings, I've been nervous, but somehow, I'm not nervous at all."

"I'm glad," I said, giving one final adjustment to her dress strap.

"Okay, Elliot, you ready?" the planner asked, handing me my bouquet.

"It's not her first rodeo," Mom teased. "She knows exactly what she's doing."

I turned to her. "You look beautiful, Mom. See you on the other side?"

She nodded. "See you on the other side."

I took a deep breath and started to make my way through the center of the crowd. Even though most of these same guests had been to at least one of Mom's many weddings, there didn't seem to be a dry eye among them. Like they knew too, this time was different.

I glanced to my left. Dad was sitting on the end, positively beaming at me, his iPhone at the ready, and snapping pictures as I advanced toward the dock. He gave me a small, proud wave as I passed.

The band switched songs, now playing a soulful steel-drum version of "Somewhere Over the Rainbow," the gentle melody floating in the air. On my right, Matty, in a light-pink button-down and khaki pants, was watching me, the way you watch someone you've known your whole life.

Instinctively, I looked for Leo in the first few rows, where I imagined he'd be sitting, and a fresh pang of sadness speared through me when I realized he wasn't there.

The sun dipped low, casting a shimmery hue across the water as Sonja stepped onto the walkway, barefoot and radiant. She looked younger than

I'd seen her in years, not because of the makeup or the perfect golden hour lighting, but because she was lit from within. Glowing. Her smile was unguarded, unburdened, and utterly unflappable.

She walked toward Keith, who waited with tears in his eyes and his heart written plainly on his face. And to my own surprise, I felt something unshackle in my chest. A deep, genuine swell of happiness, not for the idea of love or the pageantry of it, but for her. For this version of my mother, who had risked her heart yet again. Who had fought for joy. Who looked so free.

The ceremony was short and sweet, punctuated with personal vows that made the guests laugh and sniffle in turn. Keith promised to always stock the freezer with Mom's favorite mango Popsicles and never raise his voice at her in anger, and Sonja swore to pretend to be just as excited about the Red Sox as he was even though she was a native New Yorker and vowed to meet this new chapter with both hands open. When they kissed, the crowd erupted in applause, a celebratory whoop carrying across the water.

The Caribbean band kicked in with a joyous calypso, and as the newlyweds made their way, hand in hand, down the dock toward the reception, conch shells blew, flower petals rained, and I found myself clapping along with everyone else, genuinely, gratefully, with something that felt suspiciously close to hope.

The reception was like something out of a wedding magazine spread: effortless, twilight lit, and impossibly romantic. Strings of light bulbs crisscrossed between palms, slowly coming to life as the sky deepened to indigo.

Friends and family mingled, drinks in hand, linen clothes fluttering in the breeze. The air smelled of salt and roasted garlic, of citrus and grilled fish. A ceviche bar stood beside a carved wooden canoe filled with fresh fruit and coconuts, and farther down, guests gathered at a jerk chicken station, where flames licked the air and the spice made eyes water and mouths beg for more.

By the makeshift dance floor, couples kicked off their shoes and moved to the beat, the sand cool beneath their toes. It was celebration at its purest, easy and warm, the kind of evening you wished you could bottle and keep forever.

I found Matty by the bar, nursing something dark in a lowball glass, his tie loosened and his pastel button-down rolled to the elbows of his tanned forearms. I made my way over to where he was and nudged him with a gentle elbow. "Hey you."

He hesitated, clearly unsure if the greeting was meant for him, then gave a soft laugh. "Hey you, back. You look beautiful, El, and your mom seems . . . well, she seems really happy."

"Thanks," I said, signaling to the bartender for his attention with my empty glass. "I think she is."

"She deserves it. She's certainly had her fair share of frogs," he joked.

"Frogs would actually be high praise for most of them," I quipped.

He nodded. "True. But no matter how bad it got, she never stopped believing in love. That's always been Sonja's superpower."

"I never thought of it as a superpower before, but yeah, I guess it is. I think perhaps she found her prince, though." I glanced over to where Mom and Keith were locked in a slow dance.

The bartender set down my glass of wine as a charged quiet stretched between Matty and me. Finally, he cleared his throat and said, "You know, I didn't mean to ambush you by coming here . . . to Belize. But something inside me wanted to . . . no, needed to see you. It's been such a long time, and yet I still think about you every day. I can't tell you how often I wonder if I made the biggest mistake of my life."

"Listen, we don't have to—"

"No, we do. If not now, then we may never get the chance, and I have to say this. I came all the way to Belize to say this. Look, I know it's not an excuse, because what I did was unforgivable, but you have to understand, things between us weren't perfect. I should've faced it head-on and talked to you. I see that now. But I was twenty, reckless, and when the only woman I ever loved kept me at arm's length, I started believing it was my fault . . . something I was doing wrong or wasn't giving you. So I went looking for what I thought was missing with someone else. I fucked up, plain and simple. You never let me fully in, El. Never. There was always a part of you I couldn't reach, no matter how hard I tried." Tears pooled in his eyes. "And I tried. I swear to God, I tried."

My mind flashed back to a conversation Matty and I had about our plans for after our college graduation. We both wanted to return to New York, him to pursue a career in finance, and me, something in media. This was before the radio show had taken off, but even then, I knew most of the best opportunities would be there.

Matty used to pull up apartments on StreetEasy and imagine us living in one of them. He'd joke about what we'd be able to afford, the dog we didn't currently have but would adopt one day so that we could take her for long walks in Central Park, the corner coffee shop where they'd know our order, and the rooftop where we'd drink wine on Friday nights and feel like we'd made it.

It was a fun fantasy, yet I could never bring myself to indulge in it with him. I'd push it away, change the subject. Anything to avoid committing to any kind of a future with Matty. Not because I didn't love him, but because I did. I loved him so much it terrified me. I was terrified of losing him, of him disappointing me, of him leaving. Of all the things I'd seen and lived through that had shaped my fear. The closer we got to the end of school, the more I withdrew. I knew he'd likely propose before we graduated, and the thought filled me with mounting dread.

He swirled the brown liquid, the bright maraschino cherries spinning at the bottom of the glass. "I couldn't escape the feeling that you were already bracing for the ending. Like you always had one hand on the rip cord, just in case."

I blinked. Instinct and defensiveness told me to lash out at him, to deny it outright or say he was misremembering it all. But somewhere deep in my chest, a tiny, reluctant voice whispered, *He's not wrong.*

I *had* dismissed his conversations about anything serious. I *had* continuously dodged the subject of what we wanted for our future because love had always felt like something with an expiration date.

Like a light bulb flickering on in a room I'd been stumbling through in the dark, I finally saw more clearly than ever before. How I'd pulled away the closer we got. How I'd started retreating when things began to feel too real. Not that it gave him a free pass to betray me, but suddenly, his actions made sense like they never had before.

Watching the pooling tears now falling freely from Matty's eyes, something inside me shifted. I was ready to forgive him. It wasn't about excusing what he did or pretending the hurt wasn't real. Forgiving Matty meant finally admitting that we were *both* flawed, *both* scared, and *both* trying to protect ourselves in the only ways we knew how.

I breathed out the truth I'd been holding back. "You weren't wrong. I did have my hand on the rip cord. I was afraid. I think I've spent my whole life trying to avoid the fall."

Matty now looked like a weight had been lifted from his shoulders, his posture easing. "I'm sorry I wasn't there to catch you. I should have been. I didn't know how to show up for you then. But I know now." He paused, eyes steady. "El, I'm still in love with you."

My breath caught, but I didn't flinch. "Matty . . ."

His amber eyes met mine, full of longing and regret. "I'm not sure I ever stopped."

"You don't mean that. It's been over five years."

"What's five years compared to the rest of our lives?" he challenged.

I shook my head gently. "I'm not the girl you loved back then. And you're not the same either."

He reached for my hands. "I know. That's the point. We're not who we were, and that's exactly why we might have a chance now. No illusions, no pretending. Just the truth. I think we're finally standing in the same place. And I think you still love me too."

"Some part of me will always love you, Matty. But I'm not *in* love with you. Not anymore."

"Then I sincerely hope you find happiness with someone else. You deserve it."

My thoughts went straight to Leo and everything he'd forced me to confront about myself, about love, about trust. I didn't know what we were now, but I knew one thing: My heart had learned to beat differently.

I met Matty's eyes. "I have met someone . . . and he changed everything."

He swallowed hard, his Adam's apple bobbing. "I see," he said, his voice barely steady.

I reached out to take his hand and gave it a squeeze. "Watching my mom . . . and even my dad, learn how to be in the same room again after everything has been eye-opening. They've found peace. A way to more than coexist, but to actually return to the friendship they had before everything fell apart. I want that too. I want that for us."

I didn't see Hurricane Matty anymore. He wasn't the all-consuming storm that had torn through me and left only wreckage in his wake. He was my childhood friend—someone I shared a lifetime of memories with, someone I'd always keep a place for, even if that place had changed.

He must have felt the same. "You know," he said softly, "there's always going to be a space in my heart for you, even if it's not the shape I imagined. I'm just glad I get to be part of your world again."

"Me too," I whispered.

We sat in silence for a beat, holding hands, the breeze lifting the hem of my dress and the pulse of music beckoning us back to the celebration. Closure wasn't always loud or dramatic. It was sometimes just two people looking at each other and quietly choosing to forgive.

And with that small, seismic shift still settling in my chest, I saw the wedding planner give me a little wave, my cue to deliver my speech, and I pressed a gentle kiss to Matty's cheek before I rose to head toward the mic.

Chapter Thirty-Four

Standing to address the crowd, time slowed. Instead of reading from the speech I'd worked on, I folded the paper and held it in my sweaty hand. This time, I was going off script, feeling a bit more ready to speak from the heart.

"Hi again, everyone. As you know, I'm Elliot, Sonja's daughter, and I wanted to start by thanking you all for coming to celebrate the marriage of Mr. and Mrs. Banner. I wasn't totally sure what I wanted to say today after my *colorful* toast last night. I'd considered sharing a handful of quotes about love and maybe a few funny anecdotes." Glancing over at Mom, at Dad, and at Matty, their smiling and supportive faces, I breathed out, "But now, I've decided to go in a completely different direction.

"It's a bit hard to explain, but all I know is that this week, I think I've finally come to understand what real love looks like. It's not grand gestures or sunset walks on the beach. It's someone showing up when they don't have to. Holding your hand when you're at your worst. Calling you out when you're hiding. It's the quiet kind of love. Steady, present, and brave. I realized I've spent so much of my life afraid of all the ways love can hurt us, can scar us, can change us, that the thought of jumping in with both feet seemed like the craziest idea in the world. But I've learned through some very hard lessons that love, the right kind, doesn't ask you to be perfect. It just asks you to have the courage to open your heart and try.

"So today, I'm not just toasting my mom and her new husband. I'm toasting the woman who refused to stop believing in love, even when at times it seemed to break her. I'm toasting to her optimism, her bravery, and her willingness to leap, even without a net. Love is about having faith. Even when it's hard. Even when it hurts. Actually, especially then. She's taught me that letting people in—I mean *really* in—isn't weakness. It's actually the hardest, strongest thing a person can do."

I didn't realize I was crying until a falling tear hit my forearm. Wiping my cheek, I glanced at Mom and Keith and gave her a wink. She was beaming, her head rested on his shoulder, and he kissed her forehead almost to punctuate my point.

I raised my glass high and looked out into the crowd. All the faces lit with genuine happiness and excitement for the new couple made my heart swell, and an actual lump formed so solidly in my throat that I found the next words almost impossible to get out.

"So everyone please help me in celebrating Mr. and Mrs. Sonja and Keith Banner, to the couple who proves it's never too late for a new beginning. May the best parts still be yet to come."

As the final words of my toast settled over the crowd, applause broke out, and I caught a glimpse of Mom with tears in her eyes and a wide, beautiful smile on her face. Keith leaned over and kissed her gently as the band fired up a gentle ballad, the kind meant for slow-dancing under string lights and open skies. I stepped down from the small platform, exhaling as if I'd been holding my breath for weeks.

Then I heard a voice behind me. "May I have this dance?"

I turned my head. Dad stood there, hand extended, eyes steady but softer than I remembered them ever being. I hesitated, caught off guard by the gesture, but then I slipped my hand into his, and he led me onto the sand-smoothed dance floor. We swayed together to the music for a few moments, the beat of the steel drums wrapping around us like the tropical evening air. I wasn't used to this kind of closeness with him, this dance with the man who'd once left a silence so deep I'd mistaken it for indifference. But here he was, offering something I'd stopped expecting:

presence. I let my head fall lightly to his shoulder, not because we were suddenly fixed or because everything had been forgiven. But because for this one moment, we were both still here. Trying. And for now, that was enough.

The rest of the wedding reception passed in a dazzling haze of conga lines, carefree dancing to reggae-spun pop songs, and the clink of tropical drinks. I took silly family selfies with Keith, Shira, Allegra, and Cannon, watched as Mom and Dad led a rousing rendition of the YMCA, took one too many Banana Hammock shots with Marin, and Matty twirled me around the dance floor like we were seventeen again.

We kept the party going until the sun crept up over Ambergris Caye. The guests peeled off one by one, half dancing, half dragging themselves for a little shut-eye before checkout. I made it back to my own villa, feet throbbing, headache blooming . . . But my heart, though fuller than I ever remember it being, was still missing a pretty big piece.

Leo.

What we could be, what we almost were. And now that I'd glimpsed it, the thought of letting it go felt impossible. But it was time to leave Belize behind, and with it, the version of me who didn't believe she deserved a life full of love.

After grabbing the last of my bikinis drying out on the lanai, I adjusted the strap of my bag on my shoulder, took one last look at the empty villa. I wasn't leaving with souvenirs or shells or trinkets. I was leaving with something better.

Less weight, less fear, and just enough hope to carry me home.

Chapter Thirty-Five

The door creaked open with a familiar groan as I stepped into my apartment, suitcase wheels *thunk*ing softly against the hardwood and Pickles in her carrier in hand. Everything smelled faintly of old takeout and stale coffee, like it had been waiting patiently for me to come back and resume my regularly scheduled life.

But it didn't feel the same.

I dropped my bag, took two steps in, and froze. Something was off. Not messy or ransacked or changed exactly, but off in the way a dream starts to dissolve the second you wake up.

The picture frames on my bedside table were the first to catch my eye. The Polaroid of Marin and me at Coney Island was back in its old spot. The one of Leo, windswept and laughing, gone. I turned slowly toward my nightstand. Empty. The photo of the two of us under the Eiffel Tower, the one where he was kissing my cheek while I wore that ridiculous beret, vanished, as if it had never existed.

In its place was nothing but a thin layer of dust.

Scooping Pickles out of her carrier, I sat on the edge of my bed and raked her soft fur under my fingers as I stared at the bare tabletop and felt a hollowness expand inside my chest. Not panic, not grief. Just . . . silence. Like the echo of something beautiful that had already slipped through my fingers.

Maybe Leo really was never here.

Or maybe the harder truth was that he had been, and it had meant something. Something that changed me in ways I hadn't been ready for. I used to pride myself on not needing anyone. I was sharp, self-sufficient, and unshakable.

But now? Now there was a Leo-shaped ache I couldn't explain away, and I didn't know what to do with it other than try to get on with my day, let alone my life.

Setting Pickles back in her cage, I gave her some carrot sticks I found in my fridge drawer and started to unpack my suitcase, sorting my clothes into two piles: one for the wash, the other for the dry cleaners. I put away my toiletries, lining them up on the shelf like I always did. The fridge was nearly empty, so I made a quick list on my Notes app of what I'd need to grab later.

Then I pulled my laptop from my carry-on and set it on the kitchen table. I still hadn't made any real progress on the next episode of *Love Is a Four-Letter Word.* So between that and how I'd left things with Ravi before I flew to Belize, where he told me in no uncertain terms I needed to figure out what I actually wanted, I wasn't exactly looking forward to going into the studio later.

I inhaled sharply and set my fingers down on the keyboard.

C'mon, Elliot, a rant on the disasters of destination weddings, this is the type of hot take you can write in your sleep.

Only, the words weren't coming. Every time I tried to string together a sentence about the overpriced nonsense or the inevitable family drama that comes with that many days trapped in endless group texts and the forced fun of daily excursions, my thoughts kept drifting back to zip-lining with Keith and how he coached me through my fear when I nearly backed out. Then to Dad and me reeling in that monster mahi-mahi.

I thought about how Matty consoled me after the fight with Mom, no questions asked. Then the mah-jongg game on the beach, where Mom and I mended fences between shuffles. Most of all, I thought about the wonderful day I spent with Leo exploring Belize, just the two of us.

And I couldn't help but wonder if these kinds of destination weddings weren't actually just a messy, imperfect way to foster the sort of connection that only happens when you're away from real life for a few days. A kind of trauma bonding that brought people together despite themselves.

But that wasn't the brand of revelation my listeners expected, not from me. It wasn't a punchy take that 'love-cynic Elliot West' was known for. And so I reached down deep into the pit of misanthropy and did my best to pull up all the sarcasm and righteous indignation I could muster, spewing it onto the page like one long unfiltered exhalation.

I wasn't sure if it was muscle memory or just plain desperation, but eventually the words took shape well enough for me to email them off to Ravi and hope they passed for something close to acceptable.

Pushing open the studio door, I half expected to find Ravi hunched over the soundboard, clutching one of his usual snarky mugs. Instead, he held a glossy white one that read Thank You for Being Awesome in a sunshiny-yellow script.

"Hey, how was the wedding?" he asked brightly as I stepped inside, the unexpected warmth in his tone catching me off guard.

"Good. It was . . . surprisingly good."

"Glad to hear it!"

I dropped my bag by the door and gave him a confused look. "Rav, you okay?"

"Yeah, I'm great, why?"

"Um, maybe because you were pretty pissed off at me before I left for my trip."

"I was?"

"Very."

He shrugged. "I mean, sure, I'd love it if you were ever on time and if you occasionally answered your phone or checked your email, not to mention let me finish a sentence without interrupting. But those are just my usual Elliot gripes. I don't remember there being any full-on explosions before you left."

Now, I was genuinely confused. "What about the post–Valentine's Day show? The on-air *Mamma Mia! Immersive* inquisition? My appearance on *Good Day, Manhattan*?!"

"Oh, yes, that's right, *Good Day, Manhattan*."

There it was. I closed my eyes and prepared for another unleashing of his hellfire.

But instead he said, "Yeah, I guess you could've plugged *Love Is a Four-Letter Word* and the upcoming book a little bit harder. The execs would have loved to see a bigger jump in presale numbers, but other than that, you pretty much killed it."

I squinted, one eye open and waited for more. Wait, what? I killed it? I was pretty sure after my on-air admission about Leo that Ravi was ready to fillet me alive. Ever since Leo magically appeared in my life, work had been one long string of screwups. Ravi had every reason to be furious with me, but he wasn't? This didn't make any sense.

Until I remembered that when Leo disappeared, so did everything he'd shaken up in the past few weeks. He never surprised me with the *Mamma Mia!* experience on Valentine's Day. And because he never surprised me, I was never confronted on air about our date or the fact that I was some kind of lovesick hypocrite.

He never supported me, challenged me, or cherished me. Because that version of us never existed, I never unraveled in real time on *Good Day, Manhattan*.

None of it happened.

Apparently, the Sirius deal was still solid. The book contract firm. Ravi wasn't the least bit pissed at me. Everything was exactly as planned. Not meeting Leo in Paris had landed me right where I wanted to be, no loose ends.

And yet, somehow, it all felt . . . off.

Ravi took another sip from his mug. "Had a chance to skim your notes for today's show. Looking good. I went to my college roommate's wedding at a god-awful all-inclusive resort in Cancun last year, and let's just say, I'm still recovering from the sunburn, the secondhand embarrassment, and the crippling wallop to my credit card. Your take is spot-on."

"Oh, good. Glad you liked it."

"A lot. Anyway, I left some copy on your desk if you want to do a quick read-through. New advertiser, HelloFresh. See you in the studio."

I wandered into my office, picked up the sheet from my desk, and read it aloud:

You'll get fresh ingredients and easy-to-follow recipes delivered right to your door. No awkward grocery store run-ins with your ex. No "dinner for two" pity freezer meals. Just delicious, stress-free cooking designed for people who've realized they're the best company they'll ever have. So go ahead and light a candle and toast to the fact that you don't have to share your fries. Because the only thing more satisfying than a great meal . . . is getting to eat it alone.

I shook my head and set down the paper. Is this really who I was? Someone who peddled the idea that solitude was the prize? That being alone was the ultimate flex? I knew that marriage and the traditional idea of "happily ever after" didn't necessarily define happiness, but did I really believe that shutting everyone out was the answer either?

Ravi poked his head into my office door. "Ready?"

I nodded, printed the script for today's show, grabbed the advertiser packet from my desk, and followed him down the hallway to the studio. The ON AIR sign glowed red, casting a faint halo in the corner of the booth. I slid into my usual seat, the one with the scuffed armrest and a lingering trace of coffee soaked into the padding. Wrapping my fingers around the microphone, I drew in a breath that didn't quite reach the bottom of my lungs.

Ravi settled into the sound booth, leaned over to the speaker, and gave his usual spiel. "Okay, El, system's all checked. Remember, watch your time with the callers during the first segment. We've got a hard break at ten past for a sponsor mention and commercial. Okay, live in three . . . two . . . one." He held up three fingers before tapping the mic and giving me a quick nod before the light flipped to green.

I glanced down at my notes and cleared my throat. "*Heeeelloooo*, my loyal listeners, I'm back from Belize. Slightly sunburned, emotionally dehydrated, and ready to dish! For those of you who missed the memo, I've just returned from my mother's destination wedding. Yes, the woman who once grounded me for sneaking off to a Dave Matthews concert just pledged eternal love to her fourth—yes, *fourth*—husband under a canopy made entirely of palm fronds and delusion. Anyway, we've got a jam-packed show today. Hot takes, cold truths, and that familiar and ever-lingering taste of regret. Let's dive on in."

Ravi hit play on the show's intro music, then pointed to me when it was time to take over again.

"If you hadn't already guessed, today's hot topic: destination weddings. Pinterest fantasy . . . or hostage situation? I definitely have my perspective. What's yours?"

I looked down at the long bulleted list of destination wedding transgressions in my notes, trying to decide where to start.

- The lie of "casual beach" formal
- The $27 poolside mimosa
- Being emotionally waterboarded by steel-drum covers of Ed Sheeran songs
- Family photos staged to look perfect when the people in them were anything but

All of them were a good place to jump in, but the one about family seemed like it had the most legs. I adjusted my headphones and leaned into the microphone. "Okay, let's get this party started with a conversation about the awkwardness of putting all your family members on an island with literally no escape. I've mentioned this before, but my dad left me and my mom when I was young. Now imagine he and his whole *new* family—wife, kids, the works—showing up at the wedding of the woman he left, a.k.a.

my mom. Two people who haven't exchanged so much as a text in over two decades, unless it was about me, now sitting side by side at the pool, sipping mai tais like old friends. And if that wasn't enough drama, guess who else shows up? My ex. Yes, *that* ex. So there I was, surrounded by my dad's new family, my mom's new husband, and the boyfriend ghost of my past, trying to act like I was totally fine when really it was a personality endurance test. I was the piñata, smiling for photos, taking hits, and quietly wondering if I could book a one-way flight home without anyone noticing. And no plot twist here: I could not."

Ravi gave me two thumbs-up, like I'd just delivered a sermon he'd been waiting his whole life to hear, but my mind . . . my mind drifted.

Back to the wedding weekend.

Back to the thoughts that had made this segment almost impossible to write without lying to myself. Because the messiness, the awkward silences, the forced proximity, the accidental reveals, the truths I didn't ask for, turned out to be exactly what I needed.

I'd seen it with my parents, who somehow managed to share space without blame or broken glass. I'd seen it in my mom, choosing love again without apology. I'd even seen it in myself, finally confronting what happened with Matty, and my part in it all.

The trip didn't break me. It exposed me for the fraud that I was. The girl who could analyze love to death and dismiss it without ever really understanding it. The one who could keep control, keep score, and keep her distance without ever admitting she was actually lonely.

"Alright, loyal listeners," I began, the sarcasm easy, automatic. "What do you get when you mix one destination wedding, an ex, and a lifetime of unresolved family tension? Apparently . . . a breakdown in paradise. I went to the wedding with one singular goal in mind: survival. To stay out of the way, keep it superficial, and feel absolutely nothing. What I didn't expect . . . what I didn't expect . . . was to feel everything."

I exhaled and met Ravi's eyes, which were wide, confused, and very much saying, *What the hell are you doing? This isn't in the script.*

I gave him a tiny shrug and kept going.

"Turns out, emotions don't really care about itineraries. They don't care if you're ready or not. Because here's the thing, when you go into something like family drama, or really any relationship, trying your best to stay numb, life tends to hand you a defibrillator to shock you back to life."

I readjusted in my chair, staring up at the ceiling as if the right words might be written there. "But somewhere between the ceviche and the mayhem, the chocolate tours and the arguments that cracked me open, I realized that maybe . . . I'm not as invincible as I thought. Maybe protecting myself all these years from love, from disappointment, from vulnerability, maybe that's what's been keeping me stuck. I realized I've been moving through life with blinders on, missing not just the good stuff, but maybe even the best stuff."

A silence settled in the booth, heavy and alive, like the kind that only happens when you're about to say something that really matters.

"So, yeah. I felt everything. Old heartbreaks, new hope, nostalgia, anger, awe, regret, longing—you name it, I went through it like a twelve-course tasting menu. And I came back not with answers, but with this one annoying little truth I can't seem to ignore anymore."

I looked straight at the mic, heart hammering. "Maybe love isn't a scam. Maybe it's just a messy, flawed thing shared by messy, flawed people fighting like hell to weather the storms and still dance in the downpour. Maybe it's just a terrifying, unpredictable, wildly inconvenient leap of faith. And maybe I'm finally ready to stop sitting it out."

The last words snagged in my throat, thick with the weight of everything I might've missed by seeing love and life as all or nothing. I'd been clinging to a world drawn in black and white, and now this epiphany happening in real time on air caused a sudden ache to burrow inside my chest, knowing how much I'd lost by shutting love out. But not anymore.

All the years I'd spent building walls had only kept me from the things I needed most, and I was done with pretending not to care. It was too tiresome, too draining, and no longer true.

"So if you're out there listening, sitting in your own fortress of doubt, maybe today's the day you stop building walls and open the damn door. I did. Even if I'd been kicking and screaming, I did it. And the view? It's different. Brighter. Less lonely. More alive. I won't pretend it's easy. But now I know it's worth it. And maybe that's the real lesson. That love *is* a four-letter word. And that word . . . is hope."

Tears I hadn't expected wet the corners of my eyes, and I brushed them away with my knuckle before they could fall. Ravi, on the other hand, looked horror-struck, jaw clenched, lips tight, and fiercely pacing in the small studio space. From the look on his face, I knew I'd very possibly just blown up the show, and probably my whole life along with it.

Chapter Thirty-Six

After receiving a late-night email telling me the Sirius execs wanted to see me first thing in the morning, I didn't sleep a wink. I knew there'd be backlash after my epic on-air one-eighty, but I just didn't realize it would come so soon. The stakes were higher than I'd ever imagined. This deal wasn't just a contract, it could be a turning point. The money alone would be huge, a complete game changer, the kind that reroutes your entire future.

But I knew if I really wanted to *change* my life, I couldn't keep walking the same path. Not after everything I'd learned.

The elevator dinged open on the thirty-sixth floor. I stepped out and faced the glass doors of their sleek office space, the word Sirius etched boldly across the surface.

Expelling a heavy breath, I made my way into the hallway, my boots squeaking louder with every step. The receptionist gave me a tight smile as she continued chatting away on a phone call and nodded me toward the open door to the conference room.

I craned my neck inside, spotting three people already seated at the table: Greg, head of programming; Elise, head of advertising; and Lauren, Sirius's general counsel.

Great. The big guns.

Walking in, I tried to smile to hide my panic, a vicious thunderstorm hammering in my chest and swirling down into my gut. I pulled out the chair they gestured to across from them, but before sitting down, I cleared my throat.

Opening my mouth, I had hoped to offer the team a warm hello, instead I instinctually launched into a mounted defense. "Look, before you say anything, I know. I went off script. Way off. It was messy, it was emotional, and yeah, completely off brand. But I couldn't fake it anymore. I couldn't keep pretending to be this detached version of myself just because it makes good radio. When I think about the world right now, all the fear, the division, the loneliness, I realize it doesn't need any more cynicism. It needs something to believe in. And I didn't realize how much I needed that too. And if it means the deal's off the table . . . then I'll have to live with that. But I'd rather lose it all than keep selling something I don't believe in anymore."

Silence.

Elise leaned back in her chair, a slight smirk playing at her lips. "Anything else?"

I nodded. "Well, yeah. In fact, now that you mention it. Ravi had no idea that I was going to go rogue like that. I'd given him different show notes that he'd green-lit. Please don't take out any of my missteps, if you'd call them that, on him. He's really good at his job."

Greg folded his hands on the table. "Is that all?"

I nodded. "Yeah. That's it."

"Well, I think everyone in this room can agree that your show yesterday was quite a departure," Greg said.

Elise was nodding, her expression tight. "Not exactly what our partners are paying top dollar to be associated with."

The reality of the situation was hitting me. As much as I'd tried to prepare myself for the very real possibility that they might pull out of this life-changing deal, actually sitting there and watching it unfold was something else entirely.

"No, of course, I completely understand."

Elise's disapproval gave way to a smile. "That's what made the spike in numbers so unexpected."

My head snapped up. "Wait? What?"

"Why don't you take a look at this for a minute." Greg unfolded the cover of his tablet, tapped the screen to life, and spun it around so it faced me.

I leaned over the table studying the screen and blinked at him. "Um . . . I'm sorry, but what is this?"

"These are the numbers for yesterday's show."

The screen showed a graph with a very steep, very promising upward arrow.

"Highest ratings you've had in two years," Greg explained. "Social media threads were on fire. The show was trending within fifteen minutes of you going off script. The fan-mail inbox is apparently overflowing. People are calling it the most powerful episode in the show's history."

"You tapped into something. Something raw. And you're right. Given the current climate of the world right now, people are tired of cynicism. They want to feel something. They want permission to believe again. And somehow, you, our queen of detachment and disillusionment, gave them that," Elisa said, a look of astonishment crossing her face as if she couldn't quite believe it either.

I stared at them, and it took me a few seconds to collect enough saliva in my mouth to speak. "So wait . . . you *aren't* nixing the deal?"

"Hell no!" Greg said, now beaming. "We want *more* of that. Not the whole show, obviously. We still need the bite and the fire. But now, we know you've got layers. And we want the audience to see them too."

I felt my knees wobble a little as I finally plopped into the nearest chair.

Elise crossed her arms and leaned forward. "We always knew you were good, Elliot. But now? You may have tapped into what people are *really* hungry for."

My heart thudded loudly in my chest, the rush of it making my face flush with heat. For the first time in a long time, I wasn't guarded and closed off. And instead of getting punished for it, I was being . . . celebrated.

Lauren slipped a packet from her leather folder and slid it across the table. Hands trembling, I lifted the pages and scanned the first one. They were giving me everything I'd asked for. A three-year contract stacked with more zeroes than I'd ever seen in my life. The show would have national syndication, a prime-time placement, and best of all, I retained full creative control over *Love Is a Four-Letter Word.*

For a second, the words blurred. I blinked hard, letting it all hit me. This was everything I'd worked for. This wasn't just a deal. It was validation. I'd made something that mattered. That reached people. And now, I was being trusted to keep going, on my terms.

"A copy's already been sent to your agent," Lauren said, smiling warmly, "but we wanted to make the offer in person."

"I'm speechless, which doesn't happen to me often," I joked.

"Let's hope not," Greg said with a smile.

We rose from the table and shook hands, the kind of firm, congratulatory grip reserved for people who'd just sealed something big.

After thanking them for the incredible news, I walked out of the room in a daze, the door clicking shut behind me. The receptionist gave a polite wave, still mid-call, but I was too stunned to do much more than blink back. My heels clicked down the hallway toward the elevator, and my hand reached instinctively for my phone. I wanted to call Leo. To tell him.

But he wasn't in my life anymore.

Still, I didn't put the phone away. Instead, I opened a new group text and typed in a list of names—Ravi, Mom, Dad, Shira, Keith, Allegra, Cannon, Marin, Jada, Stella, Izzy, and even Matty. People who had been part of the journey, in one way or another.

I did it.

Love Is a Four-Letter Word was picked up by Sirius.

Three-year deal.

Full syndication.
Next stop: everywhere!

Then I hit send.

◆ ◆ ◆

Marin was waiting at her apartment door with daisies, champagne, and a smile so wide I could practically see her molars. Before I had a chance to speak, she threw her arms around me and squealed.

"Oh my God, El, you did it! You're going to be like, actually famous. Like *famous* famous! Promise you won't forget about me when you're rubbing elbows with Jimmy Fallon and the rest of the late-night hosts and celebrity guests."

"Are you kidding? I would never forget you! I may need a plus-one to all the fabulous events I'll get invited to, so get your party pumps ready."

"*Ooh*, I haven't needed my party pumps in like a decade. Now I'll finally have an excuse to take them, and me, out of retirement," she said as she led the way inside. "Jada texted that she's running a few minutes late, but Stella should be here any second."

Marin already had the mah-jongg table set up, the tiles all face down, ready to be stacked. I set my bag on the floor next to my usual seat when Stella burst in the front door, arms full of two boxes of Baked by Melissa mini cupcakes and a bottle of champagne. "*Ahhh!* Elliot! That show. I was walking to Pilates, earbuds in, and then your whole on-air love-and-hope confession hit. Suddenly, I'm tearing up in the middle of Madison Avenue. Oh, and the contract! Sweet Jesus, tell us everything!" She tossed the goodies on the counter and practically plowed me down with an enthusiastic hug.

Her excitement reignited my own, and I still couldn't believe it was real. It was the sort of thing I dreamed about in college while I ate cold, day-old pizza and wondered if my Communications degree would ever be worth anything. And now? Now it was real. Tangible. The DocuSigned PDF sitting in my inbox like a glittering, too-good-to-be-true plot twist.

"Let's at least wait for Jada so she doesn't have to repeat the story a zillion times," Marin suggested as she popped the bottle of cold champagne she had in the fridge and replaced it with the one Stella brought to chill.

And as if on cue, Jada flung open the door and squealed as she shuffled in with a handful of treats and chucked them on the counter with the others. She flung her arms around me, jumping up and down until Marin and Stella joined in, and the four of us, entangled in a group hug, bounced like idiots in excitement.

"Okay, so *now*, tell us everything!" Stella repeated, grabbing the flutes Marin had just poured and handing them out. "But most importantly, what's the going rate for baring your soul live on air these days? Please tell me it starts with six figures!"

I scrunched up my face and slowly held up seven fingers which caused them to scream like we were teenagers at a boy band concert.

"I don't think I'll be retiring to the South of France anytime soon, but it's enough to at least cover the therapy and wardrobe change I'll need for leveling up," I joked.

We made our way to the table and took our usual places and began building our walls, two rows of nineteen, carefully arranged.

"Cathartic *and* capitalistic?! Girl, you are livin' the dream!" Jada joked as she arranged the tiles on her rack.

"Don't get me wrong, the money is . . . well, it's incredible, but more than that, they liked the show. The numbers and ratings were the highest ever. Can you imagine? People actually enjoyed my unraveling!"

"The unraveling *was* the show," Marin said, raising her glass. "That's why people listened. You stopped performing and were just authentically *you*."

"I didn't even mean to be. It all just kind of spilled out," I admitted, eyes misting despite myself. "I was just . . . tired. Of pretending. Of acting like I had it all figured out. Of building my whole brand around this version of myself who was so guarded."

I took a sip of champagne and settled into the familiar hum of clinking tiles and the warmth of the friends who had stitched themselves around my life in spite of my former walls.

We started the Charleston, passing unwanted tiles back and forth until we each settled into our individual hands. Marin made the first move, quickly discarding a North tile, which Stella quickly snatched up, revealing her pung before discarding a Five Dot.

I guessed Stella was going for a Wind hand. No surprise there. She always played it safe, building her line steadily instead of chasing flashy combos.

The game went on like that for a while, each of us picking up and throwing out in turn. Me, more focused on trying to decipher their hands based on what they put down rather than on my own strategy.

But then I remembered what Mom said to me that day on the beach about why I rarely won. I was always playing defense, too guarded, too afraid to take risks because I was so busy worrying about how other people's moves might affect my own.

I wasn't putting together my own hand. I was just reacting, protecting myself from every possible threat. I glanced down at my rack, a jigsaw of combinations and possibilities. But if I was going to win, if I was even going to try, I had to pick one. Pick one and, despite what might come my way, try to build on it, make the best of what I got, and see what happened.

The game went on, each of us snatching the suits and pieces we needed, with Stella hoarding the Winds, Jada seizing a Joker, and Marin taking forever whenever it was her turn, weighing each decision like her life depended on it.

And suddenly I could see it, move by move, my hand coming together, until all I needed was one last tile to win.

Then Stella threw out a Two Crack, the singular tile I needed to finish my pair and declare victory.

"Mah-jongg!" I cried, seizing the last piece of my puzzle.

Marin leaned over to check the hand against the card. "Yup"—she nodded—"you got it."

"El, your first win, huh? Nice!" Stella smiled and clapped me on the shoulder. "You should go play the lotto or something. Today is most definitely your lucky day."

I used to think staying a step ahead meant staying safe. Reading the room, anticipating moves, protecting myself—that was how I got through it all unscathed. But in mah-jongg, like in life, playing defensively hadn't just held me back from seeing my hand, it kept me from truly playing at all.

And I knew now it wasn't about luck or skill. It wasn't about having the perfect tiles or making the smartest moves. It was about being brave enough to commit fully, without holding back.

Like Leo had with me.

Love doesn't survive in halves. Eventually, it needs a whole heart.

I floated home from Marin's high on sugar, laughter, and the heady buzz of my first mah-jongg victory. The evening air was crisp in that early-spring-in-New-York way, and for the first time in what felt like forever, I wasn't bracing against it. My skin hummed with something close to joy. Something earned.

The new show, the contract, the freedom to be *me* on air—it should've been enough. And it *was*, mostly. I was standing taller, breathing deeper, and actually letting people in without flinching. I had rewritten the narrative I used to cling to like a childhood blanket. But as I pushed my apartment door open, Leo's absence hit me. It wasn't a sharp ache or some gaping hole in my heart, more like the absence of a song I hadn't realized I'd been humming along to until it stopped playing.

I dropped my keys, kicked off my shoes, and flopped onto the couch, pulling a throw over me. My fingers acted on their own, opening Instagram before my brain could stop them. I tapped onto Leo's profile, still unfiltered and perfectly *him*. I flicked through a few of his pictures from Morocco and other countries he'd visited until I reached the posts from our summer weeks together in Greece. A candid shot of him laughing, shirt half buttoned, sun glinting off his sunglasses. I remembered that moment. I'd taken the photo. He'd just made a terrible joke about how emotionally complex baklava was, given all its layers, and I'd rolled my eyes so hard I nearly gave myself a headache. Picture after picture of us on crystalline-blue-water beaches, tipsy on ouzo and the delirium of our chemistry together.

I scrolled. Our cappuccino-foam mustaches. One with our snorkeling masks on. One of a heart he'd drawn in the sand with our initials in the middle. My vision blurred with mist and memory, and I swallowed hard past the tightness in my throat. Blinking away the tears, I realized I'd fought so hard to be whole without him, and now I knew I *was*.

But standing here, confident and self-assured in my own strength, I also realized I missed the hell out of him. Not to fix me. Not to complete me. But just because I very much wanted him in my life.

I stared at my phone for a long minute, Stella's words from earlier echoing back to me: *You should go play the lotto or something. Today is most definitely your lucky day.*

Then, without giving myself the chance to back out, I found his number, tapped the call button, and held the phone to my ear.

It rang once.

Twice. My heart was beating fast, my stomach full of butterflies.

And then—

"Hello?"

His voice was comforting, like a perfect cup of tea. Warm and familiar.

I swallowed hard, then smiled.

"Leo? Hi," I said. "It's me."

Chapter Thirty-Seven

About six months later, that autumn, a bookstore in Brooklyn known for its author events and signings was set to host me for a reading of *Love Is Dead, Let's Have Brunch*, now newly retitled *Love's Not Dead, It's Just Brunching*. I would be lying if I said I wasn't a little nervous. I'd invited everyone: Mom and Dad, Keith, Shira, Allegra and Cannon, Izzy, Matty, and of course, Marin, Stella, and Jada. And every single one of them came, ready to celebrate my accomplishments and support me like family should.

The room buzzed with that cozy pre-event electricity, bookish types claiming seats, wine being poured in plastic cups, the smell of old parchment, and the hum of excitement all wrapping around me like an embrace. I stood near the podium, trying to remember how to breathe normally.

Mom and Dad walked toward me side by side, like it was the most natural thing in the world. Keith followed behind, chatting with Shira and Allegra. And for a moment I just stood there, taking it all in, this version of life where people were genuinely there for me. Where everyone set aside their hurt, their history, and whatever might've kept them apart to simply show up.

"Are you ready for this?" Mom asked, pulling me into a quick hug. "It's a full house. You've got real fans, El."

"I'm so proud of you," Dad added, placing a hand on my shoulder. He was beaming. "Even if I don't totally understand the brunch part."

I let out a laugh and shook my head. "It's meant to be funny, cheeky, Dad."

He winked. "Well, you're the writer. What do I know?"

The stage was set with an embarrassingly large photo of me, boldly emblazoned with my name. Below it, the tagline read HOST OF THE HIT SIRIUSXM RADIO SHOW LOVE IS A FOUR-LETTER WORD. It felt surreal and incredible, taking in all the reminders of how far I'd come to get here.

Once the Sirius deal was inked, I'd finally faced the mountain of editorial notes I'd mostly skimmed over (a.k.a. run from) in Belize. Predictably enough, the feedback echoed the same refrain: more balance, dial back the bitterness.

The notes and red lines were clear. It was one thing to be opinionated, but apparently, I was coming across like a grumpy sitcom character. The tone? "Too heavy-handed." The message? "Too dark." What they were looking for was more nuanced optimism to cut through the cynicism. Something for today's already overwhelmed and exhausted audience. Something a bit brighter than I'd originally envisioned.

It was time for a book makeover, a brutal one at that. So I locked myself in my apartment, tore the chapters down to the studs, and rebuilt it one hopeful sentence at a time, made easier by the fact I had finally taken the step to see a therapist, to address the wounds I'd long ignored, and because Leo was firmly back in my life.

He'd been more than a little surprised to hear from me when I'd called him after Belize. I'd expected him to still be angry after I stood him up in Paris all those months ago, but instead, he expressed how often he'd wanted to call, in all those months, how many times I'd crossed his mind. It surprised me how quickly we slipped back into an easy rhythm. Our time apart hadn't changed the way we fit together—it had only made me realize how much I'd missed it.

How much I missed *him*.

Since inviting him back into my life, we talked nearly every day despite his nonstop travel and my chaotic schedule. No matter the hour, we carved out quick moments to connect. The earliest hours of dawn. The wee hours of night. Nothing was off-limits, and the need to hear his voice felt like a magnetic pull drawing us together from opposite sides of the globe, but as strong as they'd ever been.

At first, pretending those weeks the spell had given us never happened felt like some kind of lie. That gray period that didn't exist for him. And since he didn't have those memories, I had to remind myself to fill in the gaps, to hold the space for what had been lost. But eventually, we found our footing again, settling back onto fertile ground ready to be planted with new memories and fresh beginnings. Weeks passed, pages turned, and life began to feel whole again. Like any good story, healing demanded both time and the courage to share it.

Now, standing in the cozy Brooklyn bookstore filled with the scent of cedar and leather-bound classics, I faced a packed room. Clutching a marked-up copy of my book, I inhaled, gathering my courage, and leaned in to the mic. "Hi, everyone, I'm Elliot West. Thank you so much for coming out to see me tonight." I cleared my throat and shifted the pages in my hands. "If you've been to any of my past readings or listened to my show, you've probably heard me talk about my Ten Commandments of Love and Dating—rules that, let's just say, came from a place of serious self-protection. And honestly, I don't regret them. That version of me needed those guardrails. But the truth I've come to realize is that while love in whatever form—romantic, familial, or otherwise—isn't any guarantee of happiness . . . neither is pretending you don't need it."

I opened to where I wanted to start and smiled. "So allow me to introduce: Elliot West's Ten (Revised, Slightly Wiser, and a Bit Less Jaded) Love Commandments. Number One: *Thou shalt not abandon thyself in the pursuit of someone else.* Love should expand you, not erase you. Number Two: *Thou may put thyself first—but leave space beside you.* Independence isn't isolation. Let someone sit close to your fire and relish in its warmth, not extinguish it. Number Three: *Thou shalt remember: Vulnerability is not weakness.* Let them see your heart. If they flinch, they're not your person. Number Four: *Thou shalt not confuse peace with boredom.* Healthy love can be electric and steady. Choose the kind that lets you exhale."

Marin was nodding along, while Izzy and Shira raised their plastic cups of punch in a gesture of cheers. I continued, "Number Five: *Thou shalt honor red flags—and also green ones.* Look for the good, but don't ignore what your gut says isn't right. Number Six: *Thou shalt not ghost thy own needs.* Speak up. Be clear. Don't shrink to make love fit where it doesn't."

Catching Matty's eye, it struck me that he wasn't here to reclaim something we'd lost, like he perhaps had been in Belize. Instead, he was here because he believed in me and wanted me to win, even if he wasn't the one standing beside me anymore.

And that, I realized, was its own kind of love.

I went on, "Number Seven: *Thou shalt stay open-minded and open-hearted, even when scared.* Armor keeps pain out, but also joy. Love is a risk. Wear sunscreen, not chain mail." Finding Mom in the crowd hand in hand with Keith, her face brimming with both contentment and pride, I gave her a little wink. "Number Eight: *Thou shalt give second chances sparingly—and never to the same person twice.* Growth is welcome. Repetition is not. Number Nine: *Thou shalt know the difference between butterflies and warning signs.* One makes you feel alive. The other makes you lose sleep. Learn the difference."

As the crowd murmured in response, warm and receptive, I heard the faint chime of the bell above the bookstore door. The sound was soft, but it cut through the noise like a secret only I could hear. Framed in the doorway, a little windblown, a little late, but still the most grounding presence in the room.

Leo.

Leo.

I wasn't sure how he knew or how he'd gotten here, yet this time I knew it wasn't a spell, but an altogether different kind of magic instead.

A wide smile broke out on my face, and I was hardly able to contain it. "And lastly, Number Ten: *Thou shalt believe in love. Not the perfect version, but the one who puts in effort to make it work.* The kind where two flawed people show up, try hard, laugh often, and hold hands anyway."

His attention was locked on me, and it was almost like everyone else in the room completely disappeared. I felt the words rise up in my throat, the conclusion to my talk already crafting itself.

He came. Despite the long flights and his packed schedule, despite the distance and every reason not to, he came. Just to be here. Just to see me. And it wasn't flowers or grand gestures or even a perfect timing kind of thing.

It was effort. It was intention. It was proof that when he said he cared, he *meant* it. And that, more than anything, told me I hadn't been wrong to believe in what we'd rekindled.

"Because sometimes," I said, glancing back to the crowd with tears in my eyes, "the best kind of love isn't the one you plan for—it's the one that finds you anyway."

Applause broke out and I barely registered it. I was already stepping down from the small stage, weaving through the crowd, my heart thudding like a drum as I closed the distance between us.

Leo smiled, just a fraction, as I reached him. "You were amazing. I'm sorry I'm late," he said softly, voice rough at the edges.

I didn't answer. I just threw my arms around his neck and kissed him. The girl who once ran from love now ran toward it. And just like that, I let myself write a different ending to my own story. One that was imperfect. Unsure. Messy.

Because this time, the ending was just the beginning.

Epilogue

The cold bit at my cheeks as we strolled through the glowing streets of Paris, our breaths visible in soft clouds that curled into the winter night. Tiny white Christmas lights draped the bare trees along the Seine, blinking like stars as if the city itself was trying to outdo the sky. My hand was tucked into Leo's coat pocket, fingers laced with his, and every few steps, he'd lean down to kiss the top of my head like he couldn't help himself.

With New Year's Eve only a few days away, the city, though chilly, was still aglow in festive holiday charm, which just added to the whimsical vibe emanating off every café and street corner.

We'd spent the last few hours wandering aimlessly, our only agenda being crepes and champagne. Mine had been dusted with powdered sugar, the citrus tang of lemon sharp against my tongue. Leo's had Nutella and strawberries and was, naturally, better than mine, though he insisted it was only because I kept stealing bites.

We passed accordion players and laughing children, lovers pressed against stone walls beneath hazy lamplights. It was all so achingly, unbearably romantic that if it hadn't been real, I would've rolled my eyes at the pure cliché of it all.

But it was real.

We were real.

And though I never found any clear explanation for what had happened with the tarot card reader or why the magic had chosen me, all I knew was that I was grateful it had. That window gave me a glimpse into a life I didn't know I was missing out on and a chance to finally open myself up to a whole new world of possibilities.

Leo and I reached Trocadéro, the plaza directly across the Seine, just as the Eiffel Tower lit up for the nine o'clock sparkle, its diamond-like shimmer reflecting in the river below. I stood there, completely breathless, not from the cold but from the ache in my chest, this fierce, deep, wildly tender thing that had taken root ever since Leo reappeared in my life.

He turned to me, his face lit by the golden strobe of a city in celebration. "You know," he said, brushing a stray hair from my face, "this is where I imagined we'd be when we were supposed to meet last year."

I swallowed hard. "I know. I think about who I was back then. The me who never showed up."

"All that matters is that you're here now," he said gently.

"Yes, I am *finally* here."

And I was there. All of me. Every last piece he'd waited for. Every last piece I'd been so afraid to give him.

Leo reached into his coat pocket with his other hand and dropped to his knee. Just like that. No elaborate speech. No dramatic lead-up. Just him, in the middle of Paris, with a look that shattered every wall I'd ever built.

"Elliot West," he said, his voice steadier than mine would've been, "you've made me believe that second chances and love, the miraculous kind, are absolutely worth waiting for. I've known I loved you since the day—"

I held up my hand. "Wait. I'm not ready."

Leo froze, his mouth still partway open. I could see his face fall, but before he moved to stand up from the ground, I shook my head, dropped my bag to the cobblestones, and crouched to kneel beside him. My heart was pounding harder than I'd ever remembered, and after pulling a pair of men's sneakers out of my tote, I placed them in his hands. "I had a plan too."

He blinked. "What? What is this?" He untied the bow that kept the tissue paper in place and looked up at me, puzzled. "Um . . . new trainers?" he asked, staring down at a brand-new pair of Nike sneakers in his size.

"I was planning on proposing to you."

"You were?" His face softened, a smile overtaking his confusion.

"Remember that story you told me in Mykonos? About Atalanta?"

It was the very same story he had reminded me of during that last epic fight in Belize before he'd disappeared. Of course, the Leo on this timeline had no memories of Belize *or* that argument, but I hoped he'd at least recall telling me the myth over dinner in Little Venice on the night of our first date.

"The girl who was trying to outrun the world," he affirmed. "I remember."

"But Meleager didn't try to beat her," I said. "He ran with her. Kept pace."

Leo searched my face. "He wasn't trying to win. He just wanted to show her he was there, right alongside her."

Taking the sneakers from him and placing them next to us, I reached for his hand. "Exactly. And I want to spend the rest of my life running with you, Leo. Not ahead, not behind. Just with you."

His fingers tightened around mine. "What do you say?" he asked. "Maybe we do this next part together."

"What do you mean?"

"Instead of me proposing to you or you proposing to me, what if right here and now we simply promise to choose one another in all the ways that matter. Because I do. I do choose you, Elliot, to be my partner, both in sparring and in life, my lover, my confidante, my mirror, and my best friend."

"And, Leo, I choose you to be my partner, even while knowing there will be good times and bad, that I will weather the storm with you and hold your umbrella and be your safe haven. I want you to be the person I run to and the home I return to. I never want us to lose sight of how there was always an invisible thread pulling us back to one another and that magic is just what we call it when something impossible becomes undeniable."

Leo smiled, his eyes creasing in the corners, and he brushed a gentle thumb over my cheek. "If there's magic in this world, Elliot, it's you standing in front of me, choosing me back. That's all I'll ever need."

I threw my arms around him, laughing and crying at the same time as the Eiffel Tower burst into its next glittering sparkle. The small crowd that had gathered around us clapped and cheered, though I hardly noticed. It felt like the whole world had stilled just for us at that moment.

As we kissed beneath the twinkling Parisian night, I realized this was the life I had never dared to believe was possible. It was imperfect, full of forgiveness, hard but real, and fiercely beautiful. The joy it held burned so brightly that even the darkest shadows felt worth facing.

Because in a city built on love, I'd found something even stronger—the courage to finally embrace it.

Elliot West's Ten (Revised, Slightly Wiser, and a Bit Less Jaded) Love Commandments

1. *Thou shalt not abandon thyself in the pursuit of someone else.*
   Love should expand you, not erase you.

2. *Thou may put thyself first—but leave space beside you.*
   Independence isn't isolation. Let someone sit close to your fire and relish in its warmth, not extinguish it.

3. *Thou shalt remember: Vulnerability is not weakness.*
   Let them see your heart. If they flinch, they're not your person.

4. *Thou shalt not confuse peace with boredom.*
   Healthy love can be electric and steady. Choose the kind that lets you exhale.

5. *Thou shalt honor red flags—and also green ones.*
   Look for the good, but don't ignore what your gut says isn't right.

6. *Thou shalt not ghost thy own needs.*
   Speak up. Be clear. Don't shrink to make love fit where it doesn't.

7. *Thou shalt stay open-minded and open-hearted, even when scared.*
Armor keeps pain out, but also joy. Love is a risk. Wear sunscreen, not chain mail.

8. *Thou shalt give second chances sparingly—and never to the same person twice.*
Growth is welcome. Repetition is not.

9. *Thou shalt know the difference between butterflies and warning signs.*
One makes you feel alive. The other makes you lose sleep. Learn the difference.

10. *Thou shalt believe in love. Not the perfect version, but the one who puts in effort to make it work.*
The kind where two flawed people show up, try hard, laugh often, and hold hands anyway.

ACKNOWLEDGMENTS

From Beth: For my husband, who reminds me every day that the real magic is found in love, laughter, and the life we've built together. For my mah-jongg crew. And, as always, my beautiful Hadley Alexandra.

From Danielle: For my parents, my family, and my friends—*thank you* will never be enough. I am so grateful to share this life with all of you.

From both: To the wonderful Jill Marsal, Angela James, Maria Gomez, and the Montlake editorial team: Thank you for working your "magic" behind the scenes to help bring this story into the world.

ABOUT THE AUTHORS

Beth Merlin earned her BA from the George Washington University and her juris doctor from New York Law School. A lifelong New Yorker, Beth loves anything Broadway, romantic comedies, and a good maxi dress. When she isn't writing, you can find her spending time with her husband, daughter, and two cavapoos, Sammy and Scarlett, at home or at their favorite vacation spot, Kiawah Island, South Carolina. She and Danielle Modafferi are the coauthors of *Life Derailed*, *Heart Restoration Project*, and *The Last Phone Booth in Manhattan*. For more information, visit www.merlinandmod.com.

Danielle Modafferi, a high school English teacher and pun enthusiast, earned her MFA in writing popular fiction from Seton Hill University and, shortly after, founded Firefly Hill Press in 2016. By day, she helps her students discover the magic of language, and by night, she's a writer and publisher on a mission to unleash her creativity and help others do the same. Danielle loves making memories with friends and family, traveling to faraway (and some not-so-faraway) places, and snuggling with her Yorkipoo, Liam, who is also, incidentally, her biggest fan. She and Beth Merlin are the coauthors of *Life Derailed*, *Heart Restoration Project*, and *The Last Phone Booth in Manhattan*. For more information, visit www.merlinandmod.com.